COLEEN NOLAN

Envy

PAN BOOKS

First published 2010 by Pan Books
an imprint of Pan Macmillan, a division of Macmillan Publishers Limited
Pan Macmillan, 20 New Wharf Road, London N1 9RR
Basingstoke and Oxford
Associated companies throughout the world
www.panmacmillan.com

ISBN 978-0-330-51698-3

1 3 5 7 9 8 6 4 2

A CIP catalogue record for this book is available from
the British Library.

Typeset by Ellipsis Books Limited, Glasgow
Printed in the UK by CPI Mackays, Chatham ME5 8TD

Envy

...n is a member of the world-famous girl group The Nolans, who chalked up massive record sales in Britain and Europe, selling nine million records in Japan alone – which is even more than The Beatles! Coleen joined the band at the age of fifteen. Among their various hits, their single 'I'm In the Mood for Dancing' has become a cult classic. The sisters reformed in 2009 for a sell-out tour and new album.

Now an established television presenter with credits including *Dancing on Ice Friday*, *This Morning*, *Secret Guide to Women's Health*, and *The Truth About Eternal Youth*, Coleen is also one of the lead presenters on ITV1's multi-award-winning daily chat show *Loose Women*. Coleen also writes a popular column in the *Daily Mirror*. *Envy* is her first novel.

Also by Coleen Nolan

Upfront and Personal

Mum to Mum

For all the women who
inspired me along the way

Prologue

Inside Studio 9, the warm-up man strode across the floor of the *Girl Talk* set, whipping the audience – almost all women – into a frenzy. 'Here they are,' he boomed, 'the ladies you love. Let's hear it for Julia Hill, Karen King, Lesley Gold, Cheryl West and Faye Cole.'

The audience rose to their feet, clapping and whooping, as the women walked on to the set of their popular late-night show. One by one they took their places behind the distinctive pink neon-lit desk. Still smiling, Faye turned in her seat, her face now in profile to the audience. 'Why did he say my name last again? Who put him up to that? You know I hate being last; it's bad luck,' she hissed through bright red lips.

'Darling, he's simply announcing us in order of popularity,' replied a beaming Julia, four seats along and the furthest away from Faye. 'We can't help it if you're the least loved.'

'Can you two just shut up? I've got the headache from hell,' Lesley muttered through a slew of apricot lip gloss, smile fixed in place, mouth barely moving, managing to pull off the kind of trick a top ventriloquist would be proud of.

'More like another *hangover*, Lesley,' Cheryl said.

Karen was the only one who kept quiet as the director began his countdown. 'We're live in five, four, three – roll opening titles – two, one ... and we're on air. Twenty seconds on the titles . . . seventeen minutes to the first break.' The warm-up man punched the air and the audience went wild as the show beamed into millions of homes.

'Hello! And welcome to *Girl Talk*,' Julia purred. 'Settle back for your nightly dose of the best news from the *best* of friends.' She paused and shot a dazzling smile at the others as the director cut to a close-up of Lesley, ever the professional, smiling back despite her pounding head.

Karen King gazed at the women on either side of her and braced herself for another hour of fake friendship, played out in front of millions.

'On tonight's show, let's talk men . . . *unsuitable* men. The kind with trouble written in big letters all over them . . . the kind that should carry a government health warning,' Julia said. 'You know the type – charmer-meets-cheat . . . gets that shifty look every time his mobile phone rings. Never asks you back to his place. Always pleads poverty. So, Lesley, do you know anyone like that?'

Lesley gave the audience a knowing look. Her head was killing her. She would take more painkillers in the break; the fast-acting, heavy-duty ones she got on prescription and kept for emergencies. 'Julia, I don't know anyone *not* like that.'

Cheryl pulled a face. 'Those guys – I can spot them a mile off.'

Lesley grinned. 'Me too. Doesn't stop me going there, though.'

Faye piped up. 'I so used to be a sucker for a bad boy – until I met my wonderful husband.' A murmur of approval went through the studio audience. 'And,' she said, not quite making eye contact with the others, 'I can't tell you what a relief it is to know I've found the perfect man.'

Lesley turned to her. 'Trust me, there is no such thing.'

Cheryl raised an eyebrow at Faye. 'If you ask me, men are genetically programmed to be unfaithful.'

Julia peered along the desk at Karen. 'You're very quiet. We're all dying to know what *you* have to say on the subject.'

Karen mustered a cool smile. '*I* think the signs are usually there from day one and what it comes down to is whether or not you choose to see them.' She was thinking of her husband, Jason. 'My trouble is I tend to give people the benefit of the doubt, always look for the good, play down the bad – and I get the feeling some guys think that means you're a soft touch.' She gave a tiny shrug. 'Usually, it's the people you're closest to, the ones you think you can trust, who give you the most grief.' Now it was the women beside her she had in mind, recalling how just a few weeks ago they had all been friends – real friends – in spite of being very different characters. And then in one night, at the Dome Awards, jealousy and ambition had turned things ugly.

Suddenly she had the strangest feeling – an odd prickly sensation right between the shoulder blades – almost as if a well-manicured hand was poised, ready to plunge a knife into her back the second she dropped her guard ...

One

Karen agreed to slip that together I find your dress that figured around evening garage. If you had one hard the presence it around then perhaps what. This was a sleep, the best at house. That's my own. We're dying to know what you have to say on the subject with innocent one smile. Around me spare around there from one year and what you try away to learn to is aside to melt the charge an the moors, and was rather wet art precede.

Karen pulled up the zip on her brand new size-12 dress, the silk lining cool against her skin. The dress had caught her eye as she browsed online, trawling through collections by every designer she had ever heard of and a few she had not. Although she must have spent hours looking at hundreds of dresses, as soon as she saw the one by Kyri she had to have it. As it happened, Kyri had a showroom in London not far from where she lived, so she could have arranged to go in and try the dress on, maybe see if there was something she liked more, but she preferred the whole virtual shopping experience. Taking her clothes off in changing rooms was something she avoided if she could.

When the dress arrived, shrouded in scented tissue paper in a fancy box with a ribbon, she had a moment of panic. It was exquisite: elegant, classy, feminine. It was also ... well, tiny. Karen held it up, convinced they had sent the wrong size. She swallowed. No way could she get into such a slinky little number, yet according to the label it was indeed a size 12. She stepped into it, holding her breath as she tentatively pulled it up, the fabric gliding over her curves. It was perfect, just right, accentuating her new hourglass shape. She laughed with relief. Of *course* the dress was tiny – so was she these days. It had

4

been so long since she wore a 12 she still had moments when she couldn't quite believe it.

Now, feeling the scarlet silk slip rather than stretch across her hips, she was aware of every pound she had lost. She would never have dreamed something so figure-hugging and flattering, with its nipped-in waist and sexy little side-slit, was for her. It really is amazing how having your heart broken works better than any diet, she thought, as she smoothed and tightened the straps to give her more support. She might have dropped four dress sizes but she still had her boobs – they weren't going any-where, unlike her lousy, cheating, good-for-nothing husband. She knew she wasn't over Jason yet but she couldn't carry on crying at home any more. Seeing *them* splattered all over the party pages of celeb magazines attending the opening of an envelope told her *he* wasn't staying in so why should she?

She had never got this glammed up when they were together, mainly because he insisted he liked her looking natural. Ha! 'Natural' was the last word anyone would use to describe Hannah Blake, a glamour model barely out of her teens. Nothing about that bitch was natural, Karen thought, getting agitated. She looked in the mirror and did her breathing exer-cises, counting backwards from ten in a calm tone until she felt normal again.

'I will not think about him tonight,' she said out loud. The Domes, television's most prestigious awards evening, was about having fun – and boy, did she need some. Besides, the show's booker had told her Jason would definitely not be there so it was a good opportunity to forget all about him for at least one night. Normally she avoided awards dos like the plague, not least because she could never find anything even vaguely attract-ive to fit her size-20 frame. So-called plus-size fashions just made her feel mumsy, which was ironic considering that after more than twenty years together Jason had still claimed he wasn't ready for children. It was a double shock then to open *heat* magazine and discover the tart he ran off with was up the duff in two minutes flat; either he had matured very quickly or she had planned her little accident all along ...

She shuddered as she remembered coming home one day to change, after getting ketchup on her white shirt from a sneaky Big Mac, and running into Hannah on the landing, her hair damp and smelling of Karen's shampoo, her tiny body swamped in Jason's dressing gown. The girl had smirked as she let the robe fall open, giving Karen an eyeful of firm, young, fake-tanned flesh. Resisting a powerful urge to throw her down the stairs, Karen instead stormed into the bedroom to confront Jason, who was on his back, naked, eyes shut, a stupid post-coital smirk on his face. He managed to scramble clear just before she took a swing at him with the empty champagne bottle at the side of the bed. *Their* bed. For a long time after-wards it drove her crazy wondering just how many times Hannah had been there, making herself at home, using Karen's things.

'STOP IT!' she berated herself. It was so annoying the way her thoughts constantly drifted back to her errant husband. It had been six months now; she should be able to control it. She reminded herself again she wasn't going to let thoughts of Jason and *her* ruin her big night.

People always made such an effort for the Dome Awards, and this was the first time it would be broadcast live on TV, so there was an added incentive to pull out all the stops. Karen was nervous. She picked up her phone and typed a message: **Can't wait to see you all tonight! XXX**. Then she flipped through her address book and sent it to Julia, Lesley, Cheryl and Faye. Her phone began to beep almost instantly with messages back saying pretty much the same thing. She smiled.

It would be the first time the girls had been together since the five-month summer break. As soon as the show came off air Lesley had gone somewhere hot for some serious tanning, while Julia went straight to a beauty boot camp in a remote part of Brazil and Cheryl got to work on a fitness DVD. She wasn't sure what Faye had been up to. This time next week they'd be at work and back on air again, but the Domes was a chance to let their hair down and have some fun. Although they were up for two awards – individually nominated in the Most Popular Entertainment Presenter category, and the show as Most Popular Entertainment Programme – she didn't think they'd win. Not that she minded: she just couldn't wait to get out there.

The other girls had been her saviours throughout the nightmare of Jason's cheating with the bimbo slut he'd run off with. It was the *Girl Talk* girls who propped her up on air night after night as the tabloids got their teeth into her love-rat husband. That was in the late spring. By the time he'd moved out, a few weeks after the story of his affair first surfaced – supposedly to get his head together – Karen was at breaking point. He never told her he was moving in with Hannah; she read about it in the *Sun*. The girls had rallied round and kept her going, refusing to let the whole sorry saga drag her under. She had missed them over the summer.

They would be so shocked when they saw her. Shocked but pleased. When she'd first noticed she'd lost a whole stone just from crying she threw herself into exercising and denied herself all the tasty treats she loved. If she was going to be miserable, at least she didn't still have to be fat. All the working out, the endless salads and going without chocolate had been worth it. Inside, her heart still ached, but as she dusted bronzer on to her cleavage and checked her reflection she smiled again; she hadn't looked this good in years. Her long hair shone, the glossy black fringe bringing out the green in her eyes, gleaming tendrils snaking over her pale shoulders. After running her fingers through her hair she dabbed her favourite Annick Goutal fragrance behind each ear and she was off.

Tonight it all changes, she told herself. She was right about that, although she could never have predicted how.

Two

Bloody hell, Lesley thought, as she noticed she'd already laddered her stockings just putting them on. She rummaged in her drawer for a replacement, tossing odd stockings and patterned tights on to the bed. Damn, they were her last sheer pair and she didn't want to wear any of her longer dresses so she'd have to go bare-legged in one of the coldest Septembers she could remember. Oh well, at least she'd been for a waxing session a couple of days ago. She rubbed some shimmer on and decided that would have to do the trick. Stepping into vertiginous stiletto heels, she slipped on her favourite black mini-dress. She'd had the dress for twenty years and it still looked amazing, pulled her in right where she liked and showed off just enough leg and cleavage without looking tarty. She loved the fact it was slashed low both front and back. No way could she wear a bra – not that she needed to. She still had great boobs. Maybe some tit-tape, though, just in case.

She emptied the remains of her odds-and-ends drawer on to the bed. A few more mismatched stockings fell out, along with some hair grips and a giant pink sponge roller. There was a wispy black teddy, a red satin suspender belt she didn't wear any more because it cut into her, and some frayed frilly knickers that were past their best. No tit-tape. Never mind.

She stood in front of the full-length mirror and gazed at

herself. In her heels she was at least six feet tall and her legs went on forever. She checked her rear view. The fabric clung to her, emphasizing her tiny waist and curvy bum. Lesley was lucky: a slender size 10 with curves in all the right places and never a day's workout in her life. Well, not in a gym anyway. She tossed her mane of blonde hair. It fell in soft waves halfway down her back. Thank God for extensions. Strange to think she spent more on having her hair done every three months than she had on the dress. Her mum had always said, 'If you can't afford, don't buy,' but she disagreed. She did take her mum's advice on buying the best quality you could, though, just not about saving up first.

The dress had been a good investment: even now it still felt new. Two decades and a hell of a lifetime ago she had found it in a boutique in Islington and blown two months' rent on it, lived on soup for weeks, but it had been worth every penny. The woman in the shop had said it was a classic, made to last, and she was right. Lesley had still never seen anything since on the Gino Gardini label, although she had searched far and wide. As for the shop in Islington, that was long gone.

As she fastened a heavy silver cross studded with amber around her neck – another one-off, from a designer on the Portobello Road – Lesley thought of her mother and wished she was still alive. She would have *loved* her shoes, six-inch stilettos in the softest black suede and trimmed with feathers that sprouted from the ankle strap and ran all the way down the heel. They made Lesley feel like an exotic bird displaying its finery to lure a mate, although she was pretty sure it was the males who did that.

Her mum would also have laughed at how Lesley had saved the dress but conveniently lost five years from her age. Officially, she was now forty-three. 'Keep 'em guessing,' her mum would have laughed through a haze of Benson & Hedges smoke. She loved her cigarettes, puffing away, defiant to the end. A heart attack had done nothing to stop her lighting up, despite dire warnings from her consultant. 'Too late to worry now,' she used to say. Lesley had definitely inherited her stubborn and slightly reckless streak.

When she was a girl her mum had told her she could be whatever she wanted to be. They might have come from a two-up, two-down in Brixton but that would never do for little Lesley.

'What are you, my darlin'?' she'd ask her just before Lesley went to sleep each night.

'Oh Mum, don't be silly.'

'Come on – let Mummy hear it,' Linda would trill in her Cockney smoker's drawl.

'I am a special little girl.' Lesley would giggle and pull the covers over her face to hide her flushed cheeks.

'That's right, darlin', and one day the whole world will know it.' She would tuck her in, plant a tobacco-scented kiss on her forehead and leave the door open a smidge, just the way her little princess liked it.

Lesley smiled, lost in the past for a moment, then frowned as it dawned on her she was very much in the present. She didn't really want to go tonight but could almost hear her mum telling her to *get back out there and show 'em what you're made of*. She had always hated awards ceremonies. In fact she had always hated late-night TV too, which was bizarre since that was where she found herself these days. And not just on any old dross; she was on the hottest show of the moment, up for two awards at the Domes, which was why she had to drag her old bones out and show all the fuckers who'd laughed when her career stalled that she was most definitely back on the ladder.

Girl Talk might not be what she was into – personally she could think of better things to do last thing at night than curl up in front of the box – but millions of women were tuning in and the more than respectable audience had made it a hit, a great big one. The truth was the show had saved her, really. Sometimes she needed to remind herself to be a tad more grateful but it was still a bitter-sweet victory. Just a few years before, when she was at the top of her game, offers starting to come in for plum film roles, she would never have been seen dead even as a *guest* on a show like *Girl Talk*, let alone presenting it. Her mother had drummed it into her that she was destined for great things and she believed her. Only under duress would she have swanned in, talked about her fabulous acting career and die-hard fans, graciously accepted the wild applause, and then no doubt flounced off and hit the clubs. That had been her life before her fall from grace and she had loved it.

As Karla Kane, Lesley had once been soap's brightest star, the big-hearted landlady who for six years had been adored and envied, on and off screen, in equal measure. She'd thought she was untouchable but in the end all it took to bring her down was an eighteen-year-old shelf stacker, some sex toys, a small mountain of cocaine, a hidden camera and an exposé in the *News of the World*, and it was all over in a flash. Drug-taking was an absolute no-no. Splattered across the tabloids, she was swiftly sacked and humiliated. No drama would touch her, no one was willing to audition her, and her hopes for a series of her own were dashed; no one would even talk to her or return any of her calls. She was well and truly finished. Or so it had seemed.

At first, *Girl Talk* was just a short-term contract, a means of paying the bills. By the time they called her she was so desperate she'd have done almost anything. Since she was the last one to be approached at almost no notice, it was obvious she wasn't their first choice and guessed someone else had pulled out, leaving them in the lurch, but a break was a break and the producer at the time was a young gay guy who had loved her on *Spitalfields* and said such a brilliant talent deserved a 'second chance'. Condescending, but sweet, she'd thought to herself as she'd thrown her arms around him in the campest manner she could muster, thankful that queens loved a bit of scandal. What had happened to her was probably no more than a typical night of the week as far as he – and possibly the odd disgraced Tory MP – was concerned.

Things moved fast; they made her an offer and Lesley – not really in a position to haggle – said yes. The next day she was on set and suddenly she was a *TV presenter*. Three short years on and she was up for Most Popular Entertainment Presenter at one of television's most prestigious awards ceremonies. All the girls had been nominated in that category, not that Lesley really expected any of them to win. They were the new kids on the block really, as was Channel 6, up against the likes of the *Loose Women* lot over at ITV. Still, it was acknowledgement that they were now a force to be reckoned with, taking on the big guns, which was something she would never have imagined.

She opened her compact and did a final make-up check, dabbing an extra dot of concealer under each eye. You could never be too careful, not with everyone filming on high-definition these days. She had piled on the kohl, going for a smudgy, smoky, sex-kitten look. Glossy gold eyeshadow flecked with glitter and luscious false lashes completed the effect. Her eyes were almost exactly the same shade as the amber stone in her necklace.

Never in a million years had she expected anyone to watch *Girl Talk*. It was only scheduled to be on for six weeks, to fill an empty slot when the host of a late-night chat show was yanked off air after thousands of viewers complained and the *Daily Mail* launched one of its campaigns over what it deemed 'lewd and reprehensible behaviour' and 'the erosion of broadcasting standards'.

Using the old chat-show set, *Girl Talk* did a quick rehearsal and before anyone could say 'Live from London' they were on air. They read the papers for gossip, chatted about anything and anyone – especially men – and went out live, which gave the show an edge and made it unpredictable. It was a sort of girls-chatting-down-the-pub-type thing and Lesley fully expected it to bomb. Maybe Channel 6 did too, because there was no hype, no publicity at all, but almost immediately word got out and women all over the UK switched on – and stuck with it. *heat* made it their TV Hot Pick and in the space of six weeks *Girl Talk* was the surprise hit of the year, catapulting the girls – all of whom had seen their stars wane in recent years – to stardom again. None of them was even a proper presenter, apart from Julia, but somehow the mix worked. Since then they had never come off air apart from their annual summer break. As she touched up her lip gloss for the umpteenth time and rummaged for her bracelet in a bag crammed with more make-up than the beauty hall at Harvey Nics, Lesley thought, You couldn't make it up really.

While it may have been women looking for something other than news or sport or a Steven Seagal film to watch late at night who first caught on to the show, the media circus wasn't far behind and suddenly Lesley was actually popular again. People stopped talking about The Incident and focused more on how good she was looking. Now, almost three years to the day since the show had launched, they just might scoop a top gong at the Domes, *Loose Women* permitting. Lesley had refused to attend the first two years, but this time the producers insisted because of her individual nomination – a first for her and the other girls, although Julia had been nominated the year before – so she couldn't really say no.

Anyone who was anyone went to the Dome Awards, which ranked as *the* event of the year in TV circles. It had been four long years since Lesley had last seen some of the people who would be there and she had a score to settle. Thanks to being 'hot' again she finally had the power to get even with the bitch who'd set her up. She had been on the case for quite a while now and according to the guest list the one person she most wanted to see would be there, lording it on the *Spitalfields* table.

Three

In the pristine, white-walled surgeon's room Dr Joel Reynolds, tall and handsome, in his late forties, was 'working' on Julia Hill. As the empty syringe exited her cheek, Julia was instantly focused. He was always surprised at how unaffected by the injections she was. He knew no other client like her.

'Show me,' she said, and gestured impatiently at her face.

The nurse glanced at Joel, waiting for him to nod before handing Julia the mirror as the electronic bed whirred and manoeuvred her body into an upright position.

Julia's angry face swivelled towards them. 'It's not enough. I said I wanted to look late twenties.'

Joel's voice was soothing. 'Julia, if I put any more in you'll look unnatural – people will be able to tell.'

She pulled the mirror closer and inspected his handiwork. 'Listen to me: every media tart in town will be at these awards tonight and I have to be perfect.'

Trying to be helpful, the young nurse at the side of the bed placed her hand on Julia's arm. 'How about an oxygen facial and some hydro cosmetics? I could do your make-up myself.'

'Fuck the hydro and fuck you!' Julia screeched, her voice shaking. She turned on the doctor. 'What exactly is she doing here anyway?' Before he could answer Julia rounded on the nurse, who had taken a step back and looked shaken. 'Make-up is useless, it does *nothing* any more,' she spat. 'You stand there with your twenty-year-old skin and tits like rocks and think *you* can advise *me*? Get this stupid little girl out of here!'

The nurse stepped back in shock as Joel gestured for her to leave. 'Julia, you can't speak to my staff like that . . . You have to be realistic. I mean, there's only so many procedures you can have in such a short space of time otherwise you risk—'

She cut him short and brought her face close to his. 'You've done very well out of me, haven't you, Joel? I've sent you clients here, clients there . . . you've got this brand-new clinic' – she gazed about her – 'which clearly hasn't come cheap. Your suits are Savile Row instead of that high-street trash I found you in, and judging by the way that toddling nurse was mooning over you you've found yet another young tart happy to bend over your designer desk. You think you're a proper Mr Big Shot these days, don't you?'

Joel shook his head. 'Julia, stop it – you're being ridiculous.' He hoped the interruption might shut her up but it was useless; she was in full flow, her breath on his cheek, her face practically touching his now.

'Shhh . . . I'm talking now, so time to listen up . . . You do know all this can come crumbling down as fast as it went up . . . if people were to know about *your past*,' she hissed in almost a whisper.

Joel glanced around, nervous, making sure they were still alone, then lowered his voice. 'You wouldn't. And besides, who's to say anyone would believe you?'

'Oh, they'd believe me all right, because I'm *famous*, Joel, which makes what *I say* count. *You*, on the other hand . . . well, that's a different story . . . All your fancy clients, what would they think if they knew your grubby little secrets?'

'OK, that's enough,' Joel said, defeated. 'Get back on the bed.'

Julia smiled. 'Good boy. Now do as you're told and fill me up – I need to be flawless.'

Julia lay back as Dr Reynolds reached for his syringe. 'You're going to regret this,' he muttered, sinking the needle into her skin.

'No I'm not; I need it,' Julia replied, gritting her perfect porcelain teeth as the filler oozed into her forehead.

But it wasn't just the filler he was talking about.

Four

Faye nibbled on two dry crackers and sipped from a large glass of equally dry white wine as she studied her reflection in the mirror.

'Not bad. Not bad at all,' she said, as she turned and admired her rear view. The dress, in purple shot silk with a beaded bodice and short net skirt, had cost a small fortune and she had felt a touch guilty when a transaction for a cool £6,000 popped up on her black Amex, although not for long. The dress looked good on her slight, lithe frame, and showed off her toned legs. That was Pilates for you. She gathered up a handful of glossy red hair and piled it on her head. She might wear it up, give herself a bit of extra height. The dress was fabulous. She spun round. A sheer chiffon panel covered her back. Yes, it was perfect, and it was ages since she had splashed out. She deserved it. She worked hard and if she didn't indulge herself, who would? Not Mike, certainly. She looked at her wedding-ring finger, at the monstrous and still beautiful ten-carat glittering stone, remembering when he'd given it to her and said he'd love her forever, how she'd believed him. *Again*. No fool like an old fool, she thought.

She really should have known better. It wasn't like she hadn't been there before. Their friends, having seen them split up and get back together more times than anyone could remember, had nicknamed them Taylor and Burton. Mike was always promising to change, although it never lasted long. It wasn't other women he cheated on her with; his 'mistress' was his job as an ITN war correspondent. She'd begged him to give it up after he'd been shot in the leg and spent months laid up. Back on the front line, when he saw two of his co-reporters die in a bomb blast, Faye felt sure he'd finally come to his senses and call it a day so they could start a family. But it was too late: by then he was addicted to the thrill of it, so while he was out in Kabul being shot at, she was home alone in Balham, watching his reports and waiting for the call every war wife dreads.

He claimed he did it because he wanted to make a difference, but recently she had noticed that he was never happier than when he was doing one of those live links back to the studio. It was written all over his stubbly, battle-worn, sunburned face. He loved the way the press bigged him up as their brave poster boy. The women's mags voting him sexiest man on television hadn't helped either. Faye couldn't move these days without someone telling her how proud she must be and what a wonderful man he was, so fearless and dedicated, so *selfless*. Huh. Not dedicated enough to put his wife first. Ten years of worry and coping for months at a time on her own was long enough for Faye to know he was unlikely ever to change now.

Of course she'd had the odd fling before, but nothing serious, just the warmth of a body on a cold night when she was going out of her mind with loneliness. This one was different though. This time she was actually in love, and Mike had no idea. Not that he would believe it even if he knew. Actually, no one would believe it; she barely believed it herself.

'Faye?' A voice rang out from the bathroom, breaking her chain of thought.

'Coming,' she called, slipping the dress off, putting it back on its hanger and wrapping a towel around her naked body.

'Can you give me a hand?'

Faye walked into the large, white-tiled room where Cheryl West, her co-host on *Girl Talk*, lay up to her neck in soap suds in the bath.

'You've been in here ages – we're going to be late,' Faye said.

'Only the dross arrive early, Faye. The real stars always make the biggest entrance at the last minute, and this is our year, so we don't need to flog ourselves on the red carpet all night.' She sipped at a glass of red wine and luxuriated in the bubbles. 'This time we can just enjoy it and take our time.' She ducked her shoulders under and came up again, water running off the gleaming ebony skin. She had fastened her hair up in a topknot and a purple strand fell on to her brow. Faye gazed into emerald eyes and felt her stomach lurch.

She looked at her watch. 'It's already five, you know.'

'Plenty of time for what I have in mind.' Cheryl put down her glass and whipped off Faye's towel in the kind of fluent abracadabra motion that would have made Paul Daniels proud.

Faye laughed, dropped her watch on the side of the wash-basin and climbed into the bath as Cheryl pulled her into a soapy embrace.

Five

Inside the chauffeur-driven Mercedes Julia perched almost mannequin-like on the back seat, determined not to crease her dress. She had taken great care over her appearance and wanted everything to be perfect. Although she was older than the others she still graced the most covers and had been the only one to feature in a spread on classical beauties in one of the high-end glossies, flanked by Keira Knightley and Kate Beckinsale. She studied her reflection in the window of the car, admiring the high cheekbones and flawless skin, the rosebud mouth and sparkling turquoise eyes. Her contemporaries were Madonna, Michelle Pfeiffer, Sharon Stone, and she had no doubt she could give any of them a run for their money. She suited her hair short and this new cut, what her stylist called 'choppy with attitude', had taken years off. She ran a hand through the front, teasing it into brash platinum spikes. Sharon Stone meets Sarah Harding. The girls would be impressed, she just knew it.

As the driver slowed in front of the Grosvenor House Hotel, just yards from the drop-off for red-carpet arrivals, Julia spotted two *Hollyoaks* girls in barely-there dresses. Showing off acres of adolescent flesh, they were turning this way and that as the photographers went crazy, their flashbulbs lighting the night sky. Julia said, 'Go round the block again, Jeff. I don't want to be early.'

The car accelerated and pulled away. 'Tacky bitches,' Julia muttered under her breath. She wasn't about to see all her effort to look her best go down the pan as two teenage tramps upstaged her. As the limousine cruised past the back of the hotel she felt a sudden pain shoot across her top lip and pulled out her compact mirror to check her face. Perfect, she thought, as she studied her newly plump lips and dewy, childlike skin. Joel Reynolds may be difficult but there was no questioning his genius. She wondered whether she'd been too hard on him and decided to call, let him know how pleased she was with his work.

The phone rang twice before a voice invited her to leave a message. Bastard! Julia knew he had cut her off. How dare he? She would have to deal with his attitude once and for all – but that would have to wait as the car drew to a stop at the edge of the red carpet, now thankfully minus the *Hollyoaks* tramps. Julia was ready to make her entrance. Jeff swung open the door and she stepped out into the night.

'Julia, over here . . .' 'One to me . . .' 'This way . . .' 'To me, Julia!' The paparazzi jostled and shouted as she worked the carpet, loving it, feeling alive as the flashbulbs warmed her skin against the cold night air. She posed coyly, chin tilted down – something she had seen Anna Wintour do – not wanting to look as if she was trying too hard, and was just about to do her classic over-the-shoulder look when she felt the cameras begin to turn towards the latest arrival on the red carpet. Blinded by the flashbulbs, she couldn't quite see who was causing all the fuss.

The moment Karen's foot hit the carpet the cameras went crazy. She hadn't known anything like it since the early eighties when her band, the Thunder Girls, had toured Japan and been chased by fans and paparazzi everywhere they went. The paps yelled at her. 'Karen!' '*Karen!*' '*Karen!*' Damn, she thought, struggling to see with all the lights popping in her eyes. The steps were steep and as she took a tentative step forward she prayed she wouldn't go head-first. Steadying herself, she managed an awkward pose, trying to remember what Lesley had once told her about keeping her shoulders back and putting one hand on her hip. She had never been any good at red carpets, would normally just put her head down and make a run for it, like a suspect dodging the press on the way into court, hating to get in anyone's way.

The photographers usually took a polite picture as she went past, just being nice, making it clear they weren't all that interested. A size-20 Karen didn't sell magazines. Tonight, though, was a different story. Tonight was extraordinary.

'Karen, is that *you*?' Jackie Martin, the producer of *Girl Talk*, hurried towards her, hitching up a strapless black dress that skimmed the floor. Thrilled to see a friendly face, Karen threw her arms round her and the women hugged.

The look on Jackie's face made it clear she was shocked by Karen's astonishing transformation. 'Oh my God, you look amazing!' She stood back and took a long, appraising look.

'Stop it!' Karen laughed as they both stepped to one side to let Tamzin Outhwaite have her moment with the paps. 'Seriously – do I look OK?' Karen knew she sounded nervous and was annoyed at herself, but Jason had shredded her confidence and she needed reassurance.

Jackie looked her up and down again. 'No, actually, you really don't look OK.' Karen's face fell. 'You look *fabulous*! You look like a different woman. Have you seen the other girls yet?'

'No, I just got here.' Karen smiled and, starting to relax, slipped her arm through Jackie's.

Jackie scanned the carpet and spotted Julia, who was now watching them from the edge of the press pen. 'Oh my God. Don't look now, but you and Julia are wearing exactly the same dress!'

Karen froze. 'Please tell me you're joking.' She clutched at her arm, not daring to turn towards where Jackie was pointing and waving.

Jackie gave her a comforting squeeze. 'Nope, I'm afraid I'm not.'

'God, she'll go mad!' Panic welled up in Karen as she raised a hand in a limp wave at Julia. Julia waved back, smiling, apparently not in the slightest bit bothered at the clash of dress. Karen's shoulders, rigid with tension, relaxed. She let out a sigh of relief.

'No, see, she's smiling!' Jackie said. 'She'll see the funny side of it. Oh look, here comes Lesley.'

The girls turned to watch as a pair of glistening pins emerged from a black taxi and Lesley sashayed across the red carpet, tossing her hair and pouting.

Inside, tired of smiling and waving at people who were just blurs, Julia peered around the room, trying to spot someone she knew, but bad laser surgery in the nineties had left her with appalling vision. On TV she only wore contacts as she would never be seen dead in glasses, but her eyes had felt irritated and, knowing they were on table six, right in front of the stage, she had chanced going without them – a decision she now felt was a serious mistake. She had just waved at the *Girl Talk* publicist and mouthed a flirty Missed you, darling, at him, only to discover she was actually batting her eyelashes at Calum Best, who was over in two seconds flat. 'Have we met?' he asked, holding her hand and looking puzzled. Fortunately he was distracted by a stunning brunette who flung her arms around his neck, squealing.

Julia blinked, straining to pick out someone she knew. About the only thing that was crystal clear was that her face felt most odd. Not only was her lip aching but now her cheeks were tingling and she was getting worried. She felt hot as she wandered down the corridor towards the ladies' room; once inside and sure she was alone, she studied her reflection close-up in the mirror. She let out a dramatic sigh of relief: she looked fine, but definitely did not feel right. Reaching into her purse, she found her contact lenses. Sore eyes or not, she wasn't going to be guessing who people were all night. She slipped them in, wincing, not able to feel the skin around her eyes as she steadied her fingers on her cheekbones to pop the plastic lenses over her corneas. Very weird indeed.

It *must* be OK, she told herself. She'd had Botox and fillers dozens of times before with no adverse effects. Fishing in her bag for painkillers, she took two, swallowed them without water, applied a fresh coat of gloss to her lips with another wince, and left the room.

Six

Inside the ballroom, no expense had been spared. All 150 tables were beautifully styled, with lavish flower arrangements and ice sculptures in the shape of award statues. The stage was decked with sparkling curtains and a jewel-encrusted staircase that led to the podium where the show's host, Phillip Schofield, would soon be presenting the ceremony live on Sky1. About half the guests were already seated, while others milled around the room, drinking champagne and discreetly eyeing the competition as wine waiters in stiff white jackets buzzed around filling glasses. Thanks to her contact lenses Julia had found the *Girl Talk* table and was sitting with Lesley and a handful of the show's production staff.

Lesley sniffed at her wine and waved at a waiter. 'Darling, could you bring me a bottle of Laurent Perrier Rosé please?'

Julia shot her a look that said, *I hope you're not planning to get hammered.*

'Oh, please! It's an awards do; don't tell me you want to drink this crap all night?' Lesley winked at the waiter and gestured at the house wine on the table as Julia shrugged. Lesley watched as the waiter scurried off to get her champagne.

She giggled. 'Nice arse!'

Julia rolled her eyes and looked around at the gathering.

Spotting Lorraine Kelly on the opposite side of the room,

Lesley nudged Julia in her direction. 'I swear she only turns up to these things if she expects to win. That's another one down the drain then!'

Lorraine noticed the women looking at her and gave them a friendly wave. Lesley and Julia gave her their best Stepford Wives smiles.

'I swear she's got the luck of the Irish,' Lesley said.

'She's Scottish,' Julia pointed out in a long-suffering way.

Jackie made her way towards them. 'Hi, girls!' she said, almost throwing herself into a seat. 'God, I'm knackered! What a palaver today, but worth it, because I think you're in with a very good chance tonight.'

Julia and Lesley exchanged a curious look.

'I'm not supposed to breathe a word,' Jackie said, leaning forward, her voice dropping to a whisper as she tucked a gleaming red curl behind her ear, '*but* the Domes execs called and requested several compilation scenes from the show *and* checked that all of you were coming tonight. Now, they only do that with winners so we *must* have won one of the awards!'

'That's great!' Lesley laughed. 'I'm glad I came now.' She spotted Faye and Cheryl across the room and waved. 'Oh look, there's the girls – let's tell them!'

Jackie looked panic-stricken. 'No! I wasn't supposed to say anything and you'll need to look surprised when the cameras pan over to you, so not a word.'

Faye and Cheryl made their way through the room and reached the table, waving and blowing kisses as they went.

'Fancy seeing you here!' Cheryl pulled two chairs out for herself and Faye.

Faye scanned the table. 'Where's Karen? She *is* coming, isn't she?'

Jackie gave her an enigmatic smile.

Julia looked at her quizzically. 'Well?'

'Well what?'

'Well, where *is* she?'

'Didn't you *see her* on the carpet?' Jackie asked curiously as Julia shook her head. Jackie looked puzzled. 'But you were waving ... Oh, well she's here all right and I don't think you'll be able to miss her.'

Faye looked worried. 'Oh God, what do you mean? Is she wearing something awful?' She leaned over to Cheryl. 'I told you we should have come together. She'll be really upset if the mags take the piss out of her again for turning up in some shapeless tent.'

'She's a *big girl*, Faye. I'm sure she can take it,' Julia said, helping herself to a glass of Lesley's bubbly.

'Very funny.' Faye gave Julia a disapproving look.

'That's not what I meant!' Julia said in mock hurt. 'I just mean she's used to it by now. And anyway I'm sure she looks fine. Assuming she hasn't been comfort-eating her way through the summer break, that is, and ended up even bigger.'

'We should be there for her, that's all—' Faye said before suddenly breaking off, startled.

'What?' Julia sounded a tad annoyed.

Faye dug Cheryl with her elbow and gestured towards the entrance of the ballroom where Karen, in all her slim, trim, size-12 glory, was standing.

'Oh my *God*!' Faye squealed and jumped to her feet, waving. 'Over here!'

Julia and Lesley turned just as Karen strode towards them, weaving through the tables.

Lesley screamed. 'Look at her! She looks amazing!'

Cheryl was also on her feet. 'Karen? She's so . . . different!'

Jackie laughed. 'I know! I saw her on the red carpet; they were going mad for her! I almost didn't recognize her at first. Julia, doesn't she look *fab*?'

All the girls except Julia were now on their feet as Karen reached the table. Faye threw her arms around her as heads turned and the room, practically buzzing off the energy of her entrance, looked on.

'Karen! I can't believe it – my God, you kept that quiet!' Faye laughed as the two women hugged.

Karen beamed, her cheeks flushed from all the attention.

'You look fantastic, well done, babe,' Lesley said, raising a glass to her from the opposite side of the table.

'I hope Twatface is here tonight – he'll die when he sees the new you!' Cheryl said, also hugging her.

Karen held up a hand. 'He is off the agenda. We are not going to talk about him or even think of him tonight. Let's just leave him to his sad, pathetic life and have some fun.'

'That's more like it – go, girl!' Cheryl filled a glass and handed it to her.

'Why didn't you say anything?' Lesley said, coming round to Karen's side of the table. 'It must have been hell losing all that weight on your own.'

'It was! But I wanted it to be a surprise! God, I've missed you lot!' As Karen smiled she couldn't help noticing Julia was not joining in the conversation.

Jackie gave her a nudge. 'Julia, doesn't Karen look amazing?'

'She does indeed, Jackie,' Julia said, 'but we've got to work out a little problem.'

Karen managed an awkward smile. 'The dress. I know, what a nightmare,' she said, apologetic. Jackie pretended to be shocked as Lesley burst out laughing and Faye and Cheryl stifled giggles. Only Karen sensed that Julia was genuinely annoyed.

'Karen, everyone knows *I* wear red at awards. It's *my* colour. I've *always* worn it.'

Karen seemed to shrink into herself. 'God, Julia, I'm so sorry, I just didn't think. I saw the dress and loved it and never even thought about the colour ... I'm really sorry.'

Julia, sensing the other girls' eyes on her and the tension in the air around the table, tried to soften her tone.

'It's just if you'd told us you had a *waist* these days I'd have called and checked what you were planning to wear so we wouldn't clash!'

Karen's face went red with embarrassment under Julia's icy gaze.

Jackie stepped in. 'You both look different in the dress, and Karen wasn't to know, so it's nobody's fault.'

'If she'd told us she'd had such a makeover, it might have been less of a shock,' Julia said.

'I wanted it to be a surprise.'

'Well nobody likes a show-off, dear,' Julia said sweetly, downing more champagne.

'Excuse me,' Karen mumbled and walked away from the table. Jackie set off after her, shooting a look of disgust at Julia.

Cheryl leaned across the table. 'What did you do that for? You've really upset her.'

Julia merely smiled, prompting Faye to chip in.

'You know she's had a hard time over Jason, and we're supposed to be her friends. So what if she's got the same dress as you? It's hardly a hanging offence. Get over it and stop being such a bitch!'

Julia smiled again. Faye appealed to Lesley, who was distracted by something on the other side of the room. 'Lesley, aren't you going to say anything?'

'Sorry, I've just seen someone I need to speak to. I'll be right back.' With that she left the table and made her way to the corner of the room where she could see her former *Spitalfields* co-star and real-life nemesis, Sasha Gates.

On the far side of the building, a good five-minute walk from the main ballroom, Karen ducked into a deserted bathroom. Seconds later Jackie came in after her.

'Why is she being like that with me?' Karen sat on the edge of an elaborate brocade sofa that seemed out of place in the powder room and wiped tears from her eyes.

'She's just a bit jealous. You know she likes to be the centre of attention. Think about it: you've not only turned up looking drop-dead gorgeous but you're also wearing the same dress. You've got to see the funny side. The fact she's so pissed off is a compliment really.'

Karen managed a small smile and Jackie grinned at her. 'There we go! Come on, get yourself together; we've got a big night ahead of us, so don't let anyone spoil it for you.'

'Maybe you're right. Now she's had her say she might just calm down.'

Jackie nodded. 'You know what she's like – bark worse than her bite and all that.' She peered at herself in the mirror and pulled a face. 'I think I might have overdone the fake tan. If anyone asks, I've just come back from Barbados.' She straightened her slinky black dress and smoothed her red curls. 'Right – ready to go back in?'

'You go on ahead. I'm just going to redo my powder.'

'Thank God for waterproof mascara, eh?' They both giggled. 'Sure you don't want me to wait?'

Karen shook her head and got out her compact, blotting the shine on her nose and cheeks with the fine translucent powder. She took several deep breaths. That was better. Maybe she would just give herself a moment before going back into the ballroom, run through a few positive affirmations. I am calm and serene, she told herself, standing at the sink with her wrists under the cold tap. I deserve to be happy. Right, she said to herself, drying her hands, get back in there and stop being such a baby.

As she made her way back along the hall towards the ballroom she kept her head up and her shoulders back. I am calm, she said over and over. I am serene. Rounding a corner, a broad smile on her face, she bumped slap bang into Jason and his tramp of a girlfriend.

Jason did a double-take. 'Karen?' He took a step closer. 'Is that *you*?'

She lowered her head and tried to hurry past but slutty Hannah, in a skimpy frock, practically see-through and barely big enough to cover her bump, was in the way. Jason put a hand on Karen's bare arm, sending volts of shock and alarm through her body. She shook herself free. 'Can you let me get past, please?' Miraculously, her voice was clear and firm. 'I need to get to my table.'

Jason took a step back and gazed at her in admiration. 'You look absolutely fantastic ... I mean, I almost didn't recognize you.' He gave a low, appreciative whistle. 'Really, you look *hot*.'

Hannah tugged at his sleeve and said something in her whiny voice that Karen didn't catch.

She felt her stomach lurch. She wanted to tell Jason *he*

looked ridiculous, with that half-dressed *thing* on his arm, but she seemed unable to speak. I am calm, she told herself, frantic, her heart thumping inside her chest. I AM calm.

You are *not*, a second voice in her head countered.

'Well, it would be lovely to stay and chat,' she said eventually, hoping Hannah wasn't too dense to appreciate the sarcasm, 'but I really have to run. We've got two nominations tonight and I don't want to miss all the fun.' She brushed past Jason and another disconcerting crackle of electricity surged through her.

Julia was standing outside by the fire escape. She felt hot and fanned herself with one hand while using the other to hold her phone to her ear.

'Joel, this is my *fifth* call. I need to speak to you and I *know* you're getting these messages.' She paused. 'Something serious is happening to me so call me back or else. *Please.*' She slammed her flip-phone shut, almost breaking it in two, and put a hand on her forehead. She could no longer feel parts of her face. 'Oh no,' she said out loud and began to ferret frantically around in her bag until she found her compact. She steadied herself on the wall and slowly opened the compact to check her reflection. 'Thank God.' She still looked fine, a bit shiny as she was sweating with stress, but a quick dab of powder would fix that. What it wouldn't fix was the strange numbness now sweeping down her neck.

'What on earth has he done to me?' She cursed under her breath and fanned herself again. Joel, please call me back. She gripped the phone, willing it to ring. Stop panicking, Julia, she told herself. You're getting all worked up over nothing. As long as she looked good for the next few hours, that was the main thing; the rest she could deal with once she'd got through the night.

She looked at her watch – 7.45. The awards would go live in fifteen minutes and she needed to get herself camera-ready. She couldn't risk being caught with an expression like a sweaty smacked arse if they didn't win anything.

She regretted being so obviously rattled at the table earlier. So what if Karen's had a revamp, she thought? It's no big deal, good for her. She'll pile it all back on in a few weeks anyway, she reasoned, which brought a smile to her throbbing lips. And, yes, they were in the same dress but she still looked by far the best and, if anything, magazines might compare them and give her the thumbs-up while Karen would get the 'could do better' card. Maybe she had overreacted at the table, been a bit over-the-top. She wouldn't normally show her feelings so obviously but all this business with her face was stressing her out. If she was going to enjoy the evening at all she had to get in the party mood. And she knew just how to do that.

Fishing in her purse, she found her trusty old friend: a small white wrap guaranteed to turn even the worst of times into a celebration. It was her emergency stash. She examined the packet – a little hard as she hadn't needed to use it in a while – but once she rustled it between her fingers it soon loosened up to produce some grains of the good stuff. Turning her back to the staircase, she dug a long red fingernail into the powder, scooped up a small amount then snorted it discreetly up her delicately reshaped nostril. She gagged a little as it hit the back of her throat and her blood began to race, but instantly she felt like the good version of herself again. She was going to go back in that room, be nice to Karen, and show them all she wasn't such a bitch.

Just as she was about to slip the wrap back in her purse she paused, checked her watch again and, knowing it would be ages before she would get a chance for a top-up, did another scoop and snort, only this time a much bigger one, almost finishing the packet. As the taste filled her throat once more she really felt ready; in fact, suddenly she felt invincible.

'Julia, my girl, it is show time,' she said breathlessly as she snapped her bag shut and descended the stairs into the crowd, feeling like a queen sweeping through a court packed with admirers on her way to her throne. I am the best, I am the most beautiful, she chanted to herself as her mind raced and her emotions pulsed. Maybe she *had* been excessively harsh with Joel, she thought, a wave of benevolence consuming her as she entered the main room.

She was smiling to herself and it struck her people might think her expression odd but she merely chuckled and muttered, beaming away, not caring what anyone thought. She was lucky really: unlike some people who became weird on drugs, she softened when she took cocaine, always had. She reasoned she was a nice person really and flashed a radiant smile at total strangers as she walked back to her seat, waving at people she vaguely recognized on other tables.

'Watch out, girls, Ms Hill is in the mood again,' she giggled to herself as she felt another rush hit her body. Ooh, that was a strong one. She hoped she hadn't taken too much.

'Karen, darling, I just wanted to apologize for earlier,' she said as she took her seat. 'My mind was elsewhere when you came in and obviously I was a bit annoyed about Kyri lending us the same dress, but I know that's not your fault.'

Karen was about to point out that she had bought her dress,

got it off the internet, but Julia silenced her, placing a hand on her arm.

'And you know we're all so, *so* proud of your weight loss, don't you?! She really does look great, doesn't she, girls?'

Faye and Cheryl nodded as a beaming Julia twitched her nose twice. They exchanged a knowing look with Jackie while Karen, oblivious, rose to her feet to hug Julia.

'Thank you! That really means a lot. And I'm sorry about the dress. No harm done anyway!' She went to put her arms around Julia but was met with a polite air kiss as Julia waved an arm erratically in the air.

'Waiter! More champagne! Let's celebrate Karen no longer being second only to whales on the Greenpeace protection list!' Julia laughed and waved her glass around, spraying champagne on Karen's dress without even noticing.

Karen smiled although Julia's comments stung; she didn't want to make a big deal of it but she couldn't believe what a cow she was being. As she sat down she could feel the eyes of the others on her, urging her to let it go.

'Where is Lesley?' Julia asked dramatically. 'Don't tell me – she's shagging that cute waiter already!'

The women gestured to the corner of the room by the staircase, where Lesley was talking to Dan Kincaid, an infamous male model and well-known womanizer on the celebrity scene, while edging ever nearer the *Spitalfields* table.

'Oh my God,' Julia said. 'Clear the decks! There'll be breakages if those two get together. He's as bad as her.' The women watched as Dan drew closer to Lesley, who seemed in a world of her own.

'She doesn't look very interested,' Faye said.

'She must be ill!' Jackie said, laughing in disbelief.

'Well, not in *him*, anyway,' Cheryl said, as she noticed Lesley's gaze was fixed on *Spitalfields'* biggest star and Lesley's sworn enemy, Sasha Gates. She raised an eyebrow at Jackie. 'I smell trouble brewing. Shall I go over and bring her back?'

'I'm sure she can handle herself. Now where's that waiter? I need another drink,' Julia said. Still smiling manically, she began to fidget with her glass and scan the room for a passing drinks tray.

Jackie leaned towards Karen and whispered, 'If we win I want you to make the speech.'

Karen leaned in closer to her. 'I can't – Julia will want to do it.'

'Look at her, she's in no fit state to get on that stage.'

Karen tried to protest but Jackie cut her off. 'You're doing it and no arguments.' She glanced at Julia, wondering how best to get her out of the room without making a scene.

Just then, Julia stood up. 'Where's the bloody service?' she shouted as people turned to stare at her. Suddenly she didn't feel jolly, she felt rather messed up; she really needed another drink to take the edge off that coke. Oh God, I'm losing control, she thought, as a little more slipped from the back of her nostrils and down her throat, almost making her gag. Try as she might she just couldn't sit still for much longer.

Seven

COLLIN SOLIN

Joel Reynolds lay with his eyes closed on the sofa in a spacious living room where the walls, floors and even the furniture were white. The only variation in the room was courtesy of the black Bang & Olufsen stereo and the sixty-inch plasma screen mounted on the wall. Joel did not like clutter. He did not like complications of any kind. And he did not like Julia Hill.

'I'm warning you, call me back *or else.*' Her voice echoed around the stark room as he played the messages through a speaker connected to his answering machine.

'See what I'm talking about?' he said, turning on his side to face Laura Lloyd, an investigative journalist from the *Sunday*, who sat taking notes in a nest of scatter cushions on another immaculate white sofa. Laura was an unusual-looking woman, not conventionally attractive but striking, almost masculine, although that might have been down to the fact she was wearing a starched white shirt and paisley-print tie teamed with a black waistcoat. Her fair hair was pulled back off her face in a severe ponytail and as far as Joel could tell she wasn't wearing a scrap of make-up. She frowned and two vertical lines appeared in the centre of her brow – a novelty for Joel, who was used to dealing with Botoxed women – then removed her glasses.

'Are you prepared to take this the whole way, Joel? Because

39

once I start working on this the entire paper will be aware of it, so if you try to pull out it might just backfire on you,' she said, straight as a bullet.

Joel didn't flinch. 'She's pushed me to this. I know the risks. A connection to a celebrity scandal could send every pair of Manolos clicking out of my clinic and straight through the doors of my nearest rival. But I'm prepared to risk it. It's about time she got a taste of her own medicine, so yes, I'm sure.' He gave her a reassuring smile, although the truth was he did feel anxious. Taking on Julia was definitely a scary prospect.

Laura eyed him up and down. Damn, he was a sexy man, not that he'd ever look at her, she knew that for sure. It was the Julia Hills of this world that got to sleep with the likes of him. Julia must have really worked his buttons to push him to bring his story to her, considering the risks involved for him. And while it would take more than reports of a few abusive messages to bring down one of the queens of late-night TV, it was enough to start the ball rolling. To think she was once a Julia Hill fan seemed bizarre considering she was now on a quest to damage her reputation. Not that she felt bad about it; Julia was well known in the industry as a grade-A bitch. As it happened, Laura didn't need to listen to other people's accounts of her atrocious behaviour to know what she was like. Oh no, she had first-hand experience of Ms Hill, and it had not been pleasant.

Twenty years on, she could still remember the encounter like it was yesterday; her thrill as an eighteen-year-old junior on *Woman and Home* magazine when she'd been given Julia as her first celebrity interview. The editor knew Laura admired Julia, who at the time was presenting a popular breakfast show, *Rise and Shine*, and was the face everyone in Britain chose to wake up to. Laura tuned in every day and it was with great excitement that she set off to *Rise*'s central London studios to do the interview, arriving a good half-hour early for her 10.30 appointment. Having been kept waiting hour after hour until it got to 2.30 p.m., she began to get the feeling that maybe she had been forgotten. By then, not having dared leave her seat in the corridor in case Julia came out and she missed her, she was desperate for the loo. She crossed her legs and tried to think of something else but it was no good. She knew she couldn't hold on much longer, not helped by the water cascading constantly down the fountain in the studios' reception area. It was agony, sheer torture.

She collared a charming but harassed-looking male assistant, about the same age as her and by the look of him also new to the scene. 'Should I come back another time? I mean, it's no problem to reschedule.'

'I'm really sorry you've been kept waiting. I know you've been here ages. I'll see what's holding things up,' he said before going behind the velvet rope that cordoned off the studio from the corridor. Laura leaned against the reception desk, legs crossed, wondering if she had time to hobble to the toilets and relieve herself. That bloody fountain! She eased herself back into her seat. Seconds later she heard high-pitched screaming, getting closer as Julia Hill burst through the door and rounded on her.

'How *dare* you order me out here?' She practically spat in Laura's face.

The shock of Julia's attack went straight to Laura's bursting bladder and to her horror she wet herself. Feeling the heat spread, soaking her legs, she wanted to cry with shame as the male assistant stepped between the two women.

'I didn't say that, Julia,' he said, his voice calm. 'I just said she'd like to know if you were coming out to do the interview today as she's been waiting rather a long time. Several hours, in fact.'

Laura suspected he was as intimidated as she was and couldn't believe he was trying to help. Naive as she was, she knew it was a bigger risk for him to be involved in what was clearly becoming a 'situation'. She was snapped out of her mind-ramblings by a whoosh of air as Julia spun around and turned her attention to the assistant.

'And who the fuck are you?' she shouted in his face; he too looked shaken by her rage.

'I'm the new assistant producer,' he said as she closed in.

'What's your name, you moron?' Julia spat.

'James.'

'Well, James, I'd go and collect your things because once I go upstairs and tell them the way you and your little friend here have just been abusing me you'll be fired. So you might as well leave now.' She smiled as his face fell. Up close Julia reminded Laura of Joan Crawford in that scene in *Mommie Dearest*, and she was grateful there were no wire coat hangers nearby. She could only imagine what she could do with one.

Julia then turned to Laura, who was trembling. 'And where are you from?'

'Manchester,' Laura murmured.

Julia barked in her face, 'No, you stupid bitch – the publication?'

'*Woman and Home* magazine.'

Julia looked her up and down. 'You're a bit ugly for them, aren't you, darling?'

Laura, still rooted to the spot in her damp chair, felt tears running down her face as Julia towered over her.

'Once I speak to your editor you'll be fired too, so you've each learned a lesson today, haven't you, children?'

They both looked back at her as she sneered her final words to them – '*Nobody* orders Julia Hill about' – and with that she shot them a look of utter contempt and stomped off down the corridor, shouting at the stylist, who had been hovering in the background the whole time but valued her job too much to intervene. 'Call Caroline now!' was the last they heard as Julia disappeared from view, her stylist running along behind.

James trudged across the corridor and sat beside Laura.

'I'm so sorry, James, I didn't mean to get you into trouble,' she said through sobs that filled the reception. Hating herself even more than she'd done when bullies picked on her at school, she tried to say something else but the tears choked her.

James knew things were bad for him but seeing how upset she was he instinctively put his arm around her. 'It's not your fault,' he said, giving her a squeeze and sounding braver than he felt. 'I'm sure it will be OK.'

Caroline Canning, the show's producer, appeared through the swing door at the end of the corridor, talking on her mobile as she moved towards them. James got to his feet. Caroline, an attractive woman in her late thirties, wore an expression that indicated she had been there before, many times.

'I'm sorry, James,' she said as she reached him, placing a hand on his shoulder and giving it a pat. Her face indicated his fate was indeed a *fait accompli*.

Laura couldn't believe what was happening right in front of her, that a few hours before she'd been on top of the world, and now she would probably be sacked from her job *and* she had managed to get someone else the boot too, and all because some second-rate talk-show host thought she was God. She had stayed quiet too long. Suddenly she felt herself rising from her seat, deeply thankful she was wearing black trousers and hoping the wet patch didn't show.

'Look, he didn't do anything wrong. He doesn't deserve this, and, to be frank, neither do I.'

Caroline raised an eyebrow. She gave Laura a sympathetic look. 'I think it's best if you just go back to your office.'

Laura was incensed. 'But that's not fair – none of this is right.'

Caroline's benevolent expression toughened a fraction. 'Sweetheart, this is TV, not the schoolyard – fair doesn't come into it,' she said, not unkindly, as she turned to face James again.

'Look, I'll put in a word for you at Channel 4, they've got a new show called *The Big Breakfast* starting and I'm sure they'd love to have you on board.' She shrugged. 'These things happen, so don't worry about it.' She gave James a weary smile and started walking down the corridor, then turned to Laura again. 'It would be better for you to just go back to work and forget this ever happened.'

'But she said I'm going to be sacked too!' Laura tugged at the soggy fabric of her trousers, now clinging uncomfortably to her legs.

'Go back to work, talk to your editor, and I'm sure it will be fine.' And with that Caroline left the two of them alone in the corridor.

By now both Laura and James looked shell-shocked, as if they'd just witnessed an accident and were not yet sure how to react. James was first to break the silence.

'You'd better go and speak to your boss before she does,' he said, managing a shaky smile.

Laura took in his anxious, chiselled face and blue eyes. Even though she knew he wouldn't be interested in her and that she'd probably never see him again, she felt a sudden irrational love for this young boy who had tried to protect her. As he walked away she couldn't help thinking how nice his bum looked in his faded Levi's. She stammered, 'Will you be OK?'

'Sure, you heard her, I'll get something else,' he said, pausing to flash a big smile. 'I'll be fine – we'll both be fine.' He spoke with such certainty it made her want him to be the father of her children. 'Remember, we're a lot younger than types like her and she won't always be on top. One day it's going to be the turn of the little ones like us.' He flashed another smile and walked away down the corridor.

'Thank you,' she called after him and, gathering her things, made her way out of the building, berating herself for letting such soppy fantasies fill her head over someone she didn't even know. On her way back to the magazine she stopped at home to shower, change and gulp down a cup of strong coffee.

Back at the office, she was shocked that the editorial team appeared totally unfazed by the day's events. It turned out the editor knew exactly what Julia was like and had decided that Laura – who they all thought was a bit green – needed 'toughening up'. So she had sent her off, fully expecting Julia, notorious for hating juniors, to have a go at her. Laura, astonished and thinking of her ruined Joseph trousers, thought it was beyond cruel.

'But if she's like this in real life why are we writing flattering articles about her?' she shouted, shocked at her outburst.

'Because that's the business we're in, Laura: the fame game. It's what we *do*.' Her editor seemed genuinely perplexed by the young girl's naivety.

'Well it's not a game I want to play.' Laura spoke with a conviction that truly surprised her. She may only have been eighteen but she knew the whole thing stank. There and then she quit the magazine, much to her colleagues' shock, and vowed only to work for publications that wrote the truth about so-called celebrities and exposed them for who they really were, not the sugar-coated fake veneers they peddled for all their worth.

Over the years Laura had done the odd bit of digging into Julia's past as she worked her way up the tabloid ladder. When *Rise and Shine* was axed Julia had disappeared to front a current-affairs show for a channel based in Hong Kong for the best part of a decade before popping back up on *Girl Talk*, so no papers had really been all that interested in her until recently. Laura was sure that was all about to change now *Girl Talk* was a massive hit and her profile was high again. But while plastic surgery secrets were of some interest they weren't exactly front-page news, and certainly not enough to ruin her. She would need something bigger if she was to stand a chance of taking her down, and with Joel's help she might just find enough to do it. He had known Julia for twenty-five years and was much more than her cosmetic surgeon; he was also the closest thing she had to a confidant. Joel knew more about Julia than anyone, Laura was convinced of that. She reached inside her Dior bag and pulled out a digital voice recorder, placing it on the table between them.

'Ready?' she said, trying not to be distracted by the shape

of his jaw. Joel nodded as she pressed the record button. 'Good, then tell me everything you know about her.'

Joel took a swig from his wine glass and started at the very beginning.

Eight

For the first time ever Lesley's mind was not on the gorgeous man right in front of her. She was trying to listen in on the conversation her former co-star Sasha Gates was having with some sad sycophants who were hanging on her every fake word, but Dan Kincaid just kept on talking. Loudly.

'You really were the best thing about *Spitalfields*, no seriously, I mean it, I can't believe you left,' he said, now totally breaking her concentration.

'I didn't leave,' Lesley said sharply, still glaring at Sasha.

'Well, you know what I mean. It's no good without you, I haven't watched it since you left.'

His last comment actually got Lesley's attention and she turned to look him over in the unsubtle way she was known for, taking in the brown eyes, olive skin and messy bed hair that practically reached his shoulders. Lesley wondered if he had any Italian blood. That could be interesting. She appraised the broad shoulders and bulging pecs pushing out from under his jacket, the narrow waist and hips – he was at least six-three, six-four, still taller than Lesley even in her skyscraper heels. Finally, her gaze travelled down the long thighs in slim-fitting jeans and back up again, passing over the famous bulge which had seen him voted Top Hottie in Trunks in *heat* magazine's Well-Hung Studs collection. Yes, he was gorgeous, and she really should be flattered he was chatting her up in a room full of women half her age. Under any other circumstances she'd have happily dragged him back to her hotel – or even the nearest toilet – ripped that shirt off to reveal the gorgeous bod he flaunted in the tacky coffee ads that had brought him fame, and shagged him rotten. But timing was everything and right now she wouldn't be sidetracked, not even by someone as tasty as him.

Turning again in Sasha's direction, Lesley licked her lips to check the status of her lip gloss – an unconscious habit often misconstrued as a sexual sign. Dan noticed and a flush spread up from his neck, until he worked out she wasn't actually paying him any attention.

He was utterly baffled as Lesley zoned out from him and would have walked away right then – but she was so damn sexy he decided to have one more shot. 'So, what are you doing now?' he asked, again interrupting Lesley's snooping.

Bloody hell, she raged in her head, wishing he'd keep his voice down.

'Late-night TV, and I'm up for an award tonight,' she said without looking at him. She felt bad she wasn't really joining in the conversation but basically Dan was just a way of killing time until Sasha was alone. Suddenly the women talking to Sasha – fans, she bet, considering the way they were fawning – made their exit and she had her chance.

'No shit! That's amazing,' Dan said. 'Maybe I can buy you a drink later when you win—' He was still mid-sentence, mustering every ounce of charisma he had, as she began to move away from him.

'Sorry, Dan, there's someone I need to speak to. I'll catch up with you later.' Her words trailed off as she slipped away and prowled towards where Sasha was standing.

His eyes stayed on her killer legs and peachy bum as she shimmied away, flicking a coil of golden hair over her shoulder. Well and truly smitten, he called after her, 'Make sure you do, because I'll be waiting.' Fuck! What an idiot. That was so uncool it made him sound positively desperate. Why on earth had he done that?

Dan couldn't believe it as he watched her go. No woman had ever walked away from him, or for that matter shown zero interest in him. It wasn't so much that his feelings were hurt – well, actually, they were – he just couldn't fathom it. Was he losing his touch? It was well known around town that Lesley had a thing for younger men and was, by all accounts, a bit of an animal. He imagined she was a sort of female version of himself and from what he'd read in the Sunday papers he was sure she'd be amazing in bed. Plus, she was so well known for being an easy lay that it made what had just happened triply confusing.

He looked around, checking to see that no one had witnessed his pathetic display, and when he was convinced he was in the clear slowly moved towards the safety of the bar, where he was guaranteed to pull at least one *Hollyoaks* bird, if not two. They would take his mind off Lesley, surely?

Damn, the bitch had clocked her, Lesley thought, as Dan's raised voice caused Sasha to turn round. She'd wanted the pleasure of witnessing the shock on Sasha's face as she confronted her. Instead she'd had time to compose herself.

Lesley moved quickly, closing in on her prey like a cat with a cornered mouse, her eyes locked on Sasha's.

Sasha threw her arms out, half in greeting, half in the hope of attracting attention. Neither worked.

'Lesley! How lovely to see you, darling.' Sasha's voice was loud and theatrical, desperate for someone to notice what was going on and come to her rescue.

Knowing exactly what her game was, Lesley closed in tighter, effectively blocking all exits. 'Lovely to see me, my arse, you lying bitch,' Lesley hissed, her voice low.

Sasha's eyes flashed panic. 'Lesley, this is a packed room and I don't want any trouble.'

'Oh, I'll bet you don't,' Lesley said with menace as she flicked her hair and clicked her acrylic nails together, the scratching sound making Sasha wince. '*I* didn't want any trouble, did I? But we don't *always* get what we want, *do* we?' She continued to stare right at her enemy.

Sasha dropped her gaze. 'Look, I know there's been some bad blood between us in the press and it was *terrible* what happened to you so no wonder you're bitter, but I honestly don't know why you're taking it out on me.' She made an unconvincing attempt to look wide-eyed. 'You're wrong if you're trying to suggest I was in any way involved.' Her knuckles turned white as she clutched the sequinned purse she was holding.

'Let's just cut the crap, shall we?' Lesley drew even closer. 'I just came over here to tell you that I *know* it was you.'

'*What* was me?' Sasha winced, now feeling thoroughly trapped. Where was that damned assistant with her drink?

'You know exactly what I'm talking about, you phoney bitch. I can see right through you.' Lesley found herself on the verge of laughing. She had dreamed about what she'd say to Sasha if she ever got her alone and the fantasy version had been pretty similar to what was actually going on. In fact, seeing Sasha reduced to a quivering wreck made it even better than she had imagined.

'Listen, what happened had nothing to do with me, so stop looking for someone else to blame and try the nearest mirror. Now move out of my way. I have to get back to my t-t-table.' Sasha almost carried off her little tirade but the slight stammer at the end of her sentence gave her away.

As she made a move to pass, Lesley stepped aside as if to let her go but discreetly grabbed her arm and gripped hard, holding her back. 'This is not a script with a let's-be-friends-happy-ever-after ending, darling, this is real life. And I just want to let you know that I'm not going to let you get away with it. So enjoy the party and everything else while you can because I'm back and I'm coming for you ... Remember, I know all your little secrets ... so, tick-tock.' She was squeezing Sasha's arm so hard she could feel one of her false nails working loose, so she let go with a harsh laugh.

Sasha fled towards the safety of the *Spitalfields* table without looking back. As Lesley watched her slide into her seat it seemed none of her cronies had noticed their little 'catch-up'. Good, she thought, although she might have felt less smug if she'd heard Sasha, just a few feet away, whispering to the people around her, '... booze-soaked old hag ... vicious psycho ... out of control ...'

All of a sudden the lights went down, the band struck up and applause swept the room as Phillip Schofield appeared on stage and the cameras whizzed into action. God! The show had gone live and she'd not even noticed. She started to hurry across the room as she knew one of the awards they were up for was one of the first to be announced. Bloody hell, she thought, weaving her way between the tables in her mega-heels – the *Girl Talk* table would have to be so far away. Fingers crossed they would win something. Wouldn't that just be the perfect end to the perfect night? Phillip Schofield chatted away in the background as she continued her walk towards the table, the girls beckoning her to get a move on as his voice boomed over the music, announcing they were now live on air.

'And to reveal the winner of Most Popular Entertainment Presenter, please welcome one of Britain's most popular actresses – Jessie Wallace.'

Lesley sank into her seat just as Jessie appeared on stage.

'God, you're cutting it fine!' Jackie shouted above the applause. 'I thought you were going to miss it!'

Lesley smiled and touched up her lip gloss just in time for the camera shot which was now on them, as the voice-over man read out the nominees and their faces flashed up on the cinema-style screen at the side of the stage. Noticing Julia downing her Laurent Perrier, Lesley reached for the bottle in the cooler between them and found it was empty. She tutted and looked around for a full one.

Julia, meanwhile, a belligerent look on her face, was watching Jessie like a hawk. 'Jessie Wallace!' she said, too loudly. 'What the fuck has she got to do with late-night TV?!' The crew at the table stifled a giggle as the girls exchanged embarrassed looks.

Blimey, thought Lesley, Julia was acting a bit odd. Actually, she *looked* a bit odd too. It was quite dark but she could swear her face had gone a bit . . . *swollen*. Then again she didn't have the best eyesight in the world so maybe it was just the lighting. Before she had a chance to pour a drink, Julia snatched the bottle and slopped wine into her glass, spilling some on the table.

'Oh God, I hate this bit,' Karen said as she too reached for a top-up. Faye and Cheryl were the only ones watching the stage as Lesley fidgeted in her seat, trying to get comfortable, and slipped her shoes off under the table. She knew she wasn't going to win so she wanted to give her toes a rest. Six-inch heels were terrific as long as you didn't actually have to walk in them.

'C'mon, girls, here we go,' Jackie squealed as Jessie reached the podium, her chirpy voice booming into the audience.

'Let's take a look at the nominations.' She stood back as clips of all the nominees ran on the giant screen.

'Oh look – it's your old nose, Julia,' Faye whispered.

'At least it's gone now, darling, unlike your saddlebags,' she spat back.

Faye looked hurt. 'I was only joking,' she said quietly as Julia fixed her with a weird stare until she looked away. Cheryl's hand went under the table and gave Faye's leg a squeeze as the camera panned across all the nominees in the audience. Feeling the lights on them, they both smiled sweetly.

'That'll be yet another one for Lorraine,' sneered Julia rather too loudly, causing Faye, stunning in her off-the-shoulder six-grand dress, to gesture for her to be quiet as she smoothed her long hair nervously. Julia just rolled her eyes as Jackie leaned over the table.

'Now come on, girls, you never know – it could be one of you!'

'Of course we know, we always know!' Cheryl said, raising her glass.

Faye laughed. 'Yes, that it's *not* one of us! My money's on *Loose Women*. Jane McDonald.'

'I'm sticking with the unsinkable Lorraine and all who sail with her. She always wins and she's bound to win yet again tonight,' Lesley giggled, joining in the toast.

Faye suddenly looked depressed. 'And to think I haven't eaten for two days to make this dress look fabulous. It's going to be Lorraine, isn't it? I can feel it in my water.'

'Well, *I* love Lorraine,' Karen said, as Lesley giggled and pulled a face behind her back, pretending to be sick, making Faye crack up and spill her wine.

'Stand by, cameras coming again – here we go,' Jackie said excitedly, and they all fixed smiles on their faces as Jessie opened the gold envelope. A dramatic pause followed before she said, 'And the winner is ... *Karen King!*'

The applause went wild as a strange hush descended over the table. It was left to Jackie to break the silence.

'Oh my God!' she screamed, throwing her arms around Karen, who looked genuinely stunned. 'Get up! You've won!'

Nine

Karen looked around the table. Lesley looked pleased for her, and Cheryl and Faye were smiling, but Julia's expression was clearly not one of delight. Karen could feel Jackie pushing her and somehow she got herself out of her chair and made her way through the crowds and applause, climbing the stairs to the stage as if she was in a dream. The noise was almost deafening and the lights blurred her vision as she reached Jessie, who gave her the award with a hug and a kiss that left a huge red lip-print on her cheek. The cameras zoomed in on it and the room clapped again as she tried to take in the fact that she'd won.

She stammered into the microphone, 'Oh my God, I-I can't believe this!'

Feeling the cameras on them, the other girls stood up and clapped and waved as Karen clutched her award.

'What the fuck?' Julia sniped as they all clapped like circus seals. 'How on earth did *she* win?' she ranted out of the side of her mouth while flapping her arms and waving dramatically. The girls sat down again as Karen started to give her speech. 'Keep smiling,' Jackie said, gesturing towards the cameras.

Lesley knew they'd have to go and pose for pictures with Karen's award, so she slipped one of her shoes back on. She couldn't feel the other one and after a failed attempt at reaching for it under the table bent down and looked under the cloth, spotting both the shoe and something else – Cheryl's hand on Faye's inner thigh. Lesley shot back up, hoping they hadn't noticed her ferreting about down there. Well, well, well, she pondered. That was a surprise. What a night this was turning out to be.

Karen could see the girls waving at her as she looked out at the crowds of familiar TV faces: Ant and Dec, Simon Cowell, Jonathan Ross, Fern Britton and all the Loose Women, smiling from their table. Everyone who was anyone was there, and they all seemed pleased she had won.

'I really can't believe this!' she said into the mike, trying to get a better look at the *Girl Talk* table, her view blurred by the dazzling stage lighting. 'I never believed in a million years I'd get this so I haven't a clue what to say,' she laughed. The audience laughed with her. 'I want to thank all the team at *Girl Talk* because this really is a group effort, so I'm going to share this with my wonderful friends, Julia, Lesley, Cheryl, Faye, and all the people behind the cameras you don't see.' She waved the award in their direction and the girls waved back and blew kisses at her again.

Smug bitch, Julia thought, smiling so hard her lips hurt. Actually her lips *really* hurt. Just as well her face was practically paralysed from all the Botox. She would never have been able to fake it this well otherwise. Oh God, *how* could she lose out to Karen? The humiliation stung.

Something must have gone on, because she had been sure the award was hers. It didn't add up. First Karen turns up with a surprise new look, she thought, then she waltzes off with the prize I deserved, and Jackie's been all over her too. Julia's mind raced with suspicion. She knew the coke was probably making her paranoid but even that couldn't explain an upset like this. She looked at Karen, still glowing in the spotlight. She *so* must have planned this: the secret weight loss, turning up in the exact same dress Julia was wearing – the timing was just too good. Clearly Karen wasn't as green as she made out. No, she was a threat and must now be treated as such. She could hear Karen's voice thanking this person and that, grating on her, making her blood boil. She drained her glass and immediately filled it again.

Back on stage, Karen was nervously trying to wrap up her rambling speech. 'I don't know what else to say other than thanks again,' she ended, making her way down the stage steps, where she was led away to the winners' room to have her picture taken in the press pen. After posing for the first few shots she had attempted to get straight back to her table so she could celebrate with the girls, but Jessie Wallace wouldn't let her go. It seemed rude to leave while she was being so enthusiastic but finally the press, bored of snapping the two of them from every conceivable angle and aware there was not the slightest chance of a knicker shot or a boob falling out, drifted away, and Karen was able to wander back to the table, where the others swamped her with hugs and kisses for all the room to see. Then the cameras panned away and they settled back in their seats.

Straining to hear over the applause as Gillian Taylforth appeared on stage to present the award for best soap, Karen was just about able to pick up bits of what Julia was saying across the table.

'What I mean is, the problem with awards these days is that they are all so political.'

Lesley gave her a funny look. 'I don't know what you mean,' she said. 'They're voted for by the audience, aren't they?' Lesley, aware that Karen was now listening, tried to steer the conversation to safer ground, but Julia knew exactly what she was doing and raised her voice a notch.

'Well they *say* that, but look at poor Catherine Tate when they gave her award to Ant and Dec. You of all people must know what I mean, Karen?'

Cheryl and Faye both turned away and focused on Gillian Taylforth. 'Oh God, here we go,' Faye whispered.

'Just don't turn round and we can't get dragged into it,' Cheryl said, as both kept their eyes firmly on the stage.

Karen noticed the others turn away and suddenly felt vulnerable. Why was Julia doing this? She hadn't done anything to deserve it. She could feel tears begin to well in her eyes and didn't want anyone to see. She blinked and sneaked a look at Julia, who was tipping her wine down her throat. Even in the low light she could see something strange going on with Julia's face. She glanced at Jackie, who was also staring. Jackie gave Lesley a dig in the ribs. They peered at Julia, her skin now puffy, swelling and blistering at an alarming rate, a lump the size of an egg popping up above one of her eyes.

'What are you staring at?' Julia shouted, causing Faye and Cheryl to break their whispered conversation and stop touching under the table. There were audible gasps as eruptions flared up around her lips. Julia looked annoyed. 'What? *What?*' she said as they all began to shuffle closer.

Jackie, sitting next to her, leaned in. 'Look, I don't want to panic you, but something is wrong. You don't look right.'

'Ha ha, very funny, I'm not falling for that one,' Julia said, laughing, expecting the girls to join in, but none of them did. 'Stop looking at me, I know you're trying to wind me up and it's not funny. Stop it. STOP IT!'

Jackie inched even closer and put a hand on Julia's arm. 'Look, we're being serious. I think you've had a reaction to something – you've got these lumps on your face. Come to the bathroom with me, Julia, and we'll sort it out.'

Julia slapped her hand away. 'I'm not stupid, I know what you're trying to do,' she said, the paranoia really taking hold. 'We're going to win the Most Popular Entertainment Programme award and you don't want me to go up and get it. I heard what you were saying to Karen before, I'm not deaf. I know what's going on behind my back with the Slimfast Queen here!'

Karen flinched as Julia practically spat the words across the table. 'Julia, there is nothing going on behind your back,' she said pleadingly. 'You've probably just eaten something bad and you're not well. Let's get you out.'

'Julia, just come with me now,' Jackie tried again, her voice soothing as she grabbed at her arm. 'You'll thank me for this.'

Julia shook her head. 'There is *nothing* wrong with me!'

The women lapsed into a shocked silence. They had never seen Julia behave like this. And by now her forehead was so swollen it had given her the appearance of a baby hammerhead shark.

On stage, Helen England, the face of Channel 6's *Good Morning Britain* and acknowledged Queen of Daytime, jaw-length auburn bob teased into spirals, was accepting the award for Best Daytime Show. 'If you could just bear with me, I have a very important personal announcement to make,' she said as a hush descended over the room.

'My god, look at her,' Lesley said. 'It's only a few weeks since she had a baby. She must have had lipo.'

'I can't tell you how proud I am to be associated with such a brilliant and successful show as *Good Morning Britain*,' she said, her pewter dress, fashioned from wafer-thin leather and clinging like a second skin, gleaming under the lights. She held the award aloft to thunderous applause. A shot of the *GMB* table, where a crimson-faced man in a dinner jacket whistled and a cork flew from a bottle of bubbly, replaced her close-up on the giant screen. Helen affected a coy smile. 'Thank you.' She gazed at the award. 'I am truly humbled to be associated with such an outstanding show and can only say how delighted I am that the viewers also love *GMB* – my *baby* – as much as I do.'

Lesley rolled her eyes. 'Oh for God's sake get on with it,' she said under her breath. As Helen's perfectly made-up face filled the giant screen again Lesley narrowed her eyes. 'I don't care what she says – if she hasn't had Botox I'm a virgin.'

'So, I'm sure you will all understand when I say I have thought long and hard before coming to a very big decision.' Helen took a deep breath, causing her breasts to swell. 'It's with mixed feelings that I've decided to leave *Good Morning Britain* at the end of the present run—'

Lesley gasped. 'Shit. Did you hear that? She's fucking off.'

'And I can think of no one I would rather see in my place on the sofa than –' she shielded her eyes from the lights and gazed in the direction of the *Girl Talk* girls – 'the very lovely Karen King! Not only is she a warm and witty broadcaster, brilliant at thinking on her feet – and we all know how important that is on live TV – but when it comes to serious interviews she also shows extraordinary sensitivity. I think we all appreciate her emotional moments on *Girl Talk* and I'm sure I'm not the only one who wept buckets when Karen interviewed the gorgeous and talented Kym Marsh.' She paused, smiling indulgently. 'In all honesty, Karen, you and I have an awful lot in common.'

Ten

As Helen swept off the stage Karen, shell-shocked, her throat dry, reached for her wine. Had she heard her right? Was Helen England really putting her up for the best job in daytime telly?

Lesley stared open-mouthed at the stage as an uncomfortable atmosphere descended on the girls. 'Christ,' Lesley said finally. 'She's full of surprises.'

Julia glared at Karen. Cheryl, turning away, whispered something in Faye's ear. Only Jackie beamed with delight.

'My God, girl, this is turning out to be your night. Oh, steady, looks like we're in for a royal visit. Her Majesty Queen of Daytime approaching at twelve o'clock.'

Karen spun round in her chair to see Helen England gliding towards her, her procession interrupted by hugs and kisses and tearful hand-wringing at every table she passed. One of the *Good Morning Britain* production assistants clung to her, shaking with emotion, as Helen, her fabulous dress in danger of being crushed, attempted to free herself. A man with a walkie-talkie and a headset finally came to her rescue, prising the girl's hands from Helen's neck.

'Look at the state of that. Off her face,' Lesley said in disgust as the girl was dragged away.

'I do hope I haven't put you on the spot,' Helen said several minutes later when she finally made it to Karen, bending and planting feather-light kisses on both her cheeks. There was a streak of mascara on her bare shoulder from the *Good Morning Britain* limpet. Karen, flushed and awkward under the scrutiny of the others, scrambled to her feet, almost tempted to curtsey in the presence of such dazzling TV royalty. 'I'm very flattered, just completely overwhelmed . . . I mean, I don't know what to-to say,' she stuttered as Helen gave a modest bow. 'I mean, thanks, Helen, that was really lovely of you.'

Helen pulled Karen away from the table. 'I would hate to think the other girls are in any way miffed I picked you out for special praise like that,' she said, wrapping an arm around her shoulder.

Karen glanced back at the table where Lesley was furiously slapping on a fresh layer of lip gloss, Cheryl and Faye were in a huddle, and Julia was waving her empty glass in the air. Jackie made a thumbs-up sign. 'No . . . I mean, they're my friends.'

'The trouble is friends – *real* friends – are so hard to come by in TV. It's worth remembering that.' She shot a look at the table. 'Oh dear, they really don't look very happy. I hope that's not down to little me.' Karen locked eyes with Lesley, who gave her a tight little smile. Helen frowned. 'Is there something wrong with Julia Hill? She looks . . . unfortunate.' Karen turned to see Jackie wrestling Julia's glass from her hand.

'I think she ate something that didn't agree with her,' Karen said.

'Is *that* what they call it these days?' Helen turned back to Karen. 'You know, I didn't get where I am by being too trusting, so my advice is, just watch your back.' She cast another mean-ingful look at the *Girl Talk* table, where Jackie was trying to heave Julia from her chair. Helen raised an eyebrow. 'Take my advice – you really don't need the kind of people who'll drag you down in your life.'

When Karen sat down Cheryl rounded on her. 'Having fun with your new best friend? How long have you two been so close?'

Karen flushed. She had only ever exchanged the briefest of hellos with Helen England in the canteen at Channel 6 and was as surprised as anyone to have been singled out by her.

Cheryl muttered under her breath to Faye, who made a *tut-tut* sound, and Julia knocked over a wine glass as Jackie grappled with her. On stage, Phillip Schofield was linking into a commercial break. 'Will somebody *please* give me a hand?' Jackie said as Julia struck out, aiming a sharp kick at the producer's shin.

Sweat ran down Julia's swollen face. The turquoise eyes were bloodshot and darting frantically about. 'Should we call a doctor or something?' asked Karen, alarmed. 'I saw a documentary about allergies and how some people can go into something called apoplectic shock—'

'*Anaphylactic* shock,' Jackie said, ducking as Julia aimed a punch at her.

'Something like that,' Karen went on. 'If you have a problem with nuts and bee stings, that kind of stuff, your airwaves swell up—'

'*Airways.*'

'And you can't breathe or anything. It's really dangerous.'

Lesley, busy touching up her make-up again, said, 'Can it kill you?'

'I think so, if you don't get medical help fast enough.'

Lesley glanced at Julia, mouth open, saliva running down her chin, livid blotches speckling her throat. 'I'd give her another few minutes,' she said, unconcerned. 'She doesn't look nearly bad enough yet.'

Julia swatted at Jackie. 'Will you take your fucking hands off me!' she screeched.

Karen got to her feet. She could probably do with some air. 'I'll come with you. How long before the next award?'

Jackie glanced at the running order. 'Ages yet.'

All around, people were taking advantage of the ad break, nipping out for a sneaky fag or to the loo.

Between them, Karen and Jackie propped Julia up and propelled her from the ballroom. 'We can slip out the back way,' Jackie said, but Julia, suddenly animated, dug her heels in. 'I do *not* use the tradesmen's entrance,' she said, eyes blazing.

Karen shrugged and they steered her towards the hotel lobby, doing their best to screen her from the gaze of curious onlookers.

Away from the dim lights of the ballroom, Julia looked even worse. 'What's happened to her?' Karen said, frightened. 'I wonder if she had the prawn cocktail. I never touch shellfish, not when I'm out.'

'It's not a dodgy prawn – she's *high*,' Jackie said, placing a hand on Julia's lumpy brow. 'Maybe she snorted some bad stuff. Even so, I wouldn't have thought it would turn her into the Elephant Man. Christ, she's burning up.'

'I *am* here, you know,' Julia said, beginning to come round.

'Do you want to sit down? Can I get you some water? Should I call an ambulance?' Karen peered at her in dismay.

'Oh, you'd love that, wouldn't you? Me carted off, leaving the field clear for you,' Julia said, rallying. 'I wasn't born yesterday, you know.'

Karen shot a despairing look at Jackie. 'I think she's delirious.'

'I am NOT delirious. I know exactly what your game is, you two-faced cow, going behind everyone's backs, sucking up to Helen smarmy England, getting her to put you in the frame for a job the rest of us would kill for. Well, it won't work, because it's not her job to give. Who does she think she is, Lady fucking Bountiful? If you think I'm going to give up without a fight you're wrong.'

'But Julia, I—'

Julia shook Jackie's hand off her arm and straightened her crumpled dress. 'That job is *mine*. I deserve it. Do you really think I've been slaving away on some shitty graveyard show with the likes of you all this time for nothing?' She gave a derisive snort. 'I just hope you're ready for a fight, because mark my words, as of now, the gloves are *off*.'

Karen gasped. 'You don't think I *knew* about this?'

'Well, didn't you?' Karen spun around to find Cheryl, hands on hips, behind her. Lesley had also appeared, followed by Faye, whose face was a mixture of hurt, betrayal and disgust.

'No, no, I promise, I had no idea,' Karen said. 'I'm as shocked as all of you.'

'Only you didn't look too surprised, if you ask me,' Cheryl went on. 'And I couldn't help noticing you'd just touched up your lippy in time for that nice big close-up when Helen England said your name. The whole thing looked totally set up.'

Jackie let go of Julia and stepped forward. 'Let's not spoil the evening, girls. Better to sit down tomorrow when everyone's sober' – she glanced at Julia – 'and back to normal, and discuss this in a rational manner. You all know Karen would never do anything underhand. She's not the secretive type.'

Julia snorted. 'No, of course she's not. Remind me, we *are* talking about the woman who managed to lose half her body weight without a word to any of us. Doesn't that strike you as a tad sneaky?'

Lesley took a step towards Julia. 'As for you . . . what makes you think the *GMB* job is yours? I've as good a chance as anyone.'

'Darling, you're never *awake* at eleven in the morning, let alone in any fit state to anchor a live show.'

'Oh, and you'd be better, would you? Have you looked in a mirror lately? You look like something out of a flesh-eating-zombie flick.'

Julia flinched and tentatively prodded her face. She still couldn't feel a thing. 'I might have had a dodgy prawn,' she said.

'That's what I thought,' Karen piped up.

Lesley shot the pair of them a spiteful smile. 'Did it have a name, this prawn – *Charlie*, maybe?' She put her face as close as she dared to Julia's. It looked ready to burst. 'Just so you know, I've got my eye on Helen England's job as well, and I'd be a bloody sight better at it than you. People want a woman they can *relate* to, someone on their *wavelength*, who speaks their language, not some . . .' she searched for the right words, 'self-obsessed *automaton*.'

'I'd think very hard about making an enemy of me if I were you, Lesley.' Julia glared at the little group and pointed at Karen. 'I intend to go head-to-head with our double-crossing little *frenemy* here for that job. And I don't expect anyone else to complicate the proceedings. Is that clear?'

Jackie tapped her watch. 'Look, can we just leave this now? We need to get back inside.'

Karen stared at Julia. Out of the corner of her eye she could see Jason, hand in hand with slutty Hannah, descending the steps and posing for pictures in front of the press pen, his hand on her firm round bum. She swallowed and hastily looked away.

'Julia,' she said, 'please let's not fall out over this.'

Summoning a thin smile, Julia told her, 'You appear to be confusing me with someone who gives a fuck.'

Karen turned away. Her feet were killing her. The girl in the shop had said YSL heels were a breeze to walk in, even the six-inch ones, which she personally wore around town all day, even in Waitrose. It was flatties that wrecked your feet and made you walk like a shot-putter, she said. Clearly she was either lying or had very peculiar feet capable of withstanding intense pain. Karen shifted from one throbbing foot to the other.

'Don't you turn your back on me,' Julia said.

As Karen began to protest she lurched forward, and somehow missed her footing. Then she was tumbling down the stairs, arms and legs flailing, dress ripping, as she bounced along in what felt like slow motion. She cast a desperate look in the direction of the girls, now upside-down and running at her as she somersaulted towards the salivating press pack, flashbulbs popping, dazzling her. She landed on her back, spread-eagled and breathless, heart pounding, head spinning, nauseous, as Julia, bounding down the stairs, came into focus.

Lesley would have slipped away if she could but Jackie wasn't having it. It was bad enough, she said, that Karen and Julia had disappeared, without the other girls doing a vanishing act as well. They were still up for Most Popular Entertainment Programme – what if they won and the cameras cut to their table only to find it practically deserted? How would that look? Lesley didn't much care: let Cheryl and Faye go up, not that they would win anyway. It was bound to go to the *Loose Women* lot and Lesley didn't begrudge them yet another award. Kate Thornton had actually collared Lesley earlier to say how much she loved her on *Girl Talk* and ask where she had got her dress. She wasn't being funny either. Lesley was so taken aback she had poured out the story of finding the dress in Upper Street all those years ago, prompting Kate to say she looked amazing and how lucky she was to still be wearing the same size as in her twenties. Again, she was being completely sincere. Lesley, charmed, had poured her a glass of bubbly and said *The X Factor* was tons better when Kate was doing it. *She* was being serious too.

Bored, as Phillip Schofield ran through the contenders for Best Sports Outside Broadcast, Lesley sank two glasses of champagne in quick succession and poured a third. The cute waiter with the pert bum swooped to ask if she was ready for another bottle. 'Bring two,' she said, 'before I lose the will to live,' and pushed back her chair, prompting Jackie to break off from applauding the team from *Channel 4 Racing* and give her a stern look. 'Permission to go to the toilet, miss?'

'No need to be sarcastic. Just don't wander off – and make sure you've got your phone in case I need to get hold of you.'

'Why don't you just go the whole hog and have me electronically tagged?'

Jackie ignored her. 'Two more breaks before the final segment. Please be back well before then.'

Lesley got to her feet and glanced in the direction of the *Spitalfields* table. No sign of Sasha Gates. Some of the soap awards were still to come; the cow was probably having her make-up retouched just in case. On her way to the toilet Lesley checked her phone and found a text from a number she didn't recognize: **u r the most bootiful woman in the room Dan**. Dan? Dan *Kincaid*. How on earth had he got her number? She smiled. He must be keen. Well, keep him dangling. She wouldn't bother to reply. Lesley's treat-'em-mean attitude had served her well so far. Just then a voice behind her said, 'Your little party's looking a bit thin on the ground. I hear it all got a bit messy.'

Lesley turned, to find Sasha Gates looking scornful.

'I had heard *Girl Talk* was an absolute bitchfest but I didn't know you actually *came to blows*.'

Lesley bristled. 'I have no idea what you're talking about.'

'I'm talking about your chums, slugging it out on the pavement outside. I mean, women fighting ...' She turned up her nose. 'It's a bit – how shall I put it? – *common*. Don't you think? But perhaps that's why you fit in so well—'

She was interrupted by Lesley slapping her hard on the side of the face. Within seconds a pink handprint began to take shape on her cheek. Lesley marvelled. She had never really believed that actually happened; it was like watching a Polaroid develop – extraordinary. Sasha, eyes wide, put a hand to her throbbing face as Lesley straightened her ring with its square-cut topaz. There would be quite a bruise. And she would be in quite a bit of trouble.

Quick as a flash she imagined herself back in the market at *Spitalfields*, cameras rolling, shooting a difficult emotional scene, having to turn on the tears in time for her close-up, and instantly her face became stricken. 'I can't believe you hit me,' she said.

Sasha gasped. '*I* hit *you*!'

'I know, that's what I said.' Lesley backed away from her. 'Women fighting ... it's so ... *common*. Just as well no one saw you or you'd be in big trouble.' She turned on her heel and walked away, pleased now that Jackie had made her stay.

For the umpteenth time Jackie checked her watch. Where the hell was Lesley? In ten minutes or so they would be announcing the winner of the Most Popular Entertainment Programme. Jackie felt sweat trickle down her back as she thought about trying to explain the night's events to Paula Grayson, the *Girl Talk* editor. She felt slightly queasy.

Cheryl leaned across the table. 'Faye's not well. I think I should take her home. Can you get us a car?'

'Once they announce the award.'

Faye pulled a face. 'I might throw up.'

'You can do what you like *after* they announce the award.'

Cheryl gave Jackie a look of disgust. 'She's not *well*.'

'She looks fine.' Jackie pressed a tissue to her damp brow and thought about Julia an hour or so earlier, being whisked away to the private clinic Channel 6 trusted to straighten out its stars in cases of extreme emotional exhaustion. What an almighty mess. She knew she should have taken that job on the Peter Andre show when she had the chance, rather than opt to work with five women.

'I'm getting my period,' Faye said, 'and I haven't got anything.'

Jackie opened her bag, dug out a tampon and tossed it across the table. 'Half an hour, *then* you can go.'

Faye shrugged at Cheryl and slipped the tampon in her bag. 'I *might* be able to last,' she said in a sulky voice.

Jackie scanned the room for Lesley and spotted her at the bar with Dan Kincaid. 'Give me strength,' she said under her breath, fumbling in her bag for her phone. As she dialled Lesley's number she saw Sasha Gates, fists clenched, advancing on Lesley from behind. Lesley's phone rang and rang as Dan Kincaid whispered in her ear and Lesley laughed, tossing her head back, a mass of blonde waves bouncing up and down. The phone went to voicemail and Jackie cursed. Sasha Gates was now just a few paces away.

Jackie pressed redial as Sasha jabbed Lesley in the back, making her spin round. She gave Lesley a shove and yanked at her dress. What the . . . ? One of Lesley's breasts tumbled out. Sasha tugged at the fabric, unleashing the other breast. The pair jiggled perkily at Dan Kincaid, who lurched forward, cupping them in his large, capable hands. Jackie briefly closed her eyes. When she looked again she couldn't work out if he was copping a feel or being chivalrous. Lesley, her face furious, looked like she was about to give Sasha a slap but Dan, hands still strategically placed, stepped between the two women. As Sasha marched off Jackie saw Dan and a giggling Lesley disappear through a door at the side of the bar, her phone still ringing in her bag.

On stage, Bradley Walsh opened a gold envelope and prepared to announce the winner of the Most Popular Entertainment Programme.

'And the award goes to . . . *Girl Talk*!'

A light shone in Jackie's face. She managed an unconvincing smile and raised her glass to the camera that was now pointing at her, its shot of the empty *Girl Talk* table filling the giant screen next to Bradley Walsh. Faye and Cheryl had seen their chance and slipped away while she was preoccupied with Lesley. Jackie closed her eyes for a moment and prayed the ground would open up and swallow her. When nothing happened she got to her feet, hearing whispers of 'Who's she?' as she made her way to the stage to collect the award on behalf of the show. Paula Grayson would kill her.

Eleven

In the back of the car Karen tugged at her dress, smoothing the rumpled fabric, trying not to think about the rip left by Julia's heel. It was the most expensive dress she had ever owned and now it was ruined, the front spattered with marks where drinks had been sloshed over her – Julia again – and a strange dark stain she couldn't identify; something greasy. She had no idea what it was or where it had come from. It was as if one of those canapés the waiters were hawking round, cute little burgers on miniature buns, had slid down her front. She had seen a few people caught out by those, mayonnaise and ketchup oozing out as soon as they took a bite; Davina McCall, bronzed and lithe in a white dress slashed to the thigh, plucking a gherkin from her cleavage. Karen had steered well clear, even though the smell was tantalizing.

She studied the dress, so perfect under its plastic cover just a few hours earlier. The stain would probably never come out. Not that it mattered. She would not be wearing it again. Not ever.

A video reel began to play in her head, one awful image after another. She saw herself start to lose her footing and go head-first down the stairs and on to the pavement, arms spread out, her face a mixture of shock and fear as she tried to save herself. She had lay there sprawled out, dress hiked up, Julia teetering above her, killer heel at the ready. To think for one mad moment she had actually imagined Julia was about to help her to her feet. But instead she had stepped over her. *Stepped over her!* At least she would have if the heel, still attached to Karen's dress, hadn't sent her flying. Served her right.

Inside Karen's head the images started to jump about and jumble up. She heard the sickening sound of her gorgeous dress being ripped open by Julia's stiletto, her own voice whimpering in protest, and a series of small explosions as flashbulbs popped. There was a glimpse of red as the sole of Julia's designer shoe lifted off the ground. Something else came back to Karen: the sudden shove in the back that had made her lose her balance in the first place.

In her mind's eye she saw the scene play out again in wide shot; the photographers in the press pen, some on stepladders, all baying, and Julia, behind her, reaching out in slow motion to knock her off her feet. How could she be so mean?

In all the mayhem, with everyone shouting and Julia's arms flailing like windmills, her studded heel way too close for comfort, Karen had cowered, covering her head with her hands. The next thing she saw was a pair of shiny black brogues inches from her face. Someone was helping her to her feet, propelling her away from the snappers, whisking her into the back of a waiting car. She sank into the leather seat, safe behind the tinted glass, tears streaming down her face. As the car pulled away, horn blaring, the paparazzi jumped clear, one or two running alongside, banging on the windows, yelling at her.

The car swept along Park Lane, pricey hotels with their commissionaires in fancy top hats on one side, Hyde Park on the other. The traffic was light and they sped on towards Victoria, Karen squashed into the corner of the seat, the leather cool against her bare legs, the scent of lemon drifting towards her from an air freshener on the dashboard. As the car idled at a red light she glanced at the rear-view mirror and locked eyes with her driver, Dave. He had said nothing since wading in to the fray to pluck her from the ground, practically carrying her to the car, which was parked, rear door open, engine running. He frowned at her.

'Are you OK, Karen?' he said.

The lights changed, the car behind tooted, and she shook her head as they accelerated away.

The whole night had been a complete disaster. She wondered if she was to blame, if maybe some vengeful god was taking her down a peg or two for daring to feel good about her new slimline self. No, that was ridiculous. She placed a hand on her ribcage and drew in a deep breath, holding it for a count of five. On the pavement, in front of a hotel, a couple, arms wrapped around each other, were kissing. She watched them, turning to crane her neck as the car slid past, the man stroking the woman's cheek. She sighed, settled back in the seat and looked up to find Dave watching her in the rear-view mirror.

'I'm sorry you got caught up in all that,' she said. 'It was really good of you but it just shouldn't have happened.'

There was a moment of silence. Dave gave a shrug. 'It's no big deal, don't worry about it,' he said, as if scraping people off the ground was the kind of thing he did every day.

She stared out of the window at a girl in a short, tight skirt and clingy vest, no coat, outside a fast-food place. A second girl with masses of hair and a tiny dress covered in big gold sequins appeared with a carton piled high with chips. Karen marvelled. It wasn't warm by any means but they seemed immune. It must be something to do with being young – not that she had ever gone out without her coat, even when she was a teenager. It was bad enough walking the length of the red carpet. The girls picked at the chips, stepping over rubbish and bits of food in the street around them. Karen shivered. Immediately, she felt a blast of warm air on her legs.

She gazed at the rear-view mirror again, willing Dave to look at her, but he kept his eyes on the road. 'No big deal!' He was being kind, that's all, trying to make her feel better. One thing was certain: 'no big deal' was not what the tabloids would be saying.

It wasn't like Dave to walk her to the door. He would usually pull up on the drive of her semi in Clapham's Old Town, wait for her to let herself in and switch off the alarm, then he'd be off. Not this time, though. As soon as he swung on to the drive he cut the engine and turned around in his seat, staring at her, all serious, for what felt like a long time. She managed a self-conscious smile, knowing she must have black mascara smudges under each eye. She touched her hair, tucked a strand behind her ear in a half-hearted effort to get it looking right again. Her knee was a mess and sore, covered in blood. Dave got out of the car while she stayed put, as if she had lost the use of her legs, and waited for him to help her out. At the front door she fumbled in her bag for her keys, struggling with the locks, finally stepping into the hall and punching the code into the alarm keypad. Dave followed her and shut the door behind him.

In the kitchen he took off his jacket and slung it over the back of a chair, loosening his tie. She perched on a stool at the breakfast bar, liking the sight of a man taking charge, looking after her, filling the kettle, finding mugs and teabags. While the kettle boiled he rummaged in the first-aid kit for plasters and antiseptic ointment.

'I'm fine, honestly, it's only a graze,' she said without much conviction. 'I'll see to it later.'

He stood with his back to her, running the cold tap, soaking a piece of cotton wool. 'Let's get you cleaned up,' he said.

She was shaking when he bathed her knee, being gentle, asking if he was hurting her. 'No, honestly, I'm fine,' she said, feeling peculiar and light-headed, reaching out to steady herself on the breakfast bar.

Dave peered at her, concerned, his face just inches away. 'Are you sure about that?'

She nodded. She could smell cologne, something lemony and woody. She had never been close enough before to notice whether or not he wore cologne. She had never noticed that his eyes were the palest grey. She had never really *looked* at him, taken in the broad shoulders, the way his mouth was a bit lopsided when he smiled, how his blond hair had a tendency to flop over his eyes. He was just Dave, who drove her round while she leafed through scripts and programme notes and made endless calls on her mobile.

'I just feel a bit weird, dizzy,' she said. 'I don't know, is it delayed shock do you think?'

'It could be. Maybe I should get you looked at, take you to casualty or something. You might have concussion.'

'I didn't bump my head.'

'You sure?' He moved closer, put a hand on her brow, kept it there a second or two. He cleared his throat. 'Do you feel sick? Have you got a headache?'

She shook her head. She did feel peculiar, though, definitely hot and bothered, a bit – what was the word? – *floaty*. Dave's hand was on her leg, the cotton wool pressed against the wound.

'Just let me sort this out then we'll see what other damage there is,' he said, smiling. 'Don't worry, I know what I'm doing. I'll have you good as new in no time.' He squeezed a blob of ointment on to the end of his finger and dabbed it over the wound. 'Is that all right with you?'

She swallowed. It was. It was very all right with her.

Twelve

He was about to go, even had his jacket on, but said he would make that cup of tea he had promised her first, and while his back was turned she slipped off the stool and went over to him. The *whoosh* of the kettle boiling meant he didn't hear her so when he turned around and found her right behind him he jumped. That made them both laugh.

She felt that funny hot-and-bothered sensation again, which she now knew had nothing to do with falling on her face and everything to do with him.

She wasn't sure how she ended up in his arms – had he kissed her or the other way round? – but suddenly Dave's lips were on hers, making her breathless, his tongue exploring her mouth till she felt giddy. Eventually he pulled away and said, 'Are you sure about this?' He held her face in his hands, gazing at her, making her think of the kissing couple they had passed on the way home. The way he was looking at her made her head swim.

She nodded and took his hand, led him back into the hall and up the stairs to her bedroom. As she pushed open the door she stopped and kissed him again. She was sure.

Dave gazed around him at the bed with its crisp white linen, a fur throw draped across the end. He suspected there was some kind of rule about drivers sleeping with TV presenters. The trouble was he had fancied Karen for ages and never really thought he had a chance. Now he was in her bedroom, she was smiling up at him and, rule or not, he wasn't about to walk away. The room was cream with splashes of gold and amber here and there, the wall behind the bed like a sheet of precious metal. Facing him was a cast-iron fireplace, a row of golden candles running the length of the mantelpiece. In the hearth was a carving of a leopard, head down, ears back. There were three paintings on the wall above the fireplace, a man's face seen from different angles.

On the floor in the far corner a lamp threw soft light into the room. Dave bent and kissed the top of Karen's head. For the first time ever she felt small and fragile as his hand moved up her back, finding the zip, tugging at it. She could barely breathe as he eased the straps off her shoulders and the dress slid to the floor. She swayed, eyes shut, woozy, his hands on her bare skin now as he began to kiss her neck.

When Jason left she had vowed that was it: no more men. That was before the weight started to fall off, though, and she got herself looking the best she had for at least a decade. Dave unhooked her bra and she had the strangest feeling, like her legs were about to give way. He pulled her close, his mouth on hers; she stood on tiptoe, undoing the buttons on his shirt as he kissed her. No going back now.

His hand was on her back, barely touching her, resting on her waist, sliding down over her— She stopped, panic-stricken. Oh my God, she was wearing her *Spanx*! Mortified, she stared at Dave as he wrestled with the hideous control pants. Baffled, he plucked at the waistband, which over the course of the night had almost welded itself to Karen's body. He stepped back, peering at the monstrosity, defeated, while Karen tried to wriggle out of his arms. Oh *why* had she left the light on!

'I've-just-remembered-there's-something-I-have-to-do-so-you-need-to-go-sorry,' she gabbled, frantic.

Dave dragged his gaze away from the sturdiest knickers he had ever encountered. 'Hey, calm down, what's wrong?'

'It's-the-thingy-I-forgot-all-about-it-need-to-see-to-it-now-before-you-know ...' She cringed. That would teach her for inviting a strange man into her bed. She had that horrible sense again of Somebody Up There putting her in her place, making sure she didn't get too big for her boots. She wished she could just disappear. Right, that was it. From now on she was going to be celibate, and as for the Spanx, they were going in the bin, bloody things, just in case she got hit by a bus. Imagine ending up in hospital and them having to bring in special cutting gear just to get them off. She would rather die. Come to think of it, she would rather die *now*.

Dave put his hands on her shoulders and gazed at her. He looked crestfallen. 'Is it me? Did I do something wrong?'

She shook her head, miserable, gazing at her feet, keeping her arms folded over her bare breasts. 'It's me,' she whispered. 'Not exactly a good look, is it?' She was ready to cry.

Dave tilted her face up. She shut her eyes. 'Look at me,' he said. 'Come on.'

She stood, eyes closed, waiting for him to say something else. When he didn't she risked taking a peek.

'You have no idea how gorgeous you are,' he said, the grey eyes serious. 'A woman like you, top of your game and all that – maybe you just don't fancy me. I mean, I'm just a driver.'

'No! I do, I definitely do. Fancy you. It's just—' She hesitated. 'The pants.'

He grinned and led her to the bed. 'You haven't seen mine yet.'

Afterwards, he went downstairs to finally make that cup of tea. She waited until he had gone then scrambled out of bed, grabbed a dressing gown and dimmed the lamp a notch, lighting the candles on the mantelpiece. By the time he returned, naked, carrying two mugs of tea, she was propped up against a pillow, dressing gown securely fastened, beaming happily. He was in great shape, no doubt about it, tall and toned with strong muscular arms and the kind of abs you only get from working out. She resolved to put in more effort at the gym.

'You have very good taste,' he said, handing her a mug of tea and getting back into bed.

She burst out laughing. 'You like yourself, don't you?'

'No, no, I didn't mean that.' He shook his head, embarrassed, and a lock of blond hair flopped over his eye. 'I mean this place. It's really amazing, the way you've done it up. It's like modern but a home, if you know what I mean. Some people have these amazing places, all designer stuff that cost a fortune, but it doesn't look like anyone really lives there.'

'You know, you can get people to "dress" your house for you: choose pictures, fill the shelves with swanky books and collections of films on DVD, box sets of *Wallander*, that kind of thing.'

'You're kidding.'

'I knew someone who moved out while his architect, designer, stylist, you name it, got cracking on creating the perfect home. Once they'd finished, he moved back in again, didn't lift a finger.'

'Unbelievable.'

She was enjoying this, sitting in bed with a good-looking man, chatting after some pretty mind-blowing sex. She smiled at him over the rim of her cup. He smiled back. She couldn't quite work out how old he was – younger than her, definitely, thirty maybe. If she was right that meant she was *ten years* older than him. She felt a ripple of pleasure. It struck her she didn't even know his last name or where he lived. Just as she was about to ask, he said, 'I used to drive Debbie Irving. Two years, to and from Elstree, all the awards, functions, formal dinners. She's got a fantastic place in Hampstead – black floors, bits of sculpture that must have cost a fortune. But it's a bit *too* perfect, if you know what I mean.'

Karen sipped her tea. She had met Debbie Irving a couple of times, once in the loos at Soho House at the press launch for a new season of *Crossing the Line*, and again a few weeks later when she came on *Girl Talk*. Karen liked her, found her funny and down to earth, not a shred of luvviness about her. She was also very beautiful and very thin, a size 8 probably without even trying. She had turned up in her skinny jeans and tucked into crisps and sandwiches in the green room, glugged a large glass of wine, not a care in the world. Debbie Irving wouldn't be seen dead in Spanx. She probably had a knicker drawer full of flimsy smalls, red and black numbers that tied at the sides.

A thought crept into her head. She looked at Dave, who was now putting his empty mug on the cabinet at the side of the bed, making sure it was on the coaster without having to be told, and wondered just how well he had got to know Debbie Irving when he was driving for her. Just how much of her house he had seen. She wondered what Debbie Irving's bedroom was like. She *wondered* if she was just the latest in a long line of conquests. Her confidence began to ebb away.

He turned to face her, pulling her close, teasing the knot of her dressing-gown belt undone. She felt herself go tense. She was thinking about that famous set of pictures, Debbie Irving on a beach somewhere in her bikini looking like a goddess. The very same pictures they had shown on *Girl Talk* when they had her on. No, it was no good. Her nerve had done a runner.

'Dave, I'm really sorry,' she said, struggling to get the words out and at the same time secure her dressing gown as he kissed her. 'Look, I think I need to try and get some sleep. It's been quite a night and I'm still feeling a bit out of it. I think it's just starting to hit me.'

He took her hand and pressed it to his mouth. 'No problem, if you're sure. I just don't want to shoot off if you've still got that concussion thing going on.'

'Really, I'm fine, I promise. I can always call you if I have a relapse.'

At 4 a.m. Karen gave up trying to sleep and went to run a bath. She poured scented foam into the water and slumped into the oversized armchair in the corner of the room while the bath filled. When she was with Jason he wouldn't let her have an armchair in the bathroom, said it was 'girly'. Thanks to him, they had ended up with a wet room, some kind of slate on the walls and floor, the whole thing grey and gloomy, like a prison cell. Definitely not intended for long, relaxing soaks. In fact, there wasn't even a bath by the time he had finished, just a huge shower that was so powerful it almost knocked her over. It was a functional room, minimalist. At the time she had said she liked it but the truth was it made her think of the kind of showers you get at the gym.

At least now she had a proper bathroom again with a nice

big tub, somewhere light and airy, with a wicker basket filled with soft fluffy towels and as much girly stuff as she wanted. She eyed the piece of driftwood on the shelf running along the side of the bath and the giant shells she had filled with pretty soaps on the windowsill. There was none of that in the wet room.

As the steam filled the room she examined her knee, where a plaster covered the cut and a bruise was starting to appear. There were grazes on the palms of her hands too, from trying to break her fall. She rubbed at her wrist, which felt tender. Dave had thought she should have it looked at, even offered to strap it up, but she'd insisted she would be fine, that all she needed was a good night's sleep. She hugged her poorly knee to her chest.

In the bath, up to her chin in water, a towelling pillow behind her head, great peaks of bubbles floating around her, she relived the moment she had locked lips with her driver. On the radio a woman was telling a talk-show host how she couldn't sleep if she had anything on her mind, the slightest thing at all; didn't matter *what* she did, it was no good, she would toss and turn all night. Karen knew just how she felt.

She still had no idea who had made the first move. It was probably her, not that she could be sure, and anyway it was hardly important in the great scheme of things. What *was* important was that she had ended up in bed with her driver, which was probably breaking some kind of professional code. For all she knew, if it ever got out she would be sacked, face public humiliation. Never mind Julia shoving her on her face; this was much, much worse.

Even so, she couldn't help experiencing a sense of delight. Let's be honest, Dave was hot, and if she was going to get into trouble she might as well at least have fun in the process. She slid under the water and stayed there as long as she could, in the hope it might make the guilty thrill she was feeling go away.

On the radio a man had called in to say sex was the way to get to sleep, the best stress buster there was. Karen thought about how she would feel when Dave, in his work uniform of grey suit, white shirt and navy tie, arrived to take her to the studio. He had already sent her a text message – **Wicked nite K x** – which she had read and re-read several times. He was right about that. It had been wicked, in every sense of the word.

It wasn't the only text to have come through. There had been one from Jackie, something garbled about Bradley Walsh and wanting to kill herself, and three from Jason, all of them decidedly slushy, which was bang out of order, all things considered. Who did he think he was? What with Jason and Julia and this business of the top job on Britain's best-rated daytime show going begging, life was complicated enough as it was. Trust her to make things worse.

Thirteen

Julia had been running for more than half an hour and she was just getting into her stride, not even beginning to flag. A cluster of small beads of sweat gathered on her brow and at the base of her neck. It was a week since the Domes and she was back to normal after that horrible reaction to an overdose of filler. Thank God for the Abbey clinic, where they'd started her on strong antibiotics. The swelling had subsided as fast as it had flared up. In future, she would pay more attention to what Joel had to say. Of course, he knew what he was doing.

She picked up her pace, felt her heart rate quicken. That was more like it. Pounding on as if her life depended on it, she kept her breath even, pushing her body, her legs striking out in long, confident strides. She saw herself running the London Marathon, out there ahead of the pack, all the other unfit celebrity losers in their silly costumes trailing at the back, dropping out after a few measly miles, not up to it, while she, Julia Hill, warrior woman, strode on, overtaking the so-called real athletes and crossing the finishing line to wild applause, TV crews and reporters swarming around her as someone draped one of those shiny blankets over her shoulders and a medal round her neck.

Lost in her own private fantasy, she pressed a button and the treadmill accelerated. The sound of her feet going *slap, slap* on the rubber belt echoed around the room as the door opened and her assistant, Kirsty Collins, diary in one hand, mobile phone in the other, took a tentative step into the room.

Kirsty, only too aware how seriously Julia took her daily cardio session, shrank back into the doorway, familiar knots beginning to form in her gut. Under normal circumstances she would rather gargle with wasps than interrupt. No, make that gargle with wasps *and* poke herself in both eyes with a sharp stick. She shifted from one foot to the other, clutching the diary to her chest, thinking about all the things she feared – having blood taken, immersing herself in a flotation tank (she had done that once and practically had a seizure), that awful fairground ride that dropped you like a stone from a great height – any of which would have been preferable to Julia wiping the floor with her. The trouble was there had been a flurry of calls from the *Girl Talk* office, the last one from Paula Grayson, the editor, who would not be fobbed off. Kirsty hesitated. She could slip out of the room, and risk Julia shouting at her for coming in for no good reason in the first place. Or she could stay, and risk Julia shouting at her for coming in when she knew she was not to interrupt her mid-workout under any circumstances. It was, after all, one of the rules Julia had presented her with on her first day:

1. *Field all calls and prepare detailed message log*
2. *No personal calls*
3. *No interruptions during JH workouts*
4. *No eating or drinking at workstation*
5. *Mobile phone to be switched on at all times*
6. *No chit-chat. Speak when you are spoken to*

*

Slap slap slap. Kirsty recalled what had happened when Julia engaged a personal trainer, Isaac Eastman, and the first thing he said was that she was putting unnecessary stress on her joints by running so hard. He told her if she was running correctly she would barely make a sound. His mistake was thinking that he was there because he knew best and Julia wanted to improve her technique. Wrong!

Having shown him in, taken him through the kitchen into the garage, now converted into an impressive mini-gym, as if leading a lamb to the slaughter, Kirsty had lingered, waiting to be told she could go. As Isaac spoke to Julia, putting a hand on the small of her back, saying something about posture, Kirsty had winced, steeling herself for the inevitable outburst.

The moment he stepped on to the treadmill to demonstrate what he meant, 99 kilos of solid, sinewy muscle loping along in virtual silence while Julia was forced to stand by and watch, he was doomed.

Julia wasn't there to watch someone *else* show off. The only reason she had hired a personal trainer in the first place was to have an audience while *she* worked out.

'Have you quite finished?' she had said as he stepped off the treadmill.

'Your turn now,' he replied, oblivious to her frosty tone. 'And remember, you're not landing flat on your feet like a baby elephant.' Kirsty winced again. 'That's why you're making such a racket.'

'Oh, believe me, that's not a racket,' Julia said. 'I would say that's actually pretty low-key, given what I'm capable of.'

He had whistled. 'It's a lot of pressure on your knees, your hips. I hate to think—'

She cut him off. 'Who asked *you*?' she bellowed.

Isaac, who had assumed he was being paid to provide an honest professional opinion, opened his mouth to say something but she elbowed him out of the way and leaped back on to the treadmill.

'I mean, do I look like I give a fuck? I couldn't care *less* what you think.'

Isaac took a step back, hands up, as if Julia was pointing a gun at him.

Kirsty had seen his CV. He had been a boxing champion, won a gold medal at the Olympics a few years back. She closed her eyes and started to pray. Dear God, please let him throw a punch.

Julia glared at him. She had heard more than enough. Some jumped-up so-and-so who made a living taking kick-boxing classes telling her what to do was beyond belief. Didn't he know who she was?

'Get the fuck OUT,' she bellowed, gripping the handrail on the side of the running machine. Isaac, confused, looked at Kirsty.

Please God, a swift right hook to the jaw, knock her out.

'Don't look at *her*!' Julia ranted. She poked him in the chest. Now, please.

'Just GO – what is it about "FUCK OFF" you don't understand?' She rounded on her assistant. 'Curse-dee, get this arsehole out of here NOW, will you?' She fiddled with the buttons on the control panel in front of her and the treadmill started up again. 'Go on, MOVE. If I have to say it again you're fired as well!' she yelled, picking up speed, her eyes now on her own reflection in the mirrored wall facing her.

Kirsty had beckoned to Isaac and the pair of them retreated, the rhythmic *slap slap* of Julia destroying her knees following them out of the room.

The treadmill slowed to a stop and Julia, steadying herself on the rail, bent forward, taking deep breaths. Christ, that hurt. Maybe she had overdone it, just a tad. She could see her assistant out of the corner of her eye, half in, half out of the room. Curse-dee standing there with the door wide open, making a mockery of the air conditioning.

'Just come in, will you, and close the door,' she said.

Kirsty stepped forward. 'Paula Grayson called. She wants to speak to you. Urgently.'

Julia gazed at the television suspended from the ceiling in front of her, Helen England gushing over the arrival of baby Lou Samuel, wishing Heidi and Seal well, fawning about the unusual name, grovel, grovel.

Julia's breath slowly returned to normal. The Marathon might have to wait. Helen England was saying what a refreshing change it was for a celebrity couple not to sell their baby pictures to the highest bidder – the same Helen England who had just pocketed a rumoured £50,000 for a feature on her and her hubby, who did a dreadful DIY makeover show, the pair of them cooing over their new baby. Rumour had it the magazine had even ripped out their hideous kitchen and put a new one in – since his makeover skills were sadly lacking on the home front – just so the happy couple could be pictured posing with a wooden spoon over a state-of-the-art stove.

'I could do your job with my eyes shut,' Julia said, dabbing at her face with a towel, 'and I'd be about a hundred times better.'

'She has a meeting at twelve so she wants to speak to you beforehand,' Kirsty said.

Julia watched Helen England cross the studio to a make-up artist with a couple of women on high stools. There had been something in the paper at the weekend, Helen claiming she had never had surgery, not even Botox, that everything about her was natural.

'I bet that was a relief to the world of cosmetic surgery,' Julia said. 'I mean, what surgeon worth his salt would claim to have worked on that? Look at the state of her.'

'I'm sorry?' Kirsty asked, baffled.

Julia turned to face her. 'Tell me, Curse-dee, has somebody died?' Kirsty shook her head. 'Isn't there a *rule* about disturbing me in here?'

Kirsty lowered her eyes to the floor, waiting for Julia to bawl her out. 'Tell me, does it surprise you to know Helen England has never been under the knife?'

Kirsty glanced at the screen. 'She looks pretty amazing,' she conceded. 'Not even the odd tweak? That's incredible.'

Julia bristled. 'Yes, I suppose it is, if you *want* to look like a wrinkled old hag, which clearly she does.'

Helen, a radiant smile on her face, appeared in close-up. Julia punched a button on the remote and switched channels. 'There had better be a very good reason for you coming in.'

'Paula Grayson. Can you call her?'

'Get her on the line after I've showered.'

'The thing is she has a meeting at twelve and wanted to speak to you first . . .' Kirsty bit her lip.

It was 11.54. 'Why didn't you say so? Get her for me now.'

Kirsty took her mobile from her pocket and dialed Paula Grayson's direct line.

'I have Julia Hill for Paula Grayson,' she said.

Julia snatched the phone from her. The theme music from *Show Us What You're Made Of*, Channel 6's talent search, blasted down the line and a voice told her to vote to keep her favourite in the competition.

'And you can fuck off too,' she said.

'I beg your pardon – Julia?' It was Paula Grayson.

Julia jumped. 'Not you, Paula, darling,' she said. 'I had a cold caller on the other line wanting me to do a survey on broadband. Can you believe it?'

'Didn't you get my message? I called half an hour ago.'

'I know and I'm *so* sorry. Little Curse-dee's only just got round to telling me. Can't get the staff, can you?'

Kirsty, peering at a list of messages in the diary, wondering which to relay and which to ditch, felt her cheeks go pink.

'I need you to get in early today,' said Paula. 'There's a meeting at five. I want to get to the bottom of that shambles at the Dome Awards, see if I can smooth things over with the new controller. Not that I'm holding my breath.'

Julia grinned. 'Yes, it was all very unfortunate. I don't think Karen's got the hang of heels, poor love. All those years in sensible flats don't prepare a girl to stay upright in proper shoes.'

'We'll talk about it later,' Paula said. The line went dead.

Julia handed the phone back to Kirsty. 'Rude bitch, hung up on me. I mean, it costs nothing to be polite, does it?'

Fourteen

In a corner of the coffee bar at the studios, Karen sat hunched over a skinny cappuccino with her best friend, Bella. The pair had met when Karen was out of work after the long-running review show she presented a music segment for was axed and Bella threw her a lifeline. In no time at all the two of them had clicked. Bella, thirty-six, with short blonde hair that went into soft, springy curls of its own accord, and eyes the same shade of green as Karen's, was loyal and down to earth, with an uncanny knack for knowing just when her friend needed her.

What a Week had been in the schedules for two years and had a good slice of the ratings. Halfway through the final season a new controller, Elliot Carew, had taken over and a sense of dread had swept through the production team. Carew, a notorious axe-man, had just gone through a neighbouring regional station like a dose of salts, restructuring and streamlining, as he liked to call it. Sacking half the staff was how everyone else put it. There had been no attempt to meet anyone, no reassuring memos, just an eerie silence. Elliot spent most of his time locked away in his executive office, door shut, while his PA, a stern young woman with a range of severe suits in grey, black and cream, her hair scraped back in a bun, a short rope of pearls at her neck, occupied an outer office, keeping guard.

For the remainder of the series Karen was a nervous wreck.

She imagined Carew reclining in a leather swivel chair in his office, watching her on a giant, unforgiving high-definition screen, ripping her to shreds.

Two weeks before the summer break he had summoned her to his inner sanctum. She had waited in the outer office with the PA, feeling sick, sure she was about to be sacked. All she could think of was going on air for the next two weeks and pretending everything was all right.

Carew kept her waiting. There was one of those big clocks on the wall to her right, which she tried not to look at. When she did it confirmed that her appointment was already ten minutes overdue. She had visions of Carew and his full diary telling her he was sorry, he would have to reschedule. Well, fuck that. Fuck him, making her wait, turning her into a bag of nerves. When the door finally opened and Carew burst out, full of apologies, she was thrown.

'I'm *so* sorry, Karen, please forgive me. That was a phone call I just had to take.' She could have sworn he winked at her. 'Come on in.'

He gestured at a sofa, waited until she had perched herself on one end then settled himself a few feet away. The TV was on in the corner, a lunchtime news bulletin, the sound dipped low.

'Is that distracting?' He got up and switched it off.

Elliot Carew assured her he was a fan of *What a Week*, could see how the show might be developed for the third season, do more location features. Karen could hardly believe it. Third season! She began to relax. He wanted to hear what she thought; where might they take the show? What about the occasional outside broadcast – get out of London now and then? She had nodded, told him she would love to do OBs, go up north. There was an appetite for it, she was sure. They had chatted on until his PA tapped at the door and told him his car was waiting to take him to his lunch appointment.

'We should have lunch,' he said, giving Karen a polite peck on each cheek. 'I'll get my Karen to fix something up.'

She had left the office elated. Surprise, surprise, Carew wasn't the bastard everyone made him out to be after all.

Two weeks later, once the show came off air and the production team were in the green room drinking champagne, scoffing vol-au-vents and talking about what they planned to do over the summer break, Karen got a call. Carew wanted her to pop in for a chat if she could manage it. Around three if that was convenient? She made her way to the executive corridor, still on a high from the final show, a couple of glasses of champagne inside her, and when she reached his office he sacked her. *What a Week* was to be axed. No one, not even the managing editor, who had just moved his family to London on the strength of another series, had seen it coming.

Bella, who was producing a regional show not unlike *What a Week* at the time, heard Karen was at a loose end and took her on. During the week she stayed with her mum in Blackpool, sleeping in her old room, going back and forth each day to the studios in Manchester, getting the train to London at the weekend. It was not exactly ideal – she missed Jason and was on less money, a lot less – but at least she was working. And being back at home, having her mum spoil her, was bliss. A proper cooked breakfast with fried eggy bread every morning. No wonder she had put on a stone in six months.

'This is what worries me,' she told Bella now. 'I know what happens when a new controller takes over. I mean, he's been here a couple of months now, long enough to get the measure of things. He's bound to want to make his mark – and that means change.' The editor of *The Arts and Entertainment Review* had already been moved sideways and rumour had it that show's presenter was for the chop at the end of the run.

Bella tore open a sachet of brown sugar and tipped it into her coffee.

'No point getting in a stew. What will be will be, and all that. At least James Almond is a programme maker with a pretty good track record – better than having an accountant running the place. And I wouldn't have thought you need to worry. *Girl Talk* is going down a storm.'

'Doesn't matter. It's not his show so he has no emotional attachment,' Karen said, feeling a twinge of envy as Bella stirred her coffee, wishing she was still allowed sugar, knowing it was a slippery slope.

Bella shrugged. 'I've been bumped from one show to another so many times I've learned not to care,' she said. 'It makes no difference whether or not you're doing a good job. It's all about whether your face fits.' She grinned, running a hand through her mop of blonde curls. 'Thankfully, for the time being, I seem to be doing something right – for a change. Mind you, that could all change.' She gave Karen's wrist a squeeze. 'You can't worry about it.'

The lift opened and half a dozen people emerged, two holding cameras trained on someone the girls couldn't quite make out in the middle of the group. A slender man dressed in black jeans and a black shirt, his skin golden, his hair gelled into neat spikes, joined the queue for coffee. He seemed to have three people with him, not including the pair filming him.

'Peter Andre's promoting his new single,' Bella said. 'Everywhere he goes these days there's a camera crew filming him being filmed. He must get sick of it but you'd never know. He's very patient.'

One of the cameras swung around on Bella and Karen. 'I think we're cutaways,' Bella said.

Karen leaned back in her seat, taking refuge behind a pillar. 'Is there no escape?'

Bella blew on her cappuccino. 'It's all right, you can come out now. They're back on Peter Andre, poor sod. I mean, how interesting can he make a cup of coffee?'

Karen spooned froth into her saucer. 'I've got something to tell you,' she said.

Bella sat up. 'This sounds interesting.'

Karen glanced at her friend. 'Just don't have a go at me.' She took a deep breath. 'I'm not sure quite how to say this ...'

Bella put her mug back on the table. 'Is there a man involved?'

Karen went a bit pink and Bella said, 'Please tell me it's not Jason.'

'Give me some credit,' Karen said, watching Peter Andre now, deep in conversation with the woman facing him, the pair of them doing their best to be natural with cameras practically poking them in the face. 'You know after the awards?' Bella narrowed her eyes. 'Well, when I got home I had a cup of tea with Dave – Dave Graham, my driver, you know?'

'That doesn't sound so bad.'

'No. The thing is ... well, I slept with him.' Bella's eyes widened. 'And I've been seeing him, sort of, ever since.' Karen bit her bottom lip.

Bella leaned across the table. 'That's brilliant! Good for you – you deserve a bit of fun. He's nice too – fit, I mean.' Bella's voice carried across the canteen. One of the cameras at Peter Andre's table swung towards her. She angled her chair away from it. 'So,' she said, her voice dropping to a whisper, 'what's he like?'

Karen giggled. 'He's *gorgeous*, really lovely. He's just so nice to me. I mean he's a proper bloke but he does really sweet things like bring me tea in bed and gives me a foot rub after I've been wearing these stupid shoes.'

'I bet he does. Well, I'm very happy for you. It's about time you met a bloke who knows how to treat you. Unlike You-know-who.'

'I know.'

'Just take things steady. I mean, there's no rush, is there?'

Karen shook her head. 'No, it's nothing serious. Just what I need, really.'

'So, things are looking up. New man ... new *job*? Has anyone spoken to you about *Good Morning Britain*? I see Helen England gave you another endorsement in some interview she did about the new sprog and how in love she is with Mr DIY. "Karen King reminds me so much of myself ..."'

'Oh, please tell me she didn't. That just means even more misery in the production meetings. No one's speaking to me to start with.' She wiped the edge of the table with a paper serviette. 'I know she means well but I wish she'd keep her trap shut. It's not helping.'

'Come on, you're first choice for the best job at Channel 6. It can't be all bad.'

'That's what I keep telling myself.' She gave a shrug. 'You wouldn't believe how many sleepless nights it's giving me.'

Bella gave her a cheeky grin. 'Are you sure that's the job? Or that hot new bloke of yours?'

Karen chuckled. 'Bit of both, I suppose.'

Paula Grayson had booked a meeting room on the fifteenth floor. She sat at the head of an oblong, highly polished table, writing something in a spiral-bound notebook. From time to time she paused and put down her pen, an elegant ballpoint, silver inlaid with ebony, and looked out of the window at the Thames.

A tourist boat, half full, a string of lights above the open deck, chugged up the river towards Greenwich, its passengers smothered in jackets, hats and scarves. It had been a sunny day but the temperature had dropped and it would be cold on the water.

The door swung open and Lesley, in a fitted white dress and studded biker jacket, with a shiny black Balenciaga bag over one arm, appeared. With her high heels and blonde hair piled on top of her head she looked positively Amazonian.

Paula peered at her over her glasses. For once Lesley didn't look as if she'd just fallen out of somebody else's bed. She didn't even have a hangover, Paula was certain of that; the fact that she had dispensed with her trademark giant sunglasses – worn indoors and out regardless of whether it was day or night, bright or dull, whenever she was feeling fragile – was a dead giveaway. Paula told Lesley to take a seat, and kept writing.

There was a pile of newspapers at the end of the table next to Paula. Lesley didn't need to look at them to know what they were: the aftermath of the Domes fiasco, which seemed to be dragging on forever. Oh well, fuck it. Too late to start worrying now. She took a seat facing the door and looked around for the customary flasks of tea and coffee, the plates of biscuits. She fancied something sweet, a sugar lift.

'Are we still waiting for the tea?' she said.

Paula looked up. 'I won't keep you long, don't worry.'

Lesley slathered a fresh coat of lip gloss on as Paula continued to write. What was that supposed to mean, 'won't keep you long' – weren't they getting anything to drink? She could murder a custard cream as well.

The door opened and Cheryl appeared in shiny purple leggings, a long purple vest and a black fine-knit cardigan, which slid off her shoulder, revealing an expanse of gleaming skin. She gave Paula a wave and plonked herself in a chair opposite Lesley. 'Is the tea not here yet?'

Paula frowned and kept on making notes.

Faye turned up in a checked shirt over leggings and a pair of black suede ankle boots, caramel hair scraped into a ponytail. She looked fresh-faced, as if she wasn't wearing a scrap of make-up, a look Paula knew probably took longer to achieve than Lesley's full-on glamour. Faye dumped a gigantic red mock-croc bag on the table, bent to give Cheryl a hug, then went round the table and hugged Lesley.

'Where's the tea?'

Lesley shrugged, touching up her lip gloss again.

'Is that a new bag?' Faye said, stroking the Balenciaga.

Lesley grinned. 'Nice, isn't it? I got it in Dubai. Cost a fortune but worth every penny.'

'Oh, it's a *real* one,' Cheryl said. 'I couldn't tell.'

'Fuck off,' Lesley said, indignant. 'You know full well it's real.'

'Funny, I saw one just like it in Primark.'

Faye sat down next to Cheryl. 'Stop teasing,' she said, pulling

103

a face and giving Lesley an apologetic smile. 'She's only winding you up. Cheryl doesn't shop in Primark.'

'Could have fooled me,' Lesley said, scooping up the Balenciaga and putting it on the chair next to her. 'They're selling those shiny leggings for a fiver.'

The door flew open and Julia, in mid-flow on her mobile, swept in. She waved at the other girls, gave Paula a dazzling smile and strode across to the window.

'I need you to do it tonight. If you needed to get away early for a special reason you should have said. What did we agree? That's right: work comes first.' She glanced at Paula. 'That's what it means to be a professional. Watch and learn.'

She snapped the phone shut. 'Curse-dee,' she announced, 'wanting to get away early for something or other.'

Cheryl caught Faye's eye. 'Still chaining the poor girl to the desk, are you?'

Julia ignored her and went to sit at the far end of the table, facing Paula. 'I'm gagging for a drink. Where's the coffee?' she said as Karen came in, looking slim in a tailored red dress. She was carrying a takeaway cup and the smell of fresh coffee drifted around the room.

'Not late, am I?' she asked, sliding into a seat next to Faye.

Paula checked her watch. 'Bang on time,' she said. 'Let's get started.'

Fifteen

Paula Grayson held up the newspapers, one at a time. The shenanigans at the Domes had landed them on the front pages of the *Sun*, the *Mirror*, the *Star* and the *Express*. The *Mail* had devoted a disapproving inside page to several pictures of Karen and Julia rolling around the pavement. Some wag on the subs desk had come up with a headline that read **GIRL TALK GIRLS PROVE ACTIONS SPEAK LOUDER THAN WORDS**. One of the paper's bitchier writers had written a snooty piece suggesting copious amounts of alcohol had been imbibed, hinting that other so-called 'recreational substances' were involved, and saying how sad – pathetic almost – it was to see grown women making such fools of themselves. They had even reprinted a picture of a teenager snapped on a night out with a pair of pants round her ankles next to the prone Karen and Julia with the caption *Binge drinking – not just for the teenagers?* Everyone wanted to know what was going on with Julia's face, although a statement from the medical director at the Abbey clinic explaining she had been treated for an acute, potentially life-threatening allergic reaction, most likely to seafood, had shut them up. Lesley flashing her boobs and Dan Kincaid groping her was also there. Someone must have grabbed that on a mobile phone, since there were no photographers inside the venue.

They had all seen the press. Somehow it hadn't felt as bad flipping through the pages in private before chucking them in the recycling bin. Now, though, with their scarily authoritative editor scowling at them, the episode seemed much, much worse.

Karen sat, head bowed, clutching her coffee.

'According to the *Star* you went out without your knickers on, Julia,' Paula said, disapproving.

'Don't knock it, darling. At least I'm on the front page.'

Lesley pored over the picture. 'Only because you're tits-up on the pavement. In fact, you're one of the few people whose tits *stay up* even when you're on your back. Lucky for you they all believed the dodgy prawn theory for that business with your face. Talk about gullible.'

'As a matter of fact—'

'That's enough,' Paula cut in. 'We did pretty well at the awards this year – amazingly well, as it happens. What I did not enjoy seeing was Jackie Martin having to collect the Most Popular Entertainment Programme award because none of you were in a fit state. Do you have any idea how valuable these gongs are, how much credibility they give the show? Meanwhile, all hell breaks loose. As if it's not enough to have you' – she turned to Lesley – 'assaulting one of the country's most popular actresses—'

Lesley sat up straight. 'Sasha Gates, *popular*? You *are* kidding.'

'I promise, I am *not* kidding,' said Paula. 'Just because you have some kind of personal vendetta going does not give you the right to take a swing at her. The fact it happened inside the venue away from the paparazzi is about the only saving grace.'

Cheryl piped up. 'If this is about people misbehaving at the

Domes, then frankly I have no idea why I'm here. Or Faye for that matter. We kept out of it.' She pushed her chair back. 'Can we go?'

Paula took a long hard look at Cheryl, all buffed and polished, acting the innocent when she knew from Jackie she had been no help whatsoever on the night, leaving with Faye before the awards ended despite being told to sit tight.

'If I were you, I would keep my mouth shut,' Paula said.

Cheryl got to her feet. 'I'm already late for an important appointment with my colonic therapist.'

'You'd better run along then,' Julia said. 'Pity the poor therapist trying to get the crap out of you.'

'That is quite enough!' Paula snapped. 'Karen,' she said, softening her tone, 'you're very quiet. What have you got to say?'

Karen glanced around the table. Lesley gave her a tiny, barely-there smile, while Cheryl, still on her feet, stared out of the window. Faye's eyes were on Cheryl, while Julia wore one of her famous if-looks-could-kill expressions.

'There were a few high spirits I suppose, nothing malicious,' she said. That was a lie for a start. What she really wanted to say was the entire night had been a disaster: Julia with her claws out from the word go, the others miffed because she had picked up the award they all wanted *and* emerged as the clear favourite to step into Helen England's shoes.

'I can understand if you overdid the champagne,' Paula said, 'celebrating your win and all that. I appreciate it was a big night for all of you. I don't mind people enjoying themselves, letting off steam. *If* that's all it was.' She no longer sounded stern. 'So, is that what happened?'

Karen shot a look at Julia, whose face now resembled a

death mask. That's where the Botox gives her the edge, Karen thought, biting her lip.

'I wasn't drunk, if that's what you're asking,' she said. 'I lost my footing.' Paula wrote something on her pad. Karen glanced at Julia again. 'That's what happened. I tripped.' The death mask slipped a fraction. Was that a smirk? An uncharacteristic wave of rage rushed through Karen. 'And I tripped because somebody pushed me.' There. She had said it. She looked straight at Julia, who glared back at her.

'Who pushed you?' Paula's voice was gentle.

'Someone came up from behind and knocked me over. I couldn't actually see who it was.' Her eyes met Julia's again. 'I have a pretty good idea, though.'

Julia sprang to her feet. 'Are you accusing me, you malicious bitch? If you're going to start flinging accusations around you'd better be sure of your facts.'

Karen removed the lid from her coffee, took a drink and eased the lid back on, not in any rush. The room was silent, just the sound of Julia's acrylic nails tapping on the surface of the table.

'Did you hear me? I'm warning you – you'd better think very carefully before you go telling people I—'

Karen cut in. 'Why – what will you do? Push me down the stairs again?'

Lesley clapped her hands, delighted. 'Is that *really* what happened? How come I missed it?'

'Perhaps you were otherwise engaged battering Sasha Gates at the time. Oh no, sorry, that was later,' Cheryl said as Faye dug an elbow in her ribs.

'Yes, well, in my defence I *was* drunk,' Lesley pointed out.

'And what about you?' Paula said, turning to Julia again. 'Were *you* drunk? Or was there something else going on?'

Julia turned to Paula, her features now arranged into what she hoped was a winning smile. Karen watched her, impressed. It was remarkable, really, how someone who could barely move her facial muscles could manage to go from animosity to something approaching charm just like that. 'I don't know what you mean,' she said, keeping her voice light. 'I'd had a couple of drinks—'

'Couple of *bottles*, more like. You necked most of my champagne for a start,' Lesley said.

'—a *couple* of drinks. It was a long night and I was poorly. Everyone was a bit tired and emotional.'

'You were off your face,' Lesley chipped in, 'and busy turning into the Elephant Man.' Her shoulders shook with mirth. 'I can't believe some innocent prawn is getting the blame for that.'

'Will you fuck *off*!' Julia yelled. 'All of a sudden you're Miss Goody-Two-Shoes. Just remind me, when did you get so high and mighty – when you were giving the nation's favourite soap queen a slapping, or when you were dragging that poor bastard in the ripped jeans back to your cave?'

Paula brought her fist down on the table. The room fell silent again.

'If I hear of *anyone* on this show taking drugs – no matter where or when – they are *out*. Do. I. Make. Myself. Clear?' She closed her notebook and got to her feet. 'You are all adults. Start behaving like it.'

Julia gathered up her things and flounced to the door, dropping a newspaper on the table, a polished black fingernail tapping the picture of Karen sprawled on the pavement with her dress hiked up. 'Is that a teeny bit of cellulite, darling? Tut tut. You know, you don't have to live with it. You need some of those special leggings – have you seen them? Support tights with the feet missing, kind of. Clever marketing, if you ask me. All you do is clomp about in them and – hey presto! – all that hideous orange peel gone. You can *clomp*, can't you, darling? Course you can.' She paused and arranged her face into what would have been a frown if her brow was not immobile. 'Can't quite remember where I saw them, that's the thing. Might have been John Lewis . . .' She glanced across the table. '*You* might know, Lesley.'

Lesley, scrabbling about in her bag, looked up, raised two fingers and went back to searching for her lip gloss.

'No? Oh, well, never mind. You'll probably find them in *Grazia*. Ciao.'

Sixteen

In the darkened room, Lesley drained the last few drops of wine direct from the bottle. Then, fumbling in her bag, she produced a lipstick and applied an even coat without the aid of a mirror. She'd got the motion down to a fine art. She was so used to doing her make-up in unfamiliar places she was now an expert; when you woke up in a stranger's house, looking for a mirror in the half-light was always more hassle than it was worth, especially if you wanted to slip out quietly – and she did. She couldn't afford a repeat of the now infamous kiss-and-tell incident that had derailed her career, and in the wake of the Domes a couple of months earlier she knew she was once more on thin ice. It was vital to at least appear good, so Channel 6 had no excuse to get rid of her. She still loved casual sex, although now she was seeing Dan there was less opportunity to go out on the pull. Still, whenever he was away on a shoot she returned to her old haunts in Soho, going for foreign pick-ups; they didn't know who she was and were therefore a less risky option.

She looked across at the man, who was still sleeping – well, less of a man, more a boy really, she thought to herself with a satisfied smile. If she acknowledged her real age she'd be forty-nine next birthday, but she could still pull them; despite everything she still had it. He looked so sexy, so young, that she was tempted to climb back in with him for a repeat of last night's performance, but glancing at her watch she noticed it was already 7.15 a.m. There was an early *Girl Talk* meeting and if she didn't leave now she'd be late, which would never do.

Thankfully she had her long coat with her so as she stood up she pulled it around her, attempting to cover what she had a feeling may soon be nasty carpet burns coming out on her knees. Luckily her legs would be under the table at work, but even so she made a mental note to wear jeans all week as she picked up her handbag and tiptoed to the door.

God, she was tired. She knew she shouldn't have come home with him. The really young ones kept you up *all* night and while it was what she'd wanted it wasn't wise, what with everything that was happening at work. Oh well, too late for regrets now. She eased open the door, took one last look at Whatever-his-name-was, and slipped out.

Seventeen

Inside her dressing room Faye faced a less than pleased-looking Cheryl.

'You know I wanted you to tell him last week,' Cheryl said. 'You need to do it when he gets back on Friday.' She smoothed the shoulder pads on Faye's shocking-pink tailored jacket with authority.

Faye pulled away. 'Are you even listening to me? He'll hit the roof if he finds out about us. I have to tell him there is no one else; it's madness to tell him everything.'

And it wasn't just Mike's reaction she was scared of. She couldn't help picturing the look on her parents' faces if they found out she was seeing her co-presenter. Her father, a retired army colonel and confirmed traditionalist, would never live down the revelation that his precious daughter was messing about behind her husband's back with another woman. As for her mother ... Faye shuddered.

Cheryl's stony expression didn't change. 'Look, you keep saying you'll do it but you never do and I'm just not prepared to wait around forever. You said you don't love him any more, so what have you got to lose?'

Faye didn't answer.

'Do you still want to be with him? Because we can end this now if you like.'

Faye put her arms out to her. 'No, you know I don't, it's just not as easy as that. We've been together a long time and he's a man who likes to think he's some kind of action hero. It would kill him if he knew I was with you. He couldn't handle it, and I don't want to hurt him more than I have to.'

'You're acting like his feelings are more important than mine. I'm not ashamed of us and I want people to know we're together. Clearly, you don't.'

Growing up on a tough estate in south London with four older brothers had taught Cheryl the value of fighting her corner. She had been raised by a grandmother who was feisty and fearless – and expected her only granddaughter to be the same.

Faye stomped over to the dressing table and grabbed her hairbrush. 'I do, but . . . it's just that I like things the way they are – private, nothing to do with anyone else. I've done the public thing with him and I don't want to let the world in on us. What do you think will happen once people realize we're together? This isn't America, Cheryl – you're not Ellen and I'm not Portia de Rossi. This is England! People might say it's OK to be a same-sex couple these days, but how many lesbians do you know who are on the telly?'

Cheryl gave her a knowing look. 'Well, I could name at least ten . . .'

'Ones that are actually *out*?'

Cheryl's smile slipped.

'Exactly.'

Cheryl put her arms around Faye, pulling her close. 'But we could change all that, we could be the first – people would get used to it. I just want to be with you properly—'

Faye cut her short. 'We *are* together properly and I do want to be with you, but I don't want to be a poster girl for lesbian rights, especially when I'm not even sure if I *am* one.'

Cheryl pulled away. 'And what's that supposed to mean?'

Aware of voices outside in the corridor, Faye lowered her voice. 'All I know is I fell in love and it just happens to be you're a woman, so I don't know what that makes me, and my head's messed up enough as it without having the world and his wife gossiping about me and making me choose a label.'

'Oh – "me" is it?' Cheryl hissed.

'You know what I mean!' Faye turned away and yanked the brush through handfuls of shoulder-length red hair.

'Fine, we'll wait, but I'm warning you, don't expect me to hang around forever, Faye. If you really want to be with me you've got to get things sorted, and I mean soon. He has to know.' Cheryl stepped away and finished her make-up in the opposite mirror, applying a coat of rich purple eyeshadow and a flick of eyeliner that made her green eyes even more cat-like than usual.

The two women leafed through show notes and avoided eye contact as the tannoy system crackled in the background.

Eighteen

'Five minutes to air, girls, please make your way to the studio,' the voice buzzed through the tannoy in Karen's dressing room. She used to get such a buzz of excitement when that call came. Now it just filled her with dread. Her hand shook as she applied another coat of black mascara. She put her own face on now that she no longer felt comfortable in the make-up room with the others. She made two more attempts to steady the brush before placing it down and letting her mind drift while still looking in the mirror.

In just a couple of months since the awards, her whole life had been turned upside-down and the atmosphere on set had become so bad that things were almost unbearable. It was such a cliché, she thought, but before that night she really had thought of the other girls and crew as family. All that seemed an age ago. Just being in the building these days felt like picking her way through an emotional minefield, bombs waiting to go off wherever she stepped, so she spent any time she had off set in her dressing room, trying to keep out of *their* way. To make matters worse, paranoia about the future of the show was spreading like an infection through the studios, so even the few normal people left were now as edgy as everyone else. It was always like this when a new controller took over a channel: no one knew who was safe, and people worried about losing their jobs are never a happy bunch at best. Karen knew that just because your show was a ratings winner didn't mean you were safe from the axe. People still talked about how Cilla Black's chat show had been dropped in the nineties despite brilliant ratings. The fact that no one had yet been interviewed for Helen England's position on *Good Morning Britain* made things even more tense.

With everyone putting on a show of unity to try and escape the cutbacks, at least the girls had stopped being outright rude to her; now they simply ignored her. At first it had felt better to be out of the rows and fights but, as time went by, being ostracized was making her feel much worse.

When the cameras were on it was a different story – they were still the best of friends – but now, the second they stopped rolling, or in the ad breaks, the small talk and banter that used to include her pointedly no longer did. Strange silences descended when she walked into a room and there was no mistaking the divide between her and the others.

As she finished her make-up, it struck her that what was actually happening was quite subtle, considering the things she'd seen them do to each other in the past. For the first series, when Julia and Lesley frequently locked horns, she was even considered the peacemaker during the backstage catfights. That was before Julia established herself as undisputed top dog and they all became friends.

On her dressing table was a huge bunch of her favourite flowers, white roses, from Jason. He had sent them every week since that night at the Domes and left countless messages, practically begging to see her, but so far she had stayed strong. She was tempted, though. How bad could lunch be? At the very least it would give her a chance to show off her new svelte shape and let him see exactly what he was missing. Mind you, looking at her reflection now in the full-length mirror on the back of her dressing-room door, she wasn't sure he would be too impressed. She would never have said beige was her colour, especially not on TV, but Philip in wardrobe had insisted what he called 'taupe' was in right now and said she looked – what was the word? – *gorge*, which was presumably short for 'gorgeous'. She checked her back view. As far as she could tell he had put her in the kind of shapeless sack she used to wear in her size-20 days. The dress clung to the back of her legs, clicking with static as she peeled it off her tights. What on earth was it made of, and since when were smocks, complete with an embroidered yoke, fashionable? They never looked good even when they *were* in fashion. *If* they ever were; she wasn't sure about that. As far as she was concerned smocks, along with ponchos, belonged on a to-be-avoided-at-all-costs list.

Philip had assured her she could wear anything these days, now she was slim. Clothes were all about confidence, he said, chiding her for questioning his professional know-how. Well, right now she wasn't feeling in the least bit confident, thanks to the circa-1970 fire hazard he'd put her in. She checked the label on the inside seam: 100 per cent rayon. Who made clothes from rayon any more?

The sludgy colour seemed to drain the life from her face. As a voice over the tannoy said, 'Two minutes to on-air,' she dabbed on a bit of extra blusher and searched her wardrobe for a scarf. That might brighten it up. Now she looked like her old headmistress. She just hoped Jason wouldn't be watching. The flowers and lunch invites would soon dry up if he saw her looking like this. Maybe she should just agree to meet him, before he ran out of patience, and over the main course drop a few hints, let him know she had a new love interest.

She was still having the most mind-blowing sex with Dave, although she was being careful to keep him under wraps and wouldn't let him stay the night. The papers would consider an affair with her driver tacky, and even though she fancied the pants off him she could not cope with yet more tabloid scandal – not with them still running those awful pictures of her and Julia at the Domes.

She winced. Maybe that was why Jason was pursuing her. He probably thought she was vulnerable, in need of some support. Well, he was right, as usual. For all his faults, Jason was good in a crisis, able to deliver just the right kind of pep talk and make her feel better, no matter what. The truth was, she did miss him. What if he really had changed? She almost laughed out loud at how ridiculous a notion that was. How could she possibly be thinking about giving him another chance after everything he'd put her through, especially as he was just about to become a father to that tramp's baby? Even so, she still felt something for him. You can't just wipe out twenty-something years of love for someone, even when you hate what they've done to you. If only he hadn't got Hannah pregnant she was sure he'd have come back, but that's men for you: such an idiot, damn him. Even if she did take him back Hannah would always be in their lives now, flaunting her back-seat bunk-up for all it was worth across the pages of *OK!* and bragging about how she got her size-6 figure back in ten days flat. God, she hated Hannah Blake. Karen had lost count of the amount of times she'd seen her naked and showing off her bump in the red-top newspapers, à la Demi Moore.

How she wished she could talk to the girls about it like

she'd done before, but she couldn't, not the way things were, and there was no way her family would understand because they all hated Jason. Her big sister Tina had seen through him years ago and begged her not to marry him. She was convinced Jason's supersize ego meant he would always put himself first no matter what, and that Karen would inevitably suffer. As for her little sister Shelly, she had always said she would support her even if she did want to be with a complete shit. Karen wondered if that would still apply with a pregnant girlfriend in the background. She could have talked to her mum; she could tell her anything. It just didn't seem fair, though, to go bleating to her, upsetting her. No, it was no good. There was always Bella, although she had no time for Jason these days, having decided he was a lousy cheat and could never be trusted again.

The tannoy crackled with the one-minute warning. She snatched up a belt and cinched in her waist. Dear God, that just made things worse. The dress crackled ominously. She had a plain red top in her wardrobe – was there time to change? Hearing the runner knock on her door she knew it was too late, that she would have to go on air looking like one of the Wurzels. Could things get any worse?

Bracing herself, she quickly left the room.

Nineteen

One by one the others entered the corridor and joined her in the long walk down to Studio 9.

Karen was first out and didn't look left as she entered the main corridor but she knew they were there. She could hear the other girls' doors closing behind her so she quickened her step to be ahead of the pack. All five women were now walking in silence. Karen felt unbelievably tense, sensing their eyes boring into her back. She wouldn't give them the pleasure of turning round only to be ignored. Pride kept her walking confidently forward, but inside she was thinking, I can't carry on like this for much longer.

As she rounded the corner, Julia, who was behind her, deliberately slowed her pace so as to be able to give Karen's dress the once-over. Perfect, Julia thought: another hideous number that would make sure she looked a right heifer next to her on the panel. The extra cash she slipped Philip, the queen in the costume department each week, was money well spent if it meant Karen's ever-decreasing figure stayed well and truly hidden. She didn't feel at all guilty, she thought, smiling to herself; Karen deserved it. She should have known her place: she was meant to be the jolly fat one, that's why Julia had suggested her and the network had hired her. She should have been grateful. After all, she was a singer, not a presenter, and *Girl Talk* was a massive break. The fact that she had taken to live TV as if she had been doing it all her life was neither here nor there. She owed Julia, and now she was trying to take on her style and steal her crown as late-night queen. Well she wouldn't get away with it. Julia was the most experienced broadcaster on the show and her role was to be in control, listened to and admired, *not* emulated, and certainly not pushed off the covers of magazines by an infuriatingly slender Karen. Just what did everyone see in her?

Helen England knew what she was doing when she made that speech, that was for sure, Julia thought. She'd always loathed Helen but now she hated her more than ever. But as much as she detested Helen, Julia knew she wasn't stupid, that by tipping Karen to take over from her she was suggesting someone who could never match her success, leaving it open for her to return if she changed her mind, the cunning little witch. Yes, Karen was popular with the chav vote but she would never be prime-time.

It would take time, and she had to be discreet, but she was slowly bringing Karen King down. The last time they were due to have their group shots done Julia had insisted on using a photographer who happened to fancy her. 'Put her at the back, darling? For you, anything – she can hold the lights if you want,' the snapper said before taking the pictures, now proudly displayed in the corridor they were walking along, Karen barely visible, squashed at the back.

Julia smiled as she looked at herself centre stage in the shot, then winced as she caught her reflection in the glass. She was looking her age, she thought. She just had to get tonight's show out of the way and then she'd pop out to call in another little favour. Joel could never refuse her.

Lesley's head thumped as she walked behind Julia and Karen, the sound of heels clacking along the floor making her brain feel like it was bleeding. She'd taken several pills in her dressing room but what she really needed was another drink, not that she dared risk it. She had only just escaped being sacked a few days ago, after an assistant producer caught her drinking at work, by threatening to (falsely) accuse him of sexual harassment if he reported her. That had shut him up but she knew she wouldn't get away with it again and was already counting down the hours until she could top up the old system. Yes, that would do the trick, she thought, her tongue flicking across the inside of her lips, almost tasting that first glass.

She didn't usually drink so much during the day but it was so bloody stressful at work now she felt she needed it to take the edge off. She'd tried hard not to get involved when the divide formed, as she didn't actually have a problem with Karen, but the others had made it clear there were only two sides to this fence and she had to decide which one she wanted to be on. Still, she tried to steer clear of the plotting and while she did feel sorry for Karen – who she could see was struggling – she had enough problems of her own to worry about. She certainly didn't want to get caught in the crossfire. She was just lucky she still had her job, since she could barely look management in the eye after what had happened with Sasha Gates at the Domes. Just as well they had succeeded in keeping it out of the press or she would have been done for. No cat had that many lives.

In truth she didn't regret slapping Sasha at all, she just regretted that she'd come so close to being caught. And as for

Sasha pulling her dress down – there were cameras everywhere these days and she felt cheap after flashing her tits to the room. But there was no question that slap had felt good; she'd been waiting to do it for years. She hadn't finished with Sasha either. In the meantime, she needed to keep her head down at work and stay out of trouble.

As she turned the corner behind Julia, her heel caught on a sticky patch of floor, making her stumble. The corridors were always dirty these days. 'Bloody cutbacks,' she said under her breath and strode on.

Cheryl and Faye shot each other a knowing look. Unlike the others, they walked side by side towards the studio entrance. They hadn't spoken since leaving the dressing room, but Lesley's little trip cheered them up. They didn't need to say anything as Cheryl gestured at Lesley's retreating back, raising her hand to tip an imaginary glass of something down her throat, and Faye swayed, pretending to stagger. They both stifled giggles. Julia flicked her head round and shot them a look which was met with innocent expressions.

Faye watched Cheryl as they walked. She was unusual-looking, her purple-flecked straightened hair cut into a long choppy style which framed her high cheekbones and set off those amazing green eyes. It was almost ten years since she had been one of the country's top sprinters, picking up medals at the Commonwealth Games, narrowly missing out in two Olympics, but she still had a strong, athletic body. She was the complete opposite of Faye, who was pale, fragile and petite. How on earth she'd ended up falling for her she had no idea. Maybe it was true about the attraction of opposites. Never before, not even as a girl, had she ever thought of a woman in a sexual way. Even at her posh boarding school in Ascot, when all sorts of things went on in the dorms, she had steered well clear. She remembered a pretty girl called Polly, two years her senior, suggesting they practise kissing their hands so they would be good at it by the time they met some boys. Faye had giggled as she'd kissed her own hand, blushing at how silly it seemed, but she loved boys and couldn't wait to try the real thing so she followed the older girl's lead.

'We should practise on each other,' Polly said, as they huddled behind the big tree on the school lawn.

Faye laughed. 'Why would I want to kiss *your* hand? That's silly!'

But that had not been what Polly had in mind, as she leaned in and brushed her lips against Faye's. Once recovered from the shock, Faye pushed her off.

'I'm only showing you what to do,' Polly protested.

Faye kept out of her way from then on. She had not been one teeniest bit turned on by the experience at all and had never thought of it again until the night she found herself in Cheryl's bed.

They'd been friendly on the show for some time, and Cheryl had known how lonely she was with Mike away and offered to stay over and keep her company. One night, while watching *Basic Instinct*, Cheryl had started talking about how men could never fully understand female sexuality, and Faye had somehow found herself in Cheryl's arms, before ending up in bed. It had not been planned but it felt right, and since that night six months ago they had spent every night together they could. Absolutely no one knew, and that was how she wanted it to stay until she'd worked out exactly what she really felt.

As the girls reached the studio door they waited in silence to be ushered in, then one by one switched on their smiles and entered the set. Linking arms the way they had so many times before, they smiled at the audience and at each other. It was time to put on a show.

Twenty

Above the studio were the executives' offices, and inside the most coveted corner office, with the best view of London, the controller James Almond watched a recording of the previous night's edition of *Girl Talk*. After a few minutes he propelled his leather executive chair forward, reached for the remote on his desk, and switched the sound off. He pushed the intercom button and buzzed his secretary, who was on the other side of the glass wall that kept his office private from the station's minions.

'Anne, can you ask Jackie Martin to come in please?'

'Yes, Mr Almond, right away.'

He leaned back and waited. Barely ten minutes later he greeted the cautious knock on his office door with an authoritative '*Come.*'

'You wanted to see me?' Jackie, for the last two years the senior producer of *Girl Talk*, hovered in the doorway.

'Sit down,' James said, indicating the sofa.

Jackie perched on the edge, putting as much distance between herself and the controller as possible. She had a bad feeling inside.

'As you know, in the months since I took over I've been reviewing the channel's current output and direction.'

Jackie nodded, her stomach lurching. Damn, she thought,

he's going to sack me. Why does this keep happening? She knew she should never have taken out that mortgage. Her thoughts were interrupted.

'I'm going to come straight to point.'

Here we go, she thought, shifting uncomfortably in her seat and waiting for him to utter the words she dreaded. She would call her friend on the Peter Andre show, see if they still needed someone.

'*Girl Talk* won't be recommissioned at the end of the current series and I want to move you to *Good Morning Britain*.'

Jackie couldn't believe what she was hearing, although the relief she felt at not getting the chop was quickly replaced with shock at the news that the axe was about to fall on *Girl Talk*. It didn't make sense. Surely that was one of Channel 6's hit shows? She found herself gabbling a reply. 'But it's the highest rating late-night show we have, and we've just negotiated the extension of the presenters' contracts,' she said, struggling to compose herself. After all, she didn't want to blow the *GMB* gig.

'Negotiated, but not confirmed, Jackie.' His manner was firm but calm.

'And we're getting the best ratings we've ever had—'

'Which is why the time is right to bow out. It's one of my rules – always go at the top of your game. Take a leaf out of Helen England's book. She's not a national treasure for nothing, you know.' He frowned. 'Frankly, after the disgraceful press coverage from the Domes the demise of *Girl Talk* is long overdue in my opinion.'

'But—'

James cut her off. 'But *nothing*. I've been watching the show, and they're already starting to repeat themselves. There are only so many times they can drone on about ex-husbands, hormone rage, and who shouldn't have worn what. Even some of the messages on the forums are saying they've peaked, and you know research shows that where the forums start others follow.' He paused, thinking it had been a smart move to place some entirely fictitious negative comments on the message boards. 'I'm in two minds about Karen King, though. Even my wife, who hates everyone, loves her. I'll be speaking to her and the others separately, so I don't want you to breathe a word.'

'You can't just get rid of them.'

He shrugged. 'It's a TV station, not a charity for moderately talented and slightly past-it female broadcasters.' Jackie gasped. 'We'll give them a good send-off, of course, and look for some fresh faces for the channel – preferably younger ones.'

Jackie gripped the side of her chair; she knew she should be grateful to be staying but couldn't stop herself from saying something. 'But that's the whole appeal of the show, the fact that they're not girls but women in their thirties and forties. The scores in the last three months have been the highest yet so there's no way people are going off them.'

The look on James's face shut her up.

'I've made my decision and I respect the fact you speak your mind, which is why you'll be staying with us, but when we announce the new season *Girl Talk* won't be in the line-up. It's for the best, believe me. Just so I'm clear, I do *not* want this leaking out courtesy of the presenters, so they are *not* to get so much as a whiff of this until I am ready to put out a statement. If there's a leak I will hold you personally responsible and you will pay the price. Have I made myself clear?'

Jackie stared at him aghast for a moment, then, remembering that the balance of power was weighted entirely in his favour, got a grip. 'Perfectly,' she said.

'Good. Schedule to see me early next week and we'll discuss what will be in the place of *Girl Talk* and get Anne to pull up all the current contracts. I want to see what we're paying that lot.' He gestured for her leave, signalling the end of the meeting.

As Jackie headed for the door James turned up the volume on the TV and Julia's distinctive voice, smooth as silk, not a trace of an accent, asking Twiggy something about skincare, invaded the room. James faced the screen, which now featured a close-up of the presenter. 'Bye-bye, Julia,' he said before pressing the pause button. 'What goes around comes around.'

Twenty-One

Faye hurried along the embankment, a cap pulled low over her face, a scarf around her neck, wishing she had put on a coat after all. She was only going a few yards but, shit, it was cold enough to freeze your bits off.

She passed a couple on a bench facing the river: teenagers, tourists probably, the girl squirming and squealing as the boy wrestled with her and whispered in her ear. There were plenty of people out strolling, most going the other way, towards the Tate Gallery, some with the brisk air of Londoners, others dawdling, taking pictures.

As she cut through Jamaica Wharf she passed a small queue outside the restaurant on the corner with views of the Thames. The city was heaving, no doubt about it, packed with visitors enjoying the strong euro.

Just before she reached the second-hand booksellers, their stock arranged on trestle tables on the walkway next to the river, she veered left and went in through the side entrance of the National Film Centre. A girl in a black cocktail dress, a heavy cuff studded with turquoise stones on one wrist, stepped forward and asked if she was there for the press screening. Faye said no, she was meeting someone for dinner, and the girl said she would show her to the restaurant, even though Faye had been to the NFC many times before and knew exactly where she was going.

At the far end of the room behind a roped-off area a crowd drank and talked as waiters, balancing flutes of champagne and orange juice, weaved in and out, offering refills and picking up empties.

She was a few minutes early, no sign of Mike, and the buzz of the group made her want to join in. They were all clutching some sort of glossy brochure, no doubt filled with titbits and comprehensive interviews with whoever was starring in whatever it was they were screening. She caught a glimpse of Emilia Fox on the edge of the group, talking to a woman holding a tiny recorder.

A few feet away a small mob jostled for position around someone Faye could not quite see. She craned her neck. A woman with a name badge pinned to her front stepped away from the throng, phone against her ear, and moved towards her. Faye got a good look at the cover of the press pack in the woman's hand. Suddenly she knew what all the fuss was about, or rather *who*. It was that actor, the one who was in the *Bronson* film – what was his name? They had been trying to get him on *Girl Talk* to promote his new TV series but he was so hot the publicist was being cagey.

Faye inched towards the group. Perhaps if she could have a word ... She looked to see if there was a spare press pack lying about, so she could check the actor's name and find out what the drama was, wishing she had paid more attention now when Jackie ran through the list of possible guests. Those production meetings always sent her to sleep. Shit. She could hardly wade in if she didn't even have the basics. Who was he? Ed? Ben? She hung about on the edge of the group, struggling to remember Jackie doing one of her potted guides to – Tim? Fuck. It was a period drama, she was pretty sure about that. *Little Dorrit*? No. *Tess of the D'Urbervilles*? No. Hang on . . . something clicked into place. Tom? Yes! Tom Hardy.

She removed her cap, letting her honey locks tumble on to her shoulders, put on her best smile and hustled her way to the front of the group. She could just imagine the reaction when she announced that she had managed to secure the interview everyone else wanted. *I just happened to run into him in the bar at Benugo and we got chatting, clicked, you know how it is*, was how she would put it. She might even say it had been his idea to come on the show. Genius! She could barely contain herself at the thought of bringing it up at the next production meeting, everyone bored, doing their shopping lists, sending text messages, Lesley emptying out her bag for the umpteenth time, looking for her stupid lip gloss. Faye would pick her moment, maybe just as Julia was starting to yawn, which always happened after ten minutes max. She couldn't wait to see the look on her face. Then again, it would look pretty much the way it always did. That was Botox for you.

She moved forward, nudging people, asking them to let her through, treading on some poor girl's toes, not caring, determined to get to Tom Hardy before some snooty press type whisked him away. It's dog eat dog in this game, she told herself, head down, manoeuvring her way around a stout woman in a long denim skirt with a paisley panel that looked like it had been added later. Wouldn't you think anyone coming to an event like this should have to meet some kind of minimum style requirement?

At last, she was at the front of the pack.

A familiar voice said, 'Faye! What are you doing in here?'

Her mouth fell open. There, in his usual place at the heart of the action, signing his name on the back of the stout woman's press pack, was her husband, looking as if he had just stepped out of a war zone in his regulation combat pants, dusty Timberlands, khaki T-shirt and battered bomber jacket. How he got away with turning up at ITN dressed like that she would never know.

'Where's Tom Hardy?' she said, put out.

Mike put his arm around her, steered her back the way she had come and said, 'They're saving a nice table for us in the corner. God, Faye, it's so good to see you. You look amazing.'

She scowled at him. It was just like him to turn a simple dinner date into a circus, hogging the limelight, hordes of fans around him as usual. No one had paid the slightest attention to her, even though she was on the telly every day.

'I was supposed to be seeing Tom Hardy about coming on the show,' she said, watching the press pack move off into the screening room, knowing she'd missed her chance.

'You'd be lucky,' Mike said. 'He got held up. Just as well I got here a bit early, saved the day for them – all the hacks getting restless, no star turn. So when Lou, the publicist, saw me at the bar she asked if I'd mind mingling, have a glass of bubbly, do my bit, you know.'

No, she did not know. Since when was he appointed unofficial body double for one of the hottest actors around? It made her sick. He was a news reporter, for crying out loud.

'Next thing you know one of the journos starts asking me about that stint I did on the front line in Helmand, said the footage was amazing, reminded her of *Saving Private Ryan*, so I'm just telling her about all the stuff we couldn't get in – the time the bullet grazed my shoulder, and the guy who turned a pushbike into an explosive device, parked it right outside the entrance to the camp.'

Faye sat in silence as a waiter appeared and handed them menus, followed by the woman with her name pinned to the front of her dress – *Lou*, the *publicist* – with a bottle of champagne as a thank-you to Mike for helping her out, or 'saving her life', as she put it. Faye did her best to smile and be gracious when what she really wanted to do was tell the silly cow to get real.

She was fast going off the idea of dinner, wondering how many more interruptions there would be. She only had a couple of hours before she had to get back. Frankly, she was beginning to wish she hadn't bothered, that she had gone to the canteen with Cheryl instead and had something stodgy. All of a sudden she fancied fish fingers between sliced white bread with lots of ketchup and salt, and a big plate of chips on the side. All the things she never allowed herself to eat.

She glanced at the menu. Parma ham and figs, crab ravioli – that would be a single square of pasta, guaranteed – and something or other with a red-wine jus caught her eye. She looked away. Every now and then she hankered for something deep-fried and full of fat. It must be something to do with her hormones. Trouble was, she couldn't risk eating rubbish, not after doing a Pilates video and banging on about the importance of good nutrition. She had nightmares about being snapped coming out of McDonald's in a moment of weakness, and remembered the press running a picture of Karen, preweight loss, coming out of Patisserie Valerie with a giant cake box. They had somehow managed to find out exactly what was in the box – probably by pulling the wool over the eyes of the poor girl in the shop – and wrote a piece that hinted at some kind of eating disorder, when the truth was she had actually been collecting birthday buns for one of the researchers.

'I'm on an early flight to Glasgow in the morning,' Mike was saying, 'spending a couple of days with a unit before they leave for Afghanistan. Not sure how long I'll be away this time, no more than three weeks I shouldn't think, four at the most.'

He had lost weight – all that running about in the desert, living on rations – and looked lean and fit. His arms definitely had more muscle than she remembered. She wondered if there was a gym on the base and he was working out. His hair was short, almost shaved, but it suited him. Every time he came home he looked more like a soldier. She wondered why he didn't just go the whole hog and join up.

He leaned across the table and took her hand. 'Let's have a quick bite, then I'll walk you back to the studio, have a bit of private time in your dressing room before the show.' He grinned. 'Another quick bite if you like.' The blue eyes crinkled at the corners. 'What do you think?'

She gazed at him, wanting to stay cross for Tom Hardy not being there, and blame him for spoiling her chances of getting one over on the girls, but when she looked into his eyes she felt herself weaken.

'Was that a smile?' He stroked the inside of her wrist, serious now, bent and kissed her hand, slipping a finger into his mouth.

She yanked her hand free. 'Stop it!'

'Why? No one's looking.'

'*Every*one's looking. They all want to get a better look at Mr All-Action Hero.'

He sat back in his seat, fiddled with the stem of his champagne glass. 'I've missed you, you know.'

She picked up her menu. 'Yes, well, I've missed you.'

'I mean *really* missed you – had a few of those dodgy dreams, just woke up in time, saved myself from the kind of personal explosion that can be a bit embarrassing when you're sharing a tent, if you know what I mean.'

Faye watched him do his little-boy-lost routine, eyes pleading, soppy grin on his face, and realized she was grinning too. That was Mike all over: infuriating one minute, making her laugh and charming her into bed the next.

She had a funny feeling in her tummy. Under the table he had slipped his foot out of his boot and was stroking her leg. 'Will you be*have*,' she said, wriggling, flustered. 'The whole bar is watching. Look, the waiter's coming back. Hurry up and decide what you want.'

He pushed his menu aside without looking at it, holding her gaze. 'I already have,' he said.

Twenty-Two

There was something compelling, in a nightmarish sense, about the image on the giant screen facing Karen in James Almond's office. She looked away, rooted around in her bag, got out her pocket diary and began flicking through the pages, most of which were blank, just to distract herself, but time and again she was drawn back to the screen where Julia, mouth curled, eyes blazing, was frozen in hideous close-up.

It was possibly the most unattractive still of Julia she had ever seen, not counting the one of her in *heat* magazine's Hoop of Horror, in profile, before she had her nose done, mouth open, fillings on show – she hadn't had her teeth done either then – guzzling ice cream. Instead of the usual shameful solitary hoop, Julia's picture had had been defaced with two; her nose and mouth were both circled. She had gone ballistic.

Karen had actually felt sorry for her, gone so far as to hide *heat* at the bottom of the pile of magazines in the green room, only for Lesley to dig it out and put it back on top, open at the offending page. That had sent Julia off the deep end. The pair had almost come to blows.

Karen had no doubt who'd win. Julia, tall and athletic, was a bit of a body addict – always in that gym of hers. As for Lesley, Karen was not quite sure if wrestling with champagne corks and getting jiggy whenever the mood took her really counted as a fitness regime, but maybe all that bonking explained why Lesley stayed so thin.

Karen remembered reading somewhere that sex burned off hundreds of calories, almost enough to wipe out the ill-effects of a Snickers bar, although surely it depended what exactly you got up to and how long you managed to keep going.

Her mind drifted back to the night before, Dave disappearing under the duvet, planting lingering kisses on her breasts, his tongue exploring her navel and between her thighs. She shifted on the sofa, her cheeks growing hot, and fumbled in her bag for her compact, dabbing her face with powder, hoping to tone down her rosy glow before James Almond appeared.

She glanced at the glass panel at the front of the office through which she could see James's pit bull of a PA, Anne, straight-backed at her computer, words zipping across the screen, one brusque email after another whizzing into the ether. The one arranging this meeting had been to the point: **The controller would like to see you. Please confirm you are available at 11 a.m. on the 21st.** Karen's chatty reply, saying how much she was looking forward to the meeting and asking if it was at all possible to make it slightly later in the day as she had another appointment, brought an instant response: **Sorry, it isn't.** No *Dear Karen*, not even *Best wishes, Anne* – not that anyone in the media bothered with *Best Wishes* any more. These days a brusque *Best* was about as much as you could expect, and even that was asking too much of Miss Too-Busy-for-Niceties. **Sorry, it isn't.**

Karen's phone bleeped. The message read **R u up 4 early nite? x**. She blushed and tapped out a hasty reply, resorting to the kind of abbreviations she hated in other people's texts: **U r v bad influence!** She had discovered all sorts of surprising things about Dave since the night of the Dome Awards, not least that he was fantastic in bed, always putting her first, making sure she was satisfied. Just thinking about him sent a pleasurable sensation racing through her body, although now and again she couldn't help picturing him doing exactly the same things to Debbie Irving, which produced an ugly stab of envy. She had to stop thinking like that. Even if – *if* – he had been shagging Debbie, that was all in the past. She was with that *Hollyoaks* bloke now, the one who kept popping up with his top off in *heat*'s Man Watch! He was there almost as often as Faye's husband, Mike.

She wondered if Dave compared her to the waiflike Debbie. She must stop tormenting herself, wishing she was a size 8 rather than a curvy 12. Size 12 was good, womanly. Did she really want to be skin and bone, great in one of those bandage dresses but nothing to look at once she whipped it off? No.

She glanced down and admired her flat tummy, held in place by the trusty Spanx, which she now discreetly whipped off and replaced with something lacy and a lot briefer before she got down to business with Dave. Her underwear was much more interesting these days, lots of fancy pants with bows and cut-outs. She still struggled to see herself as the kind of woman who went to bed in frilly undies, but thanks to Dave telling her she was gorgeous and sexy, she was starting to feel like a sex bomb. It was an absolute revelation. Just thinking about him sent another pleasurable sensation racing through her body. The weird thing was, even though she was in lust with Dave, she couldn't stop thinking about Jason, which was probably why she had finally agreed, after several weeks of pleading on his part, to have lunch with him. What harm could lunch do?

She put her bag on the floor and leaned back. James

Almond's office was spacious, the oversized desk some kind of pale wood, maple maybe, a computer in a glossy black casing, not a single piece of paper, no Post-its or notepad that she could see, just a neat stack of DVDs. The low table in front of her comprised a sheet of frosted glass on a base that seemed to be old railway sleepers. There were framed prints on the wall facing the desk, a simple sketch of a dove, flowers painted with bold, blocky strokes, one of those strange portraits that looked like someone had got hold of a few random jigsaw pieces and decided to make them fit, no matter what. That was definitely a Picasso. The sofa, in dark-brown leather, was enormous. She had tried sitting back and ended up flat out. At least Almond hadn't seen that, although she wouldn't be in the least surprised if there was a hidden camera on her right now and he was closeted away in some bunker, watching. She pulled a face and stuck out her tongue just as the door flew open.

'Sorry about that. Programmes to make, crises to solve, people to sack.' James Almond bounded over and sank on to the sofa beside her.

All of a sudden Karen had a horrible sense of déjà vu, of her fateful meeting with Elliot Carew all over again. James leaned back, hands linked behind his head, one knee hooked over the squashy leather arm of the sofa, foot dangling in mid-air. He didn't exactly look like a controller, with his drainpipe jeans and casual shirt buttoned to the neck, the embroidered Versace logo on the breast pocket letting everyone know it wasn't just any old shirt. How old was he? Early thirties? How come everyone in charge was so young these days?

Everything, including his belt, socks and pointy shoes, was black. For some reason in her mind's eye she saw Clint Eastwood riding into some godforsaken town, doing that thing where he walks into the saloon, doors going *swish, swish* behind him, and takes on the baddies, blasting them to kingdom come. Except *he* was the baddie, wasn't he? She chewed her bottom lip, feeling overdressed, showy, in her short tartan skirt and shiny black court shoes. She remembered she was wearing red lipstick. Shit, it was probably all over her teeth now.

'Right, *Girl Talk*,' he said, frowning at her.

Karen gave him an uncertain smile, steeling herself for the usual controller's spiel about the show being the cornerstone of the post-watershed schedule, a ratings hit, the darling of the advertisers, blah frigging blah, and not a word about taking it off air. No, the death knell would come without warning when no one was expecting it, once they had all been lulled into a false sense of complacency, moved house or remortgaged or bought new cars on the strength of a new series. She struggled to keep smiling, wishing for once in her life she could have a boss willing to be straight with her.

'Bad news, I'm afraid,' James Almond said. 'I'm axing the show.' He frowned again, picked at a thread on the knee of his immaculate jeans, studied it and dropped it into a bin at the side of the sofa. 'There you are then. No point beating around the bush.'

Karen felt as if she had just taken a massive punch right in the solar plexus. James Almond's funky office morphed into a boxing ring, Karen in satin shorts and a vest, dodging blows from the new heavyweight champion, now bearing down on her, backing her into a corner. He leaned forward and she shrank away, on the ropes now, nowhere else to go, waiting for him to deliver the knockout punch.

'Are you all right?' he said, peering at her. 'You've gone white. Bit of a shock, I know, but there's no sense pussy-footing around, pretending, when the fact is the show is coming to the end of its natural life, is there? If I told you everything was fine then pulled the plug a few months from now, just after you'd taken out a loan on a new property or one of those designer bags you girls love that cost about as much as a studio flat in Camden, you'd think I was a total bastard. Wouldn't you?'

Karen didn't answer. She couldn't. She wasn't sure she still had the power of speech. In her head she was flat out on the canvas, unconscious, her cornerman on his knees pressing a damp towel against her brow. The room started to spin and her grip tightened on the edge of the sofa as it picked up speed. She shut her eyes and held tight.

When she opened them James Almond was leaning over her, very close, much too close for comfort, in fact. She blinked and he went in and out of focus. There was another face peering at her. His PA hovered next to him, a glass of water in her hand.

'She must have fainted,' Anne was saying. 'The nurse is on her way up.'

Karen struggled to get up. She was flat on her back, sinking into the soft, squidgy sofa. Her legs struck out as she struggled to get upright. She was helpless, like a beetle that had flipped over, legs going nineteen to the dozen.

A third faced loomed above her, that of Jean Jones, the station's resident nurse. A thumb pressed against Karen's wrist. 'What exactly happened?' she asked James.

'She went as white as a sheet and keeled over,' he said.

'Karen, love, I'm going to sit you up, all right?' Jean said.

Jean propped Karen up against a pile of cushions and consulted the watch pinned to the front of her uniform. 'I'm just going to take your temperature,' she said, sliding a thermometer into Karen's mouth. Several seconds went by and nobody spoke, then Jean removed the thermometer. 'Right, young lady,' she said. 'Your pulse is fine, temperature fine, so what made you faint?'

Karen wanted to point at James and tell Jean it was his fault, giving her dreadful news, just like that, no warning, no gentle lead-in, just bam! You're fired! It was worse than *The Apprentice*. At least they got a chance to speak up for themselves before being shunted out of the boardroom and into a waiting cab. 'I don't know,' she managed to say eventually.

Jean gave her a stern look. 'Did you have breakfast?'

Karen shook her head. She had stayed in bed with Dave, got up too late to bother with breakfast, intended to get something at the studio, only there wasn't time. She hadn't eaten the night before either, hadn't fancied anything after the show, just a couple of glasses of wine before bed. What time had she got to sleep? God only knows. It was late, anyway, and then Dave had woken her up early, kissing her back, rubbing her shoulders. She wasn't sure where he got the energy, although the fact that he was a lot younger than her – a mere twenty-seven, she had discovered – would definitely help. Now she thought about it, the last thing she'd had to eat was a flapjack at lunchtime the day before, and a gluten-free one at that, no sugar, just a few oats and seeds that weren't even bound together with something sweet and syrupy, but disintegrated as soon as she ripped open the wrapper. 'I skipped breakfast,' she said.

'There you are then,' Jean Jones said, triumphant.

Anne slipped out but her departure went unnoticed as Jean launched into her famous lecture.

'The body is like a car, a finely tuned motor,' Jean said. 'Think of it like a Bentley, a top-of-the-range luxury vehicle. It needs fuel. You wouldn't go for a spin in your car, your lovely Mercedes or whatever you drive . . .' As Jean droned on Karen thought about the ancient Beetle she had bought years ago to restore and still not got round to doing anything with. Jean said, 'I don't suppose you would dream of taking your pride and joy on the road if it had no petrol, would you?' Karen shook her head. The last time she had taken the Beetle out she had broken down and had to call out the AA, who had told her, to her embarrassment, she was out of petrol, even though the gauge was on half full. The gauge, it turned out, was in pretty much the same dilapidated state as the rest of the car.

'Right, missy,' Jean said. 'You need to eat something.' She took a step back and cast a suspicious eye over Karen. 'You're not on some faddy diet, are you?'

'No, definitely not. It's just the funny hours we do – sometimes I skip meals without even noticing.'

Jean patted her own ample stomach. 'This is what lets you know when you haven't eaten,' she said. 'You feel hungry. And when you feel hungry, eat.'

Anne reappeared with a paper plate from the canteen, its contents hidden by another paper plate balanced on top. 'I've brought you something,' she said, handing the plate to Jean, who handed it to Karen.

It was a bacon sandwich. Oh bliss! She could have wept with gratitude. She hadn't had a bacon sarnie for months, not since she noticed the weight dropping off. She peeled back a corner of bread to reveal melted butter on the slice below, brown sauce smothering the crispy rashers, and she inhaled, suddenly feeling a lot better.

'You're right,' she said, sitting up straight, perky, biting into the sandwich. She closed her eyes and chewed, in food heaven.

'Perhaps we can crack on,' James said, opening a window. 'Now you've had your breakfast.'

Karen nodded. She could feel her energy levels start to rise, her fighting spirit making a comeback. 'Of course,' she said, confident, ready for him now.

Seconds out, round two, ding ding.

Twenty-Three

Karen dropped the greasy paper plates into a bin next to James's pristine sofa and wiped her hands on a paper serviette. She felt so much better.

'Ready to press on?' he said.

She lobbed the screwed-up serviette at the bin. 'Definitely,' she said, rummaging in her bag, digging out a clear lip gloss and doing a Lesley, slathering it on in full view of the controller. Screw him. If she was being sacked anyway she might as well have fun. She gave him a sweet smile. 'You were in the middle of telling me *Girl Talk* is dead in the water. Kaput. Fucked.'

She wanted to giggle. Karen would never normally use the F-word in company, preferring to say 'frigging' this or 'effing' that if push came to shove. Not this time, though. She had no intention of sparing the feelings of a man who had shown not a shred of tact when it came to hers, the heartless bastard. That she had just been in the throes of privately bemoaning the fact no one was up-front any more at the precise moment he chose to drop his bombshell was immaterial. Managers are supposed to be trained in industrial relations, able to show some sensitivity to their staff, not deliver such an almighty body blow that said staff pass out on the spot.

'Funny,' she said, searching in her bag again, not looking at him, '*I* thought we were actually doing rather well – winning awards, that kind of thing.' When James said nothing she looked up, compact in hand, flipping it open to check her reflection. She was looking a bit pale. '*I* thought the ratings were up, advertising revenue steady. I would have thought the fact we got a sponsor this year might have made a difference.' She snapped the compact shut. 'Still, what do I know? *I'm* only a presenter.'

James said, 'Just now, when you fainted' – Karen nodded – 'did you bump your head at the same time? Only you seem to have turned into Mrs Angry all of a sudden.'

'You're axing my show, no wonder I'm angry!'

'I am indeed.'

'And I wouldn't like to be in your shoes when you break the news to –' she gestured at Julia, still grimacing on the giant screen – 'because if you think *this* is angry, you're in for a shock.'

James clapped his hands. 'Priceless. You think I'll meet my match in Julia Hill, notorious ice queen? Please.' He got up and opened another window. The smell of bacon began to recede. 'I live by a strict code, Karen. Does that surprise you?' She stared at him, silent, now, not a single clever remark in her head. 'I'm sure it doesn't. Successful people usually have a set of rules, a way of staying on course no matter what. I'm sure you appreciate it's not easy getting to be Controller of Entertainment at a major broadcaster.' She began to feel uneasy. 'Anyone doing this job needs to be able to make tough decisions, keep the programme makers happy, the audience – and the board. Not easy, Karen. I won't bore you with my rules, but I will share just one with you. It's actually pretty high up on my list – second, in fact. Rule number two is: Never make assumptions about anything. Does that make sense to you?'

She nodded, distinctly uncomfortable now, sensing he was about to say something she would rather not hear.

'You're an intelligent woman, smart – an excellent broadcaster. People warm to you, unlike –' he paused and glanced at the screen again – 'some I could mention. I hadn't realized you're quite the comedian too, not until a few minutes ago. I can see you're angry about *Girl Talk* going. However, if you'd let me finish you might have been less enraged to hear that I'm looking into a proposal for a new show in a better slot. Not everyone would survive, of course.' Again he cast a glance in the direction of Julia. 'That shouldn't concern you, though, because I don't see you buried in a graveyard slot for the rest of your days. You're too – what's the word? – sharp for that. *Girl Talk* isn't the only show that's doing well. Look at *Good Morning Britain*, trouncing the opposition, taking a forty per cent audience share. I'm telling you, in these days of multichannel television, that's unheard of.'

He pressed a buzzer on the desk. There was a tap on the door and his PA came in.

'Anne, I'm trying to have a sensible conversation with Karen here about doing away with all the rubbish on our airwaves and the fact we're sitting in a rubbish tip is very off-putting.'

Karen glanced around the immaculate office, wondering what on earth he was talking about. For one crazy moment she thought he meant Julia.

'Empty the bin,' he said, 'and stop this place smelling like a greasy spoon.'

Twenty-Four

'Where do you see yourself five years from now?' asked James, once Anne had left the room.

Thrown by the question, Karen began to stutter. 'Well, I—'

'It pays to have a plan,' James interrupted, 'a clear sense of where you're going and what you want to achieve. I started out as a runner, making tea for presenters who didn't even say thank you. Never mind I had a first-class honours degree in biology; I was treated like dirt, lowest of the low, and you know what?' He paused. Karen shook her head. 'I *liked* it, because it meant I was below the radar, invisible, and that was a great vantage point when it came to observing people, seeing how things worked, separating the good guys from the out-and-out bastards.' He stared at the ceiling, lost in thought for a few seconds. 'There was one presenter, naming no names, who went out of his way to make life miserable for whoever was bottom of the pile. He thought he was *it*, whereas the truth was he was mediocre with a big mouth and an even bigger ego. He could do the job, no doubt about that, not that reading off an autocue strikes me as particularly challenging – what do you think?'

'Well—' Karen started to protest.

'Anyway, not a day went by that he didn't reduce some poor sod to tears. Not me, though. By then I was climbing the ladder, not quite junior enough to be walked over, plus I'd grown a thick skin thanks to a difficult time at the hands of one particularly snotty-nosed cow. So I was OK, but the runners, the junior researchers, third AD, and anyone who had the misfortune to come in on work experience, he crucified. What kept us going was the absolute certainty that what goes around comes around. It was practically the production motto. We knew he couldn't get away with it forever.'

'What happened? Was he sacked?'

'For a while he went from strength to strength, kept landing new peak-time shows, had all these formats developed for him, set up his own production company, took a slice of the profits, and all the time he was pissing people off.

'It became a tradition to gob in his tea. Everyone knew about it except him. So while he carried on being a grade-A shit we all told each other, "What goes around comes around."'

James got up, walked to the desk, pressed something on the keyboard of his fancy PC, studied the screen for a moment and said, 'I couldn't tell you where he is now. He'll never get through the door here, that's for sure. It took a while, but he got what was coming in the end. All those minions he tortured moved on, and one or two are doing all right for themselves.' He ran a finger across his throat. 'Game over for him. The tosser is dead and buried.'

Karen began to feel faint again.

James brushed an imaginary crumb off the front of his shirt. 'So, what's your five-year plan, Karen?'

'I suppose what I really want to achieve—'

He interrupted again. 'Because if *you* don't know, who does? You need to have a clear vision.' He tapped the side of his head. 'Are you ambitious, Karen – or a bit of a drifter?'

She blinked. She had never considered herself particularly ambitious, always believed in fate and everything happening for a reason, but she wasn't about to tell him that. She began, 'I've always been the kind of person—'

James cut in, 'What I'm saying is, if you drift along, where are you going to end up?' He paused, gazing at her, waiting for her to answer the question. She hung back, wanting to be sure he had finished, that it was her turn to speak. James kept quiet. As soon as she opened her mouth to say something he held up a hand and leaned forward. 'Think of a boat, Karen, no anchor, drifting. Not a good image, is it?'

She shook her head; a small wooden craft with creaky oars, the kind they used to take out on the boating lake for half an hour at a time when she was little, came to mind. Occasionally someone would lose an oar and start to drift, bumping into other boats, until the owner waded out and rescued them. It was only a small lake, shallow. She was pretty sure that wasn't the image James intended to conjure up.

He was silent for a moment. 'Worst-case scenario, lost at sea, never seen again, smashed against rocks.' He brought his hands together in a sudden thunderous clap, making her jump. 'Am I right?'

She swallowed. 'Well, yes, unless the coastguard sees it, manages to get a line out and tow it back in, I suppose.' She was speaking too fast, desperate to get a word in. 'I mean it all depends on *when* it starts to drift. Say it breaks anchor in a storm or something and the owner, realizing the weather's turned, goes to check the mooring – chances are he'll spot the problem.' She had no idea what she was saying. Shut *up*, Karen! Cold sweat ran down the centre of her back.

James studied her with the kind of cool detachment he had

been known for during tricky dissections in the lab at university. 'Do you need a drink of water or something?'

Her face was burning. 'I'm not heading for the rocks,' she said. 'I think my track record speaks for itself. For seven years I was part of a successful girl band. We sold more than ten million records, toured the world, picked up a Brit award.' She took a deep breath. 'So, yes, I'm ambitious.'

James stretched and rested his hands behind his head. 'Ah yes,' he said, amused, 'the Thunderbirds—'

'Girls. Thunder *Girls*. And right now I'm working hard to make a name for myself as a versatile broadcaster. It doesn't matter what I do, I always give it my best shot. I want to connect with the audience, not be someone remote they feel they have nothing in common with.' It was her turn to glance at Julia. James was nodding now. Feeling bold, she went on, 'I know exactly where I'm going.'

The corners of James's mouth twitched. 'Well that's interesting, because at this precise moment in time I just might have a better idea about that than you. You know Helen England's going and I need a new anchor for *Good Morning Britain*? Our national treasure seems to think very highly of you. So, the most prestigious gig on daytime TV is up for grabs. Think you could handle it?'

She gulped.

'This is strictly top secret for now. All the wannabes are coming out of the woodwork and they all want that job. You should see my inbox – chock-a-block with emails from agents, all of whom think they have the new face of daytime.' He gestured at the pile of DVDs on his desk. 'I can't tell you how many dreadful showreels I'm getting. Look, I think you'd be rather good on the sofa but I can't be seen to poach you from

Girl Talk. It would be completely against company policy, as you know. However, if you were to *resign* and become a free agent, so to speak, there would be nothing to stop me from offering you the *GMB* job. Do you follow?'

Karen nodded. She followed.

'This is absolutely confidential. If word gets out the job's already promised, well, let's just say you won't exactly be Miss Popularity and neither will I.' He frowned. '*Mr* Popularity. I need one hundred per cent commitment from you, Karen, and that means no surprises.' He gave her a hard stare. 'This would be a bad time to ask for maternity leave, if you follow me. So, just hand in your notice and keep your head down. This is your big chance so stay on the ball, and *no drifting*, OK?'

She gave him a weak smile. She could hardly believe it. He was offering her a way out of the misery of *Girl Talk, and* one of the best jobs on TV into the bargain. 'I don't know what to say. I mean thank you, I won't let you down.'

So the biggest prize in daytime really was going to be hers. She couldn't help wondering why she didn't feel better about it.

Twenty-Five

Lesley surveyed the gloomy restaurant through her oversized Gucci shades. As far as she could tell the place had no redeeming features. The walls' textured finish had gone out of fashion decades earlier and a coat of magnolia had been slapped on at the same time by the look of things. Even with her sunglasses acting as a filter she could see dust and the odd fossilized spider making themselves at home in the plaster crevices.

Fiddling with the napkin, which formed a neat triangle on her side plate, she noticed the tablecloth had been repaired, small patches that didn't quite match sewn in here and there. Next to a single red rose in a slim silver vase was the kind of cruet set her mother had given to the charity shop when salt and pepper mills became popular.

In the shadows at the far end of the room, a waiter in a stiff white jacket with gold buttons, black hair slicked back, a white cloth over one arm, stood to attention. Lesley let out a noisy sigh and turned to the man facing her. 'Don't tell me. We're not actually in a restaurant about to have lunch. For some reason you've dragged me to the arse-end of Victoria to visit the set of a period drama. Christ knows why, but I'm sure you're about to explain, so get on with it, then we can find somewhere decent to eat. I mean, really, Dean, is this your idea of a joke?'

She lowered her glasses and gazed at the maître d' in a smart black suit, satin ribbon trim on the lapels, who stood behind the reception desk, pen in hand, and was flicking through what she supposed was the reservations book. Not that there could be any reservations. The place was deserted. It had a weird feel to it, a bit like a museum. She began to feel uncomfortable. The maître d', who sported the same slicked-back hairstyle as the waiter, felt her eyes on him, looked up, and gave her a formal bow.

'For fuck's sake,' she said. 'I'm in a time warp. He looks like he's just stepped off the dance floor circa 1946.'

Dean Craig, head bent over the menu, said, 'The ravioli with sage and butter is excellent. Actually, all the pasta is terrific, home-made, fresh every day. The penne arrabiata has quite a kick, though, tons of chilli, so be warned.'

Lesley put her glasses back on. 'No offence, but I don't much fancy eating in a mausoleum.'

He put down his menu. 'Where would you rather eat?' he said. 'How about the Groucho, or maybe the Wolseley? I know – the Charlotte Street Hotel.'

Lesley nodded, hooking her bag over her shoulder, digging out her lip gloss, doing a quick and entirely unnecessary repair job. 'The Groucho. You'll need to get on the phone and book a table,' she said, starting to get to her feet.

'Actually, I've got a better idea,' he said, not moving. 'What about Al Dente? Nice and quiet, perfect for a tête-à-tête, a paparazzi-free zone. What more could you want?'

'It's a dump!' she protested.

'Don't be so melodramatic. This was one of the top restaurants in its day. Everyone who was anyone ate here. When Sammy Davis Jr came to London apparently he ate here.'

Lesley gave him a cool look. 'I don't suppose *his* agent got him here under false pretences and then held him captive.'

'Look, poppet, have I ever let you down?'

Lesley stared at the swirly plasterwork on the wall. A coat of paint would work wonders. 'And another thing, why am I sitting with my back to the door?' she said.

'It's a precaution,' Dean said, 'in case anyone happens to spot us.'

'Dean, I am on the *telly*. People *know* me. I am a *celebrity*. My face is on the cover of *Closer* this week, and *Hello!* So why the fuck am I practically in hiding in the back of frigging beyond?' She gave him a sulky pout. 'Anyone would think I was a criminal. You'll be bundling me out with a blanket over my head next. Just make sure you mind the extensions.' She twisted a strand of blonde hair around her finger.

'Funny you should say that, because you came *this* close –' he held up a thumb and index finger – 'to ending up in the slammer on a charge of aggravated assault for socking Sasha Gates at the Domes. Just think, you wouldn't be on one or two poxy covers, you would be on *every* magazine out there, in *handcuffs* – the real ones, not the pink fluffy things they sell in the kind of shops you frequent, by the way – and no chance of getting to the salon to have the precious extensions done for, ooh, let's see, eighteen months, maybe two years? It's only because I have turned myself inside-out and done the biggest arse-licking number imaginable that you are in a position to walk the streets freely and have a civilized lunch with your put-upon agent.' Lesley winced. 'Believe me, she was ready to see you hung, drawn and quartered. You are extremely fortunate she agreed not to press charges.'

'Oh for crying out loud, we had a tussle, that's all.'

'What you call a "tussle" meant an extra hour in make-up every day to cover up the bruises before she could go on set. You made quite a mess of her eye. Come to think of it, I'm surprised *Spitalfields* didn't hit you with a bill for overtime. Trust me, poppet, if she had wanted to go for the jugular it wouldn't be Bruno's ravioli you'd be turning your nose up at – it would be porridge.'

Lesley picked up her menu. 'If we're staying in this dump, can we at least have a drink?'

She didn't want to think about that awful night at the Domes, but it kept coming back to her in hideous detail. She stared at the menu. Parma ham to start and then the ravioli Dean was banging on about to follow. He was cross with her, she could tell. Usually he took her side, no matter what she'd been up to. She glanced over at him as he flipped open the wine list. He was the same old Dean, with his cropped hair, bleached white, and a T-shirt, probably a one-off, with the words from a song scrawled across the front. Dean, who knew how to dress down like nobody else, spent a fortune on his clothes. He wouldn't be seen dead in anything mass-produced. Feeling her eyes on him, he looked up.

'What about a decent bottle of Chianti?' he said.

She nodded. His voice still had a brittle edge to it, just like the time he phoned her late on a Saturday night to warn her about the kiss-and-tell the *News of the World* were running the next day. 'For fuck's sake, poppet,' he had said, 'if you're going to shag around at least be a bit choosy. The bloke's basically a shelf stacker in a frigging sex shop.' Lesley had kept quiet. She *knew* he was a shelf stacker in a sex shop. That was how she met him, when she was doing a bit of browsing, looking for something to perk things up in the bedroom. He had been very attentive, suggesting that Spanish fly stuff and a couple of DVDs by someone called Anna Span, who supposedly made 'respectable' porn geared towards women. Sure enough, the blurb on the cover boasted 'genuine female point of view'. Lesley had heard Anna Span on *Woman's Hour* and subsequently suggested having her on *Girl Talk*, but prissy Paula had put her foot down and said she couldn't care less if Anna Span was the first female porn director, porn was porn.

Anyway, Lesley had found it a bit of a turn-on, rifling through porn with a total stranger who was hot and less than half her age. They had arranged to meet later in a basement bar tucked down a back alley off Tottenham Court Road and after a couple of large glasses of wine (for Lesley) and three San Miguels (for Whatever-his-name-was) they had gone back to her place. Careless, really, letting him know where she lived, but it was all part of the thrill. And anyway, there were more possibilities at home than in some sterile hotel room. They had cracked open some fizz, laced it with Spanish fly, and watched a bit of Anna Span's film, then he had rummaged through her toybox and dug out a blindfold, some handcuffs and her prized Agent Provocateur whip. It was during their third session, after a few lines of coke, while she was helpless and blindfolded, that he had videoed her with a sophisticated cameraphone supplied by the *News of the World*, cunning bastard.

'I know what I'm having,' Lesley said, snapping the menu shut, giving Dean an apologetic smile, wanting to get back on his good side. She hated it when he gave her a hard time. Let's face it, when her agent showed signs of tiring of her it was a bad sign. 'You've sold me on the famous ravioli,' she said, 'and I'm sorry for being so snooty about this place.' She looked around and aimed a dazzling smile in the direction of the maître d'. 'Actually, it's nice to be away from all the poseurs for a change.'

She slid her hand across the table and squeezed Dean's wrist, admiring his chunky rose-gold timepiece. Was that a Philippe Patek? 'I'm just being a cow, ignore me,' she said, eyeing the watch. They cost how much – £20,000, £30,000? Peter Mandelson had one as well. There'd been something in the *Style* section of the *Sunday Times* about it. She was seriously impressed.

'And thanks for getting me off the hook with Stroppy Sasha, bitch of this parish. I know you wouldn't think so the way I carry on, but I do appreciate it.' Feeling a sudden rush of warmth towards him, she said, 'In fact, lunch is on me. Let's have some fizz, something decent.'

'You need to keep your nose clean, poppet—'

'I told you, I'm not doing that stuff any more,' Lesley said, offended.

'I *mean*, give the kiss-and-tell boys a wide berth for a bit. One of the best jobs in telly is on the market so chop-chop, be on your best behaviour, and leave the rest up to me.'

The champagne helped put her in a good mood but still she couldn't shake the memory of losing it at the Domes. In the past when she had done something awful under the influence – and there had been plenty of occasions – she had at least benefited from not being able to remember a thing about it. Blackouts definitely had their uses. This time, though, it was all there in graphic detail. She hadn't meant to slap Sasha Gates (had she?), just warn her off, but the bitch had goaded her. And yes, it had felt good at the time but Lesley hadn't slept that night, and not just because Dan Kincaid was the kind of guy who didn't seem to need any sleep. As the effects of the bubbly wore off, she had been tormented by the sight of Sasha's battered face. Oh God, she had actually *assaulted* the woman. OK, Sasha had come after her, not that tugging at her dress exactly constituted reciprocal GBH. If Lesley had only been wearing tit-tape she would never have fallen out. She had lain awake, her heart thumping in her chest, waiting for a knock on the door, a couple of policemen telling her to get dressed and go to the station with them. Horrible visions of being fingerprinted, a set of garish mug shots taken, and some doctor doing a blood test that showed she was several times over the drink-driving limit haunted her. She would be locked up.

It didn't help that *heat* had run a picture of Sasha, hair scraped back, no make-up, looking like she had been in the ring with a heavyweight champion. She wanted to be seen, of course, probably tipped them off, otherwise she'd have been wearing dark glasses. The story speculated that the Queen of Soap's mystery shiner was something to do with her on-off boyfriend and invited anyone who knew the gory details to ring the news team on a free number.

When nothing happened she hoped perhaps it would all just go away. It didn't, of course. It became the cause of frantic behind-the-scenes negotiations between Dean and Sasha's agent. She drained the last of her champagne and reached for the bottle, topping up Dean's glass first. She owed him. Buying lunch was the least she could do.

Not that she had finished with Sasha Gates yet. She couldn't stop until she had seen her toppled, out in the cold, off all the guest lists. See how she liked it.

Twenty-Six

In the canteen at Elstree Studios Cheryl sipped her skinny latte and picked at a low-fat blueberry muffin. Every now and then members of the *Spitalfields* cast would drift in, get a coffee and drift away again. A spotty boy, with a walkie-talkie in the breast pocket of a padded jacket with a BBC logo, patrolled, his radio crackling now and then, a disembodied voice instructing him to fetch So-and-so and get them on set.

At a table, also on his own, was the actor who played the gay one. He had nodded at Cheryl when he came in but she couldn't remember his name and had misplaced her call sheet with details of who everyone was and which scenes were being shot that day, so she couldn't check. She could have gone on the net on her mobile if she had really wanted to know, but she wasn't that interested. He wasn't one of the people she was due to interview, so why bother finding out who he was? No point making unnecessary work for herself.

She composed a text to Faye. They had fallen out over Mike, with Cheryl accusing Faye of cheating on her. Faye had hit the roof, saying how could she cheat on her lover with her husband? Not that she had slept with him anyway.

'Nothing happened,' she insisted. 'He stayed over, that's all. The thing about Mike is he takes his work very seriously, a bit like a football player, and would never ever have sex on the eve of a mission. He says it saps him of his energy.'

Cheryl wasn't sure what to believe. She couldn't help thinking it was about the most pathetic thing she had ever heard. Mike had been away, living in filth in a war zone for months. He had one night at home and Faye expected her to believe he wasn't interested in having sex with his wife. She really must think she was born yesterday. The fact that Cheryl had said as much meant things had been strained between them ever since. Still, with war breaking out on the home front between Julia and Karen, and Lesley sticking her oar in, making matters worse, it was important not to fall out. They needed each other. Strength in numbers and all that.

The last production meeting had been a case in point: Julia having digs at Karen, Lesley needling Julia, Faye giving Cheryl the silent treatment. She almost wanted to laugh out loud at the piece in *Hot Celebrity* magazine, quoting a so-called insider saying *Girl Talk* was a bitch-free zone and all the women got along on and off screen. What a joke. The fact that Karen was doing so much press around her dramatic weight loss had put everyone's backs up no end. Why on earth the magazines were making such a fuss was a mystery to Cheryl. They should have been jumping up and down ages ago when Karen was a proper fatty and shamed her into doing something about it, but most of the time they'd left her alone, just the odd snatched picture of her in McDonald's or eating an ice cream. Cheryl had made it her business to have as little to do with Karen as possible during her fat phase, without being obvious. Just having to appear on TV next to such a tub of lard had made her feel violated.

The spotty boy was back at the counter, ordering something.

She imagined Sasha Gates in her dressing room, a runner at her beck and call. She was looking forward to interviewing her later, might even slip in a cheeky question about Lesley.

Cheryl had started doing behind-the-scenes features for *Girl Talk* midway through the last series. Paula had sent her off to do a piece on the set of *Emmerdale* as a means of appeasing her when she grumbled she wasn't being given enough to do, and she had done such a good job it became a regular slot. Cheryl had a gift for getting actors to open up, filming them having their make-up done, getting changed, messing up their lines. Paula had been surprised. In fact, most of the work was done by the researcher, Natalie Scott, who was happy to stand in the cold for hours on end getting footage of scenes being shot, grabbing off-the-cuff chats with whoever was willing to talk, while Cheryl made herself at home in the catering bus or, if they happened to be in a studio complex, the canteen or green room, only showing her face when it was time for the main interviews, which were always done indoors under controlled conditions.

The *Spitalfields* shoot had been scheduled for a while, long before Lesley battered their leading lady. Still, no one had suggested they pull the plug. Maybe Sasha Gates wanted a chance to tell the world exactly what she thought of Lesley Gold. Cheryl smiled. This was going to be fun.

She tried calling Faye again but it rang a few times and went to voicemail. Cheryl was about to hang up then decided not to. 'Still giving me the cold shoulder?' she said. 'Sign of a guilty conscience, if you ask me.' She rang off, feeling less pleased than she had hoped. If she wasn't careful she would blow it totally and Faye would definitely be back with that gung-ho husband of hers. Cheryl stared at her phone, willing it to ring. Even a text message would be a start.

Natalie Scott, all wrapped up in a waterproof jacket that was too big for her, a scarf wound around her throat, her cheeks flushed from standing in the cold all morning, threaded her way through the canteen, giving the actor whose name Cheryl couldn't remember a cheery wave, showing a pair of fingerless gloves. Cheryl, in a tailored military jacket, William Rast jeans and Alexander McQueen boots, rolled her eyes. The girl had no idea. She was in London, for God's sake, not about to hike across the fells. What Cheryl failed to appreciate was that Natalie, dressed in exactly the same garb as every other member of the crew filming in the market, wasn't actually the odd one out.

'We've got some great stuff,' Natalie said, flopping into the chair opposite Cheryl, 'but we're just going to back off now, give them a bit of space before they get sick and tired of us.'

'What about Sasha Gates?'

'She's in the first scene after lunch, then there's one scene she's not in, so that's when we're going to do her. We can get into her dressing room, set up all the lights when they break for lunch, then once she wraps we'll get ourselves in and do the interview. Are you OK with the questions I've given you?'

Cheryl gave her a sly smile. 'I might ask one or two of my own.'

'It's just I had to clear everything with the press office so if you want to make changes I'll have to run it past them.'

Cheryl bristled. 'Bit touchy, aren't they? Who does she think she is?'

'Queen of the Soaps, I suppose,' Natalie said, 'which means if she wants a press officer sitting in on the interview she gets one.' She eyed the uneaten muffin in front of Cheryl. 'Are you going to have that?'

Cheryl slid it across the table. 'Help yourself.' She had never known anyone eat as much as Natalie, skinny little thing though she was. God knows what happened to all those calories she put away. Not that Cheryl minded: she had no problem with people stuffing their faces as long as they didn't turn into porkers.

'Back in a bit,' Natalie said, getting up, taking the muffin with her. 'Sure you don't want to come outside? You're missing all the fun in the market.'

Cheryl gazed at Natalie with her rosy cheeks and bulky jacket. 'Nat, when my idea of fun is freezing my butt off on the set of a programme I don't even watch, just shoot me, will you?'

Sasha Gates had been through costume and make-up and returned to Dressing Room 1 to make some calls and pick at the fruit salad the runner had brought for her. She had specifically said no pineapple and the bowl was full of it. The girl had put milk in her green tea as well. It was hard to believe she had a first-class history degree from Cambridge.

Sasha had just two scenes after lunch, both brief and undemanding, a total of seven lines, the kind of stuff she uttered week in, week out. In one, her character, Tasha Lyons, had to tell a newcomer to *Spitalfields*, Jack Burton, where to go. In another she was giving her ex, Billy Marsden, what-for. Both called for a look of indignation tinged with fury, something she could deliver on cue with the minimum of effort. Even so, she had thrown a minor strop with the press officer for scheduling an interview right before she went on set for her final scene of the day. It didn't do to be too obliging, even though the truth was she was dying to ramble on about herself for half an hour or so.

Sasha had already seen Cheryl West's questions and if that

was the best she could come up with she would run rings round her, maybe even get in a dig or two about that crazy bitch Lesley Gold, which was the real reason she had agreed to the interview in the first place. She was still looking for a way to get her own back after the altercation at the Domes, although she would have to be subtle. No sense going for the jugular, not since Lesley seemed to have worked out that Sasha was indeed the one responsible for her fall from grace.

The interview didn't get off to the best of starts. While Pete, the camera operator, was busy adjusting the lights, Cheryl decided to make small talk. 'You don't have a cor-blimey accent,' she said, surprised. 'I had no idea.'

Sasha gave her a condescending smile. 'No, well, they do call it "acting" for a reason. I've always been good at dialects,' she said, in the snootiest voice she could manage.

'Get you, sounding more royal than the Queen,' Cheryl said. 'Still a bit of Cockney twang creeping in, though. You need to watch that. Say something else – like "We are not amused." Go on.'

Sasha's smile slipped. Pete glanced at Natalie, who sneaked a look at the press officer, positioned in the far corner of the room behind the sound recordist, Simon. He raised an eyebrow as he adjusted his headphones.

'Another thing, I actually thought you'd want to do this in costume – in character, you know?' Cheryl said, puzzled, scrutinizing the frumpy satin blouse, slightly too-tight pencil skirt and cheap court shoes. 'If you want to nip to costume, get into your Tasha Lyons stuff, we can wait.' The press officer cleared her throat and shuffled her chair to one side so Simon no longer blocked her view.

Sasha went pink and glowered at Cheryl with her immaculate designer clobber, glorious cheekbones and perfect white teeth. She was winding her up, she knew it. Her gaze fell on Cheryl's nails, grotesque talons painted purple to match her hair, with some kind of design in gold etched on the top. Sasha had read about nails like that harbouring all kinds of disgusting infections and fungal infestations. She turned up her nose.

'I love your nails,' she lied. 'Are they real?'

'God no, they're acrylics,' Cheryl said, holding them up. 'I get them done every couple of weeks. I like to think they'd come in handy if anyone tried to mug me and snatch the Rolex.' She made a stabbing motion and Sasha recoiled. 'I can give you the number of the guy who does them, if you like.' She stared at the soap star's short pearly-pink nails. 'He could do something with yours. Mind you, he's a bit out there, if you know what I mean.' She stared at the shapeless blouse. 'He might be a bit *fashion forward* for your taste.'

Sasha bristled. 'I'm not into fake,' she said, sounding a bit less posh than she intended.

Cheryl gazed pointedly at her. 'No, well, not everyone can carry stuff like this off.' She tapped her nails on the clipboard on her lap, making a sharp clicking sound that set Sasha's teeth on edge and made Simon jump and fiddle with the levels on the sound mixer. 'The last time I saw you was at the Dome Awards,' Cheryl went on, 'not that we got a chance to speak. You won something, didn't you?'

Natalie shot a look at Pete, who said, 'Just about ready to go.'

Sasha, sitting up very straight, a strained expression on her face, said, 'I was up for Best Actress in a Long-Running Drama Series—'

'That's the one,' Cheryl said.

'Actually, it went to Helen Worth from *Coronation Street*.'

Cheryl frowned. 'Is she the one that runs the pub? Or the one from the factory – done up like an extra from *The Addams Family*?'

The press officer stood up. 'Right,' Natalie said, nodding at Pete, 'we're now rolling and up to speed, so whenever you're ready – Cheryl, Sasha – let's make a start.'

Cheryl smiled. 'Lesley said hi, by the way, and no hard feelings for yanking her top down. It was all the free booze, probably ... not to mention losing out to – who was it again? – Helen Worth. I mean, no wonder you got tanked.'

'I can assure you, I had most certainly not been drinking.'

'You went all cor-blimey again there.' Cheryl looked thoughtful. 'So you were actually sober and in control when you grabbed at Lesley's bazookas? God, that's priceless.' Her eyes sparkled with mischief. 'Hang on, don't tell me you're *gay*? Well, you've got no chance with La Gold. She is strictly men-only. Still, she'll definitely be flattered when I tell her you've got the hots for her ... I mean, she thought you couldn't stand her.'

In the crew's van on the way back to the studios, Pete, behind the wheel, said he had never realized just how insensitive Cheryl was. Simon, in the front passenger seat, busy tapping a post-code into the satnav, said you only had to look at her to see she was self-obsessed. 'I've worked with her on nearly all of these jobs and she still hasn't the foggiest who I am. It's not often she speaks to me but when she does she calls me Neil. I don't even bother correcting her any more.' He paused. 'And who in their right mind comes on a shoot dressed like that?'

Natalie, busy marking up the tapes on the back seat, said, 'She was doing it on purpose, all that catty stuff with Sasha. What put her back up was having a press officer in the room. She took it as a personal affront, as if they were saying they didn't trust her.'

'They didn't, and no wonder,' Pete said, coming to a stop in a line of traffic at a roundabout. 'What was she playing at?'

Natalie slid the tapes into her bag. 'There was a bit of an incident at the Domes. Something went on with Lesley and Sasha, a bit of a catfight I've heard, but it's been hushed up. Some kind of spat anyway. The word is Lesley reckons Sasha was behind some hideous press exposé a while ago that got her axed from the soap. Then Sasha floated in and stole her crown. All very convenient. Anyway, Lesley's hardly Cheryl's favourite person but sisterly solidarity apparently counts for something. Cheryl wanted to put Sasha on the spot, make her squirm.'

'Surely not,' Pete said. He glanced over his shoulder and grinned at Natalie. 'I mean, someone in TV doing the dirty on someone else? Nah, that can't be right.'

'I know what you mean,' Simon said, deadpan. 'It's far too noble an industry for such underhand goings-on. Shame on you, Nat. What were you thinking?'

She pressed a hand to her brow. 'Must be coming down with something. I take it all back.'

Twenty-Seven

Karen couldn't decide what to wear. The bed was covered in outfits she had tried on only to have a change of heart. Nothing looked right. It was only lunch, she told herself, nothing to get in such a state about. She would wear something simple, understated: her black shift dress. As soon as she had it on she wasn't sure. She looked like she was going to a funeral. She took it off and stood there in her high-waist Spanx and a fancy bra that reminded her of the kind of thing Madonna used to have when underwear as outerwear was all the rage. The Spanx came all the way up to her bra line. She turned sideways and admired her flat tummy and firm, curvy rear. These control garments were amazing.

On the TV screen fixed to the wall facing the bed, Helen England linked to an item about a man in his seventies who had recently become the proud father of twins. He was on the sofa with his wife and two of the most adorable little girls Karen had ever seen. She felt herself welling up. It was obvious Helen England was dying to hold one of the twins, who seemed utterly content in their frilly white dresses, beaming and clapping their hands, delighted with their cameo appearance on *Good Morning Britain*.

Karen turned up the volume. The mother was saying the pregnancy was a surprise and, yes, the age thing was something they had talked about but it seemed to bother other people more than them. The girls were a gift, a miracle, she said, the best thing that could have happened. Nothing else comes close, she added, gazing at her husband, who looked pretty remarkable for a man of seventy-something. He gave her a peck on the cheek and the two of them exchanged a look of absolute devotion.

Karen sat on the edge of the bed, remote in hand, feeling something ache inside. Matt Prestwick, Helen's co-presenter, was going on about the age difference and how Kevin, the father, would not live to see his girls grow up. Karen, thinking you didn't have to be an older parent to miss out on the best years of your child's life, wished he would shut his stupid face.

'I mean, when they're celebrating their twenty-first you'll be, well, not to put too fine a point on it, *very old indeed*. In your nineties,' Matt said, looking pleased to have done a simple calculation and stating the obvious at the same time.

'Oh shut *up*, you wanker,' Karen shouted at the TV. She hit the mute button. 'Insensitive moron. Can't you see they're happy? Leave them alone.'

Her baby would be twenty-three now, all grown up. She had no idea what had become of her, where she lived, whether she was married and had children of her own. She had been a child herself, barely seventeen, and frightened, afraid she would not be able to look after a baby, ashamed at having got herself into such a predicament in the first place. If only Jason had been more use, but he was adamant it was the wrong time for them to be saddled with a child. He was twenty, on tour with a repertory company, scratching a living, and reckoned the two of them bringing up a baby was about the worst thing in the world – for them *and* the baby.

He wasn't even there when she gave birth. It was just Karen, in a hospital miles from home, alone apart from the nun from the adoption agency hovering outside her room, ready to swoop in and whisk her baby away as soon as she was born. She had spent the last three months of her pregnancy with other girls in the same predicament, living in a home run by a pro-life charity, where she had consented to adoption. They had told her what to expect, said it was for the best – less chance of getting attached. Wasn't she already attached to this little person who had been growing inside her for nine months?

She had held Amy in her arms for moments, not minutes, long enough to press her lips to her baby's soft, damp hair, before a stout figure in a grey and white gown that rustled and smelled of lavender came to prise her from her arms. She didn't even have a picture of her, although she had begged for one. 'It's for your own good,' she was told. Amy, with her jet-black hair and flushed cheeks, had gazed at Karen with wide blue eyes.

She closed her eyes and was suddenly back in the hospital on the outskirts of Manchester, in that shitty room away from everyone else, walls the colour of puke, a scratched plastic beaker and a jug of water on the cabinet at the side of the bed. No cards or flowers. The staff had a brisk, matter-of-fact manner, and made no secret that having a young girl with no husband in the maternity unit was an embarrassment. She was that shameful creature, a gymslip mum. One nurse had actually called her a slut to her face.

She thought about Amy every day, had a picture in her head of a strong, independent woman, the kind who would never be talked into giving her baby away. Her version of Amy was tall, like Jason, with long black hair, the blue eyes she was born with having given way to green, just like her mum's. If she ever saw her she would know her, she was sure of that.

In the back of a drawer, held together with an elastic band, were copies of the letters she had written to her daughter and sent to the adoption agency. She had no way of knowing if Amy had even read them. Maybe she didn't want to hear from the woman who'd abandoned her, which was probably the way she saw it. Maybe the adoption agency had no idea where she was any more. People move around, lose touch, don't they? A sudden image of her precious child in a scruffy squat somewhere, drinking strong cider, track marks in her arms, begging for money, appeared. Karen shook her head, gazing at the twins on the TV, laughing and burbling, their mum and dad cuddling them. She just had to hope that one day Amy would come looking for her, that was all.

She got up and went back to the wardrobe. She would wear the black slash-neck sweater and dogtooth pencil skirt, maybe a short string of pearls: shades of Audrey Hepburn. Who was she kidding? Audrey Hepburn was probably a size zero before the term was invented.

She pulled on a pair of opaque tights and shimmied into the pencil skirt, tucking her sweater in, cinching it at the waist with a patent belt. Yes, that was it. Sassy but prim at the same time. Just the effect she wanted.

Her phone rang. Karen picked it up and watched the display flash **Bella calling** at her. She dropped the phone on the bed and chewed her lip, waiting for it to stop. She hadn't told Bella she was meeting Jason for lunch today, but somehow she would know. She had an extraordinary ability to pop up at just the right/wrong moment and catch Karen on the hop. She had called three times so far. When Karen ignored her first message she called back and left another one along the lines of 'You're up to something aren't you? Hang on – you're not meeting that shitty husband of yours, are you? Do not, repeat NOT, do this without speaking to me first.'

Karen's phone bleeped. Another message. She was just about to listen when it started ringing again. She backed away. The screen turned blue and pulsed. **Bella calling. Bella calling.** Oh God. She picked up on the fifth ring and did her best to sound breathless.

'Sorry,' she said, 'just had to run upstairs.'

'Liar,' Bella said, sounding stern. 'My radar is picking up something very disturbing to do with you meeting Mr Jerky. Go on, tell me I'm wrong – and don't bother lying because I can always tell.'

Karen began to stutter something about being in a rush.

Bella jumped back in. 'You're seeing him, aren't you?'

'Only for lunch, in a public place, lots of other people around, so nothing can possibly happen,' Karen said, everything coming out in a rush. She chewed her lip.

'Right, here's what you do,' Bella said. 'Have a car booked to pick you up from the restaurant. Spend no more than two hours with him. Do not drink. And view everything he says with absolute scepticism. He is not buying you lunch because he fancies a bit of idle chit-chat. He has an agenda.' Dead air hung between them. 'And make sure he puts his hand in his pocket. I wouldn't put it past him to palm the bill off on you, cheapskate that he is.'

When Karen walked into the restaurant almost twenty minutes late, having hung about in Monmouth Street, going into Kiehl's, buying something she didn't need, marvelling at the lingerie in Coco de Mer – hundreds of pounds for a tiny scrap of something flimsy – wondering whether to just jump in a cab and go home, she spotted Jason right away, on a high stool at the bar. He was checking his watch and, in the mirror that ran along the wall facing him, she could see his face, anxious, deep frown lines running across his forehead. She wanted to stride up to him, full of confidence, but the pencil skirt wouldn't let her. She hobbled instead, taking small, delicate steps. Jason stood up and when she reached him went to kiss her on the lips. She turned her head and he ended up planting a kiss on her ear.

'You look incredible,' he said, levering himself back on to the stool, signalling at the barman for drinks.

Karen wasn't sure the skirt would allow her to hoist herself on to the stool. She stood, one elbow on the bar, trying to give the impression she was happier standing, while the barman poured each of them a glass of champagne.

He is definitely picking up the tab, Karen thought, wishing she had worn the black dress after all. At least she could perch on a bar stool in that.

'Sit down.' Jason patted the seat next to his.

She shrugged, flustered. 'I'm OK standing,' she said, the Spanx making her feel slightly out of breath. She glanced to her left, where a woman at a table was watching them, leaning over to whisper something to the man opposite, the pair of them taking a sneaky look. Karen felt miserable. Bella was right: she shouldn't have come. 'Actually, can we just go to the table?' she said.

Jason gave her a curious look. 'I'm glad you came, babe,' he said.

'I'm not your babe,' she snapped, her face burning, 'not any more. Save that for the bimbo. I don't suppose she knows where you are, does she?'

Jason glanced at the couple at the table, who were no longer making any secret of the fact they were watching. 'Let's just go through.'

'Start as you mean to go on, fobbing her off with lies. I suppose you've had plenty of practice.' There were tears in her eyes. 'You're going to be a father, Jason. Isn't it about time you grew up?' He shifted from foot to foot. 'You should be ashamed.'

'If I'd known you were going to be like this—'

'Like what? Angry? Oh well, pardon me. It's only five minutes since you walked out, so it just might take a bit longer for me to get my head around cosy little luncheons.'

Jason took her elbow and steered her into the restaurant, to a booth at the back. Karen slid along the velvet banquette, an image coming to mind of her at home in the bedroom, admiring her reflection in the mirror, determined to let Jason know she was happy and confident and totally over him. Ha! So much for that.

A waiter swept up and handed them each a menu, reeled off the first few specials, saw the looks on both their faces and backed away, gesturing at a board at the front of the room. Karen put the menu to one side. She wasn't sure she wanted to eat any more; maybe she'd just finish her drink and go. She looked at Jason, who looked wretched, close to tears. Now she was looking at him properly, she could see he'd lost a bit of weight as well. He was veering towards gaunt, which wasn't like him at all.

He sighed. 'I am such a prat. I know I've screwed things up.' Karen wondered whose idea it was to send him out in a Sex Pistols T-shirt and ripped jeans. That would be the scrubber, no doubt. Jason, always so smart in his suits and pricey shirts, looking like he'd just fallen out of some trendy screening at the ICA. She bent down to tuck her bag under the table. To her horror she saw he had on the kind of canvas boots kids on skateboards wore. She had seen them on the South Bank, all baggy jeans, T-shirts down to their knees, and shoes just like Jason's. Good God Almighty.

'I think I had some kind of breakdown,' he was saying, 'because there's no way on this earth I would have walked away from you otherwise. Seriously.' He was wearing a chunky watch – Jason never wore a watch – with a couple of rubber bracelets, the kind with anti-poverty slogans. No. On closer inspection one was a VIP pass for something or other.

'Have you been to see a band?' she said.

He twisted the band on his wrist. 'Can't get the bloody thing off. Backstage pass for Duffy.'

Karen stared at Jason, who loved rock and big ballads, whose favourite bands were Queen and Led Zeppelin – Jason, who would argue until he was blue in the face that Paul Rodgers was the best vocalist on the planet – and wondered if he had been abducted by aliens and ended up with someone else's brain implanted. He had, in a way. It was all the work of the scrubber, who was clearly brainwashing him bit by bit.

'I'm sorry,' he was saying. The waiter appeared, hovered, and went away again. Jason reached across the table and took her hand. Karen, caught on the hop, tried to pull away but he wasn't letting go. 'I've made a mistake,' he said. 'I still love you, always have, always will.'

Her hand went limp in his. 'Stop it. You're not being fair.'

He let go. 'I don't expect it to change anything, not for you, not after what I did; I just had to tell you because it's the truth.'

He blinked, eyes welling up again, picked up his champagne and knocked it back in one go. 'I didn't mean it to come out like that.'

She reached across the table and took his hand. He was still wearing his wedding ring. Hers, inscribed on the inside with LOVE, NOW AND FOREVER, was in its box on the dressing table next to her engagement ring, also back in its box. 'Don't get upset,' she said. 'It's OK.'

Twenty-Eight

It was the champagne that did it. Karen had never been good with fizz, which always went straight to her head and made her a bit woozy. It only took a glass and they had practically finished the bottle before the first course came. Even then, keen to impress Jason, she had ordered rocket salad, no parmesan, no dressing – *just* rocket – which wasn't doing much to soak up the alcohol. There was a basket of warm bread on the table, miniature seeded loaves and soft, floury rolls. She watched Jason tear a roll apart and slap butter on it, her mouth watering, knowing if she took one it would blow the image she was so desperate to create of a healthy-eating paragon.

She chewed the rocket, not liking the taste, thinking a hefty dollop of blue-cheese dressing would improve it, or maybe a slab of goat's cheese and some vine tomatoes, while Jason tucked into crab cakes – her favourites, as it happened – dipping them in mayonnaise, popping morsels of buttery bread in his mouth. Oh, the agony!

He pointed at his food. 'These are mind-blowingly good. Want to try a bit?' He cut a corner off a crab cake and held it towards her.

She wavered. Of course she wanted to try it. What she really wanted was to send back the frigging rocket and order some

180

real food. She shook her head. 'No, really,' she lied, spearing another few measly salad leaves. 'I'm fine with this.'

'No wonder you look so amazing,' Jason said, impressed. 'You should do a fitness DVD or a weight-loss plan or something.'

He wasn't the first one to have suggested that. What advice could she give, though? If you want to lose weight get yourself dumped, what Cheryl Cole called the misery diet, which was about right. Now here Karen was, having lunch with the man who had caused her so much pain. She felt a sudden rush of panic. What on earth was she thinking? She should go. To hell with the rocket. Just get out of there.

Jason, who seemed to have an uncanny sense of timing, chose that moment to say, 'I wasn't sure you'd come, you know.' He gave her a sheepish look. 'I don't know what I'd have done if you hadn't. It sounds crazy but I can't see the point of anything without you.' She put down her fork. 'I mean it,' he said. 'You know what I did the other night?' She shook her head. 'I walked from Camden to Waterloo—'

'That's miles!'

He nodded. 'You know it's my favourite view of London, the one from Waterloo Bridge. I don't know why, I just wanted to see it. Anyway, I was leaning on the bridge, looking at the river, boats moored, the Eye all lit up, a few people out, not many – it was late, gone two by then – and all I could think about was walking home again and how I couldn't face it.'

'Weren't there any black cabs? You can usually catch one, even late at night. Or you could have just walked to Waterloo Station. Loads of cabs there coming and going, although maybe not that time of night.' She paused. 'I bet there's a night bus goes up your way. There's always a night bus.'

Jason was frowning. 'I wasn't bothered about getting home. I wasn't bothered about anything. I was ready to jump in the Thames.'

Karen swallowed, imagining one day breaking the news to Amy that her father had killed himself. 'Don't say things like that.'

'That's how I felt.' He reached for her hand again. 'I want us to give it another go.'

Another bottle of champagne appeared. Karen had decided she was already a bit tipsy and didn't want any more to drink but sat in silence as the waiter filled her glass. All this stuff Jason was coming out with was making her feel very peculiar. She needed a drink.

'What about Hannah Montana?' she said. 'I don't suppose you've said any of this to her?'

'All we do is argue,' he said.

'She's about to have your baby!'

The waiter swept up. 'All done here?' he said, picking up plates, whipping the bread basket away.

'Look,' Jason said, once they were alone again. 'I know I've made a cock-up of everything. I hold up my hands.' He raised them, as if Karen was pointing a gun at him. 'Babe, I wasn't thinking straight, having some kind of mid-life crisis, whatever you want to call it, but I'm getting help.' He lowered his voice. 'I'm seeing a shrink and I'm on medication, anti-depressants. I'm feeling so much better.'

'You shouldn't be drinking if you're on tablets.'

'The odd glass won't hurt.'

The odd *bottle* might, Karen thought, as a vision of Jason hurling himself into the Thames if things went wrong over lunch came to her. She wasn't sure she wanted to know all this. He wasn't her responsibility any more. She had moved on. Hadn't she? It wasn't so easy to wipe out twenty years' worth of memories, that was the thing.

The first time she set eyes on Jason was on the seafront at Blackpool. She was doing a favour for an old lady who lived a few doors down from them, walking her dog, a well-bred Pekinese used to lounging about on the furniture. He had trotted to the end of the road all right then refused to budge. Karen yanked on the lead, trying to drag the little so-and-so along the promenade on his backside. She crouched in front of him, saying if he went to the end of the block she would take him straight home for a chewy stick, so how about it? The little dog, who always looked morose no matter what, lay down, its face between its paws. Karen knelt on the pavement, saying right, that was it, she would drop him in it when they got back, tell Mrs Wilson just what a bad boy he had been. He raised his head and licked her hand. She sighed. It wasn't his fault he was spoiled rotten. The red bow in the dog's hair was coming undone. She secured it, a vertical ponytail sprouting from the top of his head. 'Right, Mr Chips, you win,' she said, picking him up, holding him on his back, floppy paws in the air. When she turned around she almost dropped him. There was Jason, spiky blond hair, cheeky eyes, plain white T-shirt tucked into Levi's, grinning at her. Drop. Dead. Gorgeous. She went bright red.

'Need a hand?' he said, coming over, putting out a hand to pat the dog's belly.

'Careful,' Karen said, 'he's not too keen on blokes.'

'You need to be more firm with him,' he was saying, taking

Mr Chips off her and putting him on the ground. 'No point having a conversation with him. He's a *dog* – hasn't the foggiest what you're saying.' Karen blushed again. He had heard her – talking to the dog! 'Right,' he said, 'which way are we going?'

Karen watched in disbelief as Mr Chips, tail up, began to trot along the promenade at Jason's heel. 'Come on then,' he said, and she had trotted along too.

The waiter appeared with a plate of grilled sea bass and French beans for her, and battered haddock and chips for Jason. She looked at her saintly fillet of fish and felt like asking for chips on the side.

'What were you thinking about?' Jason said, dipping a chip into ketchup. 'You were miles away just then.'

'You, on the promenade in Blackpool, making that stubborn little Pekinese walk home.'

'You didn't know I'd been following you.'

'Stalker!'

'I couldn't help it. You had that little halter top on and denim shorts, tottering along the prom in a pair of massive platforms. My eyes were popping out of my head. As for the dog – what was it called?'

'Mr Chips.' Karen eyed up Jason's meal: the pile of hand-cut chips, the fish in its crunchy golden batter. What had possessed her to order plain grilled fish? It was the kind of thing Madonna might do after a six-hour stint in the gym. Karen was not cut out for self-denial.

'Give us a chip,' she said, helping herself.

'That's more like it. I was starting to get worried.' He grinned. 'You didn't believe me when I said I was in a show.'

'I thought you were just a show-*off*.' She had agreed to meet him at the stage door of the theatre, not convinced he would turn up, but he was waiting for her. He took her hand and led her along a corridor to the dressing room he shared with another young actor, then took her front of house and gave her an aisle seat four rows from the stage. It was a quirky comedy, two best friends in love with the same girl, both tying themselves in knots trying to get her to notice them. Karen cried with laughter. Jason was terrific and gave her a cheeky wink at the curtain call.

He had his arm around her as they walked along the pier, waves sloshing against the pillars beneath them, a carpet of silver moonlight on the sea. It was perfect, and when Jason kissed her she didn't try and stop him. He was the first boy she had really wanted. He slipped his hand inside her top, stroked her back, unhooked her bra. The next thing she knew his hand was on her breast and she was shocked at how much she liked the feeling. He had hesitated but she kept on kissing him, let him know it was all right, didn't even object when his tongue went in her mouth. She was glad he was holding her because she wasn't sure her legs would support her. He wanted her to go home with him, and held up a shiny ten-pence piece.

'What's that for?'

'So you can call your mum, tell her you won't be home.' That cheeky grin again.

Her heart was racing. 'Please tell me you're joking,' she said, flattered, hoping he wasn't.

'OK. Twenty pence then.' He pressed himself against her. 'Don't tell me girls actually fall for that?'

'All the time.'

She pulled away, straightening her top, reaching inside and fastening her bra. 'Not this one.' She sat on a bench, feeling wobbly, waiting for her heartbeat to return to normal. She could happily have gone off with him, gone all the way for the first time in her life. She had already decided she would – just not straight away. If he was really interested he would wait. He stood in front of her, thumbs hooked into the belt loops of his jeans, full of himself. She had known right then, as an innocent young girl, that getting involved with Jason would mean heartache. A voice inside her head warned her to watch her step. He had trouble written all over him.

She turned a deaf ear. After all, she was young and having fun. Where was the harm? Six weeks later she was pregnant.

Now, she watched him tucking into his food as if he hadn't a care in the world, when the truth was he was dragging a whole heap of baggage around: a wife he had dumped, a child he had never met, and now a floozy he didn't want to be with. Not to mention yet another baby on the way. 'Do you ever think about Amy?' Karen said.

Jason put down his knife and fork. There were two deep frown lines running down the centre of his forehead. His blond hair was sprinkled with grey and he was starting to look his age. 'What do you think?' His voice was low. 'I think about her all the time. She's one of the reasons I'm having therapy.' He shifted, awkward. 'I don't know, the closer Hannah gets to having this baby, the more I'm questioning everything. Like why wasn't I there for you when you were having our child? What do I say to this one about his big sister? Will Amy ever meet her brother?' He sighed, fiddled with the stem of his glass. 'It's driving me mental, Karen.' He took a deep breath. 'We could try and find her – Amy, I mean. Get back together, look for our little girl, get to know her. Then, when the new baby comes along I'll make arrangements with Hannah, shared custody maybe. I want to do it right this time.'

He had it all worked out.

Twenty-Nine

Karen sat in silence in the back of the car, deep in thought, Dave at the wheel, inching along Clapham High Street, the lights changing to green for a few seconds at a time, no more than one or two cars getting through.

She should have been firm with Jason yesterday, told him there was no way on this earth she would have him back, not after what he'd done. Instead *she* had ended up comforting *him*, saying there-there, things would work out. Oh God. That was the champagne talking. She wasn't so sure any more, not now, stuck in a jam, clear-headed, no bubbly turning her brain to mush.

She glanced at Dave, who was unusually quiet. It was as if he sensed her guilt. Rain drummed on the roof of the car and she rested her face against the window, liking the way it felt cold on her skin. She had to keep her cool, not let Jason rail-road her into anything. A cyclist in Lycra shorts, flecks of mud up the backs of his legs, pulled up next to the car. His top, black and sporty with grey side panels and logos on the sleeves, was wet through. She had a sudden urge to throw open the door and tell him to get in, just to save her from the atmos-phere inside the car. He turned, caught her looking and gave her a helpless smile. She smiled back. The lights changed and the cyclist took off. One car made it through before they went back to red.

'What's going on?' she said, breaking the silence. 'Is it just the weather?'

Dave half turned in his seat. 'Search me. Bit of rain, everything backs up.'

He had wanted to come round the night before but she had put him off, made up a story about having a migraine, not that she had ever had one in her life. Dave had said she shouldn't be on her own, not if she was poorly, and offered to stop at a chemist and pick up some headache pills. Karen had said no, there was no need; if she could just get her head down she'd be fine. She was firm, almost offhand, and she could tell he was hurt, which made her feel bad. There was no way she wanted him turning up on the doorstep, doing his care-in-the-community bit, though.

Not with Jason in the house.

Now she pretended to be reading the briefing notes Natalie had prepared for that day's show. *The One Show*'s Christine Bleakley was the guest, supposedly coming in to talk about a charity appeal she was backing, but there was no way she would be able to dodge questions about Frank Lampard, not with the papers full of stories about the two of them going out together. Karen thought they made a lovely couple, Christine with her thousand-watt smile and Frank, who was bright as well as being good-looking *and* a loving son, doing that pointing-at-the-sky thing for his mum every time he scored a goal. Of course, predictably, his ex was also all over the papers, saying she still loved him. Tricky. Karen knew firsthand what it felt like to have your ex declaring undying love, that awful feeling of being pulled in different directions. When it came up on *Girl Talk* later she would be perfectly placed to understand some of what was going on in the Christine–Frank–

Elen situation, not that she would be sharing any details of her own messy love life.

She glanced at Dave again. He was peeved about last night; it was obvious from the way he had pulled on to the drive and waited in the car, not even bothering to knock at the door. Now he was barely speaking to her. Funny, she would never have said he was the type to sulk. Just goes to show.

Her phone vibrated. She had turned it to silent because there was an embarrassing number of texts coming through from Jason and she didn't want Dave getting suspicious, seeing her face light up. She decided not to read any more until she was in the safety of her dressing room. It vibrated again. Private number. She let it go to voicemail.

She had left Jason just before four in the afternoon and headed home. A few hours later, curled up on the sofa in her pyjamas, watching Katie Price have a panic attack after being knocked off her feet by a torrent of water midway through a Bushtucker Trial, four stars under her belt, on *I'm a Celebrity ... Get Me Out of Here!*, the doorbell went.

Karen sat up. She definitely was not expecting anyone. She went to the window and sneaked a look between the slats of the blinds just as Jason bent and peered through the letterbox. Letting the blind go as if it was on fire, she took several steps back into the centre of the room. In the background, Katie was being told to take a deep breath and hold it.

Jason's voice echoed around the hallway. 'Lemme in, Karen, please. I know you're there. I love you.'

He was drunk – totally wasted! She clutched her pyjama top to her throat and took a few tentative steps towards the hall.

'KAREN! Lemme in, babe, I gotta see you. Now. Now now *now*!'

She had visions of the people next door, who had only moved in a couple of weeks ago and went out to work early dressed in suits and carrying laptops, calling the police. They were probably already in bed, resting up ready for another hectic day on the trading floor. Oh for God's sake! Hurrying along the hall, she opened the door and Jason tumbled in, landing at her feet on his hands and knees. He crawled along the hall. 'Had to see you, babe,' he said, slumping against the wall.

'Look at the state of you. What on earth have you been doing?'

'Had a couple of pints.' He gave her a soppy smile. 'Just one or two.'

She shook his shoulder. 'Come on,' she said, tugging at the Sex Pistols T-shirt. 'I'm making you some coffee.'

She filled the kettle and stood, arms folded, her back to the sink, while Jason eased himself on to a stool at the breakfast bar, still giving her that silly, soppy grin. It crossed her mind the slut had chucked him out, which was why he had come crawling – quite literally – back to her.

'Trouble at home?' she said.

His shoulders shifted in a half-shrug. 'Visiting her mum,' he said.

Karen looked at him, all bedraggled, off his head, having the gall to turn up on her doorstep and make her miss her favourite programme, all because his scrubber of a girlfriend was away for the night. The cheek of it. Well, he could have his coffee and piss right off.

She poured hot water on to the coffee grains, banging a mug

on to the counter, opening the fridge and slamming it shut; Jason, arms on the counter, chin resting on them, watching her with that dippy look.

He drank his coffee black, fortified with four heaped tea-spoons of sugar, while she sat on a stool facing him, arms crossed, unsmiling, doing her best to look like someone he would be very unwise indeed to mess with. It didn't seem to work.

He gazed at her, saying the coffee was the best he had ever tasted, asking if maybe she had any biscuits, something choco-latey would be nice, because he'd not eaten since lunch, watching as she went to the cupboard and got out a biscuit tin containing Special K bars.

'That's all there is,' she said, as he picked one up and turned it over as if he had no idea what it was, which he probably didn't, never having had to worry about his weight in his entire life. 'Got any digestives?' he said, tearing the wrapper open and sniffing at the contents. 'This looks a bit on the healthy side for me.'

She glared at him. 'That's all there is,' she repeated between clenched teeth.

'Come on, babe,' he said. 'Don't tell me there's no choco-late in the house, not even a teeny-weeny bit.'

Karen stomped over to the fridge, retrieved a plastic storage box from behind a row of probiotic drinks, and peeled back the lid to reveal a giant bar of Fruit 'n' Nut, only a couple of squares missing.

'That's more like it,' Jason said, snapping off a hefty block. 'Just what the doctor ordered.'

Karen would have killed for some chocolate, but she was not about to give in, not after being good all day, and not with him watching her. She perched on a stool and waited while he ate.

It was amazing how fast a bit of chocolate revived him. In no time at all he was alert, on his second cup of coffee, talking sense. If coming out with all kinds of stuff about them getting back together counted as sense, that is.

'I like your pyjamas,' he said, looking at her over his coffee, making her blush.

They were brushed cotton, white with pink polka dots, hardly the most sexy items she possessed. Just as well, really, since she didn't want him getting any ideas.

'They're cute. They remind me of the girl I met on the promenade that day, trying to be all grown-up in her heels and her shades.'

Karen smiled. 'I've just remembered – I had great big sunglasses with white frames. I thought I was *it*.'

Jason slid off the stool and took his cup to the sink, rinsing it under the cold tap, leaving it in the washing-up bowl. 'You *were* it,' he said, drying his hands, coming over, putting his arms around her waist, nuzzling her neck. 'You still are.'

'Jason,' she said, feeling weak as his hand, under her pyjama top, traced patterns on her back.

He swivelled the chair around and stroked the side of her breast, knowing exactly what to do to turn her into a quivering wreck.

'You shouldn't do that,' she said, her voice sounding odd.

'Why not? Don't you like it?' He kissed the base of her throat, both hands on her breasts now, while Karen clutched the side of the stool. 'I'll stop if you want me to.' His fingers grazed her nipples. 'Is that what you want?'

In bed she had cried with pleasure, tears streaming down

her face, and clung to him, the hurt and fury of the last few months draining out of her body as he moved inside her. Despite everything that had happened, all the pain he had caused, the chemistry was still there. Afterwards, they had lain facing each other, Jason stroking her hair, telling her how much he had missed her, saying he was sorry, he loved her, wanted to be with her. And Karen, breathless, euphoric, soaked in sweat, crying and saying she loved him too.

Neither of them had slept and she was the one who said he should go, that they needed to sort things out properly, not just fall into bed after a few too many. Waiting for Jason to say it wasn't like that, it was nothing to do with being drunk, that he loved her. He hadn't, though. What he'd done was jumped up and got dressed, put his ridiculous T-shirt and his charity band back on, searched under the bed for a sock and said no problem, he would walk up to the High Street and get a minicab from there, barely even looking at her as he did up the button fly on his jeans.

She could feel her phone vibrating in her bag. When she spoke to Jason she would tell him she didn't like him going off like that. From now on they were going to be open and honest with each other, maybe even do a bit of therapy together. That was all a long way off, though. First, he needed to let Hannah know what was going on, come to an arrangement over the baby, let the dust settle. It wouldn't be a good idea to go rushing into anything. She needed to straighten out her head as well. Meanwhile, she wasn't about to tell anyone about last night, not even Bella.

At last they were approaching Waterloo, Dave pulling up at the roundabout next to the IMAX, indicating right. 'It's brightening up,' he said, switching off the wipers. 'Did you want to see the paper?' He picked up a copy of the *Sun* from the passenger seat and handed it to her.

'Might as well see what the gossip is,' she said, taking it, glad he was starting to thaw. She didn't want to give him the brush-off, not after he'd been so good to her. 'Sorry I'm a bit quiet. I think that migraine took it out of me,' she said.

'No problem. My mum gets them so I know what it's like. All she can do is lie down in a darkened room. Do yours make you feel sick?'

Karen nodded. 'Sick, banging head, all that.' She could feel her phone vibrate again. Another private number. She allowed herself a tiny smile of satisfaction. Well, he was desperate to get hold of her.

'Horrible, that sick feeling,' Dave said as he eased the car forward.

She flipped through the paper, which had a picture of Katie Price in a swimsuit that looked several sizes too small. Karen turned the page and saw herself coming out of the restaurant yesterday, a huge smile on her face, Jason behind her. There was another picture, the two of them facing each other on Monmouth Street, Jason with his hands on her shoulders. Then, worst of all, another image, bigger than the others, of them locking lips. It had only been a brief kiss but the picture made it look like they were snogging. Her face went scarlet. She glanced at Dave, who was now on the roundabout waiting to turn into the studio entrance, steely eyes gazing at her in the rear-view mirror. The pictures danced in front of her eyes. She hadn't seen any paparazzi hanging about. Then again, she hadn't been looking. Dave swung the car into a parking bay and she saw a group of snappers hanging around in front of the studio doors. Shit. She rummaged in her bag. Where were her sunglasses? Oh for crying out loud, don't say she'd left them at home.

As the car came to a stop they ran forward. 'Karen! Karen! Are you and Jason back on?' 'Karen – this way, love!' She clambered out, head down, stepping straight into a puddle, hurrying towards the entrance. 'You've forgiven him, have you?' 'What about Hannah?' 'What about the baby?' 'Has he left her?' 'Will you be spending Christmas together?' 'Karen!' 'KAREN!'

Thirty

Julia, first to show up for the production meeting, arrived with a copy of the *Sun* sticking out of her bag. She spread it out on the conference table, opened it at page seven, and cackled. Little Miss Prim and Proper, caught red-handed. Julia laughed again. It was so much better than she had hoped for.

She had been coming out of a facility house after doing a voiceover for a face cream that promised to improve luminosity – not that she would ever rely on a cream for that; regular peels and Botox were the answer as far as she was concerned – when she spotted Karen going into Kiehl's. She had no desire to speak to her so hung back, pretending to check her phone, waiting for Karen to appear again. When she did she took a few steps towards Seven Dials, crossed the road and started heading back the way she had come. Julia shrank into the doorway.

Halfway along the road Karen crossed over again and stood outside Coco de Mer, then turned and went back towards Seven Dials. Silly cow, still didn't know her way round London. You can take the girl out of the North ... Julia said to herself, watching Karen go back and forth.

All of a sudden she stopped outside The Grill, right in the middle of the pavement, forcing a couple to step into the road to get past, then went in. Well, well. Julia waited a minute or two and sauntered along the street, taking her time to study the menu on the wall of the restaurant. Not that she was in the least bit interested in it. No, much more interesting was the sight of Karen and her so-called estranged husband, who was planting a smacker on her at that very moment. Julia could feel a tingling sensation inside. Bingo!

She hurried away in her lace Louboutins and shiny black trench coat, hair slicked back, a spring in her step, turning heads. Julia Hill, warrior queen, on a mission. She would tip off Stuart, the photographer who did the last set of *Girl Talk* pictures, get him to give the nod to one of his tabloid chums. He could keep whatever the tip-off fee was. She wasn't bothered about that, and anyway she didn't want it traced back to her. All she cared about was dropping Karen in it.

It had worked a treat. And there was another bombshell ready to explode in the morning, since the snapper had hung about outside Karen's place and caught Jason sneaking out in the early hours. Julia poured herself a coffee as the door opened and Lesley came in. 'Seen the paper?' she said.

Lesley shook off her coat, a black ankle-length sheepskin, which she told everyone was Prada but had in fact came from M&S. Just because she was good at mixing designer and high-street didn't mean she had to tell the world.

'I don't read the papers,' Lesley said. 'Natalie does that for me, lets me know what's going on.'

Julia shoved the *Sun* across the table. Lesley popped her shades on the top of her head. 'What a dark horse,' she said admiringly.

Once she was safely in her dressing room with the door locked, Karen finally checked her phone. All those calls she had thought were from Jason were actually some reporter wanting an interview. They would pay, he said. Who had given the *Sun* her mobile number? And why hadn't Jason been in touch? Surely he'd seen the papers by now. A terrible thought occurred. What if Dave had tipped off the press? No, he wouldn't. It was no doubt as much of a shock to him as well. She felt awful. Poor Dave, after everything he had done, helped her get her confidence back. He probably thought she had been using him all along. Had she?

The phone in her dressing room rang, making her jump. She didn't want to pick it up but it might be Jackie, or Bella. They had both left messages on her mobile but she hadn't been able to face calling back. In a few hours she would have to face a studio audience, knowing they would be jumping to conclusions, thinking she was weak and pathetic for having anything to do with Jason after he had walked all over her. She had been deluged with letters and emails from women urging her to be strong, telling her she deserved better than a rat like Jason. The phone stopped ringing. She had to calm down. All anyone knew was that she had met him for lunch. They could have been talking about anything – sorting out their affairs, as opposed to having one. She closed her eyes and began breathing slowly. What did Bob the medic on *I'm a Celebrity* . . . say? Deep breath and hold it. One, two, three . . . the phone was ringing again. She gave it a wary look. It kept ringing. Eventually, she let out her breath with a gasp and picked it up.

'Please tell me this is not how it looks.' It was Bella.

'It's not. You know what they're like. They probably Photoshopped the picture, made it look worse than it is. They can do all kinds of clever stuff.'

Bella made a sound, a kind of harrumph. 'I'm coming up. I want to see you look me in the eye when you say that.'

'No!' Karen felt a wave of panic hit her. 'I'm going to the production meeting. I'll call you later, I promise.'

As soon as she put the phone down it started ringing again. She snatched the receiver up. 'Bella, I *will* call you later.'

There was a moment's silence, then Jackie Martin said, 'It's me, Karen. Look, don't worry. A picture of you and Jason is embarrassing but it's not the end of the world. Chances are you'll get a bit of stick from Julia, though. I'm sure Lesley will be behind you. So will Cheryl and Faye. Let's face it, they've all had the press dig the dirt at one time or another, so pull yourself together and come down to conference.'

Jackie hung up, picked up her programme file and went the short distance from her office to the conference room. She could hear Julia before she reached the door.

'Can you believe it?' she was saying. 'All that guff about how Jason was history and she would never ever have anything to do with him again. What a joke!'

Faye, checking her make-up in a tiny mirror, dabbing powder on her nose, said, 'The quiet ones are always the worst.'

Cheryl frowned at her. 'That's rich, coming from you.' It *is* funny, though. I mean she's such a goody-two-shoes, so straight.'

Lesley studied Faye, a sly smile on her face. 'Well, I suppose we can't all be *straight* all the time, can we?'

Faye ignored her but Lesley could have sworn she went pink.

Before the meeting, Cheryl had told Faye it was a good thing Karen was in the firing line, that the tabloids would be all over her now, so she would hardly be favourite for the *Good Morning Britain* job much longer. Faye had agreed, pointing out that while the hacks were busy keeping tabs on Karen they wouldn't be paying any attention to what the two of them were doing, which was a bonus. Cheryl went all huffy at that point, until Faye suggested she come over for 'dinner' later.

Jackie poured a cup of tea and took her seat at the head of the table. 'It would be good if you could give Karen a bit of support,' she said, looking around. 'None of us know what's actually going on. She's still married, you know. They must have things to talk about.'

Julia guffawed. 'They'd be talking through lawyers if it was all over, don't you think? It's that poor girl I feel sorry for, about to have his baby and he legs it back to his wife.'

'Yes, well, that's none of our business,' Jackie said. 'Now, let's go through the running order. We've got Christine Bleakley on tonight so that's a bit of a coup.'

'Is that her real hair colour?' Lesley said.

Julia rolled her eyes. 'Is that your idea of a probing question?'

Lesley tossed her hair over her shoulders. 'Oh fuck off, Jeremy Paxman. I ask the questions other women want answers to.'

'She's here to promote a charitable cause,' Jackie said. 'Not that we can't slip in a couple of cheeky questions about Frank Lampard.'

The door opened and Karen slipped into the room, taking the seat next to Jackie. No one bothered to say hello.

Julia reached for the coffee flask in the middle of the table and topped up her cup. Everyone looked at Karen, who lowered her eyes.

Finally, Julia spoke. 'What you need to bear in mind, darling,' she said, fixing Karen with a predatory gaze, 'is that you can't outwit the press. They have eyes and ears *everywhere* and once they smell a rat – well, there's no stopping them. They will always, always find out your sordid little secrets. Better to just come clean, I always say.'

Thirty-One

The sign on the door to Studio 9 said **STRICTLY NO ADMIT-TANCE WHEN RED LIGHT IS ON**. On the walls of the corridor leading to a soundproofed door wedged open with a weight, were framed photos of the *Girl Talk* girls and Helen England. A dust-rimmed oblong space indicated where the picture of Quentin d'Arblay, the former presenter of the recently axed *Arts and Entertainment Review*, had once hung. A series of arrows guided the audience towards the *Girl Talk* studio and a security guard with a shaved head in a white shirt and epaulettes, a walkie-talkie in his hand, made sure no one went anywhere they weren't supposed to. In front of Laura Lloyd was a woman in an electric-blue satin dress and complicated shoes held on with a huge number of buckles and straps. The dress, a tight strapless number, skimmed the woman's bottom as she took small uncertain steps, navigating cables secured under raised plastic covers. The floor, shiny and painted black, made Laura think of the kind of ice you know nothing about until you hit it and find yourself skidding all over the road. She could smell perfume and looked over her shoulder in time to see a woman spraying a cloud of Mariah Carey Pink in the air and ducking under it. 'Amanda Holden says that's the best way to put on scent,' she told Laura, who was now drenched in the stuff. Everyone, apart from Laura it seemed, had left their coats in the cloakroom. The front two rows of plastic orange seats were already occupied and she was about to head up the metal staircase that ran through the middle of the audience – the woman in the blue dress hanging back, saying she couldn't do stairs in her shoes – when she spotted an empty seat in the middle of the third row, directly facing the seat Julia Hill would occupy.

She edged past a row of short skirts, leggings and high heels and sat down, looking at the audience, all women, mostly forty-plus, some a lot older and struggling to get up the stairs to the empty seats at the back, no one at the front willing to do a swap. Certainly Laura wasn't about to. She had made an effort to dress down, chosen plain black trousers and a polo neck with a burgundy belted jacket, but she still felt as if she stood out. Anxious not to attract attention, she shoved her Chanel bag under her seat. She had scraped her hair into a high pony-tail and was wearing heavy-framed glasses and no make-up: what she called her geek look. It had served her well in the past when she needed to blend into the background.

It was twenty years since Julia had bawled her out in the reception of another television studio and left her a snivelling wreck. She could still hear Julia screaming at her: 'How *dare* you order me out here?' Julia's shrill voice filled her head. 'Once I speak to your editor you'll be fired.' The memory of not daring to sit down on the tube on the way home in her wet pants had never faded. It was the first and last time anyone she had been sent to interview had made her cry. If anything, *she* inspired fear now, thanks to her reputation for never flinching from the tough questions. Not that she was a bitch about it. Ruthless and single-minded, yes – she had to be in her game – but she only ever picked on people her own size.

She would never dream of screaming and shouting at juniors or fledgling writers, which was partly why she was so popular at the *Sunday*. There was always someone willing to pull out the cuts for her, do a bit of background reading, make a few calls, run down to the canteen to get her a cup of Earl Grey on a Friday afternoon when she was up against a deadline. Laura smiled. In some ways her bruising encounter with Julia all those years ago had done her a favour, because it taught her to treat people the way she wanted them to treat her. There would always be exceptions, of course, Julia Hill being one of them.

The woman next to Laura was telling her friend she knew someone who used hydrogen peroxide to bleach her teeth and swore it was as good as anything you'd pay a dentist hundreds of pounds for. The friend was saying that couldn't be right or everyone would be doing it, the woman telling her you just use a cotton bud, dip it in the solution, rub it on your teeth, works a treat, but if you get it on your gums it's worse than a Brazilian wax. Another woman was tearing at a packet of Werther's Originals, offering them round. Laura shook her head when they came her way. She had the feeling there were plenty of regulars in the audience.

The set was simple, just a desk with the show's logo in pink neon on the front, marbled grey panels behind it. There was a giant screen set into one of the panels at one end, in between the seats occupied by Lesley Gold and Karen King. A set of colour bars appeared on the screen, then a clock, the kind of thing that sometimes came up during *I'm a Celebrity* ... when they lost the picture. Laura peered at it. It read GIRL TALK OPENING TITS, which she presumed was short for 'title sequence', and the pointer was set at thirty seconds. TV sets suspended from a gantry high above the audience showed the same image.

A man in a sparkly gold jacket too big on the shoulders popped out from behind a black drape that hung from the ceiling at the back of the set, making a song and dance of not being able to find the join in the curtain, taking off Eric Morecambe, pretending someone had their hands round his throat. There was a ripple of applause. Laura checked her watch. She could still smell Pink. Ninety minutes to go before she would be allowed out. The woman next to her said through a mouthful of toffee, 'I love Terry Trent. He's a scream.' Someone in the row behind said, 'Oh not again, same old stuff we've heard a million times. Ho bloody ho.'

Terry Trent waved his arms and tilted his head towards the audience, one hand cupped behind his ear, which sent the applause up a notch. A girl wearing a headset, a script poking out of the back pocket of her jeans, handed him a microphone. He tapped it and bellowed, 'Good evening, LADIES!'

The entire audience, with the exception of Laura, the only *Girl Talk* virgin there it seemed, yelled back, 'Good-evening, TERRY!'

'What a show we have for you tonight.'

The woman behind Laura piped up again. 'I'm dying for the loo. I wish they wouldn't make us come in so early and sit through all his crappy jokes. No one gives a toss. It's the girls we come to see. And that Christine from *The One Show*.'

'I loved her on *Strictly*,' another voice chipped in. 'I wonder where she gets her hair done.'

'Do you think that's her real colour or does she dye it?'

'I can't remember who she danced with now,' the second

voice said. 'Matthew or Ian, I think. I get them mixed up. I was gutted when she went out.'

As far as Laura could tell no one was talking about Karen King, splashed all over the papers that morning with her ex. She sat low in her seat, hoping the warm-up man, now singing 'Happy Birthday' to a woman in the front row, wouldn't pick her out and make a big thing of her being a first-timer. She was convinced she stuck out like a sore thumb, even with her Joe 90 specs on. Everyone else was in bright, shiny clothes and lots of make-up. They all seemed to have had their hair done. Some looked as if they were going to a party, in their cocktail frocks and dangly earrings. Of course – they all wanted to be on the telly, picked out by the director as good cutaway material. She cursed. Laura, one of the few writers to shun a picture byline, had no desire to pop up on TV. Then again, aware no director worth his salt would want to cut away to the dowdiest person in the audience, she relaxed.

Terry Trent was saying, 'Lay-deeees, we are live on air in just sixty seconds so please put your hands together and give our *Girl Talk* lovelies a big warm welcome.'

The studio erupted as Julia, in a silver off-the-shoulder dress and strappy bondage shoes with impossible heels, strode out from behind the black drape. Lesley was next, in a black strapless jumpsuit and patent stilettos. Cheryl followed in a purple bandage dress that showed off a pair of legs that practically went up to her armpits, Faye trailing in her wake in skinny jeans tucked into cowboy boots and a stretchy top cut low front and back. Lagging behind was Karen King, looking like the poor relation, in some awful sack of a dress in a garish print that was meant to be a Pucci but wouldn't fool anyone.

All five women stood in a line for a moment applauding the audience before settling into their places behind the desk as Terry Trent counted down from ten to the opening titles, red lights went on over the exits and the theme music blasted out. They were all smiling, Julia like a cat who'd just been given a large saucer of cream, Lesley bobbing to the music, Cheryl and Faye waving, pointing at someone who probably turned up every night, Karen with an unconvincing smile plastered on her face. Laura noticed they weren't looking at each other. No eye contact whatsoever. That was interesting.

Kirsty Collins sat on the sofa in a T-shirt and sweatpants, feet up, bits of cotton wool between her toes, painting her nails purple, glancing over at the TV every so often, pulling faces whenever Julia appeared in close-up. She could hear the TV from the flat below, also tuned to *Girl Talk*. Kirsty dipped the volume. Karen King wasn't saying much: probably mortified by the picture spread in the *Sun*. Kirsty felt sorry for her. Privately, she hoped Karen wouldn't get back with Jason since he was clearly a shit, but then again it was up to her. She had met Karen at the press launch for the new season of *Girl Talk* and she was the only one who had bothered to talk to her. Actually, that wasn't quite true. Lesley had cornered her and proceeded to talk gibberish. She was blotto, though, so that didn't really count.

Lesley was asking Christine Bleakley if she coloured her hair and Christine, looking luscious and bronzed and more glowing than usual, said it was her natural colour, Celtic genes and all that. Kirsty played with a strand of her own gleaming hair, creating a plait, wondering if she had a bit of Irish blood in her. Karen King, on the end of the panel, was fiddling with her hair too, tucking an ebony strand behind her ear. She had the same colouring as Christine although her skin was pale, almost white. She looked tired and delicate, swamped by that sack of a dress she had on. Kirsty suspected she was still losing weight. She wiggled her toes and removed the cotton wool, and surveyed the pile of boxes in the corner of the room. She had been in the flat nearly two weeks and still had a fair bit to unpack. What with Julia on her back constantly it was hard to find the time. Anyway, there was no point yet. The first thing she planned to do when she got a couple of days free was give the place a lick of paint.

The door opened and Isaac Eastman appeared in a white vest, shorts and flip-flops, his huge frame making the room look tiny. He stood just inside the door, holding a couple of beers, and grimaced at the TV.

'Do we have to watch this?' he said, padding over to the sofa and flopping down beside her. 'It's *CSI* on Five USA.'

'You've seen it before,' Kirsty said, putting the top back on the nail polish, 'and anyway, you know I have to watch. It's one of Her Majesty's rules.'

'I don't know how you stand it,' he said, resting his hand on Kirsty's ankle. 'She's all "Do this, do that, those are the rules, kiss my ass." Man, the woman is a control freak.'

'It's not for much longer,' Kirsty said.

Isaac rubbed her ankle. 'You do know we're missing the episode about the killer who makes miniatures of the murder scene and sends them to Grissom,' he said, his voice silky. 'It's the one where the policewoman goes into the apartment as bait for the killer and dies of carbon monoxide poisoning, all the cops watching her every move on hidden cameras, no one working out the poor woman's not sleeping but dead until it's too late.'

Kirsty grinned. 'You see – you know exactly what happens. You've seen it before.' She rested her feet on his thigh. 'You've seen them all before.'

He gave her a pleading look. 'I'm hooked, babe. Have pity. I need my fix.'

'And I need to know what the old bag says on tonight's show, just in case she puts me on the spot tomorrow.'

On screen Julia was asking Christine about being pursued by paparazzi, all the while shooting sly little looks at Karen. The director, picking up on it, cut to a close-up of Karen, whose eyes were shiny.

'She's doing it on purpose,' Kirsty said, 'making her squirm.'

'Yeah well, let her have her fun because it's not going to last.' Isaac tugged at Kirsty's feet and she shifted position and snuggled in under his arm. Really, Kirsty should be grateful to Julia, since if it hadn't been for her she would never have met Isaac. They had bonded the day Julia blew a fuse on the treadmill and chucked him out. A few hours later, after Julia had left for the studio, he had called and asked if Kirsty would like to have dinner. He was the most courteous man she had met, kind and proper. Strange to think she had been a bit overawed when she met him, not sure about going out with someone who was quite literally twice her size. She would never have imagined a prize fighter could be so gentle and loving and ... just perfect.

She gazed up at him. 'Do you think I'm doing the right thing?'

Julia, back on screen, was laughing about something. He picked up the remote and dipped the sound. 'What's wrong – having second thoughts?'

'It's just, talking to the press ...' Her voice tailed off. Kirsty tugged at her plait. 'I just have visions of Julia splashed all over the papers, some awful headline, and the pair of us caught up in it.' She shuddered. 'She would go absolutely berserk.'

'Anyone who goes through life walking all over people, doing that queen-bitch routine of hers morning, noon and night, must know it's all going to come back to bite her bony backside one day. It's just a matter of time.'

Thirty-Two

Laura Lloyd sat at her desk in the spare room that served as an office and went through her notes on Julia Hill. Technically it was her day off, but she didn't believe in sitting around doing nothing. She had set her alarm for six as usual, woken up just before it went off, thrown back the duvet and got straight up. Laura was definitely a morning person. She had no qualms about getting out of bed, even if it was still the middle of the night, which it often was. Early starts were normal at the *Sunday*: the first flight to Aberdeen, an early train to Newcastle. She had been in Spain for three days the week before. The car taking her to the airport or station always seemed to be booked to pick her up at 5.30, which meant an alarm call of 4.30 at the latest. The hours had been a shock to her system to start with, being on the go for sixteen, seventeen hours at a stretch depending on what the story was and where she had to be. It was such a buzz, though, that she soon got used to it, learned to get by with less sleep and be alert, razor-sharp no matter what. Laura's tenacity and stamina soon got her noticed. She always came back with the story, even if she had to make it up. She could write a couple of thousand words about the state of a celebrity's marriage without ever having spoken to them, slipping in the odd detail that made it appear she had been in the room with them when they had their bust-up about whatever it was. It was a knack and she happened to be extremely good at it, managing to pepper everything she did with quotes – which may or may not be genuine – from 'close friends' and 'sources close to the couple'. There was never any malice in any of it, although people did tend to get upset about Laura's take on their private affairs, usually because she had an uncanny knack of touching a nerve. If she ever ran into anyone she had done a hatchet job on, she would just explain she was doing her job, no offence intended.

The Julia Hill business was different. For one thing, this would not just be an embarrassing story that would send her running off to track down the traitor(s) in her circle; this was a seek-and-destroy mission. There was no chance whatsoever of Julia surviving Laura's onslaught. For another thing, unlike any other piece she had ever written, this was personal.

Laura flipped through her notebook. It was quite astonishing how little had surfaced so far about Julia's past – although of course that was how she had engineered things, reinventing herself, deleting everything to do with who she used to be as she went along. Almost everything, anyway. She had done a pretty thorough job – there was virtually nothing in the cuts file in the newspaper library – but hadn't completely managed to cover her tracks. As Laura knew only too well, that was just about impossible. Something, a tiny clue here or there, almost always gave things away. Until a few days ago she'd had no idea where Julia was born and grew up, although from her accent she would have guessed it was somewhere in the Home Counties. Laura imagined a spoiled child, private school, parents she could twist around her little finger. Thanks to her shabbily treated and hence extremely helpful assistant, Kirsty, a very different picture was beginning to emerge. Laura had now switched her focus north and had an address in Bradford that looked very promising indeed.

She tapped the address into her computer and an image of the street appeared on screen, showing two rows of modest terrace houses with front doors that opened straight on to the narrow pavement. Number 42 was somewhere in the middle. According to the electoral register Betty Swales lived there alone. She was eighty-six. Laura had a phone number, but it would be a mistake to call and put her on her guard. Best to just turn up on the doorstep and catch her unawares.

Thirty-Three

The sound of the doorbell made her jump. Karen was in the kitchen, breaking eggs into a bowl, butter melting in a pan on the stove, determined to eat some proper food after two days of getting by on chocolate. She threw a wary glance over her shoulder in the direction of the front door and wiped her hands on a towel. The kitchen was in semi-darkness, blinds drawn. She tiptoed towards the hall. Her mobile, on the breakfast bar next to her bag, started to ring. She watched the screen flashing, waiting for it to stop. The bell went again. She poked her head around the kitchen door just as the letterbox lifted up. 'It's me,' a voice said. 'Let me in, will you?'

She edged along the wall. Damn, she thought the paparazzi had given up. On the other side of the hall the door to the living room, also in darkness, was open. All the blinds were drawn, shutting out daylight and, more importantly, the photographers who had been lurking, shoving their cards through the door, some of them even tapping on the windows. There had been flowers too, with a card that offered a five-figure sum for an exclusive about Jason. She felt like a cornered animal.

'There's no one here,' the voice said, 'only me. Come on, Karen, open the door.' She slid back the bolts and the chain and opened the door a crack. Dave, grim-faced, a woolly hat pulled low over his forehead, slipped inside. 'The snappers have gone – after some other poor sod by now probably,' he said, putting a toolbox on the floor. Karen gazed at it. 'Cover,' he said, 'just in case any nosy parkers show up. I'm here to mend the washing machine.' She looked nonplussed. 'Never mind,' he said, removing the hat and dropping it on to the toolbox.

Karen gave him a weak smile. 'I owe you an apology,' she said.

He shoved his hands in the pockets of his jeans. His leather jacket, zipped right up, with padding on the shoulders and zips on the cuffs, was the kind of thing a biker would wear. She looked through the peephole on the door. The silver Mercedes was nowhere to be seen. He saw her looking at him as he undid his jacket and said, 'Day off.'

Karen had been doing her best to avoid him since the stuff in the papers with Jason, which was difficult since they had to share a car most days. The pictures outside the restaurant had been bad enough but the ones that popped up the next day, Jason coming out of her place in the early hours, Karen on the doorstep in her dressing gown, post-coital smile in place, had made her want to hide away forever. As it was, she had to venture out and appear on TV several times a week. It was all torture. She had barely been able to look Dave in the eye and she knew, just from the disapproval coming off the back of his neck as he drove her to and from work, that he was in no mood for feeble excuses.

It wasn't like she had made him any promises, and he must have guessed the roses that came each week were from Jason, even if she did hide the cards, but still she hated the idea of messing him about. It was the kind of thing Jason would do. She should have just been straight. The chances were he'd have understood. After all, it wasn't as if they were in love. She had kept things between them light since the hefty age gap made her wary of thinking about him as someone she could have a future with. Best not to have too many expectations, she reasoned. Plus, she was pretty sure he had his secrets; he had done an 'off-diary' job for Debbie Irving a couple of weeks before, whatever that meant. And then there was the fact he always had his phone switched off on Tuesday and Thursday evenings, which was when he did tae kwon do. Fridays were off-limits as that was his night to play poker with the lads. And she had never seen where he lived because he said he would be embarrassed to show her his poky flat in Chingford.

The *Girl Talk* programme they'd done on unsuitable men a while ago came to mind: 'the type that never asks you back to his place'. She winced. It was Jason, with all his lies, that was making her paranoid. Dave was nothing like him. She should have come clean in the first place, not chosen the coward's way out, mumbling something that didn't ring true about the papers getting it wrong, then, when he said nothing, allowing an awkward silence to hang between them. The atmosphere ever since had been suffocating. The feeling that there was no air inside the car was so strong she had to have the window wide open no matter what the weather was doing. How could she have got herself into such a dreadful mess?

Dave followed her into the kitchen, where smoke was rising from the pan heating on the stove for her scrambled eggs. She ran over and whipped it off the gas. Inside, the burnt butter had turned brown and sticky. The air was acrid. As she ran cold water into the pan the smoke alarm started to bleat. She stood at the sink and covered her face with her hands. It was hopeless. She couldn't be trusted to do the simplest of things. No wonder she preferred to survive on chocolate. At least there was no chance of setting the place on fire with a bar of chunky Aero.

When she turned round Dave was at the breakfast bar. The smoke alarm screeched in the background. 'I'll open the window,' he said.

She was about to stop him, just in case there was still a stray reporter lurking, pressed against the wall ready to eavesdrop, but she let it go. Fuck the lot of them, she told herself.

Dave looked around the kitchen, taking in the dirty mugs in the sink, the loaf defrosting on the breadboard, the shiny chocolate wrapper on the floor beside the bin, the drawn blinds. He wandered over to the counter where the eggs were in a bowl waiting for a beating and opened the fridge, empty apart from butter, milk, eggs, parmesan, some ground coffee, a bottle of Pinot Grigio two-thirds drunk, and a tub of mini-chocolate brownies. He gave Karen a quizzical look.

'I've not done any shopping.' The truth was she couldn't face pushing a trolley round the supermarket the way she was feeling.

'They do deliver, you know,' he said. 'Want me to nip out, stock up on a few basics for you?'

She shook her head. 'I'm managing, just about.'

'Right,' he said, taking off his jacket and putting it on the back of a chair. 'I'll do you some grub, then maybe we can clear the air if that's OK.' As she opened her mouth to object he said, 'Not asking too much, am I?'

Thirty-Four

Karen was sure she wouldn't be able to eat a thing but the smell of the eggs in the pan and bread browning in the toaster gave her an appetite. Dave seemed completely at home in her kitchen, opening the right cupboard to get some plates, rinsing out the coffee pot, filling the sink with hot soapy water. She sat at the breakfast bar watching him, not daring to speak, feeling bad for treating him so badly. It was the first time she had cheated on anyone, if sleeping with her husband counted as cheating. She wasn't sure about that. It struck her as a bit of a grey area. She doubted Lesley would have had a problem, probably had umpteen men on the go at any one time and never gave it a second thought, but Karen wasn't like that. She liked things simple, uncomplicated, honest. It bothered her that Dave might think she had been using him for sex. Her cheeks grew warm.

He was buttering a slice of toast, cutting it into triangles and arranging it on the side of her plate next to a mound of scrambled eggs. He put the plate in front of her and handed her a knife and fork. 'Dig in,' he said, pouring coffee. She tasted the eggs, which were buttery and creamy and delicious. Dave topped her coffee up with hot milk. He was the nicest bloke she had met in a long time, thoroughly decent. He seemed to know just what she needed, and not just in the bedroom. She gave him a grateful smile. Why on earth she was still in love with Jason, who was the exact opposite of the saintly man now taking care of her, God alone knew. Feelings were the most peculiar things.

The eggs were the best she had ever tasted, or maybe it was just that she couldn't remember the last time she had bothered to eat properly. 'These are fantastic,' she said, in between mouthfuls. 'What did you do?'

'Threw in another lump of butter towards the end.' He grinned. 'That's what my mum does, and she's a wicked cook.'

Karen gazed at her plate, about to do a rough calorie count, and then gave up. She had to eat, for goodness' sake.

'I don't mind if you're giving it another go with Dickhead,' Dave said, 'but just tell me. Seeing it all over the papers ...' He gazed at her with his clear grey eyes. 'I didn't think that was your style.'

She put down her knife and fork on the edge of her plate. 'I feel awful about all that,' she said eventually. 'I thought everything with Jason was over, with him and that slut of a girlfriend shopping for the nursery. I mean, how much more final can it get? And then he starts saying he wants us to give things another go.' She held up a hand, helpless. 'If someone had told me that's what he was going to do I'd have said he could eff right off, then it happens and what do I actually do? Cave in. Almost immediately.'

Dave topped up his coffee and held the pot over her cup. She shook her head. 'It's all that history. I mean, just being with him forever, since I was a kid. There's a lot between us, loads of stuff no one else knows about, and it's hard to get my head round him being gone. I don't know how to put it. I miss him, I suppose, even though he has been a total shit.' She held Dave's gaze. 'I feel crap about messing you around and I'm sorry. It's the last thing I ever meant to do.' She looked at him in his jeans and tight white T-shirt and had a quick flash of an old Levi's ad, Nick Kamen stripping off in the launderette. 'If I'm honest, you knock spots off him. It's just ... *twenty-odd years* with someone. If there's still a chance to make things work—' She broke off mid-sentence and pushed a bit of toast around her plate, mopping up melted butter. 'I think what happens is the idea of divorce gets scarier as you get older.'

Dave was leaning on the breakfast bar, watching her. 'You don't have to tell me all the ins and outs,' he said. 'If that's what you want, fine, go for it. I'm just not sure I fancy your chances with a man who left you, got the new bird up the duff just like that' – he clicked his fingers – 'and now the novelty's worn off he thinks he just might be better off with the missus after all, no screaming kid spoiling his beauty sleep.' Karen flinched, her cheeks burning. 'I mean, what's he going to do for an encore?' He softened his voice. 'I'm not trying to make you feel bad, Kaz.' Dave was the only person who called her Kaz. 'I just don't want you landing in the shit again.'

She knew he was right and that if a friend was in her position she would be doing everything she could to persuade her not to weaken.

'It's complicated,' she said feebly.

'It always is.'

Karen lay on her back, one leg sticking out from under the duvet, and made a list in her head of all Dave's good points: heart-meltingly gorgeous, fit, great in bed, funny, surprisingly good in the kitchen. Then she did the same with Jason: charming, persuasive, familiar ... unreliable. He had always been an expert at letting her down, let's face it. She snuggled into Dave, who put an arm around her and pulled her close. His skin was smooth and damp. She planted a kiss on his chest. She even liked his musky smell and the faint hint of Joop! She hadn't meant to end up in bed with him. The way he looked at her with those slate eyes, though, had a peculiar effect. Basically, she fancied him like mad and there was still an awful lot to sort out with Jason before things would be anywhere near back on track. After all, right now he was with Hannah. Karen wondered why she was tormenting herself over him when he was still mucking her about – and probably always would – dithering, flitting between her and Hannah, keeping his options open. Dave pushed her fringe off her face and chuckled. 'You look about sixteen with your hair scraped back,' he said.

She rolled on to her stomach and gazed at him, flattered. 'Fibber.'

'Serious. It suits you.'

She burrowed into his chest. 'I'm sorry about before – you know, not being straight with you about Jason.'

'It's no big deal, but with the tabloids all over you right now you'll be lucky to keep stuff secret.'

'They don't know about us.' *Yet*. She knew if she carried on like this it was only a matter of time.

'Want me to back off while you get your head sorted?'

Did she? She sighed. 'Maybe. I don't want to muck you about.'

'That's OK, I'm cool.'

Karen wondered if the reason he was so cool was that there was someone else he could be with in the meantime. More 'off-diary' jobs for Debbie Irving, perhaps. Dave was the best thing to happen to her for ages and she could just be about to throw it away on the off-chance Jason might come back. *Might.* And just how likely was that, when he had her exactly where he wanted her? She had to get tough, make him decide once and for all. And if she lost Dave in the process ... ? Well, it was better than doing a Jason and keeping him hanging on.

'Perhaps we should stop – you know, seeing each other. Just until ...' Her voice tailed off. 'Sorry.'

'Nah, don't stress.' He propped himself up on an elbow. 'Are you OK about me driving you?'

'Of course!' She hated the thought of not seeing him at all.

He nodded. After a moment of silence he said, 'I could always have a word if you like.'

'How do you mean?'

'You know, man to man – let him know he's acting like a right tosser, bang out of order.'

Karen wondered if Dave's idea of 'having a word' involved a Jet Li-style kick to the sternum or some kind of karate chop to the back of the neck. She imagined Jason stumbling around, battered and bruised, in Epping Forest after his man-to-man chat with Dave. 'It's OK, but thanks anyway.'

'No sweat.' He sat up and stretched, lacing his fingers together, the bones making a series of explosive cracks. 'I just hope your old man's worth it,' he said. *Crack, crack.* 'I mean, once a dickhead, always a dickhead.'

'You're not angry are you?'

'I told you, I'm cool.' He gave her one of his lopsided smiles. 'I'm gonna miss you, though.'

Thirty-Five

On the train heading north, Laura Lloyd worked out a schedule of everything she needed to do in Bradford. She would call at the local paper first, where she had arranged to trawl through some cuts in the archive library. The chances of finding anything useful were slim but it was worth a look and since the offices were just over the road from the train station it made sense to start there. From there she would head up Manningham Lane and knock on the door of number 42 Garden Court, which conjured up an image of a quaint little street in a leafy suburb, not the grimy terrace revealed by the internet street view. She had no way of knowing what she would find, whether it would be a sweet old lady happy to invite her in and natter over a cup of tea, or some ferocious dragon who would tell her where to go. It was a distinct possibility that Julia took after her mother, in which case there would be several expletives and the door slammed firmly in Laura's face. She smiled. No point worrying.

Unlike most hacks, who disliked doing doorsteps with all the uncertainty and the fifty-fifty chance of being told where to go, she relished the challenge and almost always managed to worm her way in. In fairness, the person on the receiving end usually had no idea she was from a newspaper. Once you told them there was almost no chance of getting in. She never knew exactly how she was going to play things until the door opened and she got a look at whoever she was dealing with. Once or twice, especially in the north, where people seemed friendly and trusting by and large, she had claimed to have moved in up the road and – how stupid! – locked herself out. That usually worked quite well.

It never ceased to astonish her just how much people were willing to reveal about themselves to someone they had only just met. It seemed she had the kind of face people trusted, which was ironic really as while they confided in her she was committing to memory everything they said, as well as details about their home – Jeremy Kyle on in the background, net curtains, a bit of peeling wallpaper above the skirting board, that kind of thing – which she would scribble into a notebook as soon as she was out of range. Complete strangers spilled all sorts of juicy stuff, often without her even having to ask, and almost always without understanding the significance of what they were saying. Where Betty Swales was concerned, though, Laura would go easy and just hope she was in a talkative mood. As it happened, she had a soft spot for elderly people, did a bit of shopping for the woman in the flat below hers, which she hoped no one would ever find out about: as a hard-nosed hack it was definitely not in her interest to earn a reputation for doing good.

The train sped along the east-coast main line towards Leeds. The last time Laura had been up that way was for a piece about a woman who had kidnapped her own child in the hope of scooping the reward money. Laura had spent days traipsing around an estate in Dewsbury knocking on doors – a fair number of people telling her where to go – until she found someone willing to talk. The promise of a couple of thousand pounds definitely helped. She had come away with a blistering exclusive.

As the train hurtled towards Grantham, the woman opposite, bright-eyed and with a mass of wiry silver curls, took a Thermos and a foil parcel of sandwiches from a shopping bag and offered them to the man sat next to her with a gentle smile. Laura listened to them chirp away at each other, him pouring steaming tea into the cup that came with the flask, the two of them taking it in turns to have a drink.

Laura caught the woman's eye and gave her a smile. Whenever she saw a couple who still seemed happy in their twilight years it gave her a warm feeling inside. The longest any of her relationships had lasted was a year. She had begged Tony not to leave but he was adamant, accusing her of putting her work first – it was true, she did, but she had no choice if she wanted to keep her job. There was no room for anyone less than one hundred per cent dedicated and professional at the *Sunday*. That didn't mean she wanted to be alone. She was desperate to share her life with someone, to come home at the end of one of those fourteen-hour days and smell dinner cooking.

She closed her eyes and slipped into a fantasy where she was in the bedroom taking off her work clothes while her other half ran a bath and poured her a glass of wine. As she daydreamed she found herself transported into a fabulous flat with a huge open living space, all pale-wood floors and windows that covered an entire wall. She was high up and beyond the window was a balcony with a view over the Thames. The man handing her a glass of chilled wine was Joel Reynolds.

She opened her eyes, startled. She had dreamed about him a couple of nights before, the two of them cuddled up on that huge leather sofa of his, flames leaping about behind the smoked glass of the fancy fire built into the wall, angular lamps throwing soft light around the room. The TV was on, *Girl Talk*, Mariah Carey the studio guest, seated on a throne in a pool of golden light, looking soft and luminous while everyone else appeared grey and on the haggard side. Laura knew where that had come from. There had been stories all over the papers about Mariah's infamous diva demands, Kate Garraway claiming the singer turned up with her own loo roll, an entourage that out-numbered the entire studio crew and had two people on hand to lower her on to the GMTV sofa so as not to crease her dress. Laura had to hand it to Mariah. Even her *dogs* had their own entourage.

Laura closed her eyes again and Joel popped up right away, this time climbing into a bath filled with scented foam, the two of them kissing, sliding under the water, coming up laughing. She shook herself. Get a grip, Laura! Having a crush on some-one she was working with on what could well be the story of her life was hardly professional.

Joel Reynolds sat in the armchair of his consulting room in Harley Street, eyes shut, his feet up on a padded footstool, steeling himself for the onslaught. He always felt sick before Julia arrived for an appointment these days, his stomach working its way into a series of painful knots. Laura had told him that what she called Operation Julia was now on the news-paper's features list so there was no going back. His mouth felt dry. There was a soft tap on the door and he said, 'Come in.'

His nurse, Donna, in an immaculate white uniform that looked more high-end shop assistant than health worker, appeared carrying a large pink bone-china cup on a matching saucer. 'I've brought you some peppermint tea,' she said, 'to help settle your stomach.'

When he had hired Donna to replace his last nurse, driven away like all the others by Julia Bitch-From-Hell Hill, he had suspected a nurse who was also a reiki master and trained in reflexology of being a bit on the cranky side. In fact, she was proving a real boon, the kind of nurse who deserved to be called an angel. She had remained calm throughout her first encounter with Julia, despite being shouted at, called an insolent brat and ordered out of the room. Her sin had been to 'stare' at the paranoid presenter. Donna was the most unflappable person he had ever encountered, with the possible exception of Laura Lloyd, who had ice running through her veins as far as he could tell. Pity she was such a cold fish, since he rather liked her.

The knots in his insides began to loosen as he sipped his tea and Donna put on a relaxing CD of Native American chants and rhythmic beats. So Julia Hill was on her way. So what? She would rant and rave, complain, insult his nurse, hint in her usual dark way at blackmail if he failed to please. He had heard it all a thousand times before. He would take a leaf out of Donna's book and remain calm. Julia's tantrums were all about her temper and insecurities and nothing to do with his skills as a cosmetic surgeon. That's what he needed to remember once she started stamping her feet. He thought about the pictures of her after the Domes episode, face bulbous from a serious overdose of filler, and chuckled. Well, he had tried to warn her.

Donna went to wash her hands at the sink in the corner. 'T minus five and counting,' she said over her shoulder.

Joel got up. 'Columbia, this is Houston advising you to stand by for lift-off,' he said in an American accent.

Donna chuckled. 'That's more like it,' she said.

He gave her a grateful smile. 'You're a miracle worker,' he said. A buzzer sounded on his desk. He made his face serious. 'We have ignition,' he said, sounding American again. 'In ten, nine, eight . . .' He and Donna went to face the door, side by side. She gave him a mock salute. 'Seven, six, five—'

The door shot open and Julia strode into the room. 'What's this – a reception committee?' she said, flinging her coat on to the chair Joel had been stretched out on moments ago. Donna picked it up and put it on a hanger.

'There's a new treatment out, something to do with injecting your own blood into your face,' Julia said, pulling a sweater over her head and tossing it on to the chair. Donna picked it up and found a satin hanger for it. 'It's called Dracula Therapy.' Joel frowned. 'I mean it's not really, obviously, that's just what the papers are saying, but it's to do with separating off some kind of serum from the red blood cells and adding loads of vitamins and minerals and what-have-you. Apparently it's amazing, takes years off.' She folded her arms. 'So, can you do it?'

Joel tugged at the cuff of his jacket. 'I did read something about it. It's not widely available here.'

'Can't you do a course or something, get up to speed? It's going to be the next big thing.'

'I'll certainly look into it,' he said, 'now you've brought it to my attention.'

Julia held his gaze, not sure if she detected a whiff of sarcasm, but he merely gave her a pleasant smile. 'Right then, let's get you on the couch, and you can tell me what you want today.' As she lay down he glanced at Donna. 'You're looking great, you know,' he told his most difficult patient. 'Absolutely fantastic.'

She watched him suspiciously. Was he being funny? Joel never complimented her. Well, well, perhaps it had finally sunk into that dense skull of his that the customer was always right. Donna wheeled a trolley with needles and supplies of botulinum toxin and various fillers to the side of the couch. Joel switched on a lamp above Julia and pulled a magnifying glass down so that he could inspect her face. He had to stop himself from flinching at the sight of Julia, now twice her usual size, staring up at him. She really did look amazing, although she was definitely getting that overdone, frozen look that comes from endless tweaks. With any other patient he would suggest they ease off, maybe do a gentle blue-algae peel to freshen them up, leave the Botox alone. Not with Julia, though. There was no telling her, as he knew from bitter experience.

Donna handed him a syringe and he began the task of injecting her around her eyes, all over her forehead, the lines that ran from the sides of her nose to her mouth. Julia kept her eyes open throughout the procedure, at one stage telling Donna to 'switch off that dreary New Age wailing'. Joel worked on, untroubled, squeezing filler into her top lip, creating the exaggerated pout she liked so much. Old trout, he thought and began to hum, content in the knowledge that Julia was on borrowed time. Laura Lloyd was on to her and would show the bitch no mercy. He peered at Julia's swollen mouth. She was about as animated as one of those 'real dolls' sad blokes who couldn't find a proper girlfriend paid thousands of pounds for.

Beneath his cool exterior there was no doubt his nerves were

beginning to jangle. In no time at all Laura would have finished her story, Julia would be exposed, and it could easily
rebound on him. The worrying was keeping him awake at night,
but it was too late to do anything about it now.

He just had to hope his most difficult patient didn't take
him down with her.

Thirty-Six

It was 13 November, the one day of the year Lesley always, without fail, woke with a clear head and no strange man in her bed. She pushed her eye mask on to her brow and reached for her watch. It was just after seven, ludicrously early by her usual standards, but she was wide awake and ready to make a move. She made a mental note to cut down on her drinking, sat up, slipped her feet into a pair of Ugg boots that served as slippers, stretched, and switched on the giant TV on the wall facing the bed. A reporter, all wrapped up, his cheeks ruddy, was standing in the dark explaining that the street behind him remained off-limits, that the authorities were not yet letting people return to their homes. A caption in red on the screen said *LIVE*. In the studio, warm and comfortable on the sofa, John Stapleton said to wait just a minute because they were now able to go live to a community centre where local people had spent the night.

Lesley padded over to the window and peered around the curtain into the garden. The storms had not so much as grazed London, not even any rain overnight as far as she could tell. She remembered the news the night before, an elderly woman being carried to safety along a flooded street, and thinking about her own mum, dabbing at her eyes with a tissue. It had been exactly ten years since a massive heart attack killed her, and Lesley still missed her. The only thing she was grateful for was that her mother had not been alive to see her fall from grace, although she had a feeling she would have been less shocked than everyone else and would probably have taken it in her stride. Whenever Lesley got into trouble she had simply tucked her up in bed with a hot-water bottle and fed her Heinz tomato soup and floury white rolls, which somehow seemed to do the trick. Thinking about it she felt a catch at the back of her throat.

Downstairs an enormous bunch of lilies stood in a jug of water in the kitchen, their pungent scent escaping into the hall. Lesley made a pot of tea, toasted a bagel and had it with smoked salmon and cream cheese for breakfast. She toasted a second bagel and smothered it in butter and blackberry jam. It never seemed to matter what she ate, she stayed rake-thin. Then again, she never really ate that much, usually made do with a Berocca and a couple of paracetamol and codeine for breakfast, then by lunchtime, once she had a glass of wine inside her, she seemed to lose her appetite.

She showered and put on a pair of black skinny jeans and a black cashmere sweater, backcombed her hair and swept it into a funky beehive style, and pulled on a pair of stack-heel suede boots. She was going for a solemn, sober look but at the same time she wanted to do her mother proud. She could just hear her coming out with one of her pep talks, quips about dressing for success, never showing her face without her lipstick on, and only ever wearing flat shoes indoors or, at a push, on the beach. Before she died, when Lesley had landed a starring role in *Spitalfields* and was on all the covers of the celebrity magazines, her mum's favourite saying had been 'Knock 'em dead, girl.'

*

The car dropped her at the entrance to the cemetery and she slipped on a pair of Gucci shades and stepped out into the wind. A gust caught at the lilies, rustling their cellophane wrapping. Lesley turned her back to the wind, buttoned up her jacket, pulled on a pair of red leather gloves and set off for her mother's grave. She skirted round the small chapel at the top of the drive and turned along a narrow path past elaborate headstones. At the point where a sleeping angel lay stretched out on a stone altar she stepped on to the grass and walked between several rows of graves until she reached the white marble slab that was her mother's. Lesley sank to her haunches and arranged the flowers in the metal vase in front of the headstone. The entire plot was enclosed by a low chain which hung over a neat gravel border. Lesley had planted chrysanthemums, which bent their bright heads in the wind. People were sniffy about chrysanthemums these days but her mum had loved them and the little front garden of their home in Brixton was full of them. The fact they flowered late into the year meant there was almost never a time when her mother's grave was without blooms.

'I've brought you lilies, Mum,' Lesley said, dropping to her knees and turning up the collar on her jacket. 'I could smell them all over the house this morning.' She watched a man in a cap and a wax jacket in front of a faded grey marble cross pull up weeds and drop them in the compost bin next to the wall. 'The show's doing well and there's a job coming up on *Good Morning Britain*. Dean says I'm in with a chance if I behave myself.' She giggled. 'When did I ever do that?' A lock of blonde hair blew across her face. 'Blowing a gale today,' she went on. 'I've got a meeting later. Keep your fingers crossed, it's important.' The knees of her jeans were damp when she got up. 'I'll see you soon, Mum,' she said, bending and planting a kiss on the headstone. 'I really miss you.'

She adjusted the pot with the lilies, wedging it into the gravel, and headed back to the car.

Natalie had no idea why Lesley had suggested meeting in a Moroccan café in Brockley in south London. Talk about middle of nowhere. Still, she was a humble researcher and it was not her place to argue with a star presenter. She had been alarmed when three weeks earlier one of the runners had interrupted an edit to say Lesley wanted to see her in her dressing room. It could only mean she had messed up and was in for a bollocking. Her editor, Steve, had folded his arms and said, 'Oh dear. What have you done to upset our resident star alcoholic?'

Natalie had squirmed in her seat. 'I don't know,' she said in a small scared voice. 'I've not really had anything to do with her lately. Too busy with all this behind-the-scenes stuff for Cheryl.'

'There you are then. You're not giving her enough attention. They're a touchy bunch, you know, don't like being left out.'

Natalie had dragged her feet all the way from the edit suite to the dressing-room corridor. Maybe she could come up with an idea for Lesley, something that would give her a slot of her own, like Cheryl. Outside Dressing Room 2 she took a deep breath and knocked. The door opened and Lesley popped her head out, looked up and down the corridor, then yanked her inside. The television was on, Helen England wearing one of those aprons with a curvy woman in a bikini on the front, flirting outrageously as a guest chef did something clever with squash.

Lesley flopped on to the sofa and patted the seat beside her.

'Can you believe this is the top-rated daytime show in the country?' she said. Natalie, not sure if she was meant to reply, kept quiet. 'At least she's doing us all a favour and buggering off.' Lesley sat forward in her seat. 'She's thinner than she was, don't you think?'

Closer magazine had put Helen England on its cover, a picture of her now in a fitted dress next to one taken three months earlier in a baggy T-shirt over sweatpants. It wasn't a fair comparison but she did look a lot slimmer. 'The show needs a bit of glamour if you ask me,' Lesley grumbled. 'Imagine being stuck at home and having that frumpy cow shoved down your throat every day. No wonder the ratings are on the way down.' They weren't, as far as Natalie knew, but she wasn't about to say so.

Lesley swung round, tucking a foot under her bottom. She had a job for Natalie, she said, something she wanted her to do out of hours, and she would pay her well. Natalie saw herself dressed like a cat burglar letting down Helen England's tyres or defacing the *Good Morning Britain* billboards, giving the presenter a moustache. She braced herself.

Lesley said, 'You know how to find things out, don't you?' Natalie nodded. 'Well, see what you can dig up about Sasha Gates. As much dirt as you can.' Natalie opened her mouth to say something, but Lesley kept talking. 'She's swanning around as if butter wouldn't melt, thinking she can destroy people's lives and get away with it. Well, she's wrong and we're going to show everyone what an evil cow she really is. Sasha Gates has a terrible secret.' Natalie's eyes widened. 'Something she will do anything to keep under wraps because if the public knew what she was really like they would want her off their screens faster than you can say "Julia Hill is a prize bitch".'

She glanced at the screen, Helen hugging the chef. 'Oh for fuck's sake, get a room,' she said. 'The fact is, Sasha's desperate to keep her murky past hidden.' Natalie could feel her heart racing. 'And that's where you come in,' Lesley said. 'Natalie, you are going to help me expose her for what she really is.' She sat up, triumphant.

Natalie stared at her. She wasn't sure she wanted anything to do with this. If she got a reputation as some kind of grass she would never work again. Then again, there were ways of getting stuff into the open without anyone ever finding out who had lit the blue touchpaper. It was just a question of standing well back. 'What is it?' she whispered.

Lesley frowned. 'What's what?'

'You know – her secret.'

Lesley shrugged. 'I have no idea. That's what you're going to find out.'

Natalie gasped. 'I thought you already knew! What if she's squeaky clean?'

Lesley looked blank. 'She is *famous*, Natalie, a *celebrity*. Her ugly mug is all over the magazines.' Lesley shuddered. Sasha Gates had even managed to pop up in the *Style* section of the *Sunday Times*, although how was anybody's guess since she wouldn't know style if it came up and slapped her in the chops. 'She *will* have skeletons in her walk-in closet, in amongst all the tat, I guarantee it. It's up to you to find out what they are: drugs, threesomes with glamour models and footballers, sneaky blow jobs under the table in nightclubs when no one's looking.' Lesley had done all of the above, and much more besides. 'You know the kind of stuff.' She took her wallet from her bag and extracted a wad of notes. 'Five hundred quid,' she said, stuffing them into Natalie's hand. 'Just to get you going, cover expenses.

Let me know what you find, and be discreet. On no account phone me or email me about any of this. We'll meet up from time to time, see how you're getting on. I'll let you know when and where.'

Thirty-Seven

Natalie had got a bus and two trains to Brockley. On the high street her eye was drawn to an old ballroom where film lighting trucks were parked up and beefy men with metal clips dangling from the belts of their cut-off pants ran cables up the side of the building. As she drew close she noticed a tea urn on a table next to the entrance, along with a stack of disposable cups, cartons of milk, a bag of sugar and a tray of biscuits, three to a packet. Every drama shoot was identical. A black rubbish bag hooked on the end of the table lifted in the breeze. She approached a bloke in cropped combat trousers with CASINO ROYALE CREW across the back of his T-shirt who told her it was some new drama with Robbie Coltrane, not that the big man was on set that day, and pointed her towards the café she was looking for.

Ten minutes later, at a table half hidden by a pillar and with a large cappuccino in front of her, she turned the pages of her notebook, adding a few jottings in the margin, not sure any more whether she was a programme researcher, an investigative journalist or a private eye. This brief of Lesley's had turned her world pretty much on its head and she wasn't entirely sure about the ethics of what she was doing. Now she had got her teeth into it and was finally getting somewhere, though, she was on a bit of a high.

In Natalie's twelve months at *Girl Talk* she had never really got to know Lesley, who was in a booze-fuelled world of her own most of the time, and not the most approachable of the five women. Karen was warm and friendly, while Julia was to be avoided at all costs and Faye had a cool, unattainable air about her. Natalie spent more time with Cheryl than the others, working with her on a shoot practically every week, not that she would claim to have got to know her. There was a distinct air of 'us and them' about Cheryl. Schmoozing was reserved for fellow celebs while researchers, runners and the like were only there for fetching and carrying. Not that she was hard work. She just had her pecking order, which, in fairness, was the same for most of the celebs Natalie had encountered. In the past she had written Lesley off as a hopeless old soak. These last few weeks, though, she had begun to change her mind. Two clandestine meetings had followed their initial dressing-room chat and even though there had been little to report – no sordid affairs, drugs scandals, no quickies in the VIP section of Mahiki – Lesley had shown up on time, not a whiff of alcohol on her breath, listened to what Natalie had to say, bunged her another wad and told her to keep digging. Now her patience had paid off, because Natalie had something very juicy indeed for her.

The weekend before she had got the train to the south coast and called on Edward Draper in Worthing. On the way she had walked along the main shopping street and wandered into a bargain emporium which had at one time been a thriving grocery business. She had a map in her hand as she went, not that she needed to look at it because she had already memorized directions to Manor Avenue. Large houses, mostly detached, built at the turn of the twentieth century as far as Natalie could tell, faced each other. Tall, mature trees lined the pavement.

Smart cars occupied the drives. Number 90, with its yellowing net curtains, mucky windows and peeling paintwork, was shabby compared to the rest. The garden was well tended though, with its neat lawn and rose bushes in the borders. The towering hedge that divided the property from next door had been given a short back and sides. Natalie took a deep breath and undid the wooden gate. She hadn't worked out what she was going to say. Maybe she should go away, think about it and come back later. She pulled the gate shut and dropped the latch into place. No, she wasn't being paid to be a mouse. If she had still been working for a newspaper she would have been straight in there. TV had made her soft. She opened the gate again, walked up the drive and rapped on the dusty door. It was a minute or two before it was opened by an old man with a dressing gown on over his clothes.

The house had a stale, neglected air about it, worn carpet on the stairs, no sign of anyone having gone round with the vacuum for months, if not years. In the kitchen there were free-standing cupboards, a door with glass panels that seemed to be a pantry, and a stainless-steel sink under the window. A big square pine table covered in bills, shiny leaflets for pizza delivery, supermarket special offers, a dirty plate and a glass fruit bowl containing a few coins and a ball of string was pressed against a wall. The place was freezing. Edward Draper seemed to think Natalie had come to ask him about switching to a different energy supplier, even though she had done her best to explain she was a freelance feature writer (only a small lie, she reasoned). When it had finally sunk in he said she looked just like someone who had been round the week before telling him he was paying too much getting his gas and electricity from two different companies.

Natalie had sat at the kitchen table and told him she was putting together a profile piece on Sasha Gates. He listened and nodded but clearly had no idea what she was talking about. A fluffy black cat strolled in from the hall and leaped on to a saggy armchair next to the pantry door. She tried again. Still Edward Draper remained blank.

What followed that day had been nothing short of extraordinary and now she could hardly wait to fill Lesley in.

Lesley arrived at Brockley's El Bleu café twenty minutes late in her trademark dark glasses, half a ton of lip gloss and perilous heels. Natalie wondered if she had been on the sauce the night before, but could not detect any of the usual signs that she was the worse for wear until she removed her glasses to reveal pink eyes.

'You'll have to give me a minute,' she said, 'let me get some coffee inside my system. It's a difficult day for me.' She didn't elaborate and Natalie didn't like to probe. Lesley blew her nose and dropped the tissue into her bag. As she slicked an unnecessary layer of gloss on her lips a cup of frothy coffee with a chocolate heart on the surface was placed in front of her. 'Perfect,' she said, managing to empty two small sachets of brown sugar into it without disturbing the heart.

Natalie played with the froth on her drink, suddenly excited about her news.

'Right,' Lesley said eventually, putting her cup down. 'Give me the latest.'

Natalie took a deep breath and began to explain that she had been to Worthing to see Edward Draper, an old chap living on his own in a sprawling, neglected house a couple of streets from the seafront. The state of the place – cold, damp and stale-smelling – was evidence that Mr Draper, who had had his own grocery shop in the town centre at one time, was now experiencing extreme financial hardship. Lesley wondered where Natalie was going with all this but stirred her coffee and let her carry on.

'The place is *grim*,' Natalie said, 'no central heating and a poky little kitchen. He doesn't even have a cooker, just a microwave that looks about fifty years old. No washing machine. I went upstairs to use the loo and it was like the Arctic. One of the windows in the bathroom is out and he's taped the back of a cornflakes box over the gap, not that it makes any difference. His clothes are dirty and falling to bits, although you can tell they must have cost a bit in their day. I had to go to the shop to get milk before I could make a cup of tea. I bought him a few bits and pieces as well because virtually all he had in the fridge was a tin of cat food and a tub of margarine.' She picked up her cup. 'It was really sad. Poor bugger, scraping along, just getting on with it. He didn't moan once when I was there.' She drained the last of her drink. 'To be honest, it shocked me to find someone living like that, especially when there's no need.' She paused. 'Not when your daughter's one of the highest-paid actresses on TV.'

Lesley gasped. She had read an interview with Sasha Gates talking about the pain of both her parents passing away within a year of each other, long before she had landed her first TV role. 'The sneaky little witch,' she breathed. 'And she said her dad was dead.'

Natalie shook her head. 'I can confirm that he is most definitely alive *and* unwell. Poor sod, his telly doesn't work and he never reads a newspaper, which explains why he has no idea what his celebrity daughter's doing. As far as I can tell, he had some kind of breakdown when his wife died and took to wandering about half dressed, plodding along the seafront in the rain, nothing on his feet, that kind of thing. He ended up in an institution for a while. He was still in touch with Deirdre – sorry, *Sasha* – at that point, remembers her visiting him when he was in hospital, bringing clean pyjamas and bottles of Lucozade, the *Telegraph*. When he was well enough to go home she came and picked him up.'

Lesley listened in silence, a picture forming in her head of Edward Draper shivering in his shabby clothes, no food in the cupboard, while his daughter was living the high life. Without warning her face crumpled and she began to sob.

Natalie, horrified, leaned forward. 'What is it – what have I said?' She glanced in the direction of the counter, where the waiter was at the espresso machine with his back to them. Lesley dug a pack of paper tissues from her bag and wiped her face, slipping the Gucci shades back on. She looked ashen, her mouth twisted. Natalie went and got a glass of water, which Lesley gulped down. With her face streaked with tears she looked like a lost little girl.

Lesley stifled a sob. Sasha Gates was even worse than she had imagined. She was the kind of woman who pretended her dad was dead when all the while he was scraping by in squalor. Lesley, whose own father had skipped back off to Canada before her mother even knew she was pregnant, felt sick and sad and angry all at the same time.

'Sorry, I'm a bit raw today,' she said eventually. 'It's the anniversary of my mum dying. I always have a bit of a wobble anyway but, I don't know, it gets to me when I hear about old people abandoned by their family.' She sniffed. 'I would give anything to have my mum back. Are you absolutely sure about all this?'

Natalie nodded. 'One hundred per cent. It's a fantastic story – national treasure turns her back on her poor old dad. So ashamed she even pretends he's dead. And, wait for this – that house of his, which is probably worth at least half a million quid even in its current dilapidated state – is going to her when he actually does pass away.'

Thirty-Eight

Faye was getting ready for her one-to-one Pilates session. She was running late because, having stopped to check her emails, it had taken her ages to wade through Mike's latest missive, in which he told her about 'Ganners' (Afghanistan) and the FOB (forward operating base) and IEDs (improvised explosive devices). It was more like something he would write on his blog for ITN than a personal message to his wife. Then again, she could hardly blame him. Her messages were pretty impersonal too, mostly to do with *Girl Talk* and what the gossip was. She had actually mentioned the latest story the mags were running about Brad and Angelina – anything to keep things light and impersonal and as far from the truth about what was going on in her life as possible.

Increasingly, she felt bad about cheating on him. Fair enough, the odd fling on either side could be overlooked, just about, when they were apart for weeks at a time, but what was going on between her and Cheryl was intense. She was relentless. With Mike away, she took every opportunity to pile on the pressure.

Faye's stomach in her snug Pilates pants was bloated. Stress, definitely. Did she love Cheryl? Yes, in a way, she did. Enough to walk out on her marriage and let the world know she was gay? She closed her eyes. That was something else.

*

In a beauty salon in Chelsea, a discreet little place with frosted windows and private booths even if you were only having a manicure, Cheryl admired her nails. Usually she had them painted whatever the hot colour happened to be, although lately she had been sticking with black or purple, which went with virtually everything she wore. Today, though, her nail technician had suggested something new and was applying tiny leopard-print transfers. They were the latest thing according to *Grazia,* where a grinning Katy Perry was pictured, her cat's face now on a transfer on her nails. Faye would probably turn up her nose at such things since she was unimpressed with what she called gimmicks, not that Cheryl cared. She had wanted the two of them to spend the morning together, go for a leisurely lunch at the Bluebird on the King's Road, but Faye had said no. Too busy with her precious exercise class. Cheryl had been going to tell her about meeting James Almond and how he had practically promised her the Helen England job, but now she thought she might keep it to herself. She would know soon enough anyway, once she resigned and it was all over the papers. That might just be the kick up the backside Faye needed.

Julia stood in front of the mirrored wall in the gym in a vest and a pair of tiny running shorts, admiring her toned body, her powerful, athletic legs. Perhaps they were a bit too muscular, not that there was much she could do about that. She examined her face. Joel had done a great job on her lips but was still dragging his heels on that Dracula treatment she wanted, probably hoping she'd forget all about it. She frowned. Her face remained impassive. Damn, that Botox was good. She would need to consult him about how to make sure she looked as good at the finish line as she did at the start when she took part in the London Marathon. Having taken the plunge and signed up she was now in serious training, running like the clappers every morning. Everything she had read about doing your first marathon suggested taking professional advice, joining a running club, having the support of a team. That wasn't her style. She had found a website that told her everything she needed to know about long-distance running. The fact that the author had dropped dead while out on a run was slightly off-putting but, Julia reasoned, he probably had what the doctors called an underlying health condition. She stepped on to the treadmill, programmed it for an hour and started pounding the rubber.

Lesley, barefoot, wrapped in a dressing gown, knelt on the bathroom floor, elbows on the toilet seat. She felt dreadful, properly, seriously ill. She had thrown up already and still the nausea would not go away. Her forehead was on fire and she was clammy, sweat running down the back of her neck. She sagged against the wall and pressed her face against the tiles, which were lovely and cool and made her feel better for a moment. Then the nausea swept over her again. Someone had told her ginger was good for sickness and she knew she had some but didn't feel up to crawling downstairs to find it. It was all too much.

A thought burrowed into her head. Maybe she wasn't ill: maybe it was just a hangover. No. This wasn't like any hangover she had ever experienced. She should call her agent, see if he could get a doctor to come round, someone who could be trusted not to blab, just whisk her off to a private clinic under a false name.

Minutes ticked by and gradually the sick feeling in her stomach began to subside. She crawled along the landing to her bedroom, dissolved two painkillers in a glass of water, knocked them back and got under the duvet. Her whole body shook. She felt around at the side of the bed and switched on the heated blanket. Every movement made her head thump. If she died they would find her, smelly and unwashed, the bathroom a mess. There would be tests. They would look at what was in her system, tell everyone how much alcohol she had consumed. *The equivalent of two bottles of vodka, blah blah.*

She forced herself to remember the night before, hooking up with that German boy, knocking back vodka, then tequila and champagne, then more vodka. He had followed her into the toilets and they'd had rough, crazy sex against the wall of one of the stalls, not that she could remember much about it, just someone banging on the door at one point, telling them to get a move on. It was all coming back to her. Where the hell had they been? Some seedy club with strippers and topless girls serving overpriced drinks, in Soho as far as she knew, not that she would have been able to find it again. As for how she'd got home, it was a complete mystery.

The painkillers were doing their job, taking the edge off her headache. She poked her head out from the duvet. There was no need to call Dean, no need to dial 999. It was the booze, as usual, making her feel like shit. How on earth did she think she would ever cope with *Good Morning Britain*? She glanced at the photo in the silver frame on her bedside table. 'Sorry, Mum.' Her voice was weak, rasping. 'I'm going to get a grip, I promise.'

*

The night before, Bella had turned up on Karen's doorstep with a bottle of wine and a bag full of Marks & Spencer food. 'Look at you,' she had said, 'wasting away.'

Karen had taken it as a compliment but Bella was concerned. 'You do *not* need to lose any more weight,' she had said, unpacking her shopping, popping some kind of lamb dish and a carton of rosemary potatoes in the oven, taking the lid off a tub of miniature cocktail sausages and plonking them on the breakfast bar. 'When did you last eat?' she said, pulling open a drawer, searching for the corkscrew.

'When did you get so bossy?' Karen said, tucking into the sausages, savouring the taste of something that by rights was off-limits to anyone keeping an eye on their weight. She felt like an invalid, with people popping in to make sure she was all right: Dave cooking her eggs, Bella bringing dinner. She would have a full-time carer before long if she wasn't careful.

Bella had poured them each a large glass of wine and sat down facing Karen. 'OK,' she said, 'spill the beans. What exactly is going on with that jerk of a husband of yours?' She popped a sausage into her mouth. '*Ex*-husband, I should say.'

Karen had pulled a face. 'We're not divorced yet, and I have no idea,' she said. 'I haven't seen him since the brown stuff hit the fan last week. Right now he's with The Bimbo, licking his wounds, lying through his teeth about how the papers got it all wrong, making promises he doesn't have a hope in hell of keeping for all I know.' Even as she said it, she hoped she was wrong. She managed a wry smile. 'Before you ask, he did spend the night. And yes, we did have sex.'

Bella closed her eyes. Karen held her breath, fully expecting a dressing-down, but all her friend said was, 'You know what, it's up to you. It's easy for me to say dump him when it's not my problem. I was thinking about it the other night, all the tosspot blokes I've gone out with, hung on in there, put up with all kinds of shit, practically begging them to be with me even when it was obvious they were worse than useless.'

'Brian.' Karen took another sausage.

Bella opened the oven and checked the contents. The scent of rosemary wafted through the kitchen. 'No one could tell me anything where he was concerned. So, with that in mind, all I'll say is: be careful, and maybe think about what you might be telling me to do if it was my mess and not yours.'

'It's complicated,' she said, echoing what she'd said to Dave. 'All that history.' No one, not even Bella, knew about Amy.

'I get that. I know it's different when you're married. It's still no excuse for him walking all over you, though.' She got up and went to the fridge. 'Why do I bother putting the bottle away when I know we're going to finish it long before it loses its chill?'

Karen laughed. 'It's all part of the illusion that we're dainty drinkers, the kind who make a small glass of wine last all night, as opposed to the kind that can polish off a whole bottle without any help.' She glanced towards the recycling bag in the corner. 'Actually, I've been doing a bit much of that so now I'm staggering my empties, only putting a couple out at a time, just in case the press come back and start going through my rubbish. It wouldn't be the first time.'

Bella peered at the lamb bubbling away in the oven. 'So, what's happening? Are you having His Majesty back?'

'I don't know. It depends.' Karen sighed. 'You know what he's like. I haven't heard from him in days. He's meant to be ending things with You-know-who so we can give it another go, not that she'll give up without a fight.' She sloshed her wine around in her glass and her face took on an anguished look. 'To be honest, I don't know how I feel. It's hard to get things straight in my head any more.'

'Well, if you do take him back I hope it works out, really I do.'

Something in Bella's voice told Karen she didn't think there was the remotest chance it would.

Thirty-Nine

Jason woke up with a crick in his neck from sleeping on the sofa. Ever since those pictures had surfaced in the press Hannah refused to let him sleep with her. Not that he particularly wanted to, since she was barely speaking to him, but he was too old to doss on furniture night after night. He gazed around the flat, which belonged to a friend of his who let him rent it for next to nothing. The fact was, it was a bachelor pad: just the sofa he was sleeping on, a plasma TV taking up half the wall, and a Bose music system in the living room. Jason had liked it to begin with, feeling like he was dispensing with clutter, making a fresh start, a hot young chick on his arm. He sat up and rubbed his eyes. On the wall to his left was an Arsenal shirt, signed by the team and framed. That was the only thing that gave the place a bit of character. Otherwise, it was grey, black and white. No one in their right mind would consider bringing up a baby here, Hannah said. She was stamping her foot about wanting to move, find a place out in the suburbs, somewhere like Totteridge, wherever that was, with a garden. He happened to like Mayfair and, as for Hannah, all of a sudden the thought of building a future with her and the child she was about to give birth to was losing its shine.

He sat on the edge of the sofa in his Armani boxers and a

Ramones T-shirt with the sense that he was banged up, no way out, and only himself to blame. He rubbed his face. God Almighty, what a mess. In the kitchen Hannah clattered about, making a dreadful din, dropping cutlery into a drawer, putting plates away. He was surprised they had any crockery left the way she threw it around, and all to let him know she was in a foul mood. There was really no need. The fact that she had booted him out of the bedroom, walked through the living room without so much as a 'good morning' and made herself coffee (he had heard the kettle boiling) without offering him one, was a pretty good sign she was less than happy.

He sighed. All this was his fault, although in fairness it had never been part of his plan to get her pregnant just weeks into what Hannah called 'their relationship' and he had thought of as a fling.

In the beginning it had been a massive boost to his ego to be seen with a girl half his age. Karen had let herself go, he told himself, and the two of them were treading water. No wonder he had strayed. It was fun going to clubs, mixing with a young set, ditching his old wardrobe in favour of jeans that cost £200 by designers he had never heard of, and the kind of T-shirts that looked vintage even though they were brand new. He was getting his hair cut at a trendy place in Soho now, and using moisturizer. He had even been for his first facial and could have sworn it took ten years off him. That's what the girl in the salon said, anyway. Maybe he was kidding himself.

He got up and went to the bathroom. It was as stark as the rest of the flat: oversized white tiles on the walls and floor, a shower in a glass box, frosted-glass shelving covered in cleansers and serums and facial scrubs and heaven-knew-what, all in fancy pots that cost a fortune. Hannah was not one to scrimp on her beauty products. On the window ledge above the sink – an oblong contraption with the kind of odd, modern taps he hadn't been able to turn on to start with – were his things: a razor, shaving mirror, facial scrub and, in a manly black and silver pot, moisturizer. If he had to pack and get out in a hurry it wouldn't be difficult. Running along the wall opposite the shower was a mirror. He turned to face it. In the harsh spotlights sunk into the ceiling he looked every year of his age, and more. His skin was tired and grey and his eyes had a puffy look. He had never been bothered about the bags and the crow's feet – barely even noticed them – but now they depressed him. Perhaps he needed to see that surgeon everyone said was brilliant at eyes, ask around and find out what Louis Walsh had done to give himself such a fresh-faced look on *The X Factor*. Old Louis was looking pretty good.

Jason ran the cold tap and splashed water on his face, thoughts of the baby arriving and sleepless nights swirling around in his head. He had just been told his role in a long-running drama series as a brash, womanizing hospital consultant – a handful of episodes to start with – was being extended and he now had a precious twelve-month contract, which translated into early starts most days and late finishes. The thought of it, learning lines, being woken at all hours, made him feel ill. Hannah had made it clear she expected him to do his share of night feeds and nappy changes and he, rashly, had said of course, he would definitely pull his weight. That was months ago when they were getting on and the baby still seemed a long way off. Now it was real and he was under pressure with this role, the prospect of going back to Karen was more appealing than ever.

He glanced at himself in the mirror, one eye shut, hoping to create a more palatable reflection, water dripping off his chin on to the grey mat under his feet. It was no good. He looked just the same, only with a squint that made him look as if he had been in a fight.

In the narrow galley kitchen Hannah crashed mugs into a bowl of soapy water in the sink. Her bump made it awkward for her to reach the dishes, and it wasn't like her to do the washing-up by hand and risk a disaster with her acrylic nails, but he supposed the dishwasher was a bit too quiet for her liking when she was in a strop. Soap suds and water splashed against the tiles. He edged past her and clicked the kettle on to boil.

'Fancy a cuppa, babe?'

Crash. A mug landed on the draining board.

'I'll make some proper coffee, hot milk, if you like.'

'Please yourself.'

He bent to get a pan from the cupboard and brushed against her.

She flinched. 'Watch it, will you?'

'Hannah, can we just sit down and try and sort things out?'

She picked up a towel and dried her hands. 'No, we bloody well can't. You're the one who's made it like this, shagging your wife on the sly, so we'll talk when I'm good and ready.'

'Babe, I told you, I *didn't* shag her, honest. We were just talking. You do want me to sort things out, don't you – for us?'

She gave him a cold look, frowning at his crumpled

Ramones T-shirt. 'Don't you think you're a bit old to be wearing stuff like that?'

Karen screwed up the empty sweet wrapper and dropped it into the bin, where it joined a Pringles carton. She pulled a paper tissue from the sleeve of her top and arranged it over the rubbish so that nothing else was visible. On the dressing table was a huge vase of white roses. They had come that morning with a card that just said *Start again?* It was typed in a font that was meant to make you think it was handwritten. He must have ordered them online. They were beautiful, but she wished for once he would actually go to a florist, choose a card, and write something personal on it, like he used to. 'Start again?' Start *what* again?

She was determined not to put herself out for him. Why should she, with the way he was behaving? That was why she was in saggy velour tracksuit bottoms and a hooded top that didn't even match. Her hair was swept back, caught up in a simple band and trailing over one shoulder. She had no make-up on, just a smidgen of powder to take the shine off her nose. As she turned sideways to check her reflection in the full-length mirror she noticed her stomach was flat even though she wasn't wearing her trusty Spanx. Bella was right about her losing more weight, which was hardly surprising considering she was stressed to the eyeballs and just picking at food, not really eating any proper meals. Perhaps a full-time carer wasn't a bad idea after all.

Jason turned up right on time in a bobble hat and scruffy tracksuit, a rucksack slung over one shoulder, also looking like he'd made a conscious decision not to make an effort in case it got her hopes up. When she saw him she wished she had dressed to the nines just to make him feel bad. He stepped into the hall and she backed away, letting him know a kiss was definitely not on the agenda, then made him take off his shoes, a pair of smelly old trainers, and leave them on the mat just inside the door. Jason gave her a curious look. She could have sworn he was smirking as he padded along the hall behind her to the kitchen, his big toe poking through a hole in his sock. Something tugged at her. She would never have let him go out in socks that were dropping to bits.

She picked up the kettle. 'There's coffee, or would you rather have tea?' she said, in the kind of voice that made it clear either would be too much trouble.

Jason unzipped his rucksack and pulled out a bottle of wine wrapped in a shiny silver cooler. 'I brought this,' he said, putting it on the counter, digging into the bag again and producing a box of cheese twists and a tub of plump green olives stuffed with almonds. Karen put the kettle back on its base as he crossed to the draining board and dried the glasses she and Bella had used the night before. She watched him open the wine, pour it, stick the bottle in the fridge and move towards her.

Before she knew what was happening his arms were round her waist and he had her pinned against the corner unit. The marble edge of the worktop dug into her back as Jason's face bent towards hers, then stopped tantalizingly an inch or two away. She gazed at the familiar laughter lines around his eyes, the tiny scar on his forehead that no one else noticed any more, the flecks of grey in his hair. It was no good. She still loved him. Her arms went round his neck and she pulled him towards her, searching for his lips. Oh God, she was meant to be telling him what she thought of him, that enough was enough and he should go, leave her alone. Blah blah blah. Her tongue slid into his mouth and he moved his head back, stroking her face, eyes like mercury looking right inside her.

'Start again?' he said.

Forty

'You're going back to him, aren't you?' Cheryl, hands on hips, shot Faye a hostile look.

Faye ran a hand through her hair, exasperated. 'That's *not* what I said. And anyway, "*going back* to him" implies I *left* him in the first place, which I did *not*.'

'Only because he's never here, which means you can *play* at leaving, have your fun with me until Local Hero comes home, then run back and do your dutiful-wife thing.' She shuddered. 'Doesn't it bother you leading a double life?'

'It never seemed to bother *you* until now.'

They glared at each other. Cheryl crossed to the opposite side of the room and flopped on to the sofa, burying her head in her hands. 'I just want to know what's going on, where I stand.' Her voice was muffled.

Faye inched towards the other sofa and perched on the edge, a low table with a frosted-glass top and a giant wooden fruit bowl at one end separating her from her lover. The only sound came from the TV, where the *Loose Women* lot speculated on whether relationships could ever really get back on track after an affair.

Faye hugged herself, looking round the room at the quirky modern furniture, the lacquered floor a shade of purple so dark it looked black in a certain light. The sofa she was sitting on

– black leather on a tubular frame, based on some classic German design she had never heard of – squeaked indecently every time she moved.

It had been fun to start with, sneaking round to visit Cheryl, chilling out in a house that was a designer's dream, bang on trend and about a million miles away from her own place. Once she stepped through the door it was as if she became a different person, someone bolder and more interesting; the kind of woman who got it on with another woman, for a start. No wonder she had fallen for Cheryl, a brilliant sprinter, sassy and capable, who had only turned her hand to a bit of telly for fun, unlike Faye, who couldn't think of a single thing she would be able to do if she wasn't a presenter. Come to think of it, she wasn't much good at that either, always shunted to the end of the *Girl Talk* desk, last into the studio at the start of the show, not even in her seat before the applause had died away. Cheryl was always getting offers to do other things: a guest slot on some sporting show or other, a celebrity column in one of the magazines, *Strictly Come Dancing*. She had just been offered a plum job helping London prepare for the 2012 Games, *and* a lucrative deal to be the face of a health drink. She was a good presenter too, a natural, and had proved versatile doing all those extra interviews and mini-location features. Faye, meanwhile, trailed along behind her, struggling to get a word in edgeways on *Girl Talk*, Julia butting in, talking over her the whole time.

Then there was Mike, award-winning war correspondent and part-time poster boy, soon to present a Children of Courage award. Where would it end – and why wasn't *she* ever asked to do the odd extra bit of something here and there? The hot topic was Helen England's decision to leave *Good Morning Britain*, everyone speculating about who would take over, yet not a single person had even hinted Faye was in the running. She clenched her fists. In Mike's email that morning he had said he was up for the next Comic Relief Kilimanjaro trek, and knowing his luck he'd be sharing a tent with Robbie Williams or Ricky Gervais; as if his profile wasn't high enough as it was. Rumour was Cheryl Cole had been approached to do it again, which made Faye want to weep. It was about time she worked out why she kept hooking up with people who were so much more successful than her. It was a pattern, and a worrying one.

Cheryl emerged from behind her hands. 'I thought you were happy. I thought *we* were happy. You've been funny with me ever since that last night Mike was home.' She gave Faye a searching look. 'Are you sure nothing happened between you?'

Faye looked away. 'Of course I'm sure. How many times do I have to tell you?'

'Look me in the eyes and tell me you didn't have sex with him.'

Faye flushed. 'I hate it when you do this, get all heavy-handed, acting like you own me.'

'I'm just trying to get a straight answer.'

'And you think if you nag the life out of me I'll own up to something I haven't done?' Faye wished she had just gone home after Pilates now instead of stopping at the deli and picking up smoked salmon and a punnet of raspberries as a peace offering. She would never have guessed Cheryl was the paranoid possessive type. Then again, she had good reason. Despite what she had told her, Faye *had* slept with Mike and the sex had been brilliant. In fact, being back between the sheets with her husband had made her wonder if she really was in love with Cheryl after all. Maybe it was just the sense of danger, the novelty of forbidden fruit. There was no doubt Cheryl knew how to turn her on, but then again so did Mike. They had hardly got any sleep that night. Something about him heading off to a war zone, never quite sure when he would be back, gave their love-making an added intensity. OK, her marriage was far from ideal, but that didn't mean it was a total write-off either.

She glanced at Cheryl, who had the TV remote in her hand and was channel-hopping. Judge Judy, gavel in hand, filled the screen for a fraction of a second followed by Dr Phil talking to a tearful Sharon Osbourne.

What Faye needed to do was shift things with Cheryl on to a more casual footing, because the truth was she was not willing to ditch Mike and come out. The very thought of it made her stomach churn.

It was rare that Lesley was at a loss for words, but this was one of those occasions. Dan Kincaid had just made a suggestion that sent shockwaves through her entire body. She gripped the stem of her glass. 'Say that again.'

He rested his fork on the side of his plate. 'I asked if you'd be my date at an opening at a gallery in town.'

Lesley frowned. She didn't really go on dates. She went on the pull. What did he think they were – a couple? She glanced around the restaurant, just a few tables occupied, Nico the maître d' over by the door taking someone's coat, the waiter vanishing through the swing door of the kitchen, thankfully no one within earshot. She had her reputation to consider.

It was the second time she had been back to Al Dente since Dean Craig had taken her, for spite as she had thought at the time. Of course, as always, he just had her best interests at heart. Thank God she had him, otherwise the chances were she would have ended up in a gutter somewhere a long time ago.

To her amazement Al Dente had actually grown on her, mainly because, as Dean had said, it served the best ravioli she had ever tasted, and was well and truly off the map as far as the paparazzi were concerned. While Lesley liked being photographed as much as the next celeb, there were times when she just wanted a bite to eat in peace and Al Dente was ideal. Nico fussed over her, produced a complimentary Kir Royale the moment she stepped through the door, and gave her the best table. It was hugely liberating to be able to take off the Gucci shades with no fear a paparazzo would pop up, snapping away, determined to get the most unflattering shot he could. When Dan had called and put her on the spot, suggesting they meet for lunch at the Wolseley, she had panicked, knowing someone would spot them, put two and two together. The last thing she wanted was to have the gossip columns saying they were dating. It would make it much harder for her to go out and pull other men for casual sex. So she'd told him to meet her in Victoria instead. He seemed puzzled but did as he was told.

'Isn't there anyone else you could take on your *date*?'

Dan gave her one of his dazzling smiles. 'Of course, any number of people. They're queuing up.' He leaned back in his chair, his face suddenly serious. 'That's not a joke, by the way. I do have several hotties in a holding position but it just so happens I'd rather take you.'

Lesley swallowed. By unspoken agreement, she and Dan had arrived at an arrangement that suited both of them, with lots of wild no-strings sex as and when they felt like it. Beyond that they didn't really spend any time together. In fact this was the first time they had met like this, which was odd. Lesley had wondered if 'lunch' was a euphemism for something else.

Usually when they got together during the day it was for a quickie.

She trailed a piece of ravioli through the buttery sauce and popped it in her mouth. Dan sipped at his wine, not taking his eyes off her for a second. He was definitely up to something and it was making her nervous. Resting her fork on the side of her plate, she hoisted her bag on to her knee and felt about for her lip gloss. Dan watched, intrigued, as she applied a fresh coat of Tempting Touch. She picked up her wine, the lip gloss leaving a waxy pink bow on the rim of the glass. He was still looking at her. She scrabbled about in her bag and produced a mirror, studying her reflection, keen to know what it was that had caught his eye. Nothing, as far as she could tell. She snapped the compact shut. 'What's so funny?'

He smiled. 'You are – doing your lippy when you're only halfway through your pasta.'

'What's wrong with that?'

'Nothing. It's just – how can I put it? – unusual.'

'I don't feel dressed if my lips are bare.'

He gave her an odd little look, as if her lip-gloss addiction was somehow charming and cute and irresistible. 'You know, you're a funny girl.'

Lesley almost blushed. It was a long time since anyone had called her a girl.

Julia gazed at the gossip magazines spread out on the table in front of her. Lesley, in those idiotic sunglasses, the ones that made her look like something out of *The Fly*, gazed back from almost every cover. According to the magazines, 'industry insiders' had revealed Lesley was being tipped for the *Good Morning Britain* job. Julia could not fathom it. How could an addled old alcoholic in a semi-permanent stupor be a contender for a plum presenting job? She studied Lesley's bee-stung pout and wondered if she'd had some work. Lesley claimed she wasn't into cosmetic procedures and Julia suspected no surgeon would go near her, not with all that booze in her system. Her lips did seem suspiciously plump, though. Maybe it was just the angle and all that lip gloss. Julia felt a stab of envy. There was no way Lesley could step into Helen England's shoes, which made it all the more galling that *heat* and *Grazia* seemed to think she just might. For one thing she was incapable of *anything* in the morning – everyone knew that – and for another she was hardly woman-of-the-people material. Then again, Julia, known mainly for her acid tongue, might not exactly fit the bill there either, but she could work on it, cultivate a more caring image.

She checked her BlackBerry. No missed calls, no email from James Almond. She had been trying to get a meeting with him for ages, requested lunch, put in an embarrassing number of calls to ask if she could swing by for a chat, nothing major, twenty minutes max would do. He never got back to her and Anne, that snooty assistant of his, just gave her the same brush-off every time, said she would see what was possible bearing in mind his full diary. Julia had even turned up at his office on some pretext, thinking she would catch Anne off-guard and worm her way in. It was no use. Anne, not in the least bit ruffled by Julia appearing out of nowhere, simply turned her away. The door to the controller's office was shut tight but Julia was sure it was Helen England's bouncy auburn bob she could see through a gap in the blinds. Anne had promised to get back to her. That was more than a week ago.

Julia had no idea why James wouldn't see her. She was pretty sure Karen had already been summoned and according to the grapevine he had also asked to see Lesley. It could just be he was letting them down gently, of course. That was possible. One of the magazines had unflattering shots of Karen, Julia and Lesley on its front cover with a lurid headline that claimed a catfight had broken out among the *Girl Talk* presenters, all vying for Helen England's job. Other likely candidates included Fiona Phillips and Myleene Klass, apparently. Cheryl was also in with a chance, it seemed, although Faye didn't even rate a mention. Julia wasn't in the least bit surprised about that.

It drove her round the bend the way she was being blamed for everyone falling out at *Girl Talk*. Anyone would think she was some kind of monster. A 'source close to the women' claimed the production meetings were glacial these days and that off-air they all avoided each other. One so-called 'insider' said the atmosphere behind the scenes was atrocious and that Karen King was on the verge of cracking up thanks to Julia's relentless bullying. She wanted to know who the sneak was that was leaking all this stuff, plotting against her. Well, let them get on with it. It would take a lot more than a few made-up stories to give Julia Hill sleepless nights.

She had woken early, gone straight downstairs and pounded the treadmill for an hour, and now she had time to kill before the car came to take her to the studios.

She drummed her nails on the surface of the table and scrolled through the contacts in her phone, wondering if there was anyone she could arrange a last-minute lunch with. It struck her that there was just one person she was remotely close to and that was Joel Reynolds, although it was hardly a friend-ship. The only reason he dropped everything and took her calls was because she had something on him. She scrolled on through entries for colonic irrigation, dentist, hair stylist, masseur, nail technician, and that amazing girl at the Urban Retreat spa who did her eyebrows. There was no ex still in love with her and good for the odd date when she was desperate, no one she was in touch with from her schooldays, not a single person who had known her before her career took off. Then again, the whole idea of reinventing herself was to cut all ties with her past so she could hardly complain about it now.

She gazed around the room, with its turquoise walls a couple of shades darker than her eyes, and bold Hockney prints featuring Californian swimming pools. A shoal of ceramic fish in neon pink and green swam towards the ceiling and a pinboard, covered with backstage Polaroid snaps of Julia with celebs on various shows, hung on the back of the door. Her favourite was the shot of her and Joan Collins, side by side, having their make-up done before Joan appeared on *Girl Talk*.

One wall was taken up with shelves filled with back issues of *heat* and a row of celebrity autobiographies. There were expensive hardbacks on health and beauty by Liz Earle, Josephine Fairley, Gillian McKeith, Dr Murad and Leslie Kenton, and a well-thumbed make-up manual by Jemma Kidd. In pride of place was Julia's collection of books on cosmetic surgery: *Plastic Fantastic*, *Plastic Makes Perfect*, *Cosmetic Surgery for Dummies*, plus several box files stuffed with press articles on the latest procedures. Tucked away on the bottom shelf were her guilty pleasures, in the form of real-life crime stories about the Yorkshire Ripper, Dr Shipman, the Black Panther, Fred and Rosemary West, plus a signed Andy McNab box set.

Julia got up from the desk and went to sit in an oversized, bright-pink wingback chair in the corner of the room. She picked up the remote and put the TV on. There was Helen England, giggling, wafting her script over her face as if she was having a hot flush. It only seemed like five minutes since the woman had given birth. Shouldn't she be at home changing nappies or something? Simon Cowell, naked, a towel draped over his rude bits while a beauty therapist pressed strips of wax to his hairy chest, appeared on screen. Julia leaned forward in her chair. Surely not. Perhaps it was a charity thing; Simon doing his bit for Comic Relief. There had been tons of stuff in the papers showing him leaving the *X Factor* studios, shirt unbuttoned, the once hirsute chest now smooth, the backs of his hands miraculously hair-free. The *Daily Mail* had speculated on how much he forked out in a year to keep himself groomed and come up with a figure of £24,700, which included teeth-whitening, Botox and waxing. It didn't strike Julia as over the top, bearing in mind he was a multi-multi-millionaire and presumably had money to burn. A sequence of stills of Simon, his face contorted with pain, flashed before her. No, hang on, it wasn't Cowell, just a very convincing lookalike, having an all-over Brazilian by the look of things. Very good. Almost had her fooled.

Helen England wiped tears of laughter from her eyes. Julia couldn't bear her, all that chuckling and simpering and pretend crying. The woman was an utter fake. She hit the mute button. The thought of Karen King doing that job or, God forbid, Lesley Gold, made Julia want to hurl the remote at the screen.

She needed to get to James Almond. *Urgently*. She would wage a full-scale charm offensive, leave him in no doubt that she was the best candidate for the job. She gazed at the BlackBerry again, checked to make sure she had a signal, and began composing an email.

Forty-One

James Almond was out of the office for the afternoon, meeting with an independent production company to discuss a proposal for a new reality show. At least that's what it said in his diary. Anne had booked a black cab to take him to an address in Dean Street, in the heart of Soho, but he gave the driver new instructions. Soon they were heading away from the West End, along the Embankment towards Chelsea, the cabbie moaning about the traffic, saying you need the patience of a saint to drive in London these days, Oxford Street's diabolical, tailbacks all the way, stop-start end to end. And as for the fancy new pedestrian crossing at Oxford Circus ... well, that snarled things up good and proper for weeks – and for what? All to make life easier for the hordes dawdling about doing their shopping. What about the motorists? That's what he wanted to know. It was hardly worth having a car any more, the amount it cost to park, traffic wardens taking pictures and slapping you with a ticket the second you go over your time. The cabbie rambled on until James interrupted and asked to be dropped off outside a bar just round the corner from the King's Road. Once the car pulled away he nipped back along Camera Place and stepped through a revolving door into an imposing red-brick mansion block.

A vase filled with white gladioli stood on a solid mahogany

table against the wall facing the entrance. Above it was a large mirror in an ornate gilt frame. James saw himself reflected in the glass as he emerged from the revolving door, coat undone, briefcase in one hand, phone in the other, and crossed the marbled floor. A frail old woman in sheepskin bootees and a camel coat that was much too big for her struggled to restrain a small black poodle that lunged at James, tail wagging. He dodged the dog and made for the staircase at the end of the lobby, racing up to the third floor, pausing to get his breath back before strolling to the end of the corridor, where he rang the bell of apartment 303. There was the sound of a chain being undone and the door opened. He took a long, lascivious look at the woman facing him, taking in the ludicrously short see-through nurse's outfit that clung to her magnificent breasts. He stepped inside and dropped his briefcase, kicking out to slam the door shut behind him.

Helen England, in black stockings held up by a frilly garter with a red cross that matched the one on the front of her nurse's hat, and shiny white high heels with a Perspex platform at least an inch thick, slowly started to unbutton her uniform.

'Have you been a good boy?' she asked sternly. James, practically in a trance, not for a second taking his eyes off the breasts, now bobbing tantalizingly in front of his face, said, 'I've been very good, I promise.'

Helen fastened his mouth to her breast. 'Let Mummy give you some milk then.'

Forty-Two

Karen couldn't help thinking she would be better off telling Jason she wouldn't sleep with him until everything was sorted with Hannah, instead of falling into bed with him whenever he showed his face. It was sending out the wrong signal, making him think it was OK to cheat on her, rub her nose in it, then come back once the thrill of a younger, cheaper model had worn off. What if he was playing games with her and had no intention of leaving The Slut? She lay on her back, hands behind her head, picking out the glow-in-the-dark stars she had stuck to the bedroom ceiling after Jason had moved out. A couple of days later she had decided stick-on stars were a bit childish, but by then they were stuck fast and she hadn't been able to peel them off. They would probably be there forever now. She moved on to her side and buried her head in Jason's pillow, breathing in his scent. As long as she had known him he had used the same distinctive black soap. She would know it anywhere.

The bedroom door opened and he appeared, bare-chested in his boxers, carrying mugs of tea. He was still in good shape, with his broad shoulders, strong arms and narrow hips. He didn't exactly have a six-pack – which Karen thought was a sign of vanity anyway – but his stomach was nice and flat. Not even a hint of a paunch. His face looked tired, though, and there were telltale bags under his eyes.

He got back into bed and lay on his side, his face close to Karen's. 'You can't keep doing this, coming here, having sex with me, then going back to her. It's not fair. I need to know where I stand, where all this is leading.'

He sighed. 'I know. It's the baby. I can't just abandon her without trying to make things right first. If I can sort things out properly, keep the split as amicable as possible, stay on good terms, well, it's going to help us in the long run.'

Karen gazed at him. It was just like Jason to think he could somehow make everything all right. Granted, turning on the charm had got him out of plenty of scrapes in his life, but there had never been anything on this scale. Right now he was in it up to his neck. It was obvious he hadn't the faintest idea just how big the fallout from dumping Hannah was going to be. It was a mess of epic proportions, even by Jason's standards. The idea of that scheming little slut being reasonable – *amicable* indeed – made Karen want to laugh, in a grim, hollow kind of way. She could see her now, ranting and raving, throwing things, once it sank in that he was actually leaving.

That's if he really was leaving. Something stabbed at her insides and made her stomach lurch. She knew that feeling well: pure, undiluted fear. Hadn't he broken her heart once? She wasn't a betting woman, just the odd flutter once a year on the Grand National, but even she knew the odds of him doing it again were stacked against her. She swallowed. Her mouth was dry. She wanted to drink some of the tea Jason had brought her but the way he was holding her made it tricky to move.

He kissed the tip of her nose. 'What are you thinking about?'

This was her chance to spell it out, own up to feeling horribly insecure, afraid he was playing with her. Tell him what really scared her was that once Hannah had the baby – *his* baby – he would go running back. It had taken Karen months to pick up the pieces after he left, slowly putting herself back together again bit by bit. If she was honest, she wasn't even sure she was over the hurt yet, not completely, and Jason coming in and out of her life like this wasn't helping. There was no way she could go through all that heartache again. She stroked his face, feeling scratchy stubble on his cheek. He was smiling, a hopeful, tender smile that made her want to cry. She buried her face in his chest. 'I just want to be happy.'

'We will be happy – we *are* happy. Aren't we?' He wrapped his arms around her. 'I know none of this is easy. It's about the biggest fuck-up it could be and it's my fault.' He kissed the top of her head. 'That's why I have to put things right, and I will. Trust me. You do trust me, don't you?'

Did she? 'I just don't think you have the foggiest what it's going to be like getting away from her, malicious little cow that she is. Seriously, if you think she'll give up without a fight you're kidding yourself. She's on to a good thing with you and there's no way she'll just sit back and let you walk out, especially once she knows you're coming back here. She is going to make so much trouble. Trust *me*.'

Hannah stood in the kitchen, eating praline and chocolate ice cream straight from the tub. Funny, she didn't even have a sweet tooth before she got pregnant and, in any case, constantly counting calories meant the most indulgent she ever got was fat-free frozen yoghurt, and even that was a rarity. In the last few months, as her bump had grown, she had begun craving all the sugary, fatty things she would never have gone near in her old pre-baby life. She just hoped her taste buds would go back to normal once she gave birth. She would never get her figure back if she was stuffing her face with crap all the time. She had actually got up in the middle of the night and eaten a whole carton of cold custard, a large one. Heaven help her if the press went through her rubbish. It was full of the kind of stuff fatties eat. Still, she was eating for two and her hormones were all over the place, not helped by Jason running off to that whale of a wife of his. Not that Karen was a whale any more. In fact, Hannah was the one waddling about, while Karen seemed to be getting skinnier by the day. She had seen a shoot in *Fabulous* magazine at the weekend, Karen in a Ralph & Russo dress of all things, the journalist simpering on about how radiant and gorgeous she looked. Well, all Hannah had to say was she had either been airbrushed or was wearing very good underwear. Or both. There was no way Karen King *unaided* could carry off the body-con look.

Hannah hated being big. She had invested in a good maternity wardrobe and even with a massive bump she managed to look good, but the truth was she couldn't wait to get back to her usual size 6. Not that she admitted as much. In every interview she gave she cooed about the joy of carrying Jason's baby, how she was thrilled to be giving him the son he had always wanted, hoping Karen was reading, twisting the knife and loving it. She had stripped off and done Demi Moore-style shoots and the pictures kept popping up all over the place. The *Sun* had even used one on page three.

She loaded her spoon with ice cream. She had kept her cravings to herself as well, claimed she was lucky because her body only wanted good things like berries and watercress. Her biggest sin, she said, was a weakness for avocados but she made it a rule never to have more than two a week. It was all rubbish. If the chocolate-digestive wrappers and Häagen-Dazs cartons in her wheelie bin ever came to light ... She should put stuff through the shredder really, just to be safe, but she couldn't be bothered and anyway, there was nothing she could do about the ice cream cartons. They were meant to go in the recycling bag but she double-bagged them and dumped them in the bin where they couldn't be seen. The second this baby was born she would get the best personal trainer Jason's money could buy and start working out. She wanted to see her body snap back into shape – *ping!* – and if it took too long to shift the fat she would pay for liposuction. Correction – Jason would pay for liposuction. OK, it was cheating, but she wouldn't be the first. She had already done a 'How I Got My Figure Back' deal with *OK!* so she couldn't afford to mess about.

She put the ice cream back in the freezer and went into the bedroom where the wardrobe was open and Jason's clothes lay in a pile on the bed. He really should know better than to mess with her. What did he think she would do – put up with it? Allow him to walk all over her? Humiliate her in the press? Not in a million years. He had actually had the nerve to come home with Karen's scent all over him. Hannah recognized it – she used to have a sneaky spray in the days when she was first seeing Jason and they had sex in the bed he shared with his wife. She closed one of the wardrobe doors and checked out her reflection in the full-length mirror. Even her face looked fat, God help her. Where the hell were her cheekbones? Well, she wasn't going to worry about them. Right now she had other things on her mind. She went to the window and peeped through the blinds. The paparazzi were already gathering, leaning on the railings, smoking, drinking coffee. Good.

It was *Coronation Street* that had given her the idea, the

episode where Liz McDonald got her own back on her ex, Lloyd, after he kept bringing his new piece into the Rovers, winding her up. Liz did what any self-respecting woman would do and hit him where it hurt, chucking his precious record collection on to the cobbles. No mercy. His face was a picture. Hannah would give it another half-hour then Jason's collection of one-off designer T-shirts would start heading for the pavement two floors below. She sat on the bed and picked up the scissors. She would cut them up first, naturally.

She picked up the one with the song lyrics on the front and a hand-written message from Paul Rodgers, some ageing rocker Jason seemed to worship, on the back. She was well aware it was unique, irreplaceable. Jason went on and on about it, saying one of these days he would have it framed, keep it pristine forever. She felt a twinge of something – guilt? – as she began to hack at it. Next was the Iggy Pop one she had bought him for his birthday, although strictly speaking he had bought it, since everything went on his credit cards. She wavered. Since she was emotionally attached to this one maybe she could keep it. No, that would just be a sign of weakness.

She began slashing away, making a jagged cut up the front from hem to neck. Gradually she worked her way through the pile, getting into a rhythm, starting to enjoy herself. It was actually quite therapeutic. She used to think women who trashed their blokes' clothes were bunny boilers but now she could see why they did it. Of course she had the added thrill of knowing the press would be snapping away as she chucked them out of the window. By the time Jason turned up all his stuff would be strewn around Grosvenor Square. Well, that was his lookout.

She spent a minute or two psyching herself up, smudging her mascara, creating a messy tear track on each cheek, putting on an expression of abject misery, then drew the sash window open, leaned out, gave the paparazzi a chance to start snapping away, and hurled an armful of her lover's clothes into the street.

Forty-Three

It was late afternoon when Lesley emerged from Dan Kincaid's flat on the ground floor of a substantial, white-painted Edwardian terrace just off the Fulham Road and two minutes' walk from Gordon Ramsay's restaurant, Aubergine. They had been there for dinner the night before, Dan's treat, and the food was sublime. They had even been papped as they left and she hadn't minded in the least. Barely a week since Dan had badgered her into being his date at the gallery opening, Lesley had done a complete about-turn and was now practically living with him.

It was extraordinary, and yet she was able to pinpoint the precise moment her feelings had changed. It was when Dan had said, 'You're a funny girl' that did it. The words, and the way he looked at her when he spoke them, had caused the defence mechanism she relied on to keep men at a safe emotional distance to falter. For years it had worked perfectly until Dan and his heart-melting ways sparked a breakdown.

As she descended a flight of tiled steps to the street where a silver Mercedes, engine running, waited to take her to the studio, she searched in her bag for her lip gloss. Damn, she must have left it in the bathroom. Mouthing at the driver to give her a minute she hurried back to the front door with its matt-grey finish and stained-glass panels, past the ornately trimmed miniature privets in zinc planters on each step.

Although Dan had left hours ago for a shoot across town in Bermondsey, she had her own keys and as she let herself in, punching a code into a keypad that stopped the alarm in its tracks, a warm sense of belonging went through her. She could hardly believe she and Dan were an item and that she actually preferred being with him to prowling the bars and clubs around Greek Street for no-strings sex. To her astonishment, sex *with* strings was a lot more fun than she had supposed. She nipped into the bathroom, noting with satisfaction her face paraphernalia cluttering up the windowsill, the racy red slip hanging from the back of the door. As she grabbed the lip gloss from the edge of the sink and went to slick on a fresh layer she was seized by a childish desire to let Dan know how she felt. Before she could stop herself she was using the wand from her favourite pillarbox-red lippy to draw a heart with an arrow through it on the bathroom mirror. She put *L* at the pointy bit of the arrow and *D* at the other end. Then, before she could change her mind, she reset the alarm and locked up.

As the car moved away along Limerston Street, Lesley leaned against the cool leather upholstery and glanced out of the window at a mansion block where a man in a white boiler suit was polishing a brass nameplate. Coming out of the entrance and bathed in light from lamps blazing overhead was none other than James Almond, looking flushed and dishevelled and, well, as if he had just engaged in hot and sweaty sex. Lesley knew the signs only too well.

She sank low in the seat as James, phone pressed to the side of his head, scanned the street, waving at a black cab that sailed straight past. Lesley was sure he lived out of town. In which case, what was he doing? Or more to the point, *who* was he doing? She smiled to herself. He had always struck her as much too proper and stuffy to fool around, but maybe it was all an act. She waited until her driver turned into Chelsea Park Gardens, then said, 'Ian, you don't happen to know the name of that road we just came along, after we passed the bar with the tables outside?'

'It's Camera Place,' he replied. 'We pick up from there. Helen England's got a flat in the mansion block on the corner.'

Lesley smiled but kept her voice casual. 'I thought she lived in the sticks, in Buckinghamshire or somewhere.'

He shook his head. 'Not during the week. She stays in town at least a couple of nights. Reckons it's a lot more handy.'

I bet she does, Lesley thought.

Forty-Four

Having your private life splashed all over the press went with the territory of being on television almost every night of the week. Julia knew the score. The celebrity magazines were insatiable, pouncing on the slightest whiff of scandal and drawing conclusions that may or may not have been true. It was hard to tell; they always sounded convincing, but who were these anonymous sources and so-called 'friends' who seemed to know all the ins and outs of other people's lives? Julia knew it was in the interests of every celebrity to make sure the magazines had a constant supply of gossip, which was why she employed a publicist. Not just any old publicist either – *the* publicist. Tom Steiner was one of the most powerful men in the media, tirelessly drip-feeding juicy titbits and exclusives to every publication with an interest in *Girl Talk*, making sure Julia got her fair share of covers and features. More to the point, every story that ran was approved by him. Tom was expensive but, as far as Julia was concerned, he was worth every penny.

She was as vain as the next celebrity and loved all the press attention, good and bad, but at the same time she was also paranoid about anyone digging too deep. There was so much of her past that could never come out. Ever. If people knew the truth ... well, it didn't bear thinking about. She would be destroyed. Still, she had done a pretty good job of reinventing herself and making sure her old self was dead and buried. It was Tom Steiner's job, aided by a biography that was only loosely based on fact for the last twenty-five years of her life, to keep things that way.

Julia hadn't always been a glamorous, high-profile presenter and she would rather die than disclose certain things. She had seen other celebrities ruined for a lot less. Look at Lesley. If she'd had Tom Steiner on board it would have been a different story. He knew exactly what he was doing, placed the odd negative piece, kept the press onside and, more importantly, made sure nothing about any of his clients ended up in print without his say-so. The editors knew the value of a Tom Steiner tip-off and went out of their way to stay in his good books. If he put his foot down about something they almost always backed off.

Requests for interviews with Julia were usually filtered through Tom but the *Sunday* made a direct approach. The email from Laura Lloyd, one of their top features and investigative writers, said the paper wanted to run a profile piece with pictures and would Julia be interested?

Julia was flattered to be propositioned by what she regarded as a serious newspaper. As it happened, she had the *Sunday* delivered, and liked the idea of being the subject of one of their in-depth pieces. Laura Lloyd had been upfront: *Girl Talk* would not usually appeal to their readers but all the speculation about the *Good Morning Britain* job had changed things. Laura felt Julia would have more to say than her co-presenters – offer some intelligent comment on the changing face of broadcasting and the role of the older woman on television, perhaps. Julia was cock-a-hoop. She loved the idea of the others slugging it out on the cover of some tatty magazine while she got a double-page spread in a decent Sunday newspaper. She had run it past

Tom, who felt that on balance it was a good thing and might just give her the edge over the other women in the race for Helen England's job, although he warned her there would be no copy approval. The first she would see of the story was once it was in the paper. He advised her to watch her step.

'Laura Lloyd is a tough cookie, razor-sharp as well. Just make sure she doesn't trip you up,' he said.

Julia had laughed. The idea of some hack getting the better of her was ludicrous. And anyway, it wasn't that kind of interview. Laura wasn't out to dig dirt on Julia; she was after the real story of what was going on behind the scenes at *Girl Talk*. She had even been along to one of the studio recordings and picked up on what seemed to be a chilly atmosphere between the five women. Of course, that was just her take on things, she said. Julia was the one in the know and Laura was keen to hear what she had to say. If there was anything she wanted to tell her off the record that was absolutely fine; she would simply attribute it to a 'show insider'.

Laura had suggested lunch at The Ivy, which suited Julia because it meant she would probably be photographed on her way in. She was determined to look her best and made an unscheduled visit to Joel in Harley Street the day before to top up the Botox and inject more filler into her lips. There had been something different about him which she couldn't quite put her finger on. He was – how could she put it? – *jaunty*, almost, humming to himself as he bent over her with the hypodermic. She wondered if he was on happy pills, but when she asked how come he was so full of the joys he had just given her a mysterious little smile. At that precise moment his nurse had stepped into the room and Julia could have sworn the two of them exchanged a soppy look. So he *was* knocking off the nurse.

How original. He had put down the syringe and crossed to the other side of the room, gone into a huddle with her, the two of them whispering about something. 'I haven't got all day, you know,' Julia had snapped.

That dim nurse of his had actually offered to massage her feet while she was having her jabs. Needless to say she told her where to go in no uncertain terms. It just so happened she was sensitive about her feet, which she considered way too big. She had bunions too, thanks to wearing high heels constantly. Yes, if Julia had an Achilles heel – no pun intended – it was her feet, horrible great ugly things. She glowered at Joel when he said she should really give it a go, that reflexology was a fantastic complementary therapy and did wonders for stress and anxiety.

'The only thing that's making me stressed is you paying more attention to my fucking feet than my face. Now will you just *get on with it*, for pity's sake!'

Joel had given a nonchalant shrug and carried on jabbing at her forehead. 'I'm going to put a little more around the eyes,' he said, 'just to keep that area nice and smooth.' He peered at her and she noticed two vertical frown lines in the centre of his brow. One of the leading cosmetic surgeons in the country and he didn't even have the sense to Botox himself. She despaired. 'I wasn't expecting to see you for another couple of weeks,' he said. 'Have you got something special on?'

'As it happens, yes.' Not that her lunch with Laura Lloyd was any of his business. As long as he kept her face in perfect, line-free shape, plumped up in all the right places, she didn't give a toss what he thought. She watched him working, a picture of concentration. Actually, he seemed to be lost in his own thoughts, a faint smile on his lips, still humming some ghastly tune, one of those catchy pop songs. It would be going round in her head for the rest of the day now.

'Joel,' she said. He straightened up. 'That song, what is it?'

'Oh, it's the new Westlife single. Now, what's it called . . . ? I've actually got the CD here if you're interested.'

'No I am NOT fucking interested. You are driving me mad, as it happens, bloody great racket in my ear when I'm trying to relax, so unless you know "The Sound of Silence" I suggest you just zip it.'

She chose a fitted black dress embellished with studs for the lunch. She decided on a biker jacket in soft grey leather and a pair of silver mirrored ankle boots she hadn't worn before, pacing about the bedroom, making sure she could walk in them. The last thing she wanted was to go flying on the pavement outside The Ivy. The press would love that. She sat at her dressing table and checked her make-up, applying a generous slew of vermilion lip gloss, and then peered at her reflection, satisfied. She looked every inch the top TV personality with attitude. It was vital to look the part because Laura Lloyd would no doubt write something about what she was wearing. That's why she had cleverly combined a dress from the high street with a pair of head-turning designer boots that had cost the best part of a thousand pounds. Journalists liked that kind of thing. Laura was bound to ask if Julia had a stylist and she would take great pleasure in saying no, she did everything herself.

She ran a hand through her hair, teasing it into jagged spikes. She definitely had a look of Sharon Stone, although the last pictures she had seen of the actress – in some hideous lacy dress and a trilby hat – did nothing for her. Whoever got her ready should have been taken out and shot.

A horn sounded outside. She stood up and slung her shiny red Hermès bag over her shoulder and checked her reflection in the full-length mirror. Her eyes went straight to the silver boots, which sparkled at her. Suddenly she wasn't sure about them. Maybe they were a bit much for lunch, on top of which they seemed to make her feet look enormous. Perhaps she should wear a pair of simple black court shoes instead. The horn sounded again. No, no time to change. She took a breath and hurried out.

Forty-Five

Laura Lloyd arrived at The Ivy half an hour early. She wanted to make sure they'd given her a suitable table, positioned so that Julia could preen and be on show, and at the same time with enough privacy for them to have a discreet chat. Not that Laura had the slightest interest in what Julia had to say about *Girl Talk* or whether the women were on speaking terms. Who cared about that? It was much too downmarket for her readers. All that was just a pretext for seeing Julia at close quarters, reeling her in with the promise of a prominent feature in a newspaper that was definitely a cut above the kind of publications she usually popped up in. What Laura really wanted was to steer the conversation gently round to encouraging new talent in TV and how experienced women like Julia were such fantastic role models. From there she would ask about Julia's first major presenting job and what had led her into telly in the first place. She would say her family must be proud, see if that got a reaction, and that Julia must be quite a poster girl in her home town of . . . where was it?

Laura smiled. She would let Julia rattle on, spout as many lies as she wanted, knowing the real story all along. Those were the quotes she wanted. The ones that would make her look even more foolish once Laura exposed the real Julia Hill.

Laura was in no hurry with this piece. She had all her

sources sewn up and knew no one else was sniffing round, since the rest of the world had bought Julia's lies, swallowed the fake biography and meekly towed Tom Steiner's line.

She sipped at her water and checked her watch. It was 12.15 and Julia was due at 12.30, not that she would arrive on time. In Laura's experience celebs never did, always came rushing in ten minutes late in a tizz about some 'crisis' or other. It was as if they were genetically programmed to make a big entrance – not that anyone would notice in The Ivy, where they had seen it all a million times before. In any case, Mickey Rourke had just swaggered in, hair mussed up, film-star shades, predatory smile, a killer blonde on his arm. Laura could have sworn he had his T-shirt on inside-out. Right now all eyes in the room were on him. Julia would have to pull something spectacular out of the bag if she wanted to upstage Mickey.

It was almost a week since Laura had arrived on the doorstep of Julia's mother's house in Bradford. The house was a modest stone-built back-to-back, originally intended for workers at the nearby mill. At one end of the road shirts, vests and baggy Y-fronts hung from a washing line strung across the street. Laura felt she was in some kind of strange time warp. She had stepped straight off the narrow pavement into the neat front room of number 42 and perched on the edge of a maroon sofa strewn with crocheted cushions. The arms of the sofa and the two matching chairs either side of the fireplace were draped with cream embroidered slip-covers. Facing her was a tiled fireplace where a two-bar electric fire glowed orange. Beside it in the hearth was a redundant copper coal bucket and an ornate stand from which hung tongs and a miniature dustpan and brush.

The tiny room was stifling. A big wooden clock and rows of brown bottles with typed labels containing prescription drugs dominated the mantelpiece. Against the wall, facing the window, where a greying net curtain blocked out the street, was a china cabinet filled with mugs and figurines and commemorative plates. A wall unit held bills and books and a few framed photos. An angelic little girl with blonde curls, aged about three, in a pink and white sundress, featured in one. There was a recent picture, big and glossy with a white border, unframed, curling at the edges, of Julia with Tony Curtis. Well, well. A gilt frame held two pictures of a teenage boy smiling awkwardly at the camera. In one he was lounging on the sofa Laura now sat on, hugging an eager-looking black-and-tan dog that had its paw on his chest. In the other he had his back to a stone wall, arms folded. In the corner next to the window a TV, a big old Sony, was on, and one of the *Cash in the Attic* experts was examining a vase, telling a bearded man in a brown velvet jacket it was a Lalique and at least eighty years old.

Laura hadn't been sure what kind of reception she would get, whether Julia's mother would be suspicious and shut the door in her face. In fact, she had been very helpful once Laura explained she was a writer with a newspaper, putting together a colour piece, which was true, although she didn't actually specify what the piece was about, just said something about how rare it was to find mill workers' cottages still in their original state these days.

Julia's mum had invited her in, made tea and produced home-made jam tarts, seeming glad of the company. Laura steered the conversation round to family: who was the gorgeous toddler in the photo? Oh, she said, that was when my baby was little. She had done well for herself, was on the TV.

Perhaps Laura had heard of her – Julia Hill? Betty went on to say it was all very sad, there had been a falling-out, a rift for several years. That was down to her late husband, who had a terrible temper on him when Julia was growing up, and took a dim view of his daughter's media life, branding it decadent and sinful. He had driven her away, but since he'd passed on a couple of years ago things were getting back on track. It would take time, but they were getting there.

In Laura's bag a tiny black digital recorder, no bigger than a mobile phone, captured every word as she nibbled on a delicious tart, the pastry melting in her mouth, and studied the old woman in her thick tan support stockings, a flowery pinny over a practical, calf-length navy skirt. Her grey hair was set in soft curls that had a violet cast about them and she wasn't wearing a scrap of make-up. Laura searched her face, looking for something to connect her to Julia, but couldn't find anything. Hardly surprising considering the presenter was a slave to cosmetic procedures and had undergone such a radical transformation over the years.

Laura had spent two hours with the old woman, asking the occasional question, mainly letting her reminisce, and steering her back to the subject of Julia again and again. It transpired she had suffered beatings at the hands of her father, which caused her to go off the rails in her teens. Betty Swales had come out with some belting stuff – truancy, a suspension from school, an arrest for blasting a boy in the next street with an air rifle, putting him in hospital. That had been an unexpected bonus. Laura had actually found the boy – now fifty with tattoos and a belly hanging over the top of his stained jeans – and heard the story all over again, even seen the scar on his chest from the pellets all those years ago. According to Betty, the teenage boy in the photos was Julia's older brother, now working on a VSO project in Uganda. That had thrown Laura, who had been sure Julia was a spoiled only child. She had considered pocketing the photo of the cherubic toddler in the sundress – Julia aged two and a half, according to her mum – but didn't get a chance. As she left, Betty had wished her well with her piece, making Laura feel bad, and apologized for going on about all that family stuff. 'You don't want to hear all that,' she had said, embarrassed.

Laura had been back to Bradford again a couple of days later and managed to unearth one of Julia's old classmates, a girl who had vivid memories of the two of them having an altercation in the girls' toilets one day. It seemed no one had a good word to say for her. To her surprise, Laura felt a twinge of sympathy for the presenter. She would definitely have to play down the stuff about her old man whacking her with electrical cable and locking her in her room, or the readers would side with her. That was incidental to her piece. A bonus was finding a picture of Julia in her teens in the local paper's archive. Taking into account what Joel Reynolds had already told her, Laura knew she had more than enough to hang Julia Hill out to dry. Anything else would be icing on the cake.

Forty-Six

Bang on cue, ten minutes late, Julia strode into The Ivy, huge white shades, embellished with a gold CD logo, like horns on the top of her head. Laura could hear her complaining to the maître d' about getting stuck in a jam *forever* as she weaved her way through the restaurant. Laura noted the figure-hugging dress, the biker jacket studded with tiny spikes, and the extraordinary mirrored shoes. Julia looked like something out of *Blade Runner*. As for that hideous gash of lipstick . . . Laura plastered a broad smile on her face and got to her feet as Julia bore down on her.

'I am so sorry, God, the traffic was dreadful, big snarl-up on Whitehall, buses on diversion or something, major headache.' The truth was she had actually made good time and instructed her driver to go around the block until she was acceptably late. It was not in her nature to arrive anywhere early. There was, she felt, something slightly desperate about people who turned up exactly when they were meant to. In any case, no one expected celebs to be clock watchers.

'It is *so* good to meet you.' Julia lunged at Laura, planting kisses in the air in the vague vicinity of her face. 'Did you get my message? God, I hope so. I called to say I was held up, told them to be sure to let you know. I absolutely *hate* being late.' Two tables along, Gaby Roslin, having lunch with two men in grey suits and a woman Laura had seen covering events for Sky Sports, turned and watched Julia's performance. Laura wished she would stop flapping about, getting on everyone's nerves, and just sit down.

'It's perfectly fine. I was also held up, stuck on the tube – someone jumped in front of a train on the Piccadilly line – only got here a minute or two ago myself by the skin of my teeth,' Laura lied, playing Julia at her own game. 'So really, there's no need to apologize. To be honest, I was worried you might actually get here first and end up sitting all by yourself.' Laura gave her a sweet smile, knowing she had touched a nerve. For all her brash exterior Julia, used to being fussed over and pandered to, would have been mortified to find herself the only unaccompanied celebrity in the place, everyone wondering if she'd been stood up. 'Anyway, you're here now and it is an absolute pleasure to meet you. I asked them for champagne. I hope that's OK with you?'

Julia nodded. Laura Lloyd was not what she had been expecting. She was younger for a start. In Julia's experience reporters were hard, hewn from granite, the type who would drink you under the table, sell their grandmother for an exclusive and brag about it in the press club later. Laura Lloyd didn't look the type. She seemed – well, a bit *unsophisticated*, with her plain white shirt and scraped-back hair. She didn't even have mascara on. What had Tom Steiner said? That Julia should mind her step, proceed with caution, and above all bear in mind Laura was smart: a tough cookie. Well, he had got that wrong. She decided to relax and enjoy the lunch.

'It's good of you to make time to see me,' Laura said, confident Julia had no inkling that the two of them had actually met once before. 'Especially with so much going on at the moment – I mean, all this business about a feud over the *Good Morning Britain* job . . . it must be so disruptive and unsettling.'

Julia shook off her jacket and slung it on the back of her chair. 'Not a bit.' Her voice was light. 'It's just television, and when you've been doing it as long as I have you get used to the politics, all the in-fighting. That's the way things are; survival of the fittest and all that.'

A waiter appeared and wrestled the cork from a bottle of champagne. Julia waited while he filled her glass, pausing to let the froth subside.

'It's wonderful that you can be so calm. I'm not very good at dealing with in-fighting, internal politics, all that stuff,' Laura said.

Julia lowered her gaze, sliding her chair back an inch or so. She dug around in her bag and pulled out a gold tube. Laura watched as, eyes fixed on something beneath the table, Julia slapped another blood-red layer on lips that looked set to burst from an overdose of filler. Laura imagined them going pop and deflating, oozing some kind of messy alien gunge. She thought of *Blade Runner* again. Curious to know what was proving so fascinating under the table, she leaned back in her chair and caught Julia admiring her reflection in her shoes. Laura stifled a snigger. Everything Joel had told her was true: 'utterly self-obsessed' was how he had put it. Laura set a tiny recorder in the centre of the table. This was going to be good.

It came as no surprise that Julia, given the chance to talk about herself, barely paused for breath. For three hours Laura listened with enormous patience, slipping in the odd question, as Julia droned on. In the end, desperate for a break, Laura excused herself to go to the loo, only for Julia to push back her chair and say she would come too. Laura found herself hanging around in the ladies' while Julia got out a make-up bag bigger than most women's handbags and started touching up her face. Out came the eyeshadow, something grey and sparkly from L'Oréal's Studio Secrets range – brilliant, according to Julia, and a bargain too – followed by translucent powder and a pearly highlighter, applied to her cheekbones with a fat brush. Last but not least, she trowelled on the shocking lipstick that made it look like a crazed slasher had been let loose on her alabaster face.

All the while, Laura, who had merely washed her hands, watched the performance utterly fascinated, a second recorder in her bag capturing Julia's ludicrous running commentary about where she got her skincare stuff and how she swore by primer under foundation. She could let Laura have the name of a fantastic make-up artist who did one-to-one lessons – a bit on the pricey side, but you get what you pay for. Before returning to their table Julia extracted an industrial-size bottle of Chanel No. 5 from her bag and sprayed a huge cloud in the air.

It was priceless, all of it. Laura already knew she had struck gold.

Forty-Seven

James Almond leaned back in the executive swivel chair that had come from Sweden and cost the best part of £10,000. The padded frame concealed a complicated internal mechanism inspired by the one NASA designed for the flight deck of the space shuttle. That's what the blurb said anyway. He rested a hand on sumptuous leather. Specially bred albino heifers reared on a diet rich in alfalfa and liquid chlorophyll (the blurb again) gave the hide its velvety texture. At the touch of a button the seat reclined and a footrest glided into position. He stroked the leather arms in gratitude. It was not an exaggeration to say he loved the chair. It was so ... well, *him*.

On the TV in the corner of his office Helen England was chatting to the *Good Morning Britain* agony aunt, a woman who was much too jovial for his liking – he made a mental note to look for a replacement – about achieving a balance between work and home life. His thoughts turned to his wife, Stephanie, at home in their sprawling house on a private estate in a posh bit of Weybridge, bored out of her mind, nothing to do except talk to fancy designers about colour schemes and soft furnishings and rustle up dinner on the rare nights he wasn't stuck in town on business with some executive or other. He should get a crash pad in town really, like Helen.

James had been a lowly trainee on a regional news magazine

show at the BBC in Birmingham when he met Stephanie, a coordinator with a pioneering scheme for troubled teenagers. His attachment to the features unit coincided with a series of special reports about the work of the project. He had clicked with Stephanie right away and within six months they were married. She loved her work, loved the Midlands and naively thought they would settle there, but James had other ideas. He was ambitious, rising rapidly through the ranks, making a name for himself and, inevitably, London beckoned. Stephanie never wanted to move south but she had little choice. James was on his way up, his sights set on getting right to the top. There was no way round it; he had to be in the capital.

To start with, things had worked out. Stephanie created a home for them – a one-bedroom flat in Crouch End – and James worked his tail off. The plan had been that once they were settled she would look for work. The trouble was, James was so busy, always under huge pressure, and the kind of work Stephanie wanted to do meant odd shifts, the occasional weekend stint. James couldn't see the point of the two of them working all hours and never seeing one another, especially when he was earning enough to support them, so Stephanie gave up her job. Predictably, it made little difference. They still hardly saw each other. The more successful James became the harder he worked, leaving the house at the crack of dawn, sometimes getting in gone midnight. When he was home he was tired and bad-tempered, constantly checking emails, welded to his mobile. Even on holiday work came first.

He knew Stephanie did everything she could to be the kind of wife he wanted to spend time with. She created a beautiful home, cooked fantastic meals, mixed his vodka tonics just the way he liked them, worked out at the gym every day, went blonde when he asked her to, and kept abreast of what was going on in TV. She had made it clear she was desperate for children but James never felt it was the right time to start a family. He couldn't afford to be distracted from his work, not when his career was at such a critical stage. There were televisions in virtually every room of the house so that even when they sat down to eat – it could be breakfast, lunch or dinner – the TV blared away in the background. It was essential to keep on top of things. Although he loved his wife, he had a job that brought him into contact with beautiful women who made it clear they fancied him. It was not lost on him that the attraction was less to do with him being a babe magnet and more about his mover-and-shaker status.

He thought about Karen King. He wouldn't mind a crack at her, even if she was back with her husband. There was something about her, a kind of old-fashioned decency, that he found appealing. He'd put money on her being wild in bed. The quiet ones always were. He should take her to lunch, somewhere swanky with rooms, do a bit of sweet talking and let her know she had a bright future in front of her. Surely she knew the score. It had worked with Helen. She definitely had what it took to get to the top. Warm and engaging on screen, she was probably the most ruthless woman he had ever met. At one time he would have thought that was Julia Hill, but she lacked subtlety. Helen on the other hand kept her bitchy side under wraps, managing to trample people underfoot without them even noticing. Now that was clever. She also happened to be the filthiest woman he had ever met.

Forty-Eight

Sasha Gates had been in *Spitalfields* long enough to know there were no such things as secrets in the soaps. Whenever someone was up to no good it always came out, no matter how careful they thought they were. It was just a matter of time. Months could pass and the storyline team and writers would make viewers believe a character had got away with murder – quite literally sometimes – but they never ever did. At some point their crime would catch up with them, usually just as they thought they were in the clear. It was one of those rules, set in stone, to ensure the baddies eventually got found out. It definitely kept things straightforward and created the notion that justice somewhere along the line was inevitable, which was reassuring. Sometimes Sasha thought it would be a good thing if real life was like that. Then she would think about her own secrets, the ones she would rather no one ever uncovered, and feel grateful it wasn't.

She was having a lazy afternoon, feet up on the sofa in her pyjamas, an antioxidant face mask on, a two-thirds-empty bottle of Pinot Grigio and her script for the following week beside her, and an episode of *Sex and the City* on the DVD player, when the phone call came. It was a withheld number and she wasn't going to answer but then she figured out it had to be important for someone to call her on a Saturday. It was her second line as well, and hardly anyone had that number. Sasha frowned at the phone. Just as she picked it up to take the call it stopped ringing. She waited for it to beep with a message but instead it glowered at her, silent, ominous.

A tiny alarm bell rang somewhere in her head. Who had that number? A handful of people, that's all, and they only used it if they couldn't get hold of her on her main line. She waited for it to ring again but it remained silent. Perhaps it was just a wrong number. Several minutes went by – Samantha frozen on the screen above the fireplace, head back in ecstasy – and Sasha began to relax. She hit the play button and Samantha resumed bouncing up and down on top of her toy-boy lover. It made her think of Lesley Gold, who probably saw herself as a glamorous *Sex and the City*-type character rather than the tawdry, washed-up old slapper she was. Anything in trousers with a pulse would do for her, although according to the gossip mags she and Dan Kincaid were an item, which was puzzling. They had been snapped coming out of Aubergine, and at a pavement café in Primrose Hill, Dan spooning the chocolatey froth from his cappuccino into Lesley's mouth, the two of them giggling together like teenagers. It made Sasha want to throw up. She had torn the page out and shredded it. Not so long ago she had thought Dan Kincaid was hot, hardly a one-woman man either from what she had heard, so what he was doing slumming it with a tramp like Lesley Gold she couldn't imagine. Maybe it was more of a business arrangement than a romantic relationship, the pair of them trying to clean up their respective images. Those frothy-coffee pictures looked staged to her. Really, who behaved like that? And what was the old soak doing drinking coffee? There had to be a slug of vodka in it or she'd never get it down.

The sound of her mobile ringing again made her jump. It was the second line, another withheld number. *Ring ring*. Her stomach felt odd, as if it was cramping up. She pressed the green button on the keypad and adopted a snotty tone of voice.

'Who is this?'

'Sasha, hello there, how's it going? It's Alec Dexter from the *News of the World*. Please don't hang up. I just need a word.'

'I'm actually in the middle of something important.' She could feel the face pack turning solid. Bloody cheek of the man, calling on a Saturday, and on her exclusive line as well.

'Me too, love, deadline looming and all that. Won't keep you long, though, I promise, then you can get back to painting your toenails.'

Sasha bristled. She could not remember the last time she did her own toenails. She was a regular at a salon in Knightsbridge renowned for the best manicures and pedicures in town. An awful lot of celebs went there. 'Where did you get this number?'

'It's on file, love.' In fact, Alec Dexter had got hold of it through a freelance guy who spent all his time compiling and updating an impressive celebrity database packed with snippets about where they lived, their contact numbers – not just theirs but those of anyone close to them – email addresses, car registration, info on who did their hair, where they went for Botox, their private hospital of choice and so on. You name it, he seemed to know it.

Sasha could feel her face tightening. She needed to get the frigging face mask off *fast*. She got up off the sofa. 'I really have to go. And please don't call me on this number again.'

'Just wondered, Sasha, love – have you seen your old dad lately?'

She stopped in her tracks. A sudden sharp pain made her

clutch her stomach and sink back on to the sofa. 'I think there must be some mistake,' she said, her voice shaking.

'No, no mistake.' Alec Dexter sounded breezy. 'He's alive and well – actually, not as well as he might be – and living in a bit of a shithole by the seaside last time I looked, which was . . . well, earlier today, actually. Lovely chap, mind you. Doesn't have much, scrapes along, but he's a proper gent: put the kettle on and made a brew, chatted away happy as Larry for hours.' Alec paused. 'I got the impression he doesn't get much company.'

Sasha felt as if she was about to pass out. She could hardly catch her breath and the back of her neck was hot and clammy. She put her head between her knees. The face pack had set like concrete. She would have to chip the fucking thing off.

'He's an interesting man, your dad. Not had it easy, has he? We had a good old talk about that bad patch he went through a few years back, the spell in the hospital – well, secure unit, I suppose we should call it.' Sasha could have sworn she heard Alec Dexter yawn. 'Anyway, it's a shame the two of you are out of touch. I mean, he has no idea how well you've done for yourself.' He chuckled, as if a funny thought had just popped into his head. 'You know, he still thinks you're called *Deirdre*.' Another chuckle.

Sasha felt herself gag.

'I mean, Deirdre Draper. It's got quite a ring to it, rolls right off the tongue, although I can see why you'd want to change it to something – how shall I put it? – a bit more foxy, more *now*. If you were to ask me I'd say "Deirdre Draper" conjures up an old biddy in wrinkly stockings, maybe a character out of a sitcom – *Only When I Laugh* or *Last of the Summer Wine* or something – not the tart-with-a-heart soap queen we've come to know in *Spitalfields*.'

Sasha put her hand on her brow. She could feel it burning up under the face mask. The power of speech seemed to have deserted her.

'The thing is, we're running a piece this week, an interview with your old dad. Oh, and he gave us some pictures too, family snapshots, the young Deirdre. There's a good one of you and him on the beach. That was some perm you had.'

The silence hung between them once more.

'I'm just after a quote or two, Sasha – *Deirdre* – make sure it's a balanced piece.'

She tried to open her mouth and felt the face mask pull at her skin. It was no good. She couldn't speak.

'All right then, lovely, we'll put you down as a "no comment". How does that sound?'

Sweat ran down her back. Her heart was thumping. She should tell Alec Dexter to fuck right off, let him know she would sue the backside off him *and* his newspaper if he dared to print a story about her father, but she knew there was no point. It was too late. Her secret was out.

Forty-Nine

Lesley could barely contain herself. She was having dinner with Dan at Al Dente, tucking into her usual plate of ravioli, when Natalie called to say the story was running the next day, and that You-know-who was probably throwing up with the stress of it all at that very moment. Dan asked the waiter to keep his crab linguine warm and nipped out, went to one of the vendors at Victoria Station where the early editions of the Sundays were already on sale, and bought half a dozen copies. When he returned, grinning, holding up the newspaper, Lesley's mouth dropped open.

It was so much more than she had dared hope for: Sasha splashed all over the front page, the story running across three more pages inside, exposing her as the kind of heartless bitch who callously deserted her poor old dad, now in dire straits, living in abject poverty and barely able to make ends meet, with just his cat, Fluffy, for company. Meanwhile Sasha, a.k.a. Deirdre Draper – this was too good to be true! – single-mindedly pursued her career with not so much as a backward glance in the direction of the man who raised her and paid for her to attend evening and weekend classes at a local stage school, from when she was tiny right up to the age of sixteen. Well, that was a surprise. Sasha Gates – without doubt the most wooden actress on TV, in Lesley's entirely biased opinion – had actually been formally trained. And at a school that had a pretty good name as well.

Lesley was hard-pressed to decide what she liked most about the exposé, although the photos of the young Deirdre were spectacularly bad. Those teeth! The hideous frizzy hair! She was even wearing specs – ugly heavy-framed things – in one of them. No wonder she wanted to keep all that quiet. Well, she was finished now. No way would she be able to play a loving mother on screen when she'd dropped her own dad. She would be laughed off set. Well, Lesley had no sympathy. Oh, revenge tasted good. It had taken years but it had been worth the wait. Natalie was in for a big fat bonus. The girl had worked wonders. Lesley was the happiest woman alive.

She leaned over the table and kissed Dan, slipping her tongue into his mouth. When she went to pull away he held on to her, nibbling on her bottom lip, tasting vanilla. Dan never knew what to expect when he locked lips with Lesley. She could taste of anything from strawberry to chocolate to lime. One of her lip glosses tasted exactly like pistachios.

Nico, picking up on the buzz between Lesley and Dan, hurried over to ask if they were celebrating. Could he bring champagne?

Lesley clapped her hands, delighted. 'Bring us a bottle of Bollinger, Nico. It happens to be a very special occasion.'

Nico looked at Lesley's radiant face and at Dan, who was grinning at her, the two of them holding hands across the table. 'May I ask, would congratulations be in order?'

Lesley beamed at him. 'Nico, I can honestly say that this is one of the best days of my life. Fan-frigging-tastic!'

Nico clasped his hands together and gave a small bow. 'In

that case, the champagne is on the house and I offer my very best wishes on behalf of all of us at Al Dente. I hope the two of you will have a long and happy life together. I cannot tell you how much joy it gives me to think of my favourite couple making your vows, for better, for worse—'

Lesley jumped in. 'No, Nico, we're not getting hitched—'

'Ah, I see – it's a secret. Well, if that's the case my lips are now sealed.' He made a zipping motion from one side of his mouth to the other and tapped the side of his nose. 'Nico is a man of honour, known for his discretion.' He gave another little bow.

Dan winked at Lesley. 'Probably best to keep it just between the three of us for now.' He also tapped the side of his nose.

Nico gave another little bow and went to fetch the Bollinger. Lesley gaped at Dan. 'Would you please tell me what the fuck you think you're doing?'

'Just didn't want to disappoint him. You saw the look on his face. We've made his night.'

'And what about when we tell him it was all a mistake and we're not engaged at all, just deeply in lust?' Lesley scrabbled about in her bag and pulled out a selection of lip glosses, choosing Nude Shimmer and slapping several coats on without for a second taking her eyes off Dan.

He twiddled the stem of his glass. 'And anyway, is the idea of getting hitched to me really so awful? I mean, we do make a lovely couple. Even Nico thinks so.'

Secretly pleased, Lesley spluttered a protest. 'You *are* joking, right? I mean' – she lowered her voice – '*me*, and marriage? That is one of the worst ideas I have ever heard.'

Dan laughed. 'All right, keep your extensions on. Shit, you

307

are so touchy. You have to be one of the easiest people in the world to wind up.' She gave him a huffy look. 'Now come on, let's see a smile back on that gorgeous face.'

Lesley, trying and failing to remain cool, gave him her best smile.

'That's more like it. We're celebrating, remember?'

Fifty

Jason had underestimated Hannah. He really should have seen the business with his clothes coming. She had always had a temper on her, been prone to go off the deep end and throw epic tantrums to get her own way. He was actually a bit scared of her when she let rip. She had thrown a cut-glass fruit bowl at him once. There was a coconut in it at the time, and an unripe mango, both deadly missiles. She could have killed him. Still, that was probably something to do with her hormones being all over the place. She had got pregnant pretty much as soon as they got together, saying she didn't know how it had happened because she was on the pill. The last thing he wanted was a baby but he didn't seem to have much choice. Hannah was off buying bootees the second two blue lines appeared in the window of the pregnancy test. It had taken all his acting skills to tell her he couldn't be happier, at the same time wondering if there were grounds to sue the makers of the contraceptive pill that had proved so ineffective.

The day he came home and found all his stuff in the street, Hannah leaning out of the bedroom window crying and calling him a lousy two-timing bastard, the paparazzi with a ringside seat, snapping away, he could have wept. Karen had been right to be sceptical. He had been forced to gather up what was left of his belongings under a hail of abuse. There was no point in saving stuff she had taken the scissors to so he dumped it all in a wheelie bin, salvaging only the beloved Paul Rodgers T-shirt, even though the message, scrawled by Paul with a Sharpie after a gig at the O_2, was barely legible. Steeling himself, he went inside and did his best to persuade Hannah there was nothing going on with Karen, that it was in both their interests to string her along, make sure he didn't get stung in the divorce settlement. If he could explain it in crude financial terms, she would understand. As long as he was careful he just might manage to find a way to have it all: Hannah, the baby, *and* his wife.

Karen huddled in a doorway in a deserted street just off Long Acre in Covent Garden, wondering what on earth was so significant about this spot and why Jason couldn't just have told her to meet him in a restaurant or bar – somewhere warm. Although it was sunny the wind was cold as it whipped against her bare legs, making her shiver. He had sounded excited, as though he had good news, when he phoned. Maybe The Slut had finally seen sense.

Karen glanced at the sky, which was clear and blue, just a vapour trail from a jet overhead, no sign of flying pigs as far as she could tell. She did up the buttons on her coat, a paper-thin three-quarter-length trench, wishing she had worn something a bit warmer. The wind whistled through her silk dress. At least she had put boots on, although the fact they had peep-toes wasn't helping. She stamped her feet and shoved her hands deep into the pockets of the flimsy coat.

The whole Hannah Montana business depressed her no end. She had allowed herself to fantasize about persuading The Slut the baby would be better off with them, and had already imagined turning the spare room into a nursery. In a moment of madness she had actually jumped the gun and bought the most adorable mobile to hang above a crib. She hadn't dared tell Jason in case he thought she was a bit barmy. The mobile, which had come from a fancy shop in Kensington and cost a ridiculous amount of money, was now in a John Lewis bag and hidden behind a rack of shoes in the bottom of her wardrobe.

She chewed her lip. She wasn't barmy: she was broody, and who could blame her? She wanted a child of her own. Correction – she already had a child of her own. She sighed. Where was Jason? Privately, she thought he would be lucky to see his son at all once he left Hannah. Grasping cow, she had probably already done a deal for the baby pictures. An image of herself sweating and straining alone on the maternity ward and a grim-faced nun sweeping in to wrench Amy from her arms came to mind. She blinked back tears. It would be a different story for Hannah, fussed over in a private hospital, the best of everything, a room filled with cards and balloons and flowers, someone on hand to do her hair and make-up ready for the first exclusive shots. Karen felt for Jason. He was an idiot, but it broke her heart to think he would miss the birth of his second child too.

He was late. She fumbled in her bag for her mobile phone and called him. It went straight to voicemail. 'Jason, it's blowing a gale and you've got me standing in a wind tunnel freezing half to death. Is there a point to all this? Seriously, if you're not here in two minutes I'm off, before I end up with hypothermia.'

As she hung up someone grabbed her from behind. 'Boo!'

'For crying out loud, you nearly gave me a heart attack.'

Jason nuzzled her neck. 'I was watching you, all the way

from the end of the street there as I came up, thinking you were bound to turn round and see me, and when you didn't I couldn't resist sneaking up. You should have seen your face!'

Karen whacked him with her bag. 'It's not funny, creeping up on people like that. What if the shock had made me pass out?'

'I've got my London Ambulance Service cardiopulmonary resuscitation certificate. I know all the techniques. In fact, let's have a go now.' He pulled her towards him and gave her a long, tender kiss.

Her stomach did an odd little flip. He still had that effect, even when she wanted to be cross with him. 'I've been standing here ages, catching my death of cold, trying to work out why in God's name we couldn't just have met in a restaurant. Like normal people.'

Jason put a finger to her lips. 'Because we're different, and I thought it would be fun to meet in Wild Court.' He pointed at the sign on the wall above them. 'Isn't that a fantastic name for a street? It's romantic.' It was also out of the way, discreet, not likely to be on the radar of a prowling paparazzo. He took her hand and led her into Wild Street and towards Great Queen Street, pausing on the corner. 'Don't you recognize the building?'

She stared up at the impressive structure with its pillars and gigantic studded doors. 'It's the Masonic Hall.'

'Correct. It's also the HQ in *Spooks*.'

Karen smiled. Jason had an almost childish fascination with film and TV locations. He had once taken her to a bar in Manchester that had been made to look like a glamorous waterfront location in Australia for an episode of *Cold Feet*. If he hadn't been an actor Jason would probably have been a location manager. 'I recognize it now,' she said. He squeezed her hand, pleased with himself.

They hurried along Long Acre, Karen struggling to keep up in boots she had never had to walk more than a few yards in, her toes already numb, and turned left into St Martin's Lane. He flung an arm round her. 'Worked out where we're going yet?'

Karen gazed at him. 'Are you taking me to Sheekey's?'

Every year Jason took her to the fish restaurant tucked away down a narrow lane off Charing Cross Road for their anniversary – apart from the last one, of course, which she had spent alone, working her way through a couple of bottles of wine and sobbing over him and The Slut. It had become a tradition to start their anniversary celebrations with champagne at the bar before going through to the restaurant, where they had the same table each time. Karen would order smoked-fish ceviche to start, then a nice fillet of whatever the fish of the day was to follow. Jason stuck with traditional fish and chips, mushy peas on the side, all washed down with a delicious dry white wine. The whole thing was a ritual that meant something to both of them.

'But it's not our anniversary.'

His face was suddenly serious. 'No, well, I blew the last one, didn't I? I just want you to know that's never going to happen again: me acting like an arsehole. I know there's a long way to go but I want to feel things are at least starting to get back to how they should be. So, even though it's not our anniversary, let's just pretend.'

Fifty-One

Julia was feeling very pleased with herself. It was three days since she had adopted a new beauty regime based on a breakthrough anti-ageing treatment derived from snail slime, which sounded disgusting but worked like a dream; Laura Lloyd had sent her a note to say how much she had enjoyed their lunch; and there was a picture spread in *heat* of Jason and his monstrously pregnant girlfriend, hand in hand, shopping for baby stuff in Knightsbridge. In the *Girl Talk* conference room at Channel 6, Julia interrupted as Jackie Martin outlined the topic for that night's show – women who were so-called body addicts, hooked on punishing exercise routines.

'Can't we look at love triangles and how messy it all gets when a man's torn between two women?' She gave Karen a pointed look. 'Especially when there's a baby involved. I mean, we have first-hand experience right here in this room.'

Lesley looked up from tapping an email into her BlackBerry. 'I saw something on the Discovery Channel about women being used to interrogate terrorist suspects because apparently they're better at mental torture than men, and I couldn't help thinking of you, Julia.'

Julia gave Karen a pitying smile. 'Is it very awkward, you know, having sex when he's been –' she lowered her voice – '*somewhere else*?'

Karen felt sick. In fact, she had almost thrown up that morning after seeing the shots of Jason, grinning, weighed down by Harrods bags reportedly full of designer baby clobber. He was supposed to be leaving her, for crying out loud, not playing the doting father-to-be.

'I just wondered, did anyone see that piece in the paper about how if you're single when you hit fifty the chances are you'll never find a partner?' She gave Julia a meaningful look. 'I mean, we have first-hand experience of that . . . right here, in this room.'

Julia smirked. 'Sounds like one for Lesley, if you ask me.'

'Except I haven't hit the big five-oh and I'm spoiled for choice when it comes to blokes. Out of interest, when was the last time you even got laid?'

Julia bristled. 'I prefer to keep my private life private.'

'What private life might that be?'

Cheryl glanced at Faye. 'Can we get off before World War Three breaks out?'

Jackie sighed. 'The subject tonight is body addicts. If anything else crops up I'll be in touch. Now please try to be in a better mood by the time we go on air.'

'Oh well, body addicts, obsessive dieting . . .' Julia looked at Karen again. 'Is it my imagination or are your tits shrinking?' She slid her copy of *heat* across the table. 'Keep this if you like.'

Karen felt like punching her but didn't much fancy her chances. She still had a scar on her knee, a livid pink mark that would probably never go away, from the last time the two of them had clashed, at the Domes. She decided not to rise to the bait no matter what Julia said, although it drove her mad to hear her harping on, rubbing her hands with glee, endlessly speculating about the impact the Jason/Hannah scandal was having on her chances of landing the *Good Morning Britain* job. There had already been a scathing piece by a celebrity columnist writing – no, *ranting* – in the *Daily Mail*, accusing Karen of letting down women everywhere by giving her cheating husband another chance. She was sending out all the wrong signals. Oh, for fuck's sake! Karen had never even met the celebrity in question but knew enough about her to think she was on very thin ice indeed, coming across like some kind of moral crusader. What right did someone with three children, all with different fathers, not to mention two failed marriages, have to pass comment? OK, Karen was hardly perfect and nor was Jason, but they were doing their best, trying to do the right thing for the baby *and* Hannah, not that the little tramp deserved it. She had even had the gall to pour her heart out to some tacky magazine, saying it was tough for Jason and hinting that his clingy wife wouldn't leave them in peace. It was all enough to make Karen want to walk away, go and live on a farm in the middle of nowhere – preferably where there was no TV reception – and grow vegetables. A bit like that woman from the *Mail on Sunday*, Liz Jones. Mind you, reading what she had to say about rural life it didn't exactly sound like fun, waking up to find bullet holes in your mailbox.

It seemed like everyone had an opinion about the state of Karen's marriage. Even Faye, who normally kept out of things, had stuck her oar in after one of the production meetings, saying it was the baby she felt sorry for. As if she was a paragon of virtue. It was common knowledge she played around while Mike was ducking bullets in Afghanistan.

That day Karen had gone back to her dressing room and

broken down. She couldn't take much more. To think she had actually considered them friends. The truth was they were a set of back-stabbing witches, all ready to see her go under if it gave them a better chance of landing the *Good Morning Britain* job. If only they knew she already had it in the bag. Only Lesley surprised her, coming to her dressing room one day and saying she shouldn't let all the bitching get to her. 'It's a fucking *job*,' she said. 'In *television*. It's not like what we do is even important in the great scheme of things. We're not out there saving lives. We're sitting on our backsides reading off an autocue. I mean, really, who cares? As for Jeremy Paxman' – Lesley's nickname for Julia had now stuck, which incensed her – 'let her do her worst. They'll never give that saggy old crone one of the best jobs on the box. She can't even get in to see James Almond.'

Karen was lost for words. This from Lesley, who had made no secret of the fact she was as keen to perch her backside on the daytime sofa as much as the next person, so why was she being so nice? She could have sworn she hadn't even been drinking, which was bizarre in itself. Karen wondered if she was sickening for something, but she actually seemed sharper and more together than she had for a long time. She looked good too. Half a ton of lippy as usual, but at least it was a flattering nude shade that suited her. Even though Karen hadn't been spending time with the others she had noticed Lesley was decidedly mellower these days and more than a match for Julia's vicious barbs, dismissing her with a casual 'Fuck off, Jeremy.' Ever since that damning piece about Sasha Gates in the *News of the World* there had been a spring in Lesley's step. Word was she and Dan Kincaid were serious, if the magazines could be believed. Karen was baffled at her unexpected show of solidarity. Maybe it was all just a ruse to make her drop her guard, at which point Lesley would deliver a killer blow.

Now, looking round the table at the other women, Karen took a deep breath. 'Just so you know, I'm leaving at the end of the current run.'

Lesley put down her copy of *In Style*, sat up and removed her shades. 'You're kidding? Because the tabloids are having a pop? Trust me, that's nothing.'

Karen shook her head and kept her eyes on Julia, who for once seemed lost for words. 'It's nothing to do with that. I actually gave James Almond my resignation a couple of days ago.'

Cheryl gave Faye a quizzical look. 'But why?'

'I'm ready to move on, that's why.'

Julia recovered her composure and gave Karen what she hoped was a baleful look. 'Well I'm sure I speak for everyone when I say your unique contribution, not to mention – how shall I put it? – your *distinctive* dress sense, will definitely be missed.' Her mouth twitched, suddenly leaving Karen in no doubt as to who had been behind her recent wardrobe malfunctions.

'Oh, you'll survive without me, and you'll soon find someone else to pick on.' She glanced at Faye.

Jackie, remembering her chat with the controller about the fate of *Girl Talk*, had an idea there was more to this resignation than met the eye. 'Didn't he try to talk you into staying? I mean, you're popular, the show's on a high . . .'

'No, actually, he didn't, although he did say he wants me to keep in touch after I go, see what other opportunities there might be.'

Julia, suspicious, said, 'And where exactly *are* you going?'

Karen gave her a crafty smile, the kind of smile Julia usually gave her. She was enjoying this. 'You'll have to wait and see. *Girl Talk* isn't the only show on TV, you know.'

Lesley's mouth dropped open. 'Oh my God, she's going to *Loose Women*! I bet that's it. Kate Thornton said they were looking for a new face on the panel.'

Julia turned on her. 'Since when were you pally with Kate Thornton?'

'Actually, according to Kate, *my* name's come up,' Lesley replied. That was a lie, designed to send Julia into orbit. 'Not that I'm keen.' She gave Julia a knowing smile. 'Not with another plum job right here at Channel 6 going begging.'

'You think they'll even look at you for the *Good Morning Britain* job?' Julia was incensed. 'You're not even a proper broadcaster.'

Lesley smiled. 'You have to admit I'm good, though, and people like me.' Unlike *you*, she didn't say.

Karen picked up her things, gave Jackie a look that said *Here we go again*, and slipped out as Julia told Lesley she only had a job in the first place because she, Julia Hill, had convinced the producers it would lend a bit of colour to have a washed-up soap star on board, while Lesley said the moment you started referring to yourself in the third person it was the beginning of the end.

As the door shut behind her Karen stood for a moment in the corridor, listening to the raised voices interspersed with Jackie's soothing tone. One thing was sure: *Good Morning Britain* would be a breeze after this.

Fifty-Two

With stories about her private life all over the tabloids Karen was sure she would be summoned by James Almond and told that even though she'd resigned, as he'd advised, he no longer saw a future for her with *Good Morning Britain*. In fact, when he finally did ask to see her it was to say she should keep her chin up and wait for the storm to pass.

'It may seem bad now, maybe even feel like the end of the world, but it most certainly is not. Do you know what the end of the world is, Karen?' She shook her head, miserable. 'Well, let me tell you. The end of the world is a drop in ratings. The end of the world is a sponsor pulling the plug because they no longer have faith in a show. The *end of the world* is a fall in advertising revenue. This –' he paused, searching for the right word – 'claptrap in the press about your personal life is more an irritation than a catastrophe. It's the difference between being stung by a bee and bitten by a venomous snake.' He frowned. 'Assuming of course you don't have an allergy to bee stings, in which case a single sting could prove fatal. You're not allergic to bee stings are you?'

'No, not as far as I—'

'Well then, you don't need to worry. Batten down the hatches, wait for the storm to pass and it will. I do know what I'm talking about, you know. I was in a house right on the beach in North Carolina when Hurricane Floyd hit, and do you know what I did?' Karen sat, mute, waiting for him to tell her, her head starting to spin the way it always did when she was in the presence of the controller. Was it just her, or did he spout the biggest load of crap? 'I sat tight. Neighbours in a panic, packing up their cars, driving off, getting stuck in the most appalling tailbacks, wishing they'd stayed put because actually the houses were solid enough to stand a battering. All I did was fasten the shutters, brew some *decent* coffee on the stove, and wait.' He closed his eyes for a moment. 'I was the only one who faced it head-on. Fight or flight, Karen. I cannot stress enough how crucial it is to pick your moment and, trust me, right now is not the time to run away.'

He got up and crossed to his desk, where he pulled a black folder from a tray. Karen watched him leaf through the pages. She really had no idea what to make of him. Never had she met a man with more confidence, always so sure of himself, oozing authority from every pore. He might as well have a sign above his head with the words I AM IN CHARGE in big flashing letters. No way would she want to get on his wrong side.

She wondered what Mrs Almond was like and pictured her rake-thin, head full of expensive highlights, platinum-and-diamond Stephen Webster ring on her wedding finger, an ambassador for several high-profile charities, invited for lunch with the Prime Minister's wife. It occurred to her she had never actually seen Mrs Almond, not even a picture of her in the party pages of *OK!* James was always being photographed at some do or another, usually cosying up to a celebrity like Simon Cowell or Piers Morgan.

He flopped back on to the sofa beside her and tapped his finger on the black folder. He had neat, perfectly filed nails.

Karen wondered where he went for manicures. On the front of the file a white label bore the words **CODE 001 CONFIDENTIAL**.

'This is the latest audience research, Karen, and it tells me everything I need to know about what the viewers think of our output. You know what's *really* interesting? In all my years of making programmes I have yet to see a piece of research that has surprised me. I know what the viewers think before they do because I'm in tune with them. It's a knack I have.' He flipped the file open. 'According to this the viewers are on your side.' He glanced at her. 'No need to look surprised. They feel your pain, Karen. They want things to work out for you and your shit of a husband. The reason I know this is because we specifically asked them for their opinion.'

Karen's jaw dropped.

'Shocked? Don't be. I knew they'd see things from your point of view. What's more, the ratings are up for *Girl Talk* and I don't suppose that's down to Jeremy Paxman, do you?'

Jeremy Paxman?! Even James Almond knew about Julia's nickname. Perhaps the dressing rooms were bugged. She shifted on the giant sofa, balancing on the edge. At least she had trousers on, straight legs with a flattering high waist. No chance of flashing her knickers at him today, thank God, although for a moment there he seemed to be speaking directly to her breasts. She shifted on the sofa and he frowned.

'I'm on your side,' he said, his eyes boring into hers. 'We all are. I still have plans for you. Big plans.'

Karen could have sworn he sneaked another look at her boobs. Was her top a bit see-through? She could feel heat spreading up her neck as her phone began to ring in her bag, and scrambled to her feet. 'I'm so sorry, I forgot, I'm meant to be somewhere . . .'

James sprawled on the sofa, top button of his shirt undone, jacket open, revealing an elaborate gold label stitched on the inside pocket. 'That's absolutely fine, you go ahead. We'll talk again. Over lunch. Soon. I'll get Anne to give you a call.' Karen hurried towards the door. 'And Karen' – his voice was loaded with meaning – 'remember what I said. It doesn't help to run away.'

Fifty-Three

Karen stood in the corridor, waiting for the lift to reach the twentieth floor and whisk her away from James Almond's executive suite. She adjusted her wrapover top, doing what she could to hide her lacy bra strap and the tiny bit of cleavage on show, and made a mental note to keep a roll-neck sweater handy from now on just in case he called another impromptu meeting.

Had the controller of entertainment just made a pass at her? No, it was impossible. He wouldn't. He was married. Then again, when had that stopped anyone? In her experience powerful men operated by their own set of rules. She had fended off plenty of advances in her time. Even that slug Elliot Carew had had the gall to try it on – *after* he sacked her. No hard feelings, he said, squeezing her bum. She had kneed him in the groin and left him doubled up, dirty old lech that he was. It depressed her to think James Almond might be no different from most of the other television executives she had encountered in her career. Then again, he had never given her the impression of being flirtatious, so perhaps she was just imagining things.

She reached her dressing room and gazed around it, feeling depressed. It was an oppressive little space with no window and a strip light that flickered and got on her nerves. In the corner was a bunch of white roses from Jason. She had told him he didn't need to send flowers every week but still they turned up and, secretly, she was grateful. She needed a reminder that somebody out there loved her, although she wasn't sure a bunch of flowers really counted as a sign of true love. A nice gesture, yes, but evidence of a serious commitment? Definitely not. Maybe they were just his way of keeping her sweet.

She hated how things were dragging on with Hannah, the humiliating pictures in the magazines, Jason disappearing for days at a time, expecting her to put up with it all until the time was right for him to make the break. He had to tread carefully, he said, otherwise Hannah would clean him out. Karen still had moments when she wondered if he was stringing her along. If she was honest, she still had moments when she missed having Dave around. She was glad he was still driving her, even though sometimes she felt awkward and longed to explain what was going on with Jason. Somehow she always lost her nerve at the last minute. Although Dave never mentioned her messy love life she had a pretty good idea what he was thinking just by the way those steely eyes of his looked at her.

As for work, she couldn't wait to leave. Most days she scurried back to her dressing room after the daily production meeting and stayed there until it was time to go on air, avoiding the others as much as possible. It was like being held prisoner. Luckily, Natalie had got into the habit of popping in with a frothy coffee for her every afternoon and Lisa, one of the make-up girls, was happy to swing by and do her face. She spent her spare time watching TV or old episodes of *Sex and the City* on her laptop.

The second hand on the clock above the door made a loud thud as it jerked around. She still had hours to kill before the show. She called Jason and got the message service, an impersonal voice asking her to speak after the tone. It was two days since he had been in touch. She hung up without saying anything and decided to nip to the canteen for a coffee.

On the tubular glass walkway that linked the two towers of the Channel 6 building, she saw Julia coming towards her, shades on, coat flapping, a young girl with a tray of drinks and cakes shrinking alongside her as she flew by. Karen took a deep breath, put her shoulders back and walked on, shifting slightly to the left, only for Julia to move in the same direction, advancing with long, pounding strides, arms pumping in sync with her legs, eyes impenetrable behind the dark glasses, her presence taking up so much space she was almost steering the girl and her tray towards Karen's side of the walkway. As they drew level Julia suddenly used her shoulder to shunt the girl sideways, knocking the tray with all its contents over Karen. Hot coffee and tea drenched her, and she went arse over tit on a muffin which had landed just under her foot. Karen shrieked as the hot liquid splashed against her legs and she felt the full effect of her weight crashing down on the rock-hard floor. The girl, taking in the sight of what she'd just done, fainted and hit the deck at Karen's feet.

Julia stopped, pushed her glasses on to her head and looked down at Karen. 'You really must be less clumsy, Karen; someone might slip now you've made such a mess with your elevenses.'

Karen stared at her, humiliation and rage rising in her bones. 'You vicious cow.'

'Such language! Tsk tsk, Karen, hardly appropriate for someone with daytime aspirations, although I guess it must be annoying that all your little treats have got dirty. Never mind, I won't tell anyone if you still want to scoff them.'

Karen pulled herself up using the side rail, slipping as she did so and shaking the droplets off her soaked trousers. She glared at Julia, who was smiling smugly. 'You're going to pay for that, Julia.'

'Are you accusing me of something?' Julia said in a butter-wouldn't-melt lilt as Karen drew closer.

'Yes I am, you psycho bitch,' Karen spat, body shaking from shock at the incident and now the confrontation. They were just inches apart; below them at the reception and coffee bar, tiny figures stood together in the atrium watching them. Julia looked down and surveyed the audience, smiling with delight.

'Well, what are you going to do about it, you former fatso?' She prodded a finger into Karen's tummy as if to emphasize her point. 'Whoops, nearly lost my hand in there!' She laughed in Karen's face.

Karen felt something give inside as her legendary patience finally began to run out. 'Trust me, Julia, you *are* going to be sorry you messed with *me*,' she said as she shoved Julia out of her way and strode off down the walkway.

'Oh really!' Julia called after her, smug smile still firmly in place, not at all distracted by the groan coming from the ground below as the young girl she had knocked into started to come round.

'Yes, *really*,' Karen said under her breath, and she meant it. She headed straight for the controller's office.

Karen stood in front of James Almond's desk. 'It's not the first time,' she said. 'It's been going on for months – the taunts, the snide remarks – and I'm at the end of my rope.'

James leaned back in his chair. He knew all about the episode on the walkway. It had gone round the building in seconds flat. He sighed.

'You need to do something,' Karen said, her voice shaking with emotion. 'She's a maniac. I love Channel 6, but if I can't even go to the canteen in peace I don't see how I can keep working here.'

James frowned.

'I'm serious. I want her gone. There's no way I'm taking the *GMB* job if there's a chance of bumping into her round here.'

James opened the top drawer of his desk, removed a red file, and held up a hand to silence Karen.

'This is a confidential report from the medical director at the Abbey – that exclusive and ludicrously expensive private clinic that picks up the pieces during moments of personal crisis for our stars,' he said. 'You may recall Julia Hill's unfortunate allergic reaction at the Domes ...' He opened the file and ran his finger down a typewritten page. 'I won't trouble you with all the boring stuff to do with excessive quantities of botulinum toxin A and hyaluronic acid in her face. No, what's interesting is what showed up in the blood tests *I* requested that night. They were extremely revealing, to put it mildly.'

He glanced at Karen, whose mouth had dropped open. 'No need to look surprised. Who do you think pays for all this private treatment? I think that entitles me to run a few tests of my own, don't you? There was a violent episode that night too, I seem to recall.' He slapped the file shut and put it back in the drawer. 'Suffice to say she definitely wouldn't want the contents of this file falling into the wrong hands.'

Karen wondered if there was a file in his desk on her and, if so, what was in it.

He glanced at his watch. 'Right, run along. When the press start sniffing around – which they will, since just about the whole building witnessed your little tussle – they'll get a brisk "no comment".' He drew a finger across his mouth. 'And leave Julia Hill to me. Frankly, I think she'll have more to worry about before very long than her petty feud with you.'

Fifty-Four

Julia was in the car on the way to the studio, iPod on shuffle, 'Flashdance' playing, Irene Cara telling her to take her passion and make it happen, when Tom Steiner called to say *Girl Talk* was being axed. If it was anyone else she would have assumed he'd got it wrong, but Tom was one of the shrewdest operators in the business, both ears to the ground, and if it was coming from him it had to be true. He told her he was at Sketch in the middle of lunch when a contact emailed to give him a heads-up on the press release that was going out shortly.

Julia was speechless for a good ten seconds. She made Tom read the entire piece to her. Twice. She could not take it in. Julia felt very peculiar as he spelled things out.

'*Girl Talk* has another few weeks to run and then it's over,' Tom said. '*Finito.*'

Julia thought she must have misheard when he told her Lesley and Cheryl had also resigned. 'When did that happen?'

'I have no idea, Julia. These are your colleagues, not mine.'

She couldn't take it in. When had they resigned? Why? How come nobody had told her?

There was one glimmer of hope, according to Tom. 'The statement says that James Almond is developing several new shows, so it may just be he has something up his sleeve for you. Did you actually get in to see him?'

Julia felt weak. 'No,' she whispered.

'Right, in that case, this is his way of telling you you're fired.'

'He can't just fire me!'

'I think you'll find he can do exactly what he likes. He's in charge. Now, go to work, don't do anything rash – no hissy fits – and let me see if I can put a spin on this in the forthcoming piece in the *Sunday*.'

Julia's heart was racing. She fished about in her bag for a bottle of water. Christ, she felt dreadful. 'How can I go to work now? Let him shove his fucking job up his arse, find some other mug to go on air tonight and perform like a fucking seal.'

'Look, Julia, I need to get back to my lunch. It's rude to leave the table for so long, especially when I'm not even picking up the tab.'

'Fine, don't let me keep you from your steak or whatever the fuck it is you're eating.'

'Chateaubriand, actually, pink, and I'm sharing with Marsha Hollings from Channel 4.'

'Fine, fuck off then. I hope it chokes you. *And* her.'

She hung up, hurled the phone on the floor and dug her compact out of her bag. The driver caught her eye in the rear-view mirror. 'What do you think you're looking at? Keep your eyes on the fucking road.' He looked away and back again. She could have sworn he was smirking. Oh Christ, did everyone know already?

She flipped open the compact. Her face was glistening with sweat and there was a wild look in her eyes. Her mascara, which she had paid a fortune for and was supposed to be smudgeproof, waterproof, shockproof and God-knows-what-fucking-else-proof, was starting to run. She found a tissue and tried to wipe it off but it wouldn't shift. For fuck's sake! *Now* it was waterproof. Just as well she had a pack of wipes on her. She scrubbed away at the mascara, which seemed to have acquired the properties of indelible ink. Fucking stuff, she was never wearing that again. She dabbed at her face with powder, taking off the shine, then slapped on several layers of Night Mischief, a restorative and anti-ageing lipstick, a Japanese brand that came in a gold-plated case with its own tiny mirror and had cost the best part of fifty quid. It claimed to be plum with a hint of blueberry, although it looked almost black in this light. Not that Julia cared. Anything that drew attention to her lips was fine by her. She had spent a fortune creating the kind of pout other women could only dream of, so why hide it? She checked her reflection again. That was more like it. Armour in place, she prepared to face the others.

Fifty-Five

Karen was curled up on the sofa in her dressing room, *Mamma Mia!* playing on her laptop, a packet of chocolate buttons going down a treat, when someone rapped at the door. She froze. It was too early for Natalie. Maybe if she kept quiet whoever it was would go away. A few seconds passed and the door handle rattled. Another sharp tap. She jumped as Bella said, 'It's me. Open up. You're going to want to hear this.'

Karen let her in and locked the door behind her. 'You need to have a look on the Channel 6 website,' Bella said. 'You're not going to believe it.'

Dominating the home page of the in-house internet was a picture of a triumphant Helen England under a headline that read: **STAR TURN IN U-TURN!**

Controller of Entertainment James Almond today announced that Queen of Daytime, Helen England, has agreed to stay on for another series of *Good Morning Britain*. Helen, 38, a favourite with the viewers, was due to step down after hosting the top-rated show for five years. However, it was revealed today that she has now signed a three-year deal to host a new weekly prime-time talk show for Channel 6, as well as remaining the face of *GMB*.

Karen scrolled down. When had all this happened? At the end of the piece a few paragraphs in bold type said *Girl Talk* would be axed at the end of the present series following the resignations of Karen King, Lesley Gold and Cheryl West. Her mouth felt dry. It was news to her the others were going.

'We're losing three of our star presenters and without their contributions the show simply cannot survive,' the controller was quoted as saying.

Karen stared at Bella. 'I don't understand. I was in with James yesterday and he said nothing about any of this, not a word. How long has it been on the website?'

'It went up ten minutes ago. I don't even know if word's got round yet. Almost everyone checks the home page first thing in the morning then doesn't bother again until the next day. Mind you, it won't take long for the jungle drums to start beating. Talk about a bombshell! And what a two-faced cow Helen England is. Look at the smug face on her. You can't tell me she hasn't known about this for ages, yet only yesterday she was doing a cookery item on *GMB*, going on about retiring and how she planned to become a domestic goddess once she had time on her hands. According to this, there have been so-called "lengthy negotiations" about her future so it's obvious she was never going anywhere – probably just said she'd had enough to force Almond into paying her more. Unbelievable!'

'She wouldn't want to say anything until she had it all signed and sealed, I suppose, and I don't really blame her.' Karen thought about her own discussions with the controller. What had he been playing at? Suddenly she felt sick. 'I wouldn't trust James Almond as far as I could throw him either.'

Bella said, 'You don't seem shocked about *Girl Talk* being axed.'

'He told me he was taking it off but swore me to secrecy. What was I supposed to do?' Perhaps he had tipped off Lesley and Cheryl as well. She wanted to say he had led her on, as good as promised her Helen's job, but there seemed no point. She sighed. He had completely played her for a fool. 'We've got the production meeting in half an hour. Oh God – there's going to be blood on the walls.'

Fifty-Six

James Almond faced Helen England across the oval conference table in the corner of his office, paperwork, sushi and bottles of sparkling mineral water between them. They were having a working lunch, running through a proposal for the new chat-show format developed for her. His phone had been ringing off the hook ever since the announcement went live about *Good Morning Britain* but he had given his assistant strict instructions not to interrupt.

'We could slip away, go back to my place, get down to some *family* business, if you fancy it,' Helen said, slipping off a shoe and rubbing her foot against his ankle.

'Not today, Mummy. Don't want anyone putting two and two together, do we?'

Helen's toes worked their way up his leg. 'Spoilsport.'

'You won't be saying that when your new show launches and you become the highest-paid woman on the box.'

She shrugged and picked at an edamame bean. 'Suppose not. You're absolutely sure this is going to work?'

'It can't fail. I'm the controller and it's up to me what I commission. This just happens to be an excellent proposal from a new production company whose creative team has a brilliant track record. Once *Girl Talk* goes, that leaves a gap in the schedules for something else. So, we'll have the weekly *Helen England*

Show – big-name guests from the world of music, film, sport, et cetera – and a new early-evening magazine show: quirky, whacky location reports, the great British public at their eccentric best ... you know the kind of thing.' He picked up a glob of cold rice with chopsticks.

'Is that where Karen King comes in?'

James swallowed the rice and speared a piece of tuna. 'I haven't made up my mind. I mean, she would be perfect – all that anguish and weight loss. According to the feedback from the focus groups there's not a woman in the country who doesn't feel for her. You should hear them in the one-to-one interviews, going on about *empathy* which, if you ask me, is utter nonsense since how can anyone empathize in the true sense of the word? I mean, is it really possible to know how another person feels?' He looked thoughtful. 'I wouldn't have thought so.'

Helen frowned. 'I'd just let her go if I were you. You know she's thinking of taking that shit of a husband back?'

'Even better. Think of all the women out there in crappy relationships with blokes who cheat and lie and treat them like dirt, all *empathizing* like mad.'

'"Women who give too much".' James gave her a quizzical look. 'We did something about it on *Good Morning Britain* a while back. It's very common, apparently. Loads of women do it, bend over backwards for men who basically abuse them. The worse the guy treats them the harder the woman works at getting him to love her, goes out of her way to be the perfect partner, which just makes him think he can pretty much get away with murder and she'll still have his dinner on the table as soon as he walks through the door.' Her toe slid between his legs.

'If you keep doing that we're not going to get through all this.'

She pulled a face and slipped her foot back into her shoe. 'OK, you're in charge. For today, anyway.'

'Naughty Mummy. Now, let's just focus for a minute. I didn't get to be controller by playing footsie under the table. I got here by hard graft, keeping a cool head, and getting rid of all the dead wood.'

'A.k.a. Julia Hill.'

James smiled. 'Ah yes, Julia. Only yesterday she sent a grovelling email suggesting lunch – or coffee if I'm pressed for time. Deluded fool really seemed to think she was in with a chance of your job, you know.'

Helen laughed. 'You're kidding! That menopausal old hag, fronting the network's flagship daytime show? She's bonkers.'

'According to her she would be perfect. How did she put it? Something about having the right blend of empathy and rapier-like interviewing skills.'

'*Rapier-like?*'

'According to one of her many emails currently clogging up my inbox. As you say, the woman is clearly not all there.'

Helen appeared thoughtful. 'And she really doesn't remember you from your days at City Broadcasting?'

'She hasn't the foggiest. You have to remember I was only there about five minutes before she had me fired.'

'You know, *heat* ran a piece tipping her as joint favourite with Karen King for my job.'

James laughed. 'Except there *is* no job, is there? There never was.'

Helen felt justifiably smug. In one fell swoop she had seen off the women she most feared, her only real competition. Until

Girl Talk came along she was the undisputed star of Channel 6. In the last couple of years, though, the late-night show had become so popular it threatened to eclipse her. She had not clawed her way to the top to see it all snatched away by those late-night lushes from *Girl Talk*. Of course, James couldn't be seen to axe a perfectly successful show without good reason. It had to be made to implode, hence her idea to get the women to resign one by one until he had no choice but to pull the plug. Clever, even if she thought so herself.

They sat in silence for a moment. 'James, are you sure no one's going to find out ...' A note of anxiety had crept into her voice.

He gathered up the papers on the desk. 'Of course not. What could possibly go wrong? So you've had a change of heart and can't imagine leaving *Good Morning Britain* after all. Who can blame you? I mean, look at Fiona Phillips. I bet if she could turn back the clock she'd think twice about leaving GMTV. As for the new entertainment commissions, the fact that two shows are being made by a new company will be deemed a good thing. We're always being told to give the new kids on the block a chance.'

'What if somebody works out it's actually *your* company?'

'They won't. I've gone to great lengths to cover my tracks and make sure there are no loose ends, nothing to tie me to Stealth TV. Believe me, no one knows more about this business than I do. And Stealth shows will be great telly. They'll bring in the audience and healthy advertising revenue, so everyone's happy – especially us, since we stand to make a fortune. The way I see it, I'm doing the channel a massive favour.' He stroked the arm of his chair. 'The shareholders should be grateful to me.'

'But if it ever got out ... it doesn't bear thinking about. I mean, the press would crucify us and we'd probably be done for fraud. Christ, James, we could end up in jail.'

'Relax, no one will ever know. I've told you, it's our little secret and it's going to stay that way.'

Fifty-Seven

Paula Grayson was already in the conference room, in her usual seat at the head of the table, when Karen arrived a few minutes before the meeting was due to start. There was no sign of the other women. Karen slid into a seat to the left of Paula, who looked up from her laptop. 'You've seen the announcement then?'

Karen nodded. 'Did you know he was axing the show?'

'He told me, oh let's see . . . a good minute before it hit the website. Quite the master manipulator, our James.' She managed a wry smile. 'Actually, Jackie tipped me off a while ago. Didn't like the way our esteemed controller operates. He tried to get her into bed, you know. Invited her to a so-called brainstorming lunch at the May Fair Hotel, then suggested she join him upstairs for *afters*. Very subtle.' She closed the lid of the laptop. 'Apparently there's a job for me in the new set-up, if you can believe that, assuming I want to work for the kind of bastard who takes perfectly good shows off for no apparent reason. It's ridiculous him saying it wouldn't work with just Julia and Faye left. We could have got some new faces in.

'So will you stay on?' Karen asked.

'Right now, my only concern is *Girl Talk* and making the last ten shows the best, showing the cun – sorry, *con*troller – the series still has legs; five pretty good pairs as far as I'm concerned.' She sighed. 'I'll be honest, Karen, I'm sick and tired of all the crap that goes on in TV, dealing with back-stabbers like James Almond.'

Karen swallowed. He had well and truly shafted them all.

Paula gave her a grim smile. 'What about you?'

She looked away. 'Well, I resigned, so . . .' Her voice tailed off. 'I don't really know what's next. Something will come along, I suppose.'

'*Loose Women*?'

'I wouldn't be surprised if that's where Lesley ends up.' The door opened and Faye, in leggings and a thigh-length T-shirt that said WISH YOU WERE HERE on the front, appeared. She gave Paula and Karen an airy wave and took a seat near the window. 'Is it me or is it hot in here?' She pulled her script from her bag and wafted it in front of her face.

Paula glanced at Karen. 'Have you seen James Almond's announcement?' she said to Faye.

Faye leaned across the table and helped herself to a handful of chocolate biscuits. 'I haven't seen anything. You're lucky I'm here. Gyppy tummy this morning.' She polished off a digestive.

Paula said, 'I don't suppose *that*'s going to help if you're feeling rough.'

'Sugar,' Faye said. 'I've not eaten anything today. I need something sweet.' She bit another biscuit in half.

The door flew open and Lesley appeared. 'Can anyone tell me what the fuck is going on?' She shrugged off a fur jacket and slung it over the back of the chair next to Faye.

'Is that thing real?' Faye dragged her seat away from Lesley.

'One hundred per cent authentic bunny.' Lesley picked up a flask from the middle of the table, sniffed it, and poured a coffee.

Faye gave her a look of disgust. 'I don't know how you can wear it.'

'Well, I wouldn't, only it's *Prada* and it was rather *pricey* and I didn't actually *know* it was rabbit when I bought it.' She sipped at the coffee. 'Fuck, that's hot.'

'You can't wear fur any more. Someone's bound to tip off the press and out you. Fur is cruel.'

'It's hardly baby seals, is it? I mean, it's not like I clubbed anything to death.' She lurched at the fur and petted it.

Paula narrowed her eyes. 'I do hope you haven't come straight from lunch. You know the rules on drinking before the show.'

Lesley gave her an enigmatic smile. She and Dan had got through a couple of bottles of champagne – a modest amount by her standards – at Al Dente after Dean Craig had called to tell her about the *Good Morning Britain* fiasco. Hadn't James Almond told her the job was as good as hers? She couldn't work out who was to blame – him or that two-faced bitch Helen England. Or both of them. So that's why he was coming out of her flat that day! The two of them *were* in cahoots.

The door flew back and Julia flounced in, a full-length black coat flapping open over a fitted black dress, her face as dark and threatening as her outfit.

'Jesus, Julia, did somebody die? You look like you're in mourning.' Lesley gave her an appraising look. 'Matching lipstick too. That's clever.'

Julia rounded on her. 'I don't suppose you've come across this one. You can't buy it here.'

'I'm not surprised. It looks like it should have a health warning, maybe a skull and crossbones thingy.' She slid her shades back over her eyes. 'Shit, I can't even look at it. It's giving me a headache. I hope you're not planning to go on-air like that. They'll think Cruella de Vil's doing a guest spot.'

Julia flung herself into a seat at the far end of the table. Paula said, 'You've heard about James Almond axing the show?'

Julia shrugged. 'It's actually good timing for me,' she lied. 'I have other irons in the fire, so it just saves me from having to tell him I'm not available for another series anyway.'

Faye sat bolt upright. 'What's going on?'

Lesley started clapping. 'Nice try. I had no idea you were such a good actress. You almost had me fooled for a second, pulling off a performance like that when you've just been sacked ... you really should try the stage now you've been dumped from the telly. Mind you, parts for women in their twilight years tend to be thin on the ground.' She paused for a second. 'There is *Calendar Girls* though, I suppose. They always seem to be in the market for at least one OAP.'

Faye gripped the edge of the table. '*Sacked* ... will someone please tell me what's going on?'

Julia jumped up and turned to Lesley. 'Don't think I don't know what your game is, handing in your notice without a word, you sneaky mare. What – you thought you had Helen England's job in the bag? Well, that blew up in your face, didn't it?'

'Oh fuck off. The world doesn't revolve around Channel 6, you know.'

'That's quite enough. Sit down and calm down.' Paula looked round the table. 'We still have a show to make and I'm counting on you – *all* of you – to be professional and give *Girl Talk* the send-off it deserves. The show has been very good to

344

all of you. The least you can do is get to the end of the run with a bit of dignity.'

Faye was ashen. 'What do you mean – send-off? What's happening?'

Cheryl, a coffee in one hand, her phone in the other, eased open the door with her elbow. 'You'll never guess – I've just been in the canteen and someone told me Helen England's not leaving *Good Morning Britain* after all.'

Faye scrambled to her feet, sending her chair and Lesley's precious fur flying in the process. 'Will somebody PLEASE tell me what's going on?!'

Lesley snatched her jacket off the floor and dusted it off. 'It's the end of the road, darling. We've been axed. Keep up!'

Faye went a funny shade of green and shot a frantic look at Cheryl as the room began to spin and she sank to the floor.

Fifty-Eight

Joel Reynolds sat on the edge of the armchair chewing his nails. He had lost count of the number of times Julia had called, her tone ranging from downright abusive to pleading, desperate. She just needed to talk. She had no one else to turn to. 'Please Joel,' she said, in the kind of soft tone he would never have imagined her capable of, 'please pick up the phone. Maybe we could meet for lunch, or dinner . . .' At one point he could have sworn there was a catch in her voice, although he must have been mistaken because Julia didn't do crying. Her tear ducts had probably packed up after years of neglect. Even so, he had never known her so wound up and hysterical and it worried him. He knew what she was capable of. Clearly, the news about *Girl Talk* being axed had sent her into orbit. The gossip mags had been full of it, a spread in *heat* showing Karen, Lesley and Cheryl's beaming faces next to a shot of Julia looking thunderous. Speculation was rife the girls had resigned because they had other things in the offing. Almost everyone seemed to think Lesley Gold was joining *Loose Women*; rumour had it a star vehicle was being developed at Channel 6 for Karen King; Cheryl West was being tipped to join the *Dancing on Ice* team. He wasn't sure what was going on with Faye Cole. No one seemed too bothered about her.

Joel was having an attack of conscience about pouring his

heart out to Laura Lloyd. If he had known Julia was about to lose her job he might have thought twice about blabbing to the *Sunday*. It all seemed a bit mean, sticking the knife in now she was out in the cold anyway. Then again, he couldn't have known she was for the chop and he was at the end of his rope after years of abuse at her hands. Constant bullying and blackmailing had ground him down, almost tipped him over the edge more than once. Joel remembered the time he had driven to the coast and sat in the car, rain lashing down, something dreary by Leonard Cohen on the sound system, and contemplated running away, leaving the clinic behind and never coming back.

Opposite him, Laura Lloyd lounged in a corner of the sofa, legs crossed, champagne flute in her hand. She had said nothing for several minutes, just watched Joel lost in his own thoughts and waited for him to break the silence in his own time. He rubbed his brow and gave her a thin smile. 'I feel sick,' he said.

Laura sipped at her drink. She was wearing a tight purple and black sweater dress and over-the-knee suede boots, her blonde hair arranged in a messy and flattering up-do. Three hours at the Nicky Clarke salon, some soft caramel highlights and a bill she wasn't going to think about had made her feel like a different woman: the kind of woman a man like Joel might actually look at. On the sofa next to her was a snakeskin bag that had set her back a cool £1,500 at Selfridges a couple of days earlier. She reached out and ran a hand over it. Her look said *Dressed to kill* in an expensive, understated way. She pushed up the sleeve of her dress to reveal a chunky jewelled cuff.

'You wouldn't be normal if you weren't a bit anxious.

There's always that sense of *Have I done the right thing? What will the repercussions be? Is this going to rebound on me?*'

'So it's the same for everyone?'

'Anyone with a conscience gets cold feet.' Laura held up her glass. Bubbles rose to the surface of the pale golden liquid. The truth was, for the first time in her life she was having second thoughts about a story. She was well aware that exposing Julia would rebound horribly on Joel. Once his part in her story came out, his celebrity clients, ever alert to the scent of scandal, would be off faster than you could say 'nip and tuck'. The last thing she wanted was to ruin the man she was falling for. 'You just have to hold your nerve,' she said, hating herself.

Joel winced. 'Oh God, she'll come after me.'

'She'll come after me as well, but she'll have to join the queue. There's somebody after me every week once the paper hits the stands.' For the past couple of weeks Laura had been playing for time, telling her editor she still had to stand up some of the more salacious aspects of the Julia piece, but he was growing impatient. She knew the story would have to run sooner rather than later. 'I know she'll go off the deep end but you can't take it personally.'

'It *is* personal, though – for both of us.'

'Look, Julia is a bully.' She leaned forward. 'It's time she was stopped.'

'I know. It's just . . . isn't splashing her biggest secret all over the front page a bit harsh?'

'It's called karma. You reap what you sow and all that.' By the same token, karma would ensure Joel wanted nothing more to do with Laura once his clients did a runner, leaving him with a clinic that was mortgaged to the hilt. 'Let's not worry about it tonight,' she said.

Joel decided not to tell Laura he actually felt sorry for Julia and had been tempted more than once to call her back after all the pathetic messages she kept leaving on his mobile, which he now kept switched off. Unbeknown to Julia he had got a new number and circulated it to everyone in his contacts book apart from her. Every now and then he would check the old one and there she would be, begging him to pick up the phone. He didn't dare, though, not after Laura had told him he needed to steer well clear.

She gave him a brilliant smile. 'Let's drink to justice.'

Joel picked up his glass and reached across the low table that separated him from Laura. Julia's face, her expression gruesome, stared up at him from the covers of several magazines. His glass clinked against Laura's and he threw down half his drink in one go. Almost at once he felt better. He closed his eyes. She was right. He just had to keep his nerve. Soon, one way or another, it would all be over.

'If you stick to your guns and deny all knowledge she'll never be able to prove you were behind any of this.'

Joel opened his eyes. 'Really? Won't she work it out?'

'She's not clever enough. She might have her suspicions but there are so many people she's pissed off in her long and tedious career, all she'll be left with is a long list of suspects. From what I hear, she's made life hell for Karen King over the *Good Morning Britain* job. What a fiasco that turned out to be.' She sipped her champagne. There was definitely more to all that than met the eye. Once she had finished with Julia she might just turn her attention to Helen England. And James Almond for that matter. How bizarre that he would be the boss, and how strange to think she once had a crush on him after his heroics on her behalf at *Rise and Shine*. TV must have hardened him, as these days he seemed to have acquired a reputation for being utterly ruthless.

'It's no secret Julia and Lesley Gold are at each other's throats as well. For all she knows maybe one of her *Girl Talk* buddies stitched her up to get her out of the running for a job that probably never existed anyway. I could go on. She has an impressive list of enemies.'

'What about all the calls I've been ignoring? Won't she smell a rat?'

'Your mobile was stolen and you've got a different number. There was a temp in covering for your regular secretary and she was supposed to let everyone know, pass the new number on, but she didn't do a very good job. Julia wasn't the only one she failed to contact. In fact she made such a balls-up you won't be using that agency again.'

Joel stared at her.

'You just have to make sure you're always one step ahead. Let's face it, if Julia's a mess now over what's gone on at *Girl Talk* she will be in *bits* when she sees my exclusive.' Unfortunately, so would Joel. Laura wriggled on the sofa and gave the hem of her dress a tug.

Joel drained a second glass of champagne. Laura had a point. He could worry himself sick and it wouldn't change a thing. She was smiling at him, a strand of hair escaping a clip, tumbling over one eye. She looked completely different. Maybe this was her off-duty look and the scary power dressing she usually went in for was strictly a business thing. No sign of those clunky glasses either. He wondered if they were a prop, since he was sure she wasn't wearing contact lenses. Her eyes were the most intense inky blue. Apart from a little mascara and a dusting of powder she wasn't wearing make-up, not that she needed it. What a change it made to be in the company of a woman who wasn't forever checking her face in her compact and coating her lips with some radioactive colour that gave you a pain behind the eyes. He had always thought Laura was a bit drippy, but now he was beginning to think that might be an act. She was actually a bit of a Lois Lane character on the quiet. He noticed her glass was empty and topped them both up.

Laura crossed her legs again and he got a glimpse of creamy flesh at the top of her thigh. She was wearing stockings. Again, it crossed his mind that she was going on somewhere, meeting someone. He held up his glass. 'Let's drink to you, Lois, because you are bloody brilliant.' The champagne had gone straight to his head and made him tipsy.

'Lois?' She smiled. 'Well I couldn't have done it without you, Clark.' She was light-headed too, a bit giddy. Bad move to start boozing on an empty stomach. She took a deep breath. 'Joel, can I buy you dinner? You know, just to thank you for trusting me and putting such a terrific story my way.' She crossed her legs the other way and he got another flash of flesh. 'I've actually booked a table but if you have plans I understand – I should have said something sooner. I can always call and cancel, they won't mind.' Her words were coming out too fast and a pink flush had appeared on her throat. She smiled coyly. 'I would have made it The Ivy but it'll have to be somewhere more discreet. We can't risk you being seen with me in case it gets back to Julia.'

Joel beamed at her. 'Dinner sounds great, but it's on me.' Laura opened her mouth to protest but he shook his head.

'You've made me feel like a weight's been lifted, so let me take you out. It's the least I can do.'

Laura wondered if he would still want to take her out once his reputation was in tatters.

Fifty-Nine

When the pains started Hannah thought it was indigestion. A few hours earlier she had wolfed down a curry – chicken madras, extra hot – even though Jason had said he really didn't think she should be eating spicy food in case it brought on contractions. She had laughed and told him not to be ridiculous: that was an old wives' tale. Two hours later they were on their way to hospital.

She looked around her. The room was painted a pale shade of yellow and there was a painting, a landscape, something traditional and rural with bales of hay, on the wall facing her. At the side of the bed was a cabinet in sleek pale wood, a bottle of mineral water, a couple of dimpled tumblers on a cork mat within easy reach, and a bowl of fruit. On the other side of the bed was a chair, not an ugly plastic one, the kind most hospitals have, but a proper armchair, upholstered in cream with a couple of yellow silk cushions, plumped up and arranged just so. A frosted-glass door led to the private bathroom, which was massive and had a jacuzzi bath. Hannah had no idea how much it cost to have a baby here but it was popular with celebs and that was good enough for her. Anyway, Jason was picking up the tab. It was his baby, his responsibility. Not that she was actually having the baby, not yet. She kept trying to say it was just cramp, indigestion or whatever, but no one was listening.

Now there was a consultant going through her notes and checking the latest scan, talking about her being so many centimetres dilated and generally making her nervous, while Jason was in the corridor calling the magazine they'd signed up to, telling them to get a photographer over, the baby was on its way. He also got on the phone to her agent, Steven Kirby, who wanted to be there for the birth. Hannah insisted they were all jumping the gun, she just needed something for the indigestion, but Professor Marcus Simpson was adamant: whether she liked it or not she was in labour.

'I can't be,' she said, panicking.

He peered between her legs. 'My dear girl, the baby is on its way.'

'No – I'm not ready!' Suddenly, the idea of giving birth terrified her.

He checked her notes again. 'And according to my calculations the little fella's bang on time. Now relax. You're in excellent hands.' He handed her a remote. 'Watch a bit of TV if you like – take your mind off things.'

'You don't understand – you've got to stop it!'

Professor Simpson gave her an indulgent smile. 'It's perfectly normal to be a bit anxious with your first, but there's really no need.' He took her hand and checked her pulse. 'That's fine, you're doing very well. You might just have a nice quick labour.' He winked. 'Now, leave all the worrying to us.'

Hannah was hit by a sudden wave of nausea that had nothing to do with the curry. In a few hours an awkward question that had been popping in and out of her mind, troubling her all the way through her pregnancy, would finally be answered. When she met Jason she was still seeing a footballer on and off. Damien Carlton was fit and loaded and definitely knew how to show a girl a good time. Trouble was, Hannah wasn't the only girl he was having fun with. Damien was straight with her from the word go: he had no desire to settle down, not now, not ever if he could help it. He wasn't into monogamy. Hannah said that was fine and then proceeded to pull out the stops to show him she was The One. She cooked special healthy meals just the way he liked, kept the place spotless, picked up the towels and clothes and energy-drink cartons he left lying all over and did his laundry – the delicates by hand. She took his silk shirts to the dry cleaner, arranged his collection of DVDs – including the porn – in alphabetical order, and even polished his shoes. And still he went out and picked up other women. It drove her insane. She cried and begged and threatened and gave him the silent treatment, not that it made a scrap of difference. 'Babe, you know the score,' he would say in that casual way of his, dropping his dirty Armani boxers on the floor of the bedroom on his way to the wet room.

When Jason came along she knew right away he was a better bet. To start with she kept things going with Damien, saw him on the quiet now and then while she worked on getting Jason to leave Karen, which proved trickier than she had imagined. What was wrong with him? Given the choice of a teenage glamour model or a beached whale there was no contest, surely.

She was sure she'd got pregnant after she'd stopped seeing Damien. Plus, he always used condoms. Then again, there *had* been the odd accident. She felt sick. Deep down she knew there was a chance the father of her child might just be a womanizing footballer, and if it *was* Damien's there was no way she could pass the baby off as Jason's, not unless he came from Nigerian stock and had just never thought to mention it.

The door opened and Jason bounded in, a gormless grin on

his face. 'Right, the photographer's on his way and they're sending that nice woman, Melanie – you know, the redhead who interviewed us last time: smoky eyes, tattoo on the wrist, massive bazookas – remember? – to do the chat.' He squeezed her hand. 'They're sorting out hair and make-up as well.'

Hannah's face twisted in agony. Shit, shit, *shit*. Couldn't he see she was in no mood for an audience? A sudden searing pain made her gasp for breath and lunge for the buzzer at the side of the bed to summon a nurse. A sense of dread gripped her. Jason's grinning face swam before her. It was all about to unravel, she could feel it.

Jason helped himself to a grape from the fruit bowl and gazed around the room. 'More like a hotel than a hospital, isn't it? Have you seen the bathroom? There's even a spa bath.'

Hannah panted, glaring at him. Sweat ran down her face. 'Where's the bloody nurse?'

He plucked another couple of grapes from the bunch. 'I'll get the make-up girl to do me while she's at it,' he said. 'Have you seen the bags – flipping *suitcases*, more like it – under my eyes?' He disappeared into the bathroom and stared at his reflection in the mirror. 'Christ, look at the state of me. They can always touch up the pictures, I suppose.'

He wanted to look his best in the photos, not get mistaken for Hannah's dad. Hopefully the baby would generate a swathe of positive press. All that messing about with Karen had been extremely damaging. The 'love rat' headlines had hit him in the wallet and lost him a deal for a series of lucrative TV commercials for home insurance. The company said they wanted someone reputable and trustworthy fronting their ads and hired the bloke from the Harry Enfield show to replace him. Jason had done what he could to get things back on track, getting 'a friend', i.e. his publicist, to talk exclusively to one of the Sunday papers about how tough it had been to end things with Karen, especially with her begging him to go back to her. Still, he reckoned once the baby was born he would be able to market himself as a family man, which would definitely be a plus point.

He wandered back into the room in time to see Hannah, puce, fling out an arm and almost send the fruit bowl on the bedside cabinet flying.

'Oops, steady on. Remember your breathing. One-two. One-two. Steven's on his way, should be here in about half an hour. Think you can hang on?' Hannah moaned and thrashed about. 'What about a glass of water?'

'I don't need water, you idiot, I need a frigging nurse – NOW!'

Sixty

Julia, in need of some serious pampering, had taken herself off to a spa-cum-clinic for the weekend, an exclusive place on a clifftop in Cornwall known for its first-rate therapists and innovative treatments. She had been to The Institute before and loved the strict regime, the no-fat-no-sugar-no-caffeine-no-alcohol rule, and the fact that everyone wore starched white coats and stern expressions. The Institute was beauty at its hardcore best and Julia was a sucker for it.

Doctor Hans Braun, a trim, smooth-skinned, pink-cheeked seventy-year-old who ran the place with a rod of iron, was the only person capable of bossing her about. From the moment she checked in she allowed him to confiscate her mobile phone, say what she may and may not eat and drink, and dictate precisely which treatments she would be having. Dr Braun persuaded Julia to tolerate the retch-making clay drinks that left her doubled up, convinced her insides were about to explode. When she wasn't being beaten to a near-pulp by some stony-faced former Russian shot-putter-turned-massage-therapist Julia was closeted away in her luxury suite, consuming the foul detoxifying sludge shakes delivered by one of the doctor's assistants on the dot of seven each evening. Precisely half an hour later a sharp tap on the door would signal lights-out. She would be woken with another shake and a flask of hot water with a squeeze of lemon at six the following morning.

There was no TV at The Institute, no radio and no newspapers. It was like being in a harsh, regimented cocoon where there was no need to think because someone else did it for you. As far as Julia was concerned it was absolute bliss and the results were dramatic. The Institute was indeed an extraordinary place. She visited at least four times a year and had told not a single soul, not even Joel Reynolds, about it.

For the duration of her stay she happily ate the disgusting macrobiotic food beloved of the place and spent a good deal of time on the loo in between being pummelled, kneaded, hosed down with mineral-rich seawater and slathered in something smelly called rasul mud before exotic serum extracted from the placenta of Peruvian lambs – or was it goats? she couldn't quite remember – was applied to her glowing skin. When it came to advances in anti-ageing treatments The Institute was at the cutting edge. Sometimes she wondered if the therapies, which involved needles and the kind of electrodes that made Julia think of something you would attach to a car with a flat battery, were entirely legal, but she didn't much care. She was willing to take risks for the sake of her appearance. She had undergone potentially life-threatening procedures in dodgy clinics before and lived to tell the tale.

She lay on her front in a room filled with steam, a hefty woman in giant knickers and a lift-and-separate bra pounding on her shoulder blades. Julia gasped as the woman's meaty hands made chopping motions up and down her back. Jesus Christ *Almighty* that hurt. She didn't dare object for fear her tormentor would just crank up the pain level. Julia felt the woman's hands slide down her body, deliver a series of bruising blows to her bum and come to rest on the backs of her legs. She tensed up as Olga or Eva or whatever her name was dug her thumbs into her calf muscles. Ouch! Fuck! It was unbearable – absolute fucking agony. She tried to wriggle free but the great lump just gripped her harder. Julia gritted her teeth as the woman stepped back and then bore down on her with a birch switch.

Tom Steiner didn't usually work weekends. Most Saturdays he was out on the golf course first thing, dressed in loud checked trousers in garish colours and a diamond-patterned Pringle sweater, but he could hardly get a round in now, not after his conversation with Laura Lloyd the night before.

He had put in a call to offer her an exclusive on a Premier League footballer's romance with the former daughter-in-law of his old manager. Naturally, he had asked how the piece on Julia was coming along.

'Tom, this Julia Hill piece, off the record, between you and me,' Laura said. 'I want to give you a heads-up because it's going to be –' she hesitated – 'pretty massive.'

'I should think so – right now she needs a decent spread, what with all the changes at Channel 6.'

Laura took a deep breath. 'The thing is, when I say "massive", I don't quite mean it the way you think I do.'

'I don't follow. What are you saying?'

Laura closed her eyes. 'How well do you actually know Julia?'

He could not believe what she said next and, ever since, he had been trying to get hold of the presenter, who seemed to have vanished off the face of the earth. In desperation he had woken his assistant, Louise, at the crack of dawn, and told her to go round and rouse Julia. It was no good. The place was deserted. Louise, who knew not to report back to Tom before exhausting every option, had gone along the street knocking on doors (which hadn't exactly gone down well at seven on a Saturday morning) until a woman over the road said she had seen Julia drive away the night before and, yes, she was sure it was her as no one else owned a bright yellow Porsche.

Tom had also spoken to Kirsty Collins, who said Julia had let her go early the day before but there was nothing in the diary about her heading out of town. It crossed Tom's mind that someone had tipped Julia off about the *Sunday* piece and she had done a runner. He sat at his desk and composed one of his infamous emails to the paper's editor. It simply said: You know how it works. Run the Julia Hill story and I guarantee we will not be doing business again. He considered putting 'guarantee' in capitals but since he wanted to come across as terse rather than hysterical, decided to stick with lower case.

He nipped round the corner to a coffee shop, where he ordered a large latte with an extra shot and a hint of hazelnut and sat in the sun at a table on the pavement outside. On the far side of the road a man in a navy apron over a white coat sloshed water on to the street and mopped the area in front of an organic-cheese emporium. Tom squinted into the sun and sipped his coffee. He patted his jacket pocket where his BlackBerry lay silent. 'Come on, come on,' he said, willing an email to pop up from the editor assuring him the story would be spiked. Impatient, he rang the editor's direct line. A few seconds later a recorded voice told him to leave a message or press zero to return to the switchboard. He pressed zero.

'The *Sunday*,' a chirpy voice said. 'Who would you like to speak to?'

'Put me through to Laura Lloyd.'

'Yes sir. Can I take your name?'

'Tom Steiner.' There was a pause while he waited and then he heard the phone ringing, only to go straight through to voice-mail again. He pressed zero and asked for Abigail Trent Powell, one of the showbiz reporters. 'The person at extension . . .' Shit. If no one on that fucking paper would take his call it must be bad.

By the time Julia left The Institute she felt like a new woman. Her skin gleamed and she had lost six pounds in the space of three days. Armed with macrobiotic recipes, she was full of good intentions until she pulled in at the first garage she came to for petrol and felt her resolve weakening, leading her to detour off to a little coffee shop down the road for a double-strength cappuccino. At a table tucked away in a corner she dug out her lipstick, applying a fresh slick of Tender Orchid.

She fished out her BlackBerry, which she had been going to leave off until she got home. The screen gleamed at her and she checked her reflection in it, Sharon Stone looking back as she teased her hair into ferocious spikes. Once she had the phone in her hand she couldn't resist switching it on, although she knew there would be no messages from the weekend as she only ever received work-related calls. The screen lit up and a message appeared. One hundred and thirty-two missed calls! Umpteen voicemails! The thing had gone haywire. She scrolled through the list. Tom Steiner, Laura Lloyd, Kirsty Collins. Why was Curse-dee trying to get hold of her at the weekend? It was unheard of.

Cold dread suddenly gripped her. Her fucking *straighteners*! She must have left them plugged in on the bedroom floor. A vision of them going up in flames and burning the place down came to her. Oh God, she hoped they'd managed to save her shoes. She fumbled with the phone, sweat gathering in the nape of her neck as she rang her message service and heard Tom Steiner's voice, brisk and impatient, telling her to get back to him asap. She rolled her eyes. He sounded well and truly pissed off so she could only assume he had been forced to interrupt some power brunch to call her. The next message was also from Tom, peeved, not sounding anything like he usually did, saying would she *please* call as soon as she got the message. Shit, what had got into him? Her sense of dread began to evaporate. At least the house couldn't have burned down or he would have said. Maybe a job offer had come in, something urgent, and they needed an answer right away. She didn't bother listening to the remaining twenty-six messages, just called his mobile.

'Julia – at *last*!' He didn't sound pleased to hear from her, just exasperated and on edge, like he'd overdone the caffeine.

'What is it?' she said, trying to sound unconcerned, her stomach flipping over again at the thought of the straighteners going up.

'Where *are* you? Didn't you get my messages?'

'I've been away, nice little session at a spa I know, full programme of massage and facials and foot rubs and whatnot. No mobiles, no telly and *no* newspapers since Friday—'

'Julia,' he interrupted, then stopped. She heard what sounded like a heavy sigh. Suddenly she felt sick. 'Julia, I hope you're sitting down.'

Sixty-One

Tom was known for not beating around the bush so he came right out with it. The *Sunday* was on the brink of telling the world Julia had undergone a sex change. The headline was to be **TV'S SHE-DEVIL WAS A *HE*!**

Julia sat hunched in her chair in the coffee shop, shaking, Michael Bublé warbling from a speaker above her, as Tom spelled out over the phone what lay in store. Laura Lloyd was in the throes of writing a no-holds-barred account of the operations that had transformed Alan Swales into Julia Hill. She had spoken to the medical director of the Thai clinic where the procedures had been carried out and he had described the surgery in explicit detail. Julia covered her face with her hands.

The paper had pictures of Julia as a boy in TA fatigues, and quotes from that bitch who had caught him stealing her make-up in the girls' toilet at the school disco and screamed the place down.

Julia slumped deeper in her chair as Tom said Laura Lloyd had even spoken to someone who claimed the teenage Alan had been a violent bully, blasting a neighbour with an air gun. And was it true she'd been selling her arse around town to fund the op? Julia closed her eyes. Her head spun. How had a drip like Laura Lloyd found all this stuff out?

'You need to stay away, Julia, give me a chance to try and calm things down,' Tom said. 'Keep out of London.'

'But Tom, the show ... I've got to be back for *Girl Talk* tonight ...'

'Wake up, Julia.' He took a breath. 'Look, I've had James Almond on, saying you don't need to work your notice.'

'What? He can't do that!'

'It's nothing to do with this sex-change business. No one else knows about that yet. He claims to have a dossier of complaints around the issue of bullying.' Tom cleared his throat. 'He also says he has evidence of drug abuse. Really, Julia, if I'd known about any of this I might have had more chance of helping you. As it is ...'

It was no good. She was finished.

'What am I supposed to do?' she said, her voice small.

He sighed. 'I don't know yet. It's a fucking mess. I'll do my best but I'm not promising anything. You might have to do a tell-all if I can't stop it. They'll want every gory detail, every cough and spit. It would need to be mega-bucks – it just might end up being your pension.'

Julia gagged, tasting bile in her mouth. After Tom hung up she sat at the table, coffee forgotten, staring ahead. Her brain couldn't process what was happening to her. But she knew she had to move, crawl away somewhere private and hide. Turning up the collar of her jacket, she struggled to walk back to her car. Her legs felt weak, her stomach was churning. Climbing into the Porsche, she started driving.

Sixty-Two

Julia woke up in darkness, disorientated for a moment until she remembered she had made her way, on auto-pilot, to the remote and cosy cottage she'd treasured as a secret refuge her whole professional life. She pulled herself into a sitting position on the bed where she'd passed out earlier, fully clothed on top of the bedspread.

Her brain ached as she recalled the day's events. Everything she had worked for was about to come crashing down. She would never recover. Never. She sat on the edge of the bed trembling, digging her nails into her palms. Tom had said he was on it, but how could he stop it? And no amount of spin would save her once she was exposed as a sex-swap celeb. That's what the papers would call her. She would be branded a freak. For twenty-five years she had kept her secret, maintained her image as a beautiful woman, carved out a successful career. And now this would be the end of her life as she knew it. She chewed on a nail. The press would rip her to shreds.

Who had tipped off Laura Lloyd? That was the question that obsessed her. No one *knew*. Well, almost no one. There was Joel, of course, but from what Tom had said he was going to be named as the doctor who performed her surgery. All those A-listers beating a path to his door would be gone for good the second they knew he'd been performing secret sex-change ops in Thailand. No, he had too much to lose. Maybe the Thai clinic's imbecile director had chanced upon an episode of *Girl Talk*, now running on some cable channel in the Far East, and set things in motion.

A tumbler filled with vodka and a dash of cranberry juice sat on the bedside table. She grimaced as she took a drink. She would never be able to look anyone in the eye again. Of course her career would be over – there would be no more red-carpet events and she would be off every guest list at a stroke. She'd be a pariah, a joke, a disgrace, just as she had been back at school. She forced the rest of the vodka down and filled her glass again from the bottle of Smirnoff Blue at the side of the bed. No cranberry this time. Tom Steiner had clout but there was no way even he would be able to call off the *Sunday* dogs. It had already gone too far. In a few days the world would know *what* she was.

She thought back to the day she had gone to her doctor and told him she was a girl trapped in a boy's body, seeing once again his perplexed expression and the slightest distaste in his eyes. He had sent her to a psychologist for assessment. For years she had endured hormones that made her moody and bad-tempered. She was taunted and bullied when she first started dressing as a woman, her clumsy attempts at being feminine not fooling anyone. As for the surgery, she'd saved up and gone to Thailand, funding the procedures by selling her body. The first time she'd met Joel at the clinic she'd chosen, she'd refused to believe the hippyish young man was a real doctor. But she'd come to trust him, feeling that for the first time someone really understood her, saw the woman she was meant to be. She had a boob job first, then, a few months later, was back on the operating table for seven hours while Joel worked on her face, peeling back the skin, hacking away part of her brow, reshaping her jaw, giving her a new, delicate nose. For weeks afterwards she had been in agony, surviving on fluids sipped through a straw.

Hundreds of vile clients later, back in Thailand, she had genital reconstruction. Another seven hours on the operating table while Joel hollowed out what was left of her penis after years of hormone therapy and created her dreamed-about vagina. For weeks afterwards she balanced on a rubber ring, in excruciating pain, sobbing, not knowing who she was any more. Joel had been the one person she could turn to when the changes she was putting herself through threatened to overwhelm her. For a while she hoped the two of them might get together until she saw the look of panic on his face when she tried to tell him how she felt. From then on she was careful to lock her feelings and any suggestion of vulnerability away.

She switched on her laptop. It was amazing what you could find on the internet these days. In no time at all she had established precisely how many sleeping pills she would have to take to ensure she didn't wake up. There were helpful tips on slitting her wrists – where and how to make the incisions – and how best to knot a rope if hanging was her preferred exit strategy. She thought about the banister running the length of the gallery above the sitting room at home. Perfect. One particularly macabre website offered step-by-step advice on carrying out what it called mercy killings.

Julia got her compact out of her bag and studied her reflection. Just hours ago, when she left The Institute, she had looked fantastic, her skin dewy and glowing. Now her eyes were red and swollen from crying and her skin was mottled. She looked away. It would take more than a dusting of powder and a coat of fifty-quid lipstick to save her now.

She got into bed with her clothes on and drank her way through the rest of the vodka, taking it neat. Her head began to spin and rage began to rise through her body. Before she died she had to know who had done this to her. Maybe it was Lesley, that smug, supercilious bitch. She'd been on her back for weeks, goading her, calling her Jeremy Paxman. The story had all the hallmarks of that spiteful cow *and* that bastard controller, James Almond. No wonder he wouldn't see her; they were probably sleeping together. She pictured them in bed, Lesley gossiping, dripping poison in his ear, the two of them plotting to ruin her, digging the dirt together.

Then there was Karen, who only a week ago had suggested an entire programme dedicated to the perils of plastic surgery. That had been agony for Julia. Lesley had said she could never imagine going under the knife just to change her appearance and given Julia a knowing look, then brought up a story about a teenager determined to become the youngest sex-swap patient in the UK. Julia had squirmed and done her best to steer the discussion back round to cosmetic procedures while the others banged on about how you couldn't possibly know your mind at the age of sixteen. Well Julia had, not that she dared say so.

No – hold on, it wasn't *Lesley* who sparked that whole sex-change debate, it was *Karen*. It all came back: Karen putting her on the spot, saying she was very quiet for once, and they were all dying to know what she had to say.

Julia reached for the vodka. Empty. She sat up, the movement making her feel sick. She shoved back her Egyptian cotton sheets and luxurious duvet and threw up on the solid oak floorboards. Her head was instantly clearer. Why would Karen have needled her unless she knew something? She got up. Everything began to fall into place, helped by a bottle of fifty per cent proof alcohol. Karen King had destroyed her life. And now she was going to pay.

Sixty-Three

Julia reversed out of the tree-canopied driveway, scraping the side of the Porsche on the fence, cursing, revving like mad and stalling halfway down the lane. She fired up the engine again and put her foot down, swerving to avoid a pheasant ambling about in the centre of the road. Fuck – what was wrong with the steering? It was all over the place. As she entered the quaint nearby village, a flashing sign at the side of the road recorded her speed at fifty-five. The car thudded over a speed bump, its bottom scraping against the tarmac. A man walking a dog turned to stare. Julia took her foot off the accelerator. She was in a thirty zone. She gripped the steering wheel, waited for the needle on the speedometer to drop to twenty-five and groped about in her bag, open on the passenger seat, digging out the pistol that had once formed part of her brute of a father's collection of World War Two memorabilia.

The moment she'd made up her mind she'd marched down to the den and unlocked the sturdy wooden chest where, safely away from prying eyes, she'd hoarded the few things she'd kept from her childhood, apart from her secret.

The metal was cool and smooth in her hand. She stamped on the brakes, pulling into a parking space, the engine stalling again, tears streaming down her cheeks. After five minutes, she was back in control and screeching out on to the road again. She knew what she had to do.

Karen was in bed with a mug of hot milk, watching a badly made 'who killed Michael Jackson?' doc, La Toya Jackson's plastic face and high-pitched voice wailing about the loss of her 'soulmate'. She wouldn't normally watch such rubbish, but she couldn't sleep. *Girl Talk* had been weird without Julia. No one seemed to know where she was, not even Paula Grayson, who reckoned she'd got another offer and jumped the sinking ship, but Karen wasn't so sure. Could she really have seen her off for good?

Julia's red file in James Almond's desk kept coming back to her, and even though she wasn't sure she was responsible or even knew for certain that Julia wasn't coming back she still felt a pang of guilt. Stop it, she told herself. Julia was a grade-A bitch and it was a long time coming.

She searched for her phone. Earlier when she'd been in the bath Jason had called repeatedly. She hadn't answered and only now listened in to the voicemail. It was vintage Jason: a pleading message saying he had made the biggest mistake of his life (again) and could they talk? Oh, and he missed her. Loved her. She pressed delete.

The day before, he had turned up on the doorstep in a shocking state, hair all over the place, clothes rumpled, having spent the night at Hannah's side waiting for her to give birth.

Karen made coffee and boiled hot milk while he sat at the breakfast bar, covering his face with his hands.

'Congratulations,' she said eventually, even though she felt like weeping. 'Is everything OK with the baby?'

Jason peered at her through his fingers. It was a long time before he said, 'He's not mine.'

Karen stared at him. On the stove the milk surged to the top of the pan and boiled over on to the enamel hob. She turned off the gas.

'That bloody footballer she was seeing – it's his. I tell you, babe, she's been playing me all along.' He sniffed and gave her a pitiful smile. 'All the deals we had lined up, exclusive pictures of baby Jason – two hundred grand's worth – all of it down the frigging drain.'

Karen bristled. 'So you didn't get to do your *OK!* shoot?'

'Oh, they were there – photographer, reporter, make-up, you name it – all waiting in the corridor with their banners and balloons while Hannah cooed over a baby that obviously wasn't mine.' He looked uncomfortable. 'I mean, there was no doubt about that. Anyway, everyone's flapping, I'm asking what the hell's going on, and that slimy agent of hers is on the phone to the frigging footballer breaking the news that he's a daddy and does he want to do a shoot. Can you believe it? Right under my nose! As if *he* needs the money.'

'That's awful,' Karen said, barely able to contain her fury.

'I tell you what, though – if that shoot goes ahead I want at least half the fee. *At least.* I was counting on that money. I need a new bloody wardrobe, for a start.' He covered his face again. 'Christ, this whole business has lost me a frigging fortune.'

'Poor you.'

He sighed. 'Anyway, it's over and I'm home now. Back where I belong, thank God. Tell you what, once I've had my coffee would you run me a bath? I mean, I've just spent a night in a hospital room with a jacuzzi and I never even got a chance to use it – can you believe that? I'm paying for it, of course.'

Karen had folded her arms. 'Jason—'

'Christ knows how much all that's going to cost. I've a good mind to send the bill to *him* – Mr Top Fucking Striker.'

'Jason. It's not going to work.'

'Maybe not, but I can have a go. He's on, what – a hundred grand a week? It's not like he can't afford it.'

'I mean you and me. *Us*. It's not going to work.'

He looked puzzled. 'But babe, I'm back now.'

'Well, it's too late. I've sat around for months being patient, breaking my heart, while you sort out your mess – and what happens? You come in here and all you can do is go on and on about how much you're out of pocket. Not a single word of apology.' She blinked back tears. 'Be honest, Jason, all you really care about is *you*, you selfish, greedy, headline-grabbing *pig*. It's losing out on all the publicity that really bothers you. Well, it serves you right.'

'It's just I'm in shock, babe, not really thinking straight.'

'No. I'll tell you what you are. You're a –' she searched for the right word – '*dickhead*. I just can't believe it's taken me so long to see it.'

It was after three when Karen heard a car skid on to the gravel at the front of the house. She sat up in bed and listened. The engine cut and the car door opened and slammed shut. A stone bounced off her bedroom window, causing her to jump, and for one glorious moment she thought Dave had come back – until she heard what sounded like Julia screaming at the top of her voice.

'Get down here, you fucking bitch!' Her voice seemed to

boom deeply as another stone hit the glass, this time smashing it. Karen leaped out of bed and ran to the shattered window. The front end of Julia's Porsche was in the rosebed. Beside it, Julia swayed drunkenly in her heels. She looked completely wasted and her eyes blazed as she spotted Karen.

'Open the door or I'll smash every fucking window!' Julia shouted, then stooped to grab another stone but missed her footing and fell into a bush.

Karen, heart pounding so fast she could taste blood in her mouth, ran downstairs and opened up as Julia was struggling upright. 'Julia, what the hell are you doing here?'

Julia staggered across the gravel and lunged at Karen as a light went on upstairs in the house next door. Karen screamed as Julia's hands went round her neck. 'You've killed my life and now I'm going to kill you!' Julia yelled.

More screams filled the street, this time from both of them as the two women fell into the hall, grappling each other like female wrestlers putting on a show, only Julia certainly wasn't faking her attack on Karen – she meant business. Panicked, Karen tried desperately to pull free of Julia's grip, convinced she must have worked out that Karen had complained about her to the controller.

'Get off me! Blame James, not me,' Karen said hoarsely, as Julia's large hands choked her windpipe.

'So you did it together? You scheming bitch!' Julia tried to force Karen down on to the floor but Karen raised her knee up and dug it hard into Julia's stomach. Winded, Julia let her go and, seizing her chance, Karen ran into the kitchen, where she made a grab for the phone which lay on the counter. Julia was not far behind her.

Just as Karen reached the phone there was a metallic click,

a sound she had only ever heard in movies but instantly recognized. She froze against the breakfast bar as cold metal dug into her back.

'Turn round,' Julia hissed. 'I want to see your lying face.'

Karen, rooted to the spot, couldn't believe this was happening. A few minutes ago she'd been all comfy in her pink-heart PJs, and now it seemed she was going to be shot dead in her kitchen by her deranged co-star. She wasn't meant to die like this; she was meant to be in her nineties, finished off by high cholesterol as she munched on a box of Milk Tray in front of *Murder, She Wrote*.

She had to try and reason with her. 'Julia, you need to calm down,' she said, turning round to face her slowly, still clutching the phone. She took in Julia's twitching face, which was soaked with sweat as she swayed from side to side, waving the gun in Karen's face.

Karen eyed the gun and took a step back. 'Julia—'

'Don't Julia me!' she screamed, jabbing the gun at Karen. 'Use the name! You think you're so clever, go on, say it!'

Karen's mind raced. What was she talking about? 'I swear I don't know what you mean.'

Julia stepped back and took aim. 'Stop lying! Say it, say my name.'

Terrified, Karen threw her hands out. 'I don't understand!'

'Say it. Say my name!'

Karen shouted in desperation: 'Julia?!'

Julia's face was turning almost beetroot with rage. She was now screaming so loudly Karen prayed one of the neighbours would hear and call the police.

'Don't play games with me, Karen, I've got nothing to lose

now. I came here to use this and I'll do it, I'll take you with me. How long have you known?'

'About you being sacked?'

Julia stared into her eyes, trying to work out if Karen was telling the truth or trying to trick her. She staggered back, suddenly feeling drained and drunk. 'Not *Girl Talk*! I don't give a *stuff* about the show.' She started crying, great racking sobs, her nose streaming. Karen was almost as shocked to see Julia expressing an emotion as she was to find herself on the brink of death next to her own Aga.

Julia's sobbing continued as she waved the gun dramatically around the room to emphasize her words. 'Do you have any idea what you've done? My life is *over*.' She raised the gun to the side of her head as Karen begged her to stop. 'It's too late! I'm dead now anyway.'

Karen felt sick. She wasn't just drunk, she was raving. 'Julia, please stop this, it's just a job, you'll get another one, nothing is worth this.'

Julia looked her dead in the eye. 'Are you telling me it wasn't you that told them about me?'

Karen kept her voice low. 'I swear – I don't know what you mean.' She took a tentative step forward and Julia swung the gun at her again as she tried to make sense of Karen's possible innocence.

'But you just admitted it was you and James. You're trying to confuse me.' Tears ran down her face. She tugged at her hair, which for once refused to stand to attention.

Karen answered slowly, 'I didn't know what he was going to do. He seems to have it in for you. He told me he had a file on you – on all of us, actually.'

Julia's eyes flashed. So it *was* him. That bastard controller had done this to her. Somehow it seemed inevitable that a man would be behind this. She slumped against the worktop and began to ramble drunkenly.

'As if he would have any idea what it's like being a freak all your life. You think it's easy growing up with a mother who dresses you like a girl and a father who belts you because you're not enough of a boy?' Her nose was streaming again, saliva escaping from the corner of her ragged mouth. 'And now the world will know that Julia Hill is a *him*. Well I'm not him, I'm not. Him's her, I mean I'm me, I'm her.'

Karen looked at her in shock, the words finally sinking in. Dear God, no wonder she was in such a state. 'I promise – I knew nothing about this, I swear it.' She had never seen anyone so wretched and, ignoring the gun, which was still ominously, if lopsidedly, pointing at her, she went and put her arms around Julia, whose whole body heaved and shook with sobs.

'They'll kill me,' Julia said, collapsing, the gun clattering on to the counter. 'Those bastards in the press don't care, they don't know what I went through. They'll kill me.'

Tears pricked the backs of Karen's eyes as she held on tight. Julia's arms went round her and she dropped her head on to Karen's shoulder, her body shuddering as she fought for breath.

Just when Karen thought Julia had begun to calm down she straightened like a coiled spring, grabbing the gun and running out of the house. Karen chased after her.

'Where are you going?' she shouted after Julia, who'd gathered speed and was pulling open the door of her Porsche. 'Julia, get out of the car, you're drunk! You'll have an accident.' She grabbed the door, trying to open it but Julia was too fast, flicking the keys, which she'd left in the ignition. Suddenly the car was reversing full speed out of the drive, bumping and scraping other cars parked in the street and setting alarms off as it went. Karen watched in horror as Julia smashed her way down the road and the car disappeared into the night.

Sixty-Four

Karen didn't go to bed. First she'd had to apologize to her neighbour, who had come outside in his pyjamas, holding a cricket bat aloft in case he needed to fend off a burglar. Then she'd started ringing round and within a couple of hours Lesley, Cheryl and Faye were in her kitchen, bleary-eyed, drinking coffee.

'It's all my fault,' Karen said. 'I complained to James about Julia.' She decided to come clean and tell the others exactly what had been going on. 'The thing is, he as good as promised me Helen England's job, as long as I resigned from *Girl Talk* first, and after that business with Julia on the walkway the other day I went in to see him and said I wouldn't join *GMB* unless he got rid of her first. I mean, I don't see why I should risk life and limb every time I go for a coffee.'

Cheryl straightened up. 'What do you mean, he promised you Helen England's job? He said that was my job! He said I *deserved* that job.'

Lesley had gone pale. 'The bastard. He told me *I'd* get Helen's job. Called me in, said he couldn't be seen to poach a presenter from another show, but if I resigned . . .'

Cheryl grimaced. 'Shit. Same here.'

Karen's eyes widened as the penny finally dropped. 'He really played us, didn't he?'

'The bastard told me he was setting up a brainstorming session at the May Fair Hotel.' Lesley looked indignant. 'You heard what happened to Jackie?'

Karen nodded.

Cheryl was furious. 'I was in his office one day and the dirty sod spent the whole time talking to my tits—'

'He did that to me as well!'

'So I asked him what he thought he was playing at. Course, he denied it, said he loathed any form of sexual harassment—'

'Try telling that to Jackie!'

'—and came out with some crap about having a rule that meant he would never get involved with the talent.'

Lesley's eyes narrowed. 'So how come I saw him coming out of Helen England's apartment block one afternoon with "filthy sex cheat" written all over him?'

Karen gasped. 'James and *Helen*?'

Faye's jaw dropped. 'No – I don't believe it!'

Lesley nodded. 'Trust me, I know the signs. If you ask me they cooked this whole thing up together. She was never going to quit that job. They're up to something.'

Faye nudged her. A still of Julia's face had appeared on the TV in the corner. 'Oh my God. Turn up the sound!'

The *BBC Breakfast* newsreader was saying reports were coming in that Julia Hill was in a critical condition in hospital after crashing her car in the Strand underpass in central London. A few seconds of wobbly pictures of a mangled yellow Porsche with the roof missing filled the screen. A caption read: **Mobile phone footage**.

'Oh my God,' Karen said, going pale. 'She must have been on her way to Channel 6.'

'It's just like Princess Diana,' Faye said.

Cheryl frowned. 'Look at the state of the car – she must have been absolutely plastered. What on earth was she thinking, getting behind the wheel in that state? She could have killed some other poor bastard, the stupid bitch. You know what? I have absolutely no sympathy. She couldn't give a toss about anyone else, so why should we worry about her?'

'We should call the hospital,' Faye said.

'We don't even know where she is yet,' Lesley said.

'Look, there's something else you need to know,' Karen said. 'Julia wasn't always Julia. She used to be—' She hesitated. 'Well, she went through a sex-change operation years ago and somehow the press have got wind of it. That's what sent her over the edge.' Karen looked miserable. 'She thinks that's my fault as well, that I found out and tipped off the papers.'

'A *sex change*? *Julia*? God Almighty, I feel like I've just stepped into a parallel universe,' Cheryl said. 'Think carefully, Karen – is there anything else you're not telling us?'

'No wonder it touched a nerve when I started calling her Jeremy Paxman,' Lesley said, astonished. 'Well, if you ask me, butch or bitch she's still a cow. I mean, she had a go at you in full view of the entire building – and a six-foot trannie in a strop can do a hell of a lot of damage.'

'I had no idea about her past,' Karen said, 'and even if I did I would never have tipped off the press.'

Cheryl narrowed her eyes. 'So who did?'

Karen thought about James Almond's ominous red file. 'My money's on James. I'm telling you, the guy is evil.' She took a deep breath. 'He got the clinic to run blood tests on Julia after that business at the Domes. I think he must have found out she was on hormones and put two and two together. I can just see him as the blackmailing type. I wouldn't be surprised if he's got files on all of us.'

Faye caught Cheryl's eye and her face crumpled. 'Oh my God, that's awful. We've got to stop him – for Julia, I mean.'

'We definitely can't let the bastard get away with it, that's for sure,' Cheryl agreed.

'If you ask me, none of this changes the fact she's a prize bitch,' Lesley said. 'Then again, she's still one of us, I suppose. Sort of.'

Karen frowned. 'Trouble is, it's not going to be easy pulling the rug out from under James. I mean, he's clever.'

Cheryl sneered. 'He's not that clever. He's a man, isn't he?'

Lesley folded her arms. 'Well, if he thinks his precious secret files will save him, he's in for a shock. He should have been a bit more discreet when it came to his sordid little arrangement with horny Helen. Now, all I need is a number for Tom Steiner and our bastard of a controller will be out on his ear in no time. He won't know what's hit him.' She gazed at the others. 'Have you noticed, he's always banging on about how what goes around comes around? Well, I think it's time we proved him right.'

Sixty-Five

Laura watched Joel chopping onion, garlic, ginger, chillies and red peppers, while oil sizzled in a pan. He was making what he called his signature dish, a Thai shrimp curry in coconut milk, served with home-made garlic flatbread – which was more Middle East than Far East but happened to go well – and jasmine rice. In a small bowl next to the chopping board were crushed coriander seeds, cumin, turmeric and cayenne pepper.

He'd been subdued when she arrived, shocked by the news of Julia's car crash and confused by his feelings. Although he hated her, he wouldn't have wished something like this on her. It had taken Laura a good fifteen minutes to cheer him up. Now she said, 'That smells wonderful,' and slipped her arms around his waist. Just as she was nuzzling the back of his neck her phone started to ring and she pulled away. 'It's a private number, might be the office. I'd better get it.'

Joel resumed chopping. He had never met anyone more conscientious than Laura. Her phone was never off and she answered every call she got. No wonder she was the paper's star investigative writer. He heard her voice change. 'I know.'

Tipping up the chopping board, he swept its contents into the hot pan and stepped back from the stove as the oil hissed and splashed. He wiped his hands on a tea towel, opened the fridge and took out two bottles of chilled wine, one white, one pink, holding them up for her to make a decision. 'White or—' he started to say as she put an index finger to her lips.

On the other end of the line Tom Steiner came straight to the point. 'Julia might die, so I expect you to bury your story for good. If any of this ever comes out, Laura, I will let the world and his wife know that her blood is on your hands.'

'Look, Tom, while I have every sympathy, you know I can't just kill it—'

He cut her short. 'I understand that, and here's what I propose. I have a replacement. Julia didn't crash her car by accident – I'm pretty sure James Almond had it in for her. He broke the poor woman. Now it just so happens I have a blistering story about him and Helen England. Let's just say they have more than a good working relationship. In fact, what those two get up to behind closed doors . . . well, it's enough to make your readers' hair curl. Anyway, it's all yours in return for burying everything you know about Julia *forever*. Fair enough?'

Relief washed over Laura as she scribbled something on the folder Joel kept his recipes in. The fact that his reputation was no longer in jeopardy and she was off the hook was enough to make her jump for joy. 'I don't see why not,' she said to Tom.

She hung up and turned to Joel. 'Tom Steiner shouting the odds. In return for agreeing never to publish Julia's sex op, he's given me another scoop. It seems James Almond is not the squeaky-clean controller of entertainment that full-page profile piece in last week's *Media Guardian* would have us all believe. Tom has just well and truly stitched him up.' She stared at the notes she had made on the cover of Joel's recipe folder.

'What about Julia? Did he have any update on her condition?'

'Still in a coma.' Joel was looking subdued again so she gave him a squeeze. 'She's tough as nails so I'm sure she'll pull through. White wine, I think.'

'What?'

'To go with the curry. Shall I open the bottle?'

Sixty-Six

It was ages since Karen had driven anywhere. She considered taking the Beetle, which had been parked up in the garage for months and actually started first time, but she sensed it might just conk out on the motorway, so she hired a car from a place that dropped it off for her. It had satnav, not that she had the faintest idea how to use it, but the guy showed her, even tapped in the postcode.

She picked out a slinky red jumper-dress and black leggings, slung on a necklace with giant glass beads and swept her hair back off her face. For several minutes she gazed at herself in the mirror, her certainty ebbing away. She had never worn her hair like that and couldn't work out if it suited her or not. If only she had asked the girls when they were over; Lesley could always be counted on for an honest opinion.

Karen went for red lipstick to match her top. She closed her eyes for a moment. 'It's all about confidence,' she said, repeating something Philip in the wardrobe department at Channel 6 used to say as he forced her into some dreadful frock or other. When she opened her eyes she felt better. She picked up the bottle of Annick Goutal from her dressing table and sprayed a cloud of fragrance into the air, the fresh floral scent drifting into her hair. Right, she was ready. Better get a move on before nerves got the better of her.

*

The soothing voice on the satnav told her she was now approaching her destination and to stop in twenty yards. She would find number 22 on the left-hand side, it said. She pulled up next to a parade of shops, behind a rusting Transit that had a mobile number and EDDIE'S WHITE VAN MAN handpainted in red across the back doors.

It had been sunny when she left home but now, after almost two hours crawling across London in the car, the sky was grey. Still, she kept her dark glasses on as she checked out the neighbourhood. She had imagined finding a coffee shop, relaxing and touching up her make-up, nipping to the loo, but it wasn't that kind of area. All she could see was a drab takeaway pizza place that might once have said *Orlando's*, although all that was left of the sign was the ANDO'S bit at the end. Next door was a twenty-four-hour mini-mart, its frontage cowering behind metal bars, a cab firm with an orange lamp rotating above the door, and a kebab shop (closed) with a lump of unappetizing meat on a spit visible through the grimy window. At the far end of the block was a betting shop with a board outside offering odds on Premier League games.

A newspaper cartwheeled along the pavement. In between Southside Cabs and Kev's Kebabs, a door with an entryphone and lots of buzzers led to the flats above. She glanced self-consciously at her top, which had cost a couple of hundred pounds, and at the Mulberry bag on the seat next to her, as an elderly man in a shiny sheepskin jacket, grey jogging pants and worn slippers shuffled out of the betting shop and lit a roll-up.

As soon as the old man disappeared round the corner she leaped from the car and dashed, head down, to the door, pressing the buzzer for Flat 3. 'Come on,' she said under her breath. 'Oh for God's sake, answer.'

A voice crackled through the speaker. 'It's me,' she said, sounding strained, glancing over her shoulder at a boy in baggy pants, hood up, swerving along the pavement on a skateboard. 'Karen.'

There was a moment's silence before a buzzer sounded. 'Come on up,' Dave said.

Karen pushed against the door and stepped into a passage with a stone staircase. There were mailboxes along the wall to her right. A bare bulb hung from the ceiling. She climbed the stairs, the heels of her new Miu Miu boots echoing on the stone. The air smelled of old fried food. At the top of the stairs she paused, thought about touching up her lipstick, and abandoned the idea. A sign giving the numbers of the flats told her 1–8 were on her left. Towards the end of the corridor light spilled from an open door. Dave, barefoot in worn jeans and a T-shirt with the words WE HAVE WAYS OF MAKING YOU TALK across the front, slouched against the frame. 'Looking good, Kaz,' he said. 'I like your hair.'

She stepped into the hall, on to scratchy fawn hessian carpeting. The walls were cream, the paint chipped and scratched in places. There was a large square mirror in a plain wooden frame on one wall and a row of silvery pegs with jackets and scarves hanging from them. At the end of the hall a stripped-pine door led into a small living room with an open-plan kitchen at one end. She stood next to a low sofa, cream with a rust-coloured throw draped over the back, a copy of the *Sun* open at the sports pages slung across an arm. At one end of the room, under the window, was a giant red and gold floor cushion. The TV, mounted on the wall over a modern tiled fireplace with a convector heater in the grate, was off. A window was open, making the place feel cold. Outside, traffic rumbled past.

Dave was at the sink, holding the kettle under the cold tap. He turned to face her. 'You're just about the last person I thought would ever show up here.'

She put her bag down on the sofa and went into the kitchen. 'I know. I'm sorry.'

He shrugged. 'You could have phoned, given me a chance to tidy up, get some decent coffee in. I mean, you've caught me on the hop.' He bent and opened the fridge. 'Long-life milk, if that's all right.'

'It's fine. I just wanted to see you.'

'Does this have anything to do with the dickhead?'

She looked away. 'If anyone's been a dickhead, it's me.'

Behind him the kettle started to boil. He flicked a switch on the base and it went quiet. A large red clock on the wall behind him made a loud ticking sound.

Karen blurted out, 'I wanted to talk to you. Properly. Face-to-face. I—' She paused, helpless. 'I wondered if you'd go out with me.'

He looked amused. 'Go *out* with you?'

'See each other. You know – properly.' She moved towards him and slid her hands round his waist. His back felt taut and toned. In the corner, below a cork board with cards for taxi firms and flyers for takeaways pinned to it, was a pair of battered boxing gloves.

His face was suddenly serious. 'What about hubby? Still sniffing round, is he?'

'I've given him his marching orders.'

'I bet that's a long story.'

She reached up and pushed a lock of blond hair out of his

eyes. 'Dave, I'm absolutely freezing. Is there any chance of, you know, warming up?'

He gave her his lopsided smile. 'I'll see what I can do,' he said, pulling her close.

Sixty-Seven

Damien Junior was the cutest thing. Hannah couldn't help thinking it was funny how things worked out, remembering the awful sense of panic she'd felt once he popped out after an agonizing twenty-three hours in labour and she knew the game was up with Jason. Now, just a few weeks later, she was happier than she had ever been. She had been nervous about Damien Senior, convinced he would go ballistic and demand a paternity test. In fact, to her amazement, he had jumped straight in the car and turned up at the hospital with the biggest bunch of flowers she had ever seen. From the word go he was besotted and in no doubt the baby was his – 'Look at the size of his tackle – chip off the old block,' he said, impressed. She could have wept with relief when he asked her to move back in. OK, he still dropped his dirty laundry on the floor, leaving it for her to pick up, *and* went out on the pull, but the bottom line was he loved his son. She was pretty sure he loved her too, in his own cheating-footballer kind of way. And – oh joy! – she had an Amex card again that meant VIP treatment in all her favourite shops. *And* he was treating her to lipo. She was dizzy with happiness.

Cheryl emptied a sachet of miso soup into a mug and poured boiling water on to it. She hadn't spoken to Faye since Karen had mentioned James's secret files; she worried this had scared Faye off. She hated to be the one to cave in first but there was no point being stubborn. She rang Faye's mobile. They could have that lunch at the Bluebird, followed by a lazy afternoon in bed.

'Hey, Cheryl,' Mike said. 'How's it going?'

What was he doing there? No wonder she hadn't heard from Faye. She struggled to keep the irritation out of her voice. 'I didn't know you were home.'

'Got back late Friday, surprised my lovely wife.'

Cheryl was curt. 'May I speak to her?'

'Sorry, no can do. She's having a nap and last I looked she was dead to the world. We've had a pretty exhausting weekend one way or another and I don't want her overdoing it.'

Cheryl rolled her eyes. Mike's idea of an exhausting weekend involved an hour or two's shopping in Liberty's before collapsing under the weight of his purchases in the champagne bar. She could just picture Faye next to him right now making a face and shaking her head, mouthing Get rid of her in that dramatic way she had. Cheryl checked her watch. It was gone eleven. There was no way Faye would be in bed at this time of day. If he had said she was on the Power Plate or soaking in the bath – Cheryl had never known anyone have as many baths as Faye, one of these days she would wash herself away – she might have been more inclined to swallow it, but sleeping? Not in a million years. 'Oh dear, is something wrong?' Cheryl hoped he was picking up the undisguised sarcasm in her voice. 'Poor thing's not *ill*, is she?'

'Not *ill* exactly.' He paused. 'Oh, I can tell you since you're practically family. I mean Faye's always saying you're just like the big sister she never had.' Cheryl bristled. 'She's pregnant.

We're having a baby. I knew something was up when Faye started stuffing her face with fig rolls and those sickly chocolate-peanut-butter things. Ugh. I mean, you know what a health fiend she is, how her body is a temple and all that. Then when she said she'd been off-colour, bad tummy . . . we did a test and it was positive. I know it's way too soon but we were in Liberty's yesterday and saw the cutest pair of Gucci bootees just begging to come home with us, so we had to have them.' He chuckled.

Hearing Mike Parry, hardened war reporter and bullet dodger extraordinaire, go gaga over impending fatherhood made Cheryl want to be sick.

'We've got a designer coming in next week to talk about turning one of the spare rooms into a nursery, and, of course, no more front-line duties for me, not with a little one on the way. Don't want to be caught in the crossfire with Faye in a delicate condition, do I? You know, I'm just glad it's curtains for *Girl Talk*. Couldn't have worked out better for us, really. I can see Faye as a stay-at-home mum – can't you? Veg patch out the back, the smell of baking wafting through the house, little one gurgling in the high chair . . . Hello, are you still there?'

Cheryl knelt on the floor clutching the phone, Mike calling her name, going 'Hello, hello?' into the silence and finally hanging up. She closed her eyes and gripped the edge of the sofa, bile rising in her throat.

Natalie Scott was on the train on her way back to London from Worthing, having spent the afternoon with Edward Draper. She had given his scruffy kitchen the once-over, made toad-in-the-hole with mashed potatoes and gravy, and left him a supply of groceries. Natalie had been checking on him on a regular basis ever since it came out that Sasha was Deirdre. She had wondered if being shown up in the press like that would shame Sasha/Deirdre into visiting her old dad, but the disgraced soap star was keeping well away, even giving an interview to a gossip mag hinting that if people knew what he was *really* like they might understand why she had chosen to have nothing to do with him. Well, it was up to Sasha. *Deirdre*. Natalie was in no position to judge, not the way things were with her own folks. It bothered her to think she was traipsing about acting like a long-lost daughter to some strange old man and at the same time keeping her own mum and dad at arm's length. She didn't like to think she was being hypocritical but that was the word that came to mind. It wasn't even like her parents weren't making an effort, more that she was being stubborn. Still, it was complicated.

Lesley was on the sofa with her feet on Dan's knee, dividers between her toes, painting her nails a vibrant orange. An episode of *Come Dine With Me* was on TV, the host busy making some kind of fish stew while one of his guests sat with her head on the dining table, fast asleep.

'Can you believe that?' Lesley said, sitting up and giving the bottle of varnish a shake. 'Poor bloke. Talk about rude.'

Dan stroked her ankle. 'I've got some of those olives you like, the big green ones stuffed with almonds. And a bottle of Cristal.'

Lesley gave him a curious look. 'What's the occasion?'

'We're celebrating.'

Lesley's mind raced. Oh lord, was it his birthday? No, he was a Leo so it was ages off yet. 'What exactly are we celebrating? Me being unemployed?'

Dan shifted and rooted around down the back of the sofa. 'Close your eyes.'

'I've still got to do a second coat on my toes.'

He took the nail varnish off her and put it on the coffee table. 'For once will you do as you're told?'

Lesley gave him a coy smile and shut her eyes. She loved it when Dan bossed her about.

'OK, you can open them now.'

He slid off the sofa and knelt in front of her, bending and placing a tender kiss on the inside of her ankle. Lesley shivered. Her feet were extremely sensitive, as Dan knew only too well. He gazed at her and held up an exquisite silver box studded with tiny crystals. Lesley's eyes widened as he undid the tiny catch on the front of the box and opened it. A platinum ring with a single yellow diamond glinted at her.

He cleared his throat. 'I wanted to think of something clever to say.' His voice sounded peculiar. 'But I couldn't. So, Lesley Gold, love of my life' – his voice cracked – 'will you marry me?'

Lesley's heart lurched. Marriage? That meant giving up her old ways for good. Was she ready for that? She gazed at Dan, his handsome face now clouded with uncertainty. There was definitely something to be said for settling down at her age. Then again, if she married him she would have to own up and tell him just how old she really was. Never again would she be free to prowl the seedier parts of Soho. She played with a strand of blonde hair, twisting it into a coil, feeling a flutter of panic, weighing up the pros and cons, glancing at Dan. Silence stretched between them.

Finally she said, 'I'm not a very nice person. I wouldn't make a very good wife. If you knew what I was really like you wouldn't want to marry me.'

'I do know what you're like.'

'Really, Dan, I'm no angel.' That was the understatement of the year.

'Neither am I, but I'm willing to try a hell of a lot harder from now on, so how about it? Come on, Lesley – my knees are killing me down here.'

She held his gaze. God, he was gorgeous. 'I just think—'

Dan cut in. 'Yes or no?' He rested his chin on her knee and gave her a pleading look. 'Go on then, break my heart, why don't you? Kick a man when he's down, throw the ring back in my face . . .'

'Oh, all right, you win,' she said and started to laugh. 'But don't say I didn't warn you.'

'Is that a yes?'

She flung her arms round his neck. 'Yes. Yes, yes, YES!'

Sixty-Eight

James Almond pressed a button on a panel in the arm of his chair and a set of miniature rollers began to vibrate, sending tingles up and down his spine. The screen of his computer glowed with columns of figures. Stealth TV had more commissions in the pipeline, as well as a new strand on celebrity pets on *Good Morning Britain*. The money was rolling in. He'd had to fight objections from the American Stealth Productions and Deep Stealth Productions to register his name, but it had been worth it. Stealth was perfect – it was how he operated, how he'd achieved his dreams. His chair ceased vibrating as James allowed himself a satisfied sigh. Almost immediately he shivered and jolted upright. He must *not* become complacent: he had a rule about that. After all, this was just the beginning.

The new schedule was a triumph. *The Helen England Show* would be a huge hit. Advertising revenue would go up. A bidding war had broken out among potential sponsors. The pantyliner people were willing to pay the most but James wasn't entirely sure that was the right image for the show.

Helen smiled at him from a billboard on the far side of the river. He admired her breasts, unconsciously licking his lips. He checked his watch. It was Saturday and he and Stephanie were spending the night at the Ritz to celebrate her fortieth birthday. He hadn't intended to come into the office but once he was in town the temptation was just too great. Stephanie had complained, of course, but he said he would only be an hour and told her to get a massage or have her hair done or something. That had been a mistake: she'd had her hair done the day before.

As he scrolled through the figures in front of him the ex-directory line on his office phone lit up. Strange. Who would call him at work on a Saturday? The only person who knew he was there was his wife. He sighed. For heaven's sake, could she not leave him in peace for five minutes?

'Yes?'

'Oh. Is that James, by any chance?'

Oh God, not more calls about Julia Hill. Couldn't the hacks just do a condition check at the hospital instead of plaguing the life out of him? 'That depends. Who exactly is this?'

'Petra Carson, from the press office. I'm on call this weekend and there's been a query from one of the Sundays.'

James sighed. 'Well, Petra Carson from the press office, since you're on call I suggest you deal with it.'

'It's just they're running a piece and they're keen for you to have the right of reply.'

James rolled his eyes and made a note on a pad on his desk. Petra Carson would be getting a stiff email first thing Monday morning, as would the head of the press office, Emily Eustace. 'Are you quite incapable of coming up with a suitable quote? Isn't that what we pay you for?'

Petra hesitated. 'Yes. No. I mean, it's not strictly a Channel 6 matter. That's to say it *is*, only it's not about programming or anything. It's more ... personal.' She braced herself. 'It's to do with your relationship with Helen England.'

Sixty-Nine

Lesley skipped into Al Dente, a huge smile on her face, shrugged her sheepskin coat on to the back of the chair facing Karen and applied a fresh coat of lip gloss. 'Any news on Julia?'

Karen shook her head. 'I just spoke to Tom Steiner. No change.'

Nico appeared, scooped up Lesley's coat, gave her a dazzling smile and scuttled away. Lesley flopped into her seat and glanced at the empty places at the end of the table. 'No sign of Cheryl or Faye?'

Karen nodded towards the back of the restaurant. 'Having a bit of a set-to in the ladies'. Faye's pregnant and Cheryl's put out because she didn't tell her. Apparently, Mike let it slip.'

'But that's brilliant news!'

Karen speared an olive. 'Well, we all think so, but you know what they're like, those two, practically joined at the hip. She thought since they're best buddies Faye should have told her the instant she knew.'

Lesley gave her a wry smile. She still suspected the two of them had been a lot more than best buddies for a while. 'What, like Cheryl told *her* when she resigned, you mean?'

The door to the toilets opened and Cheryl appeared, a tearful Faye lagging a few steps behind.

Lesley caught her wrist as she went to her seat. 'Con-

gratulations – I hear you're expecting. That's fantastic. Hey –
are you OK?'

Faye sniffed. 'Just a bit hormonal. I keep bursting into tears
over nothing.'

'Well, no wonder. You've got a little person in there.' Lesley
patted her tummy. 'You're bound to feel weird.' Unable to contain herself any longer, she thrust out her hand, showing off
the magnificent stone on her ring finger. 'I have news too – I'm
getting married!'

'Oh my God!' Karen jumped up and rushed over to hug her.
'I knew you two were made for each other.'

Lesley looked expectantly at a stony-faced Cheryl, who sul-
lenly replied, 'Just because I don't believe in marriage doesn't
mean I'm not pleased for you.'

Lesley grinned. 'Thanks. I think.'

Faye started crying again.

Nico scurried over, a magnum of vintage Bollinger in his
hands. 'I have been saving this for your special announcement,'
he said, the cork making a sharp *pop* as it flew over their heads
and hit the ceiling.

Karen gazed around the table as he filled their glasses. 'Look
at us, quaffing champagne like there's no tomorrow, and not a
job between us.'

'I'll pick up the tab,' Cheryl said. 'I've still got all my sports
stuff and I've been offered a ridiculous amount of money for
a spread in *Hello!*'

Faye sat up. 'What kind of spread?'

'They want to know all about what makes me tick, what's
been going on at Channel 6, finally set the record straight on
my love life . . . you know the kind of thing.' She gave Faye a
pointed look.

'No! I mean, you can't. You know how the press twists everything.'

'Not the lovely people at *Hello!* They're doing the whole thing as a Q-and-A session so there's no chance of being mis-quoted.'

Faye gave her a pleading look.

'So,' Cheryl said, 'I don't want anyone worrying – ' she paused and glared at Faye – 'about the bill.'

'Well, my gorgeous fiancé said he'd treat us to dinner tonight.' Lesley beamed with pleasure.

'In that case, I think we should let him.' Karen raised her glass. 'Let's drink to the happy couple – and our blooming mum-to-be.'

'And let's not forget why we're here,' Lesley said, checking her watch. 'Any time now the first editions of the Sunday papers will be on the streets and You-know-who will be in deep shit.'

Faye chewed her bottom lip. 'I hope Julia's OK. I hardly recognized her, lying there all pale, machines and wires around her.'

Lesley patted her hand. 'I know. I felt like putting a bit of lippy on her. She'll never forgive us when she comes round and finds out no one did her face.' She giggled. 'Mind you, I imagine she'll need some major waxing, if you know what I mean.'

'Stop it!' Karen said, laughing. 'As soon as she's a bit better we'll get a proper make-up girl in there, give her a bit of primping.' Her phone beeped and she fished it out of her bag. A text from Dave. 'That's it. The papers are on the stands.'

Nico dispatched his barman to run over to Victoria Station and buy several copies of the *Sunday*. James had made the front page and was all over pages two, three and four. The paper branded him a deviant who indulged in kinky, unnatural sexual acts with his star presenter, Helen England, a married mother of two. Outrageously, these sessions were scheduled during office hours. The paper published what it called his 'Diary of Shame', detailing his assignations – and the spurious meetings he was supposed to be attending when he was actually romping with Helen. Most damning were the pictures of him in a nappy and Helen in a sleazy nurse's outfit. Since it was see-through the paper had covered up her naughty bits – 'in the interests of taste and decency' – with solid black slabs.

Faye gasped. 'What a pervert,' she said, clapping her hands with delight. 'Can't see him showing his face at Channel 6 after this, can you?'

Cheryl frowned. 'Ooh. He's such a *gorilla* – look at his hairy shoulders.' She peered at the picture. 'What's that white stuff on his chin?'

Lesley pulled a face. 'Well, *he's* got some bizarre baby fixation thing going on and *she's* still breastfeeding, so work it out. Looks like he needs a bib if you ask me.'

They looked at each other.

Karen said, 'You don't mean ...'

Cheryl shuddered. '*Urrgh*. Disgusting.'

Lesley scanned the paper. 'It says they've been having it off for six months and that he pays the rent on that place of hers in Chelsea. How do they know these things?'

Cheryl said, 'I wouldn't be surprised if they got to her. There's too much detail here. And she comes across as the victim, almost pressured into it. So someone definitely blabbed.'

Lesley shook her head. 'But she'd never give the papers pictures of her dressed up like something out of *Carry on Nurse* – the porn edition.'

'Oh, I don't know,' Cheryl said. 'I mean she just looks slutty, whereas he looks like ... well, like he's escaped from some weirdo fetish party.' She shook with laughter. 'I knew this was going to be good, but I never thought it would be this good.'

Lesley redid her lipstick. 'Let's drink to us – more than a match for a slimeball in a nappy.' She giggled. 'I wonder if Helen ... you know, *changes* him.'

Faye covered her mouth. 'Don't, it's making me feel sick.'

Karen winced. 'Oh dear, poor old James.'

'Poor James *nothing*. What goes around ...' Lesley raised her glass again. 'Now, I suggest we get properly trashed to celebrate.' She glanced at Faye. 'Sorry, not you, sweetie. We'll get Nico to bring some fancy water or something.'

Karen held up her glass. 'Here's to the *Girl Talk* girls. We may be out but we are *definitely* not down.'

They clinked glasses. 'The *Girl Talk* girls! Out but not down!'

Seventy

Karen slipped on her shades and flipped down the visor over the passenger seat as Dave pulled up at a red light on Kensington High Street. Above them ragged pieces of cloud dotted a powder-blue sky. Her hand rested on his knee. He was off-duty, in battered denims, Ray-Ban Wayfarers and his old leather biker jacket. She was in leggings and one of his jumpers, which bore the faint citrus smell of his aftershave. A Parka lay on the back seat. The lights changed to green and he stayed put, foot on the brake, while an old lady in an ankle-length coat with a walking stick and a wicker basket on wheels crossed the road in slow motion. Karen squeezed his leg.

He glanced at her. 'You really don't care where we're going?'

She smiled. 'You decide. Anywhere's fine with me.'

'What if I said I was taking you to ... let's see – Walthamstow?'

'No problem – I trust you.' She leaned over and kissed his neck.

He gave her one of his crooked smiles. 'Go on, have a guess. It begins with a W.'

She had a pretty good idea they were going to Whitstable on the Kent coast, to a fish restaurant that also began with a W, since he had left the details lying on the printer at home. She smiled and leaned back against the soft leather headrest.

After all that business with Jason she finally felt free, as if a new and happy phase of her life was beginning. She pushed her shades on to her head, the glare on the windscreen making her squint. 'Dave, can you pull over?'

'Why, what's up?'

'I need you to stop the car.'

He swung off the main road into a parking bay and switched on the hazards. Karen unfastened her seatbelt, leaned over and gave him a long, lingering kiss. 'There,' she said, pulling away. '*Now* we can go to Whitstable.'

He stared at her. 'What are you, Kaz – a mind reader?'

'No,' she said, a huge smile on her face, 'but you are *hopeless* at keeping secrets – and that's just one of the reasons I love you.'

They moved off and she slipped her shades back on as he executed a perfect three-point turn and slid into the traffic on Kensington High Street. Bathed in bright sunlight, Karen closed her eyes for a moment, her hand resting on Dave's muscular thigh. Could life get any better than this?

www.panmacmillan.com